Potions & Peculiarities

GLORIA BOTTELMAN

Cover Design by Charlotte Slegers
Edited by Aurion Edits
First edition: November 2025
Published in the United States of America by Ravenwood Books.

LCCN: 2025916116
ISBN: 979-8-9906910-2-5 (ebook)
ISBN: 979-8-9906910-3-2 (paperback)
ISBN: 979-8-9906910-4-9 (hardcover)

To those who were told they read too much fantasy.
No, you don't.

ALSO BY GLORIA BOTTELMAN

Dark Brilliance Duology
Untethered

BEFORE YOU BEGIN

This story contains elements that may be difficult
for some readers, including: attempted sexual assault
and coercion, assault, death and murder.

Chapter One

Alora Pennigrim loved a good, enchanted lane, and the lane to Opulence Mansion was a great deal more enchanted than most. Smooth, pale stones smaller than her palm were fitted together tight and beneath her heeled boots a pleasant clack resulted, echoing against white-barked trees lining either side. They were thin but tall as towers, these trees, and nestled among them were silver-tipped ferns that glittered in the mid-morning light and signs that flashed brilliantly every few steps.

THIS WAY, they said.

NEARLY THERE.

Do NOT Stray from the Lane.

Alora gently brushed aside a butterfly come to nudge against her nose, its colors a splattered paint mix of pink and orange. Another took up residence on the bodice of her knee-length dress, its antennas wiggling with expectation.

"Those flowers aren't real, I'm afraid. Sorry to disappoint." But the insect appeared unperturbed by her confession, settling in instead for the ride. "Okay. Suit yourself." By the time she reached the end of the lane she was covered in butterflies.

Pale stone walls rose to greet her, high and wrapping, with a golden gate so intricately swirled and spired she couldn't make out what was hidden behind it. Posted directly in front was a singular guard. He stood straight and tall, a spiked crimson helmet causing him to appear stretched even higher, with golden armor heavy upon his shoulders—quite a misery, she thought, beneath the unfiltered sun. The trees had ended as the lane did, and the ferns, too, leaving only one sign remaining: *No Admittance.* Then below: *Except by Membership Only.* And below that: *Or Appointment.*

Alora adjusted the satchel draped across her chest and started toward it.

The guard awaited her approach, still as the stacked stone behind him. Nearing, Alora noted he'd not yet focused on her, his copper eyes staring straight ahead, trained upon the lane. When she stopped, close enough to note the runs in gold paint smeared across his skin, she cleared her throat in announcement. The guard, however, didn't react to this either.

Perhaps she'd been mistaken? If this wasn't a real man at all, the statue made a remarkably impressive replica.

She stepped closer, bending forward, the sun beating down on the scooped back of her dress to heat her skin in an instant. She peered up into his face—as she couldn't see if he breathed through his chest plate—and when she noticed the slight flare of his nostrils, released a rushed breath.

"You poor man! You've overheated, haven't you? Out here in all that armor, it's no wonder. I'll find you something to drink." She leaned back to peer into the satchel slung against her hip, rummaging through samples of fabrics and paints, pencils and a notebook, her fingers searching but coming up empty. She'd forgotten the bottle. Of all the days.

It was a large bottle with thick glass in a sleeve of tanned leather, stitched with florals and insects, bees and butterflies—not unlike the dress she'd chosen that morning, though the creatures covering her now fluttered their wings. And the water inside would be mountain-spring-cold, perfect and clear, so refreshing after a morning standing beneath the summer sun.

When she next reached in, she removed such a bottle.

"Have a sip of water. You'll feel much better."

At the word "water", the guard's gaze finally shifted toward her, but slower than it should have. He really appeared a concerning level of unwell. Beneath his attention, the butterflies took flight in unison, swirling around them both before vanishing into the trees.

"Can't," he croaked.

"Sure you can. It's only water, see?" She poured a little into her hand, cold and clear.

At the sight of it, the guard promptly looked one way and then the other before taking the bottle from her and drinking it dry.

"Thank you," he said, returning it. His voice, no longer parched from thirst, was a pleasant tenor. "I'd begun to dream. Of lakes and rivers and springs. I didn't notice you at all. Quite the guard, I am."

In response to such dejection, Alora couldn't help but chime, "It's the heat-fever. You can't be expected to stand outside in all that armor in the peak of summer without so much as a cloud to protect you."

He grunted and stared awhile at his golden boots, the toes pointed and curled, before finding her eyes again. Abruptly, he stood tall once more and turned out a hand, palm up and crimson gloved. "Name?" he said, and though his tone had become business-like, his eyes were soft.

"Alora Pennigrim," she replied and shook his hand.

She wondered if she'd imagined the fleeting stutter in their embrace, or the slight widening of his eyes? Then, with sudden distress, she realized he'd not extended his arm. Nor had he even positioned his palm properly; their handshake was a strange side-to-side thing.

Because he'd not wanted her hand at all, but the letter.

Her already flushed skin heated further. But when she made to draw away in embarrassment, the guard held fast. "Miss Pennigrim, yes. You're expected."

"I am," she agreed, her palm entrapped. "Eleven o'clock appointment with Mr. Merridon."

The guard dropped her hand as if coming to his senses. "Right. *Right.* I'll allow you in straightaway. Only—" His lips pursed as if the thought itself had soured.

Alora blinked up at him, and although she'd not brought along a handkerchief in her satchel, pulled one from it anyway. She held it out as he considered what he wished to say, and he took it without question, dabbing at the trickling paint.

He arched forward, his voice quieting in confidence. "Only mind your step. And your eyes. Mind everything, for that matter. And knock three times. He likes that."

"Okay," said Alora, because there was nothing else to say, really, to such instruction.

The guard nodded his satisfaction before reaching behind him to pull a lever. The adorned gate swung inward. Alora sucked in a breath.

There was nothing like it. Not in all of Enver, the town in which she currently resided, or Eirian, the town in which she was born. The pale-pebbled path continued, straight and shining. On either side, in place of trees, were manicured lawns and even further manicured topiaries. Each was different, trimmed into shapes without names and creatures she didn't recognize. It made her brain fuzzy trying to rationalize each one, so she stopped, focusing instead on Opulence Mansion itself rising beyond like a storybook castle in all its golden glory. Turrets flanked either side of its hulking expanse, a singular crimson flag stretched taut atop each, and the front steps were steep and imposing. If rumor could be trusted, the mysterious mansion held many rooms—more than any building she'd visited before, and each one unique from the last. A person couldn't enter except by membership or appointment, and as Alora could not afford such a membership card, she pulled out a letter instead.

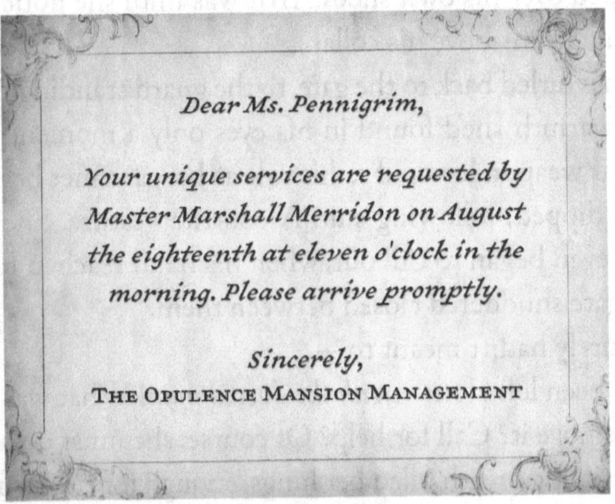

"Go on then," came a reassuring voice.

Alora, not realizing she'd been staring for an exorbitant amount of time at the scenery and then the letter, turned back to the guard with a quick smile forged and perfected to bolster confidence in those she sought to win over. "Of course. Thank you."

She stepped beyond the gate.

The mansion shone enough to hurt her eyes, and now she understood why she'd been told to mind them. Latticed windows observed her approach with a rather haughty gaze. The steps were wide before the building and led to twin, oversized doors, with no further guards that she could see. In fact, the grounds were eerily vacant. There were no birds in the hedges, no butterflies flitting about in an attempt to drink from her dress, not even a whisper of a breeze, and a strange feeling had just begun to settle in her chest when a person sprinted by. He came from behind her, running outright, his face not turned toward her at all, but staring ahead. His boots raised whorls of white glitter where they smacked. He was dressed well enough, but certainly not in any sort of finery one might attempt for an appointment such as hers, and when he suddenly fell to the ground, Alora thought he'd tripped over his own shoes. That was until she noticed the dart protruding from above his collar.

Alora whirled back to the gate, to the guard standing there. Gone was the warmth she'd found in his eyes only a moment before. An unfamiliar weapon lowered to his side as his gaze met hers, and then his head dipped, following suit. A contrite gesture. She wondered about it, even began to call out, when his hand reached for the lever and the gate shuddered closed between them.

He surely hadn't meant to—

She'd been left alone…*with the darted man!* What was she meant to do? Remove it? Call for help? Of course, she must do *something*.

A fortifying breath filled her lungs, enough for her to finally close her mouth and turn cautiously back around. It abandoned her a moment later with a startled yelp.

A rake of a size she'd never seen eased across the lawn. The unconscious man was being *dragged along* beneath it. She ran to the edge of the lane, one boot poised to step onto the grass, when the guard's words returned to her. She'd taken them for instruction, but perhaps they were a warning? Replacing her foot, she leaned instead, peering into the hedges to make out an extremely large and hairy forearm as it snaked around the man's torso, tucking him in as simple as a loaf of bread to bring home. A moment later, and both of them, including the rake, disappeared from sight.

Good god! What the devil goes on here?

But she was a *professional*. She had an *appointment*. And there was nothing else to do, really, except continue down the lane.

Chapter Two

The doors of the renowned Opulence Mansion were a hodgepodge of conflicting ideas carved in gold. Normally, Alora wasn't opposed to mismatched decor so long as it carried along a basic thread of theme at its core, but the doors, not unlike the topiaries, simply made her insides feel wrong. As far as she could tell, it didn't tell a story, and it didn't hint as to what she'd find inside once she'd dredged up the courage to knock. Or she hoped it didn't.

She'd not put the letter away regarding her appointment, and she clutched it now with both hands, palms damp with sweat. It was a hot day to be sure, and the entrance to the mansion offered no relief from the elements—which, in her opinion, was a design flaw, and if this Mr. Merridon asked for her thoughts on the matter, she'd tell him. When it came to her professional opinion on either aesthetic or functionality, she was never shy. No, the reason her palms sweat now had nothing to do with her profession, but a myriad of other things she'd rather not focus on.

So instead, as per instruction, she knocked three times. The doors swung in.

A smartly dressed woman, whom Alora would guess to be of a similar age to her mother, stood ready to greet her. Alora took in the matching gold skirt and blouse as well as the crimson vest buttoned tightly across the top. It did not complement her, with her sallow complexion that hinted at a life spent mostly indoors. "Miss Pennigrim," she said. "You're expected."

Alora held the letter between them. "Yes. Eleven o'clock."

The woman didn't take it. "I know the time. I'm management, after all, and the letter's architect." Penciled eyebrows turned down at her, examining her from piled high chestnut hair to brown boots. "Well. No gold or crimson."

Alora, who had chosen a periwinkle blue dress to bring out the ice in her otherwise gray eyes, pondered for a moment. Her hand covered a particularly large silver flower stitched across one hip.

"No."

"Hmph," sniffed the woman. "This way."

Alora, insecure now over her choice of outfit, smoothed her skirt as she walked. There were several blooms across the bodice of a dusty pink. In the right lighting, they might be mistaken for crimson. Good grief, was this to be her only color palette to work with on this project? She sincerely hoped not.

Worry could not distract her for long, though. Observance had always been in her nature, and Opulence Mansion's style certainly would not be ignored. It shouted for her attention.

The walls were textured gold paper—expensive—and the marble she walked on dyed crimson and cracked with gold veins—*more* expensive. Golden chandeliers hung the length of the wide corridor. Each one spilled yellow light onto rows of spiraled staircases corkscrewing from the floor below. There was no grand staircase. Unlike the main entrance, each set of stairs took the climber through a different door numbered with black on gold plates. And for every door on that strange second floor, there stood one directly beneath.

Alora struggled to keep her eyes trained ahead and not spinning in all directions like some broken doll, but some things could not be helped. When the fiercely-eyebrowed woman stopped, Alora's entire body smacked into her back.

"Oh! So sorry!"

A deep groove had ground itself between the woman's eyes with time, but it was impressively pronounced now. She straightened her vest in a slow and exacting fashion while she glared, causing Alora to fear that at any moment, she herself would feel the sharp sting of a dart to the neck for her blunder.

"Door Zero. Master Merridon's personal room and where he greets all his appointments. *No matter how trivial,*" she added with a healthy dose of spite. "Knock before you enter."

"Three times, correct?"

The woman only lifted her lip in a sneer, successfully slicing through what was left of Alora's confidence. *Imposter,* said that look. Good god, she was, wasn't she? Through and through. She shouldn't have been allowed past the golden gate, should have listened to the haughty windows pinning her like an insect. She wasn't experienced enough for the likes of this place. Who might she be kidding? Herself, most of all.

"When the appointment is concluded, see yourself out. Do *not* touch any of the other doors unless your desire is slow torture and permanent damage."

Alora's mouth fell wide. "Was that the fate of the man outside?"

But her question went unanswered as the woman swept away.

"Delightful," she muttered beneath her breath, and because it was likely after eleven now, and she might as well finish her flogging, she knocked three times on Door Zero.

"Enter," said a pleasant voice.

Alora glanced down the overlarge corridor and again to the entrance before easing her palm across the back of her neck. There it stayed all the while she turned the golden doorknob. Just in case.

But she dropped her hand at the room's interior.

The man behind the vast maple-wood desk was handsome, to be sure. His hair, more gray than brown, was brushed back from his forehead, and when he stood, she noticed him to be tall and broadly built. He wore a gold waistcoat with a crimson tie over a white shirt and trousers. When he smiled, it lit his entire face. He was smiling still, as he took her in.

"Miss Pennigrim, I presume?"

"Yes, sir. I received your message in the mail. It was quite beautiful, all that embossing."

If possible, the owner of Opulence Mansion beamed brighter, and Alora couldn't help the flush to her own cheeks at the sight. "If anyone would recognize a beautiful thing, I am told it is you."

"Oh goodness." Alora palmed her cheek to coax some coolness back into it. Opulence Mansion was kept at a comfortable temperature, she'd noticed, but now she felt much too warm. "I do enjoy what I do."

"Good. That is good. Forgive me, and I mean no offense, but you look rather young to have built such success in Enver. A town known for enchantment and wonder is no easy place to impress."

Alora resisted the habit of adjusting her satchel, of adjusting anything at all. "It wasn't easy, in the beginning. But small successes turned to larger ones, and now I've become comfortable with steady work and a growing portfolio."

"Excellent. Hard work builds mettle, after all. Please, have a seat. I am told it is setting up to become blazing by afternoon, and I wouldn't want your journey home to be uncomfortable. Refreshment?"

"Water is fine." Alora sank onto the buttery leather across from him—*expensive*—dragging her satchel over her head and removing her portfolio.

After depositing the glass in front of her, the man took the seat opposite. "As I'm sure you know, I am Master Marshall Merridon. So as to keep things professional, I would prefer you refer to me as 'Master Merridon', or 'Master' if you'd rather. Many others do."

Alora blinked slowly, unsure if she'd heard him correctly and wanting time to digest to be sure she had. Refer to him as 'Master'? She was a *businesswoman*. She'd rather be raked into the hedges. But she smiled politely as this was an initial appointment, and there was nowhere better to hold one's tongue. Instead, she said, "Pleased to officially meet you, Master Merridon."

"And I, you." He sipped amber liquid from a short crystal glass, brown eyes trained upon her. They were hard to read, those eyes, almost too perfectly blank. "What do you think of this room?"

"*Oh*. Well—" So they were just to dive right into it then? That suited her more than enough. She surveyed the space, examining the furniture, the decor, and the shades of each. The familiarity of using a critical eye calmed her as she inspected, to the point where she eventually cleared her throat and said, "The pieces in this room are large, almost too much so. They cause the space to feel smaller, and thus the decor, too busy. I understand you have a preference for gold coloring, but I think such a strong color would be better suited in accent pieces, rather than papering every wall."

For the first time, Master Merridon's mouth pinched. "I see."

Alora had seen similar expressions before and eased at once into her perfected smile. "But it is also a matter of the client's requests, and I do take everyone's unique tastes into account. I think in the end, you will be able to say you're more than satisfied within your new office space."

A long moment passed in which Alora felt regarded in much the same way she'd regarded the room: piece by piece. "That would be all very well, if I were interested in redecorating my office."

A chill settled over her; she felt herself go pale. "Aren't you?"

"Come. I think it's time I show you my project."

Alora stood as he did, scrambling to replace her portfolio as he made for the door. All the while, she withered with embarrassment.

A seasoned professional would have asked for clarification before such a long-winded critique, Alora!

"I think you'll find that the rumors about Opulence Mansion are untrue. If anything, they are tamer than the truth. Let us begin with Door One. Up the staircase, if you please."

Alora eyed the aforementioned stairs as if they would grow teeth and bite at her feet. They appeared either solid gold or gold-plated, though from what she'd heard of Opulence, the former was the likelier truth. They were gaudy to her personal taste, but still so extravagant that the idea of stepping on them seemed almost blasphemous. Master Merridon cleared his throat at her dallying, which prompted Alora to smile over her shoulder at him.

"My apologies. There is only so much to admire!"

Master Merridon offered her a small smile in return, though she thought she caught a twitch of impatience in the expression. "After you, Miss Pennigrim."

Alora ascended ahead of him, much to her chagrin. For the first time, she couldn't ascertain how an interview was going, and it bothered her to no end. Around and around, she followed the gold railing—definitely solid all the way through—until a crimson door with a gold plate presented itself. She paused at the threshold. "I thought I saw Door One below."

"You did. Each door below corresponds with the one above, a sort of…prequel. My favorite room," said Master Merridon. "The room in which Opulence Mansion, and myself, got its start. As you're likely aware, we operate by membership only, opening our many doors at dusk and closing them at dawn. These memberships are coveted, expensive, and limited, and soon you'll know why." The scent of whiskey and tobacco enveloped her as he stepped around, sending the door sailing inward with a flourish.

"Door One: Room of Forgotten Memories."

Chapter Three

The Room of Forgotten Memories was, in fact, a bathing chamber, with a massive porcelain soaking tub on golden feet. The walls were entirely mirrored, and the chandelier trailed strings of crystals to further reflect the light of the candles burning atop it. Alora turned slowly, absorbing her reflection from every angle. It was far more of herself than she needed to see, and she didn't dare imagine what it must be like to be bare before them.

"How…stimulating. I'm curious at the decision for so many mirrors," she said, trying not to offend, but wondering *why?* Why would anyone choose such a thing?

"Eyes are a window to the soul, would you not agree?"

"I suppose so. In a poetic way."

"And the soul is where our memories reside, molding and remolding, until we become the person you see standing here, mirrored back at you. Look closely, and you will see every moment having shaped you." When Alora made to step before such a mirror, he stopped her with a light touch to the arm. "Not now. Not with another present. This sort of thing is best done alone, unadorned. And, if one decides something to be too painful, too heavy, to continue allowing its mark on their soul, to bear with them through the entirety of this lifetime and even into the next, they may climb into the bath."

"To rest and ease the burden?"

"In a sense, though I can tell you are thinking of basic needs. No, Miss Pennigrim, this bath is part of Opulence Mansion and so it is much more. The tub will siphon one's bad memories away for eternity."

"Oh my. That is—"

"Spectacular?"

Alora wasn't so convinced. She stared at the bathtub as if it would surge, taking every memory until she'd become nothing but a shell, unfeeling, not knowing what made her.

Good gracious…

"Come along. There is more to see."

Twenty-four numbered doors made up Opulence Mansion's second floor. Alora soon visited them all.

Not once throughout her tour did Master Merridon ask for her opinion again. There were rooms designed for unique entertainments, like the Room of Fire behind Door Eighteen, and rooms designed to evoke peculiar sensations such as the Room of Lightness beyond Door Seven. The corresponding doors on the first floor offered changes of attire, if applicable, and special refreshments, if desired. By her leave of Door Twenty-four, Alora's legs protested loudly and her mind just as much.

One didn't live in Enver without expectation of enchantment, but Opulence Mansion defied normal existence. She couldn't help feeling overwhelmed.

"Master Merridon," she began, hand pressed to her forehead. "I'm afraid I still do not understand your specific requirements. Are all rooms to be redone? Or a few?"

Master Merridon paused in his descent of the final staircase. "Only one, Miss Pennigrim. I simply thought you'd like to see the rest of the establishment before encountering the project I plan for you. Many people wish they had the chance to step into the mystery of our world, but unfortunately, never will. Life can be unfair that way."

Alora lowered her hand at his choice of words. "Does this mean there are no other applicants?"

"None I would entertain," he replied, bright smile returning. "I knew from the moment we met that you were the one I wanted."

Something twinged inside her at his declaration; Alora decided it must be hunger. As of one hour ago, this appointment had become the longest interview to which she'd ever been subjected. "I'm certainly eager to learn of this project," she said, managing to do so without gritting her teeth.

Two hours ago would have been preferable, you showboat of a man.

"Allow me to show you our final room then. Door Twenty-five."

"I thought there were only twenty-four numbered rooms in Opulence Mansion?"

"Not anymore," said Master Merridon. Face alight, he gestured her to follow, and around and around they descended. "Just there."

Returned now to the first floor, Alora squinted down the remaining corridor. For all its shadows, it may as well have ended there. "I'm not sure I can make out a door."

"But it is there, at the hall's end. The soon-to-be greatest offering of Opulence Mansion." He studied her reaction closely. "The Room of Desire."

"Room of Desire," she repeated, returning his intense stare. "What sort of desires does it promise?" Her thoughts whirled from more accepted forms, such as money, to the more clandestine, such as—

At the blush having risen to the apples of her cheeks, Master Merridon chuckled. "That is the wondrous thing about desires. They are particular to everyone, and so long as a member can recall theirs distinctly, they might experience it. Perhaps even leave here *with* it."

Alora frowned. "How can that be possible?"

"The impossible thrives here, haven't you noticed?"

It was a non-answer, of course, but when she frowned deeper, he only winked at her, unbothered. It was a well-practiced wink, she could tell. One that probably charmed others into giving him precisely what he wanted. In this particular moment, his desire was clear: *silence.* "Enter it now if you like. Take your time, take notes, or whatever your process may be. As far as the remainder of the terms, you will be allotted one month to design the room to its fullest potential, a generous expense account, naturally, and payment of 100,000 evergolds by the end." Alora choked on a gasp. "Oh, and a membership. Paid in full for one year. Are you all right?"

Alora could only continue to blink rapidly, her brain a delirious whirlwind amassing around one central thought. *100,000 evergolds!* Well over twice what she earned in a year, all in a single job. She was most certainly *not* 'all right'.

"I think so. I'm only— A month?"

"Once I have my mind set on something, I like to see it to fruition as quickly as possible. I'll await your answer."

Yes! Alora wanted to exclaim. A hundred times over. But she pulled herself together at last, brushing back the pieces of hair having escaped from the top of her head during her overextended tour, and turned toward the dark corridor. "I won't be long."

It wasn't far before even the vestiges of light remaining from the main hall's chandeliers could no longer mark her way. Alora walked in total darkness, and in a slight downhill, too, if she wasn't mistaken. The flooring hadn't changed, however, as her short heels continued to clack against it as before, and the air smelled no different, though the temperature might have dropped a fraction. But that could be nerves. She wasn't in the habit of wandering into dark spaces without a light source and was surprised Master Merridon hadn't offered one. A note for her refurbishment of this space, to be sure.

"Is there even a Door Twenty-five? Maybe this tunnel burrows on forever," she grumbled, moments before her outstretched fingers touched wood. Her rushed breath of relief was loud in the dark—too loud—and before she could help it, a bout of nerves overtook her. She didn't know what might be down here: spiders or snakes or someone lurking who might hurt her. As minds were prone to do, an unwelcome memory of the running man surfaced. Did many attempt to break into this place? Had any succeeded? And where might the hairy-armed giant have gotten off to with their quarry?

She needed light and she needed it *now*, and when the flickering candle materialized in her hand, she couldn't be upset by her lack of discipline. All she felt was quick relief. Door Twenty-five. There it was, marked as all the others, and the doorknob was the same—gold and ornate. She turned it quickly and sent it inward.

At first glance, she noted the bare floors; no marble or rugs or furs as she'd seen prior. She stepped slowly in, careful, so as not to disturb anything that may be lurking. But there was nothing. Aside from an unlit lamp sitting alone on the floor, there wasn't so much as a window, furthering her suspicions she was indeed below ground. The walls were bare white plaster, and the ceiling held no adornment either. It was a plain, average-sized room with nothing to mark it but her imagination.

A dangerous thing.

Moving toward the lamp, she used the nearby matches to light it, snuffing her imagined candle and placing it in her satchel once the other flared. "A room of desires. Hmm. What to do with you?" She pulled out her notepad and a pencil, tapping its length. Master Merridon had said desires were unique to an individual. An obvious statement, but it was one she'd latched onto. She couldn't very well decorate a room to call upon every natural desire. Love, money, long life, health— No, what a nightmare. If a person sought out this room, they must already have an idea of what they wished for, and so needn't be swayed. Simple furnishings, then. No—*inviting*. Some people, not her, but some people, were skittish over admitting their desires for a host of reasons. This room should entice them to do so.

Pulling a measuring tape from the bag's depths, Alora moved about the room, jotting notes and lengths and ideas, everything else forgotten. She could picture it clearly: a thick wool rug, a chaise lounge, and soft lamplight rather than an overwhelming chandelier. The chaise would be crimson, a nod to Master Merridon of course, with thick cushions, and perhaps gold, but not much—

Alora cut off the image not a moment too soon. What a disaster it would be for an unexplained piece of furniture to materialize with no way to be rid of it or to explain it. She'd lived twenty-four years with the secret, and she wouldn't let it free now. 100,000 evergolds were on the line. *100,000!*

Stashing the notebook and dousing the lamplight, she left.

"I accept," she announced upon her return. "Oh, I'm sorry! I didn't mean to interrupt."

Master Merridon turned toward her as the stranger did. Though Master Merridon's face revealed his pleasure, the stranger's revealed nothing, as it was hidden beneath a dark cowl. Alora appreciated the tall height of the newcomer. How his broad shoulders rivaled that of the proprietor's, how he was entirely enshrouded by a high-collared black coat that brushed his knees. It didn't take any particular skill to ascertain that this was a person not meant to be seen, though Master Merridon didn't seem too put out about it. If anything, given her announcement, the shadowy man ceased to require his attention.

Alora was an unfortunate sap for mystery, especially when said mystery involved tall, darkly dressed gentlemen. *Intrigue*, hammered her heart. *He must be very hot beneath all that black.*

"Excellent, Miss Pennigrim!" Master Merridon raised two fingers in a dismissive gesture to the man beside him, who then promptly turned away. As he left, Alora caught a fascinating glimpse of a masked jaw in the chandelier light before giving her attention once more to Master Merridon.

"Before I begin, I will ask if there is anything particular you request for the room? I'll admit I'm curious as to how it's all meant to work. Take the Room of Forgotten Memories, for example. Am I to accommodate for plumbing?"

Two birds with one stone, this question was, and Alora waited, her bones vibrating. Master Merridon's mouth took on that pinched expression again. "No plumbing. I suppose seating would be my only contribution. A chair, a sofa, or perhaps a bed. Something of that nature."

A bed? What a conundrum this project is turning out to be. And so soon. She'd never had so little to go on.

"Use your imagination, Miss Pennigrim. Design it to your exquisite tastes. I'm certain it will not disappoint."

"I will do my very best, Master Merridon."

"I'm sure of it. Now, last matter of business." Master Merridon reached within his luxurious waistcoat, pulling forth a folded bit of parchment and a pen.

"Your signature, please. For our agreement."

"Of course." Alora didn't always have to sign such things, but for well-established businesses such as this, it was to be expected. When he handed both to her, she unfolded it, reading quickly. She swallowed. "A confidentiality clause?"

"Mandatory, I'm afraid. Opulence Mansion operates with a certain sense of...secrecy. I prefer it to remain that way. Also, this." From beneath his arm, a golden cloak unfurled. "From now on, you must wear it to and from."

Alora took the cloak. The material was thin and gauzy, enough that it seemed a breathable fabric. She supposed she could see the sense in it. Not that she was in the habit of telling secrets, but he didn't truly know her. Everything else was legitimate, the terms he told her clearly stated, and after a moment of struggle in retrieving her notepad to use as support, she signed her commitment to the job.

"One month," said Master Merridon, waving goodbye.

Alora returned his smile and his wave, though inwardly she wondered what need he felt in reminding her again.

Chapter Four

Summer storms were unpredictable beasts, and after leaving Opulence, Alora was foolishly unprepared to be caught in one. She certainly wasn't prepared to do so while hurrying through Enver's Mugwort Alley, the only street, as far she was aware, that refused floral arrangements to replace their storefronts' fish barrels and denied their homes' doors a fresh coat of paint. It was the least enchanting street of an otherwise enchanting town, and now she'd no choice but to either saturate the contents of her satchel or hurry into the nearest dilapidated shop in escape.

Potions & Peculiarities was scrawled in a silver script upon an otherwise black sign, its creak the result of chains hanging from rusted hooks and an unrelenting wind. In a positive direction, there were no fish barrels as sported by the shops nearby, though its window boxes appeared to be growing only weeds—and not very well. Another crack of thunder and the drenching onslaught began. With a cry over the contents of her bag and the promise of a sopping and drooping bodice over a late lunch, Alora could dally no longer. She rushed up the few steps and through the scraping door.

The shop was, unfortunately, exactly as she expected.

Judging—ah, *observing*—from the windows, she thought it would be dark inside, and it was, though the storm didn't help the matter as the sky had deepened into an angry charcoal.

A limp yellow light spilled from the corner thanks to a lamp attached to the wall, doing its best to highlight the items on the shelves. Mostly, it cast ghastly shadows. Alora needed to step close toward the obscure offerings in order to identify them, and she wondered if that was a purposeful sales tactic by the proprietor. One could never be sure with the Mugwort Alley types.

The shelves of the shop were deep and spaced far apart to accommodate all manner of things, but the aisles were narrow. Alora realized the poor functionality of this firsthand as she bent to examine a hide-covered clock. Her satchel clanged against something behind her. She spun.

A bronze candelabra teetered violently; she steadied it with a hissed curse. It was common courtesy to purchase anything one had broken, but Alora knew she could not be made to purchase this. With a base carved into a menacing scowl and its candleholders in the shapes of flames, it was far too hideous. Her fingers came away coated in some sticking substance, and she shuddered.

Grotesque piece! It's probably rotten old polish, and now I'll be stuck with the smell.

Glaring down at her soiled hands, she couldn't help her comparisons any longer. If she'd been *anywhere* within lovely Thistledown Square, she would've had a proprietor smiling over her by now, eager with assistance. Likely, she would have been offered refreshment. Certainly a least a courteous question regarding her enjoyment of the day. As it was, she wiped her dirtied fingers against her satchel and moved on—alone.

The entire place smelled oddly herby, like sage. Sage and mint and a bit like leather. As she continued down the aisle, she found the source of the leather scent: a mangy top hat and cape to match. It hung from a wiry mannequin and took up a great portion of an already crowded space. When she stood before it, an eerie feeling of watchful eyes crept over her. Enough that she jumped when the building groaned beneath the wind. Alora edged around it.

Past the mannequin were more clocks. Hourglasses and pocket watches too. A break appeared in the shelves, and she switched aisles to find daggers in etched glass cases and pocketknives on beds of purple velvet. She discovered jewelry too; old and tarnished, the stones still picked up what little light was afforded and reflected it back to her. She reached toward a crooked, bony finger with a ring wrapped around its base. Inhaling a gasp, she realized it wasn't a peculiar mold, but a real finger bone. Alora abandoned the shelf immediately with a hand pressed to her middle.

Hellish Mugwort Alley! What sort of shop displays human bones?

Around the corner, she skidded to a halt. Because here, she'd come upon something *alive*. Something that chirped faintly at her attention, its subsequent gurgles the most endearing sound she'd ever heard.

"Oh! Well, *hello*." The little green creature watched her curiously from the confines of its cage. "You're special, aren't you?"

It was, of course, quite an odd thing. The animal possessed overlarge eyes like a bat and a body composed of a gelatinous-like substance rather than bone. Combined with the two tiny arms, two fins at its end, and three horns on top of its triangular head, she fell positively head-over-heels for it.

"What are you, my darling?" Alora scanned for something to divulge its name, or at least its origin, but as with everything else, the creature's cage was unmarked. There was mystery, but then there was just plain *bad business*. Alora decided whoever owned this establishment must be lazy beyond reproach.

The creature continued to watch her steadily, offering a second gurgle at her remarks, which she didn't know how to interpret. It wriggled closer to its bars, leaving its makeshift pond.

"Are you hungry? Or only lonely? I'd like to know more about you so let me find the owner." She waggled her fingers in farewell. "Be back soon."

At the end of the row stood a peculiar humming wardrobe with a skeleton key protruding from its lock. After she managed to skirt around that, she found the shop's front counter.

Oh, Alora thought, rather dumbly, as her feet stopped propelling her at once.

A tied bundle of burning leaves sat inside a dish on a narrow countertop that stretched from one wall to the next. More sad yellow light, too, spilled from the only other lamp in the room. It highlighted the worn look of the counter. It did even better at highlighting the sharp features of the man standing bent over a ledger behind it.

Whoever he was, he appeared wholly absorbed. His pen, held in a tight grip, marked across the page, swift and harsh. Her attention flicked to his opposite hand, where it pressed into his forehead, then down to a pewter cup sitting untouched beside him. A cup that didn't so much steam as *smoke*.

He wore a black vest detailed in an alluring emerald-leaved pattern with a well-tailored black shirt beneath. Only, the buttons had been left open at the wrists and throat. It gave her the distinct impression that he couldn't or perhaps *wouldn't* be bothered with details. Something which she couldn't fathom for herself.

All in all, he looked irritated and busy, the antithesis of approachable. Which Alora promptly ignored as she made right for him.

"Don't speak to the barshet," he said, without his eyes leaving the page. "It might decide it enjoys the sound and burrow down your throat to retrieve it."

His voice was deep and rough and decidedly bored. Horrified, but also skeptical, Alora stopped mid-step and didn't even bother with a "hello" before she stammered, "But...it's in a cage."

"Little hindrance if it's motivated. It doesn't have our complicated matter of bones." Closing the ledger with a startling snap, he lifted his gaze to her.

Alora knew a boy once with brown eyes so warm she felt like she'd melted every time they focused on her. These eyes were not like those. They were an attractive color still, a mossy green, and framed by dark lashes and smudged with kohl, but they were also penetrating. Like a deep winter cold or the jab of a needle. She didn't know what possible cause she'd given for him to narrow them at her.

Her skin pricked where his eyes landed. Because even though he stared with a gaze like frostbite, he was also decidedly handsome. As in *exceptionally*. Perhaps the most handsome man she'd ever matched stares with. Her hand pressed to her throat a moment, coaxing it to widen. "*Excuse me*, but why would you have such a creature in your shop?"

"Peculiarities," he said, gesturing around. His hair was darker than hers, wet and tousled, like he'd just come in from the blowing rain. A brief and outrageous thought entered her head that she should run her fingers through it and set it to order. "Can I help you find something? A cursed ring? An heirloom dagger? A potion to poison your fiancé's former lover?" At the last suggestion, he nodded to the glass enclosure to the right of him, all manner of potions bottled and stoppered, and a sign that read: *Don't see what you need? Ask the proprietor.*

Alora's mouth fell wide in shock. "I would never kill someone! And had I planned to, I certainly wouldn't purchase my weapon in a shop easily traced. I'd be the worst sort of criminal."

"How would you do it then?"

She frowned at the lift of his lips. Scowled upon realizing he was mocking her. His hard eyes seemed to focus on her soft curves, the flared cut of her skirt, how perfectly incapable she looked of murder.

Alora was hungry and tired from her walk in the sun. Her temper had shortened rapidly because of it. She'd little energy for this smirking shopkeeper, no matter what she thought of his eyes. She scowled her fiercest before turning, certain there must be another building more amiable than this to wait out the storm, but a quaking crack of thunder stilled her steps.

"Quite the weather we're having."

Alora glanced over her shoulder, watching the shopkeeper drink from his cup.

She could spew small talk until her voice cracked when it suited, but in this moment, she would not. Instead, Alora rolled her eyes, determined to keep her back to him. That was, until she noticed a suspicious plant vining up the wall.

"Is that..." She stepped closer, enough to see the tiny blue thorns and the just-as-small blue flowers on an otherwise deep green vine. "It is! That's a Dirededron. A Grave Digger! Did you know if you jostle it the spores will settle in your lungs and kill you in a terrible way?"

The shopkeeper's expression remained lazy and unconcerned, the sight of which irked her endlessly. This was why dust encased the place, why no labels were printed, and why no more than two lamps showcased the shelves. He swirled the contents of his mug. The smoke drifted upward. "It's a good thing I don't jostle it then."

Alora could only stare. She took him in, standing there. His black trousers and black boots, his back to a rickety-looking staircase leading to somewhere above, and a doorway which must lead to either storage or a back entrance or both. Her eyes narrowed. He lifted one dark eyebrow.

"What?"

She raised her chin. "Nothing."

"You certainly aren't staring as if it's nothing."

A scoff left her lips even as her neck warmed. "It's only that I am used to paying attention to the contents of a room. I know when something fits in a space. And when it doesn't."

"Cheers to your accomplishment." He raised his cup. But while his tone had once again turned dry, his eyes seemed to skewer her in place.

"You don't fit here. Where is the real owner of this establishment?"

"I am the owner."

"A joke, surely. You couldn't be further from someone I would imagine bent behind a counter dallying in ledgers. No matter that the place is in desperate need for rearranging, among other things." She had a hundred ideas to turn this shop into something if not admirable, then at least passable. A good cleaning to start. And more lighting. Perhaps sconces, with adorable patterns etched into blown glass...

"And where do you imagine I belong? I'll ignore the jab at my configuration, for your sake." He reclined against the staircase, ankles crossed, studying her as closely as she did him. Aside from his eyes, which glittered as they speared her, he was devoid of color, endlessly dark.

It unnerved her. "In a shadowed alley. Maybe in possession of one of those *heirloom daggers* stealing others' hard-earned money."

She was only half-serious, but his lips lifted. "Nights can be very long. Who says I don't entertain both lifestyles?"

Alora ground her teeth, refusing to let him bait her. But sometimes her refusals weren't enough. She latched on. "You admit to being a pickpocket?"

"A pickpocket? In Enver? Where strangers clap one another's shoulders with a smile, and ladies sing 'good mornings' from their balconies? Hardly satisfying; they'd probably wish me well."

Alora, who'd most definitely sung aloud while watering flowers atop her terrace, blushed. A color which deepened when he made a great show of examining her person, from her boots to her head. "If I were a betting man, I'd say you smile at everyone."

She laughed, incredulous, then preened. "Yet you've not received one. You should be disappointed as I've been complimented on my smile many times."

The proprietor reached once more for his cup. "You're smiling at me right now." Alora, realizing her error, clacked her teeth together. "And you're right. I would have been dreadfully disappointed."

"Don't *mock* me."

"I've not mocked you once, Miss Whoever-You-Are. You're misreading me. In fact, it's been you who has repeatedly *judged*—"

A soft chirp cut off whatever further comment the supposed shop owner was about to say. Instead, Alora caught the widening of his eyes and the sudden stillness of his form before she turned to find the sweet barshet sitting placidly, watching her, from several feet away.

"*Don't,*" demanded the shopkeeper.

Alora opened her mouth to protest that she'd not planned to do anything but stilled when she saw his expression. The quiet horror she found there caused an icy burn to form in her own chest then. When the barshet chirped again, hopping forward, Alora shuffled back. Her hips met the counter with a jarring thud she didn't pay attention to. Should she really be so terrified of such a creature?

She wanted to ask if she should run, but he'd told her not to speak, and she didn't know how fast it could move. How fast it could claw its way down her throat. It wouldn't really, would it?

Goddammit! Why had she chosen this shop?

The barshet gurgled, and Alora watched as it began to fall within itself, flattening to the floor. What was happening to it? Was it dying?

A sharp curse left the proprietor a moment before arms snaked beneath hers, hauling her up and over the counter. A mere second later, a distinct splat was heard from the opposite side.

Quick breaths pulsed against her back as she was enveloped by the scent of vetiver. It was quite nice, despite the circumstances.

"It almost had you. It should be stunned now."

She could hardly register the strong pair of arms wrapped around her from behind, nor the feel of the shopkeeper's broad chest against her back, before they were gone.

"Wait!" she cried out, as he abandoned her for the back of the shop.

Alora clapped both hands over her mouth immediately upon realizing her mistake.

A familiar chirp sounded behind her, and she screamed. The barshet, not so stunned apparently, slithered onto the counter. It gazed up at her adoringly. Perhaps too much so? Alora replaced her hands over her mouth, determined to keep it from leaping down her throat. With one foot behind the other, she backed carefully away.

The creature would not be deterred. She observed in horror as it made to sink into itself as before. Any moment now and it would spring—

A frying pan smashed onto the countertop.

Alora screamed again, though it was muffled by her hands, and leapt backward, slamming her back into the staircase hard enough to bruise. The shopkeeper released the handle. Green goo oozed from its side, dripping from the counter's edge.

"Is it dead?" Alora whispered, hoarse, hands clutching her throat.

"Likely." Glancing her over, he turned back, pulling a handkerchief from his pocket to wipe up the mess on the floor. "Are you hurt?"

"No," she said, even as her back throbbed. She supposed it was nice he cared to—

"Good," he replied, from his crouched position. "You owe me one hundred evergolds."

Horrible man, she seethed, tossing her satchel onto a chair before easing into the one beside. *As if I'd pay him for the experience of nearly losing my voice to a creature he has no business keeping.*

"Hello, dear. Would you like the usual?"

Alora glanced up to the familiar apple cheeks and short gray curls belonging to Ellie Turkens. "Yes, thank you. But also, I was wondering if you knew of a book cataloguing rare creatures. I recently learned of one today, a barshet, and am curious to know more." Like what the proprietor of Potions and Peculiarities meant by "likely" when asked if the creature was dead.

"Hmm, let me do some investigating. Be back shortly."

Alora watched Ellie go, disappearing beyond shelves of books to ready her order. If anyone could find her information on a subject, it would be Ellie Turkens. The woman had begun El's Books and Nibbles back when she was younger than Alora, and she was at least eighty now, though you'd never guess given her energy.

Alora let her mind drift as she studied the plants nestled in crannies and hanging from the ceiling. Small butterflies and several bees flitted about them, as Ellie often left the back door open in invitation. She wondered if they'd weathered the storm inside, or if they'd come in recently now that it'd moved on.

She desperately needed the tea to be strong today. She'd love the largest cup Ellie owned, the one with blue flowers preferably—Alora's favorite color—and a single cube of sugar to cut the edge. Yes, that would be perfection.

"Oh!" Alora gasped, said cup materializing at her fingertips. She glanced around, but thankfully there was no one seated near her.

There was a man perusing the shelves, but he was behind her and thoroughly engrossed in his finds. Her breath shuddered still; Ellie would be back soon. How would she ever explain having retrieved her own cup of tea?

Not two heartbeats later, she heard the familiar laugh of the bookshop owner. As panic built, Alora could do the only plausible thing. She downed the contents of her cup in three swallows. Tongue scalded, chest afire, she hardly managed to toss the cup into her satchel where it clattered loudly when Ellie Turkens appeared at her side.

"Here you are, dear. Black tea, nice and strong today, to beat back the disruption the thunder leaves on our energies, and a warm tomato and cheese— Oh, sweetheart! Whatever is the matter?"

Alora brushed the tears from her eyes, leftover from downing hot tea like a draft horse, and gifted the proprietor a watery smile. "It's nothing, Mrs. Turkens."

"It isn't nothing if you're tearing about it. Tell me, child. Are you hurting?"

Only her tongue, but Alora couldn't very well explain that. "I met a very rude man today." Let Ellie think her common reaction to distasteful people was sorrow rather than anger.

"Ah," clucked the old woman. "Now you know what you do with rude men, don't you?"

Alora shook her head.

"Poor darling. I'll tell you now. You pull out your favorite color, freshen your lipstick nice and slow, and while they're distracted, staring right at your pretty mouth, you say: Piss off!"

Alora laughed, unable to help herself. And Ellie Turkens, her lipstick pink as petals, grinned back at her. "You'll be fine, dear. Drink your tea."

Slightly worried over what another cup of black tea would do to her nerves, Alora dutifully took a sip. It was leagues better than the one she'd imagined. Partly because it wasn't scalding hot and pouring down her throat, but also that Ellie Turken's tea was incredibly enchanted, her blends well on their way to becoming legend. Steam wafted upward in the shape of dahlias.

"And here is your book. I hardly remember what a barshet is, but it should be in there. Let me know if it isn't."

Alora finished half her sandwich before diving into the text. It was a brown book, *Rare Creatures of the West*, and it did, indeed, catalog the barshet, its bat-like eyes illustrated to peer up at her from the page.

THE BARSHET

CHARACTERISTICS: Cartilaginous endoskeleton with gelatinous covering, usually yellow or green in color. Notable by one to three horns atop its head. Hermaphrodites. Enjoys water. Brings luck if squeezed in a number synchronous with its horns.

WARNING: attracted to voices. Preference unknown but appears to be specific to each creature. If motivated, will attempt burrowing toward sound, often killing the host in the process. Avoid leaving in direct, hot sun. Will melt and perish.

Alora glared at the page as she chewed. Either the proprietor of that horrid Peculiarities shop was ignorant, or he'd lied to her. Likely he lied and the creature was happily back in its cage. To think he called her out for judging. Why, she'd been correct on every score! She swallowed another sip of tea, regarding the red floral pattern of the cup. She didn't think she'd ever been so impulsive, not since she'd learned to control her imaginings in her teenage years. First the candlestick, then the almost-chaise, and now the tea.

People admired those with vivid imaginations. They made for many creative types. Most of which ended up in this far west, whimsical town of Enver, chasing various delights and utilizing their own. But as far as Alora was aware, there were none so vivid as her own, capable of bringing into the world whatever she imagined.

It began as a child wishing for a stuffed doll, something to sleep with at night. When her parents discovered it the following morning, asking where she'd gotten it, she'd told them she'd found it. Which she supposed wasn't really a lie, considering she'd found it inside her own head. It progressed from there. Her youthful imagination conjured all sorts of things she'd wished for, from favorite sweets to hair ribbons to toys. It wasn't until she'd brought about a living thing that trouble ensued. A brown, flop-eared bunny, but one not quite right, a vital part missing—

Alora's eyes lifted to a flap of wings. Ellie's twin owls had come to lay curious eyes on the patrons. She supposed the previously dark skies must have woken them, a trickery into believing an early night had come.

"Lucille. Loretta." She nodded a hello, the birds' snow-white heads swiveling in unison as she rose. She'd another appointment which required a brief stop at home, and she mustn't linger any longer thinking of dark shops and even darker rooms.

No, those were definitely after dinner musings.

She left payment for the book and the meal, tucking the volume within her burgeoning satchel. Thinking over it for a moment, she pulled the teacup and the candlestick from the bag, placing it on the table. Ellie believed one could never have enough teacups, and as Alora wasn't of similar thought, it would probably get much more use in the bookshop. And as for the candlestick— Well, she'd gotten a little overzealous in her imaginings. Its base was solid silver and would be worth quite a lot. Also, it was heavy.

Chapter Five

This, not Mugwort Alley, was the Enver she'd fallen for. Her house was a one-bedroom flat above a print shop, with a white stone outer staircase and an overlarge terrace off the main room. She set a leisurely pace toward it as the rain had cleared, leaving the cobblestones wet and the air cooled. All around she smelled heaps of blossoms. No one went without. Barrels were repurposed to wildflower gardens, and few walls were bare of a trellis or vines climbing in sweet-scented blooms. Windowsills spilled with bright arrangements and butterflies fluttered all about, though none, she must admit, were so large or so brilliant as those along Opulence Mansion's enchanting lane. She supposed it was fitting; Master Merridon wouldn't have it any other way.

Eirian, her hometown, was several hours east by wagon, and while charming in its own right, with plenty of flowers and bees and butterflies, prairies and hills instead of forest and mountains and sea, she'd not been back since she'd left. It was not full of whimsy and enchantment like Enver. The people there were not so open-minded and far less forgiving. A scarred lesson borne.

"Harrumph," grunted the printer toward her, a broom in his hand as he swept his stoop of storm debris.

"Afternoon, Mister Zanfold," replied Alora and made her way up the steps.

Someday, she mused, she might have her own shop. A place where people could come and peruse samples and pick her brain. It would be much easier than being reachable only by letter, or a happenstance run-in, as it sometimes occurred. And she wouldn't have to carry so many things in her satchel. Only a notepad and pencil.

What a dream. One she couldn't dream of too vividly, of course, as people would balk at a sudden building materializing in any given space. And she couldn't simply will her coffers full. She had a moral compass to follow, after all.

As she fitted the key into its lock, she abruptly smiled so wide that her cheeks pulled too tight. Finish Opulence Mansion, and she could afford a lovely little spot. *Gracious, what a stroke of good fortune that fancy bit of post has turned out to be.*

Alora stepped into her home, unlacing her boots and hanging her satchel on the rack. She'd freshen up quick as could be and hurry right back out.

"Mrs. Flops," she called, entering the kitchen to pull apart some greens. "Don't tantrum. I'd told you last night my day would be hectic. Come have a bite of lunch."

Settling the plate onto the floor, Alora hurried to the washroom to reset her hair. Between the walk and the wind, she looked positively tousled, and not in a roguishly handsome sort of way. Her fingers worked quickly with their twists and pins. Placing her hands upon her waist, she turned this way and that, satisfied once more. Only—

There. She dabbed on a lipstick—a pink rose—and thought of a certain Potions and Peculiarities 'proprietor' all the while.

"Good girl, Mrs. Flops. See you for dinner." With a soft scratch between the rabbit's long white ears, Alora replaced her boots and was gone.

She didn't need any notepad or samples for this appointment as the project was nearly complete. It was only a matter of delivery now. Just two more stops and she'd be on her way. Alora walked toward the edge of town singing quietly to herself, and then louder as the buildings grew sparse. She sang until she saw green.

She'd arrived at the stable.

"Miss Merryweather, hello."

"Hello today, Miss Pennigrim. Come to fetch Mister George?"

Alora stepped within the stable door where the scents of animal, sweet hay, and musty straw overcame her. "I am. He has an important job retrieving flowers today."

"One I'm sure he'll enjoy." The stable master flung a sack of grain over her shoulder with ease, motioning for Alora to follow. "I've just let him out to pasture with the other donkeys but come have a shout."

Alora followed the stable master through the building, passing stalls of horses, sheep, and mules until she came to the gate. Ms. Merryweather flung down the grain and retrieved a rope, then she looked to Alora expectantly.

Alora cleared her throat, self-conscious over the two stable hands watching her in not-so-subtle ways from the corners of their eyes as they went about their chores.

She grimaced. "GEORGE!"

Thankfully, the kind creature didn't make her call him twice. Lumbering through the pasture, George cantered, large ears perked and eyes bright. Alora knew she possessed a weakness for large-eared creatures; she'd accepted it.

"Hello, George," she said, when he pressed his nose to the gate and snorted. "Care to visit the nursery?"

Ms. Merryweather didn't wait for his answer but flung the rope about him and swung in the gate.

"Come along, Mister George. Let's get you hitched."

Alora spared one more look for the stable hands as she followed, and though one ducked away at her glance, the other smiled and winked.

The cheek!

Why, she must wear lipstick more often.

Being as their route was so familiar, the donkey kept a comfortable pace. The pair of them had trekked this way many times. The cobblestones were larger on this road, an outlying street that wrapped the entirety of Enver. It was intersected plenty, by streets that would take her farther in, but only by three which would take her farther out. A road for the north, into the Indigo mountains, the south, down to the bustling and much-too-large capital, and the east. She shuddered. *Eirian.* Besides the lane to Opulence, there was obviously no great road to the west. Stray only a little farther that way, and one would find themselves hip-deep in glorious waves.

Enver was an enigma of a town. A person could hear tales of it their whole lives and still be shocked to silent wonder upon their arrival. She'd certainly been.

The town was situated on a far-west edge, and while most roads to other places were dirt, to Enver, in all directions, they were paved. Not little stones which released bursts of glittering dust when stepped upon like Opulence Mansion's lane, but huge silver slabs that clipped smartly beneath hooves and boots. A reminder, she assumed, to all who journeyed nearer. That they headed toward something *other*, something special.

She didn't prefer looking east. If she could have done otherwise, she would have. But the nursery was situated on that side of Enver, away from the towering white trees of Renwick Forest and on a slope that soon gave way to rolling hills and a long, winding road. A road that had brought her here not so long ago.

It was better to ignore those hills when she could help it. When she thought of them, she would remember how terrible enchantment could be. And then she would remember how terrible *she* could be.

"Oh George, these *blooms!* How will I ever choose?"

They'd arrived at the nursery, and all was made worth it. Alora weaved through the still-wet rows, touching silken petals and sniffing deeply. "If I didn't know you so well, I'd let you smell these Zanigolds, but sadly I do know you and you'd only eat them."

A pot had tipped sideways in the storm. She leaned over the old wooden table to right it, scooping dirt by the handfuls and patting it down. The yellow flower was saved, but her hands were now stuck with mud. She stared at them in a perplexed state a moment before kneeling and wiping them along the damp ground.

A pair of boots stepped not far from her fingers. It caught her off guard; not a minute ago, she'd been sure she was alone. Alora flung her hands back and her eyes up.

"Excuse m—" she began, only for the word to die a quick death in her throat.

His hair was dried now. It no longer curled on his forehead. Still, it was black and mussed with waves like he'd just raked a hand through it in vexation. Which, given her first impression, was probably so. He stood almost unnervingly tall above her, the insidious Potions and Peculiarities proprietor, and she swallowed hard in discontent at him finding her on her knees.

His eyes gleamed. Like he took amusement in discovering her beneath him. "Forgive my intrusion."

He said it in a way that caused Alora to think he didn't mean it at all. It made her teeth ache. She noticed he carried a clay pot in one arm, mostly dirt, but with one violet-black shoot.

She sniffed as she rose. "Why? It's a public nursery. I hardly own this row. Am I in your way? You might ask me to step aside."

He regarded her a moment more before reaching out beside her, caressing the petals of the flower she'd been gushing over, his arm brushing her own. Alora found herself distracted by the angular cut of his profile, his gentle stroke of the bloom between pale fingers, and bit her lip. He did not, she noted with dismay, ask her to step aside.

"Do you often react to plants this way?"

At last, his arm fell away, and she could breathe readily again.

"Flowers, yes," she replied. "So long as they can't hurt me. You'd never hear my excitement over a Dirededron, let's say. Is that what you have there? Another venomous or poisonous thing?" It was an unfair statement; it looked to be a Forget-Me-Not. Or could be, if allowed to grow, which she wasn't convinced he *would*.

The shopkeeper shifted the pot in his arm. *He really shouldn't stand so close to people*, she thought. *Not with eyes like those.* She felt hot all over and, knowing precisely why, was severely disappointed in herself. He smiled at her, slow and a little bit taunting.

"Worse."

She found that overly nettlesome, no matter if he did have nice teeth to pair with everything else. How positively *wretched*. She cleared her throat, suddenly worried her voice would come out changed. "I presume the barshet is still alive?"

"Why would you presume that?"

Alora's eyes narrowed over his tone. "After that unfortunate *incident*, I went to Books and Nibbles, and do you know what I found? Barshets can only be harmed by melting beneath the sun, but I suspect you knew that didn't you? I don't appreciate swindlers."

The shopkeeper huffed a laugh that wasn't at all jolly or nice, but dark and rude. "That hardly makes me a swindler."

"It does when you demand I pay for the creature!" Alora could feel an angry heat all throughout her. It bothered her how bothered she was by him, which only made him bother her more. She wanted to leave but couldn't. She had at least five plants to choose still.

"I didn't want you to pay for the barshet. You could hardly afford it," he said.

All at once, his gaze had softened, his voice turning almost kind.

Alora blinked at the change. "Then what?"

"A new frying pan. I can't hardly use it now after bashing that creature whilst saving your life." He *winked.* "You're welcome, by the way."

Alora's throat worked as she tried to formulate what she wanted to say. *The audacity!* Her chest heaved as she snatched the Zanigolds to her, her lips parting in fury.

The proprietor's eyes dropped to her mouth.

"Piss off!"

He startled and huffed a breath, incredulous. "*Excuse me?*"

But Alora didn't have anything else to say. Ellie Turkens hadn't given her anything else. So she stomped around him, pot in hand, and grabbed several more without focus before hopping into her small wagon and snatching up the reins.

"Let's go, George. There's a rude man here today."

She didn't want to turn back. It would have been quite stylish not to, but Alora couldn't help it. Shifting her head just a little, she caught the shopkeeper's gaze. Then his hand—brushing over his smirking mouth.

She spun around in an instant, her nose in the air. Sure, it wasn't so great as if she'd not looked at all, but it would have to do.

Chapter Six

Within the hour, Alora had become blissfully absorbed in her work. She'd finished separating the flowers—which weren't terrible picks when considering what she'd been subjected to in acquiring them—and they'd each been re-potted in attractive clay pots. She'd planned to hang them on the outside wall in a random fashion, and once finished, and pending the arrival of his oven, Mr. Whitters' new bakery would be open for business.

Without any bias in the matter, she was excited. His cinnamon buns were frosted, sugar-infected delights.

As if summoning the confection, Mr. Whitters approached on his bicycle, tufts of white hair lifting in sync with the uneven terrain of the cobbles. He slowed as he neared, smiling at where she knelt, finishing his window boxes.

"Miss Pennigrim, this is picturesque!"

Alora beamed, brushing off her gardening gloves. "Thank you, Mister Whitters. It's really coming together."

She watched him dig within the bicycle's basket and retrieve a pastry box.

"For you," he said and placed it in her hands before she could protest. Turning, he stared at the clay pots lined in a row, hands clasped at his back. "Would you like me to fetch the ladder?"

"Oh no, you've done enough," said Alora, inhaling the scents of cinnamon and cream.

The old man chuckled before waving her off. Heading inside, he retrieved the ladder while she deposited the pastries in her wagon. He settled it against the wall, both feet on the rungs, when he turned to Alora and said, "Hand me up one of those pots."

"Mister Whitters, please. I'm sure you've more important things to do. What is the status of your oven?"

"Be here in a week. A pot, Miss Pennigrim."

Alora huffed. Seeing no help for it, she handed the baker his flowers. He scurried to the top, where he hung it carefully and without mishap. Moving back down, he said, "Another."

Shaking her head, Alora selected one from the line. "You know, Mister Whitters," she began, deciding on which to give him next. "I think—"

"*Miss Pennigrim!*"

Alora leapt back on instinct as a pot whistled past her nose and shattered on the ground.

"Oh, my dear Miss Pennigrim! Are you injured? Please say no!"

Alora shook her head, attempting to calm her jagged breaths. Blood pounded in her ears. "Um, no. No, Mister Whitters, I'm fine." She bent to retrieve the broken pieces of the pot as the old baker hurried down the ladder.

"Careful of those edges," he said.

With the remains of the pot stacked precariously in her hands, she smiled at him. If it was a touch shaky, well, rightfully so. She'd nearly gotten her head split apart. "I'll just pop over to the wagon. I have a spare pot in case of such things."

Mr. Whitters nodded, clearly shaken himself. His wide eyes darted around the mess of soil. "I'll fetch a broom then."

"Sure. Good thinking."

Alora darted off to the wagon she'd parked out of the way on an infrequently used side street. She didn't have another pot. It would have been the smart thing to do, but she'd not anticipated needing one, and it wasn't as if she'd the space of her own shop yet to keep spares for later use.

"Almost finished here, George," she said in an attempt to placate what must be a bored donkey, his ears fallen back. But when she circled around to his face, she discovered he was asleep.

Smiling affectionately at his drooped eyelids, she adjusted the broken pot in her grip. Then she imagined it whole. Opening her eyes, the pot rested in her hands, good as new. She stared down at it in relief, brushing a bit of dirt from its surface where her glove had smudged it, when a wash of regret doused her cold.

Weeks had gone by, even entire months, where she'd successfully managed to repress her enchantment, and today she'd used it repeatedly. If she didn't want to be found out and her business discredited before it'd even truly began, then she needed to regather her self-control. With such a vivid brain, she could well imagine the range of reactions she would receive. Fear, over what she could bring into the world on a whim. Anger, from who knows how many dubious previous clients she'd worked alongside. Envy, of those who wished her gift for themselves and cursed her for it. And rejection, the worst of all. Because what vendors would work with her knowing she could duplicate their products with a singular thought?

She'd like to say she'd never do it, but the proof sat literally and fully intact in her hands.

She shook herself. *No, it will be fine.* She'd manage herself a little better, avoid *any* and *all* distractions. She'd get her shop.

She made to turn back when a muffled shout sounded from down the empty street. Abruptly cut off, Alora couldn't decide whether it'd come from indoors or one of the many shadowed stoops. She held her breath, listening a moment more, but when nothing else came of it, she decided it must have been an accident. Someone stubbing a toe on a bit of furniture and now nursing it back to health. Maybe a tumble down the stairs.

A hulking shadow shifted down the way. Alora stilled. When it moved again, she backed up a step herself. It could simply be someone utilizing their back door, a shortcut to whatever part of town they wished to venture to, but the prickle on the back of her neck warned her maybe not. A sudden thwack rent the air, the sound of something being hit, and Alora decided right then that she'd run for the constable. Better to be wrong than to have done nothing at all.

Her lips clamped down around a yelp when a hand gripped her shoulder. She spun around to the familiar face of the baker, his expression harried.

"Miss Pennigrim. Best you come back out of there."

Eyes wide and shifting between the now-motionless shadow beyond and Mr. Whitters, Alora followed him. Safe in front of his bakery, she rushed to ask, "Did you hear that too? Is someone in danger?"

"Yes," said the baker, his sparse eyebrows downturned in worry. "But it's not for you to investigate."

"Well that much I know," agreed Alora, setting down the pot. "My thought was to get the constable."

Mr. Whitters shook his head. "You certainly could. But it won't do any good."

"Why ever not?" Alora was sure her own eyebrows must be buried in her hair.

"*Urchins*, Miss Pennigrim. Not even the constable will mess with those miscreants." When Alora only continued staring, he wrung his hands. "Call them what you will, a gang or a cult, but it doesn't change the fact they're dangerous, and you don't want them noticing you."

"A *gang*? In Enver? What are they? Thieves?"

The baker shrugged. "Not as far as anyone can tell. Truth is, not much is known about them, and every victim of theirs doesn't remember. Some have lost entire years of their lives!"

"Mister Whitters! I've lived here almost two years. Why is this the first I'm hearing of it?"

"It isn't talked about in polite day-to-day conversation. Rather, I'm more curious how none of your friends have whispered of it. It's quite a topic of fascination among the young folk who grew up here; it's been ongoing nearly a decade at least."

Alora's mouth pressed firmly closed. Well, that was all the reasoning she required. She'd not had the time to make any close friends. Though, if she ever decided to be more truthful about the matter, it was more that she'd not even tried. Becoming a hometown pariah at a young age for a most unfortunate incident had certainly done a number on her social confidence.

"Should someone at least have a doctor see whomever we heard?"

"Yes, yes," agreed Mr. Whitters. "I'll do that. Leave you to—" He eyed the ladder with some discomfort.

"I won't be long."

"And neither will I," said the baker, a crooked finger raised in the air.

As he swung onto his bicycle, Alora flung herself into her work. She must be long finished by the time he returned lest he think to help her again.

It ended up being a hard finish to meet, however, with her inability to quit peering into the shadows every few seconds.

A gang stealing memories in Enver. Sounded a lot like thievery to her.

What a horrid idea.

But also...

What a mystery.

Chapter Seven

"Name and appointment time," requested the guard.

Alora pushed back the golden cowl of her new cloak, enough so the man might see her face. "Alora Pennigrim. No appointment this time, but here on business nonetheless."

The guard's umber eyes widened in recognition. "Right. Of course, Miss Pennigrim."

It was a warm day again, though cloud-filled, and the guard's paint didn't run upon his face, his expression clear of heat-sick. She was happy to see him fully restored. "You know, I was quite taken aback by that man the other day. Do you remember? He fell near me." The guard only watched her, wary, his posture stiff. "Are those darts—"

"Not at liberty to say, Miss Pennigrim," he said, silencing her. Alora noticed his eyes stray to the trees, the walls and then the gate before settling back onto her. When Alora opened her mouth to say that of course, she understood, he hurried on, low, "But it didn't kill him. That trespasser."

Alora breathed out on a smile, exponentially relieved. Before the guard could move to allow her through, she said, "I brought something for you."

"I'm forbidden from accepting, Miss." His hand moved to rest on the lever.

"Oh, well you won't be keeping it. I'll fetch the bottle on my way out. It's iced tea," she added, holding it out. "Though after the length of that walk, I fear it's more chilled than iced."

With a dubious expression, the guard allowed her to place it into his free hand. "Thank you."

"I brewed it on my terrace," she added, smiling.

"I've never had a terrace," murmured the guard, and his thumb stroked the bottle once, twice, before the lever turned down and the gate swung in. "Enjoy your visit, Miss Pennigrim."

Alora hesitated, then walked in slowly, her lip caught between her teeth. Because she didn't know what she'd done or what she'd said to cause the guard's forlorn countenance and the defeated way he'd said her name.

Maybe he simply didn't like iced tea.

At least no desperate strangers are galloping past me today, she noted with relief. It allowed her more time to examine the immense topiaries as she passed by, which still left her with unpleasant sensations in her chest, but at least there were no giant rakes and unattached arms lurking in the shadows. Nearly to the stairs, she paused in her next step; a topiary she hadn't paid much attention to those three days prior now commandeered it.

The base appeared afire with green branches trimmed in mounting flames. They circled around two figures, one standing rigid and unfazed while the other bent back, arms outstretched as in dance. Or rapture. Alora found herself nearing when voices brought her abruptly away. She swung toward Opulence Mansion to discover two people she'd never seen before, both clothed in gold and talking amongst themselves, oblivious to her.

Though not for long.

The man was tall and leanly built, his auburn hair swept artfully back from a high forehead. Alora appeared to have caught his attention first as his blue eyes met hers and held for several heartbeats too long. She dragged them away to the woman, younger than herself perhaps, with a clinging gown draped over her curves and loose waves of rose-red hair falling about her shoulders. She puffed on a cigarillo, her face animated as she prattled to her companion. She didn't appear to notice a thing until Alora neared the first stair.

"Oh. Oh!" Rushing down the steps so quickly Alora worried she'd trip, the girl reached her in a swirl of smoke and cloves. "Who are *you?*"

"Alora Pennigrim," she supplied, lowering her hood. She supposed she'd not needed it raised while within locked grounds. Her throat constricted on telling her business, but the girl had such an inviting countenance. "I'm new."

"New!" the woman squeaked, drawing on the cigarillo once more before shoving the entire burning thing down her bodice. With a cry of alarm, Alora lunged forward, but found her hands pushed aside with a grin. "Your dress is *decadent.*"

Tendrils of smoke twined in delicate swirls from the golden girl's gown yet, but still she seemed unbothered. "Thank you," Alora managed, as her manners required no thought. She'd worn a lilac dress today, sleeveless to balance the heat of the cloak. "Your dress is magnificent too. But it's *smoking.*"

"It's fine enough, I suppose. But I do grow sick of gold." Her eyes ravaged Alora's dress hungrily. "I'm Lennox. This is William. We work out of Door Eighteen."

Lennox's eyes were green as a new leaf and creased at their corners as she awaited Alora's reaction.

Which Alora found she couldn't give. She couldn't remember what was behind Door Eighteen to save her life. She glanced from

Lennox to William, who smiled at her with an easy intrigue, before giving up the game.

"Which one is that again?"

Lennox laughed. "I forgot already you've said you're new here. The Room of Fire." Then she plucked out the cigarillo from where it smoldered against her skin and sucked on its end. In a billow of smoke, she asked, "Which door are you?"

"Twenty-five."

Lennox's brow furrowed until William leaned in and whispered a short statement. Brightening once more, she reached out and hauled Alora in close. "You're the new door?"

Alora didn't think Opulence Mansion performers counted as off-limits in her agreement of confidentiality. She hoped they didn't.

"I'm not the new door. Only designing it."

Lennox gasped. "You're a designer. Goodness, that explains the look of you." She bit her lip over Alora's shoes before stepping back. "I'm sorry for exploding all over you. We rarely meet new faces outside of guests and those we aren't allowed to interact with except during performances. It isn't the same." Her cheeks sucked in against another draw from the cigarillo. Finished, she made to hide it away in her gown again.

"Wait!" said Alora, shaken. "Won't you burn?"

Lennox grinned, wrinkling her nose. "No. And neither will the gown catch." Proving it true, she stretched out an arm, holding the burning end of the cigarillo to the sleeve. When nothing happened, she stuck out her tongue, and Alora could only clap a hand against her cheek as Lennox effectively doused the cigarillo without incident.

"Are you impervious to fire too?" squeaked Alora, breathless, turning toward Lennox's companion.

William regarded her with the same half-smile having never retreated from his handsome face. "I'm not. Though I heal very quickly."

"But you don't feel the pain of it?"

His smile grew wide. "I feel the pain."

"We were just about to begin a practice routine." Lennox stepped nearer, her voice lowering in confidence. "Would you like to watch?"

"Is that allowed? I don't have my membership yet."

"Master is said to be occupied until opening, and so long as we avoid Madam Feebledire, it will be a fine afternoon."

Lennox smiled with every feature, and Alora found her own misgivings transforming to excitement upon seeing it. People from all over the region panted for even a drop of gossip over Opulence Mansion, and here she was, about to witness a private show! "I must do my work first, but it won't be long."

"Then it's a date! See you soon, Alora." Kissing her fingers, she waggled them at Alora before following William inside.

Alora's satchel was much heavier than the previous day and it was because she'd brought along two lanterns. One of which she lit now, using it to guide her way down the deep darkness of the unused corridor.

Madam Feebledire, management, had let her in upon knocking, her demeanor just as unwelcoming as it'd been the first day. Alora hoped the woman would find other things to occupy her time other than patrolling the hall because now that she'd met Lennox and William, she couldn't hardly contain her curiosity over what the Room of Fire might entail.

Door Twenty-five flared beneath the lantern, the gold etching reflecting the light. Alora turned the knob and entered. The room was cool and empty save for a lamp on the floor. "So, there wasn't a window in here," she said to no one, turning a slow circle.

She'd not written any measurements down for a window, but for some reason had begun to question her memories of this place in her time away from it. Now that she saw the lamp on the floor, she remembered lighting it prior. How peculiar she couldn't recall it until now; she wouldn't have brought the second lantern if she had.

Alora pursed her lips before prowling around the room. She paused to tack up a bit of wallpaper to the far wall and lay a sample of trim upon the floor. While at home, she'd already determined all of what she wanted to do to the room—and had even begun selecting her choices—when the strange sense of memories seeping from her head had her second-guessing her recollection.

She pulled out her notepad and wrote:

<u>NO</u> *window.*

Has lamp.

When she put it away, she allowed her imagination its freedom; it was always easier to do in the space she wished to transform anyway. She took the walls and papered them, trimmed every edge, and covered the floor. Once that was done, she added the finishings. The dim lamps and soft tapestries. The perfect chaise for one to lounge and dream of their most coveted desire.

She saw all this and smiled, taking care so as not to bring it all to life. She might try her best to explain how she finished such a project in only three days' time, but she would never be able to explain a fully formed and lounging person, especially one half-thought, a virtual shell. Her singular limitation.

Alora could never hope to replicate a soul.

She continued to take notes, more detailed than she'd become accustomed to due to her unexplained bout of forgetfulness, and once satisfied with her collection of thoughts, reached for the lantern.

She'd no idea how this room would be managed, no idea if she would ever use the membership that was soon to be hers, but she would complete it as promised and leave it as she did every project: more beautiful than it began.

Her fist hovered unsure over the painted wood of Door Eighteen. Madam Feebledire was nowhere to be found, thankfully preoccupied with whatever duties were appointed to management, and Alora succeeded in sneaking up the staircase unseen. But that didn't ease her nerves any. Her contract hadn't explicitly mentioned the remainder of Opulence Mansion as being off-limits to her, but it was implied in some of the wording such as:

The signee shall be granted permission to enter Opulence Mansion grounds for the refurbishment of Door Twenty-five, only. It was rather more straightforward in Madam Feebledire's warning three days ago: "Do not *touch any of the other doors unless your wish is slow torture and permanent damage.*"

But curiosity clawed at her, and Lennox's genuine smile led her to wonder if she could make a friend by month's end. A close one, like shocked Mr. Whitters had questioned she'd not had. Likely she was putting the cart before the donkey, but if she didn't go through the door, well, that was it then, wasn't it?

She knocked once, turned the knob and stepped in.

It was like stepping into an inferno. Figuratively, thank heavens.

The walls were papered in crimson and orange, iridescent so as to shimmer against an indirect gaze. It left Alora certain flames were leaping at her from the corners of her eyes, which was untrue, but part of the experience, she supposed. Divans were pressed against them, black as charred wood and cushioned thickly with pillows to maximize comfort in watching the fireplace, which was central to the room and open in both front and behind.

Alora had to walk around its edge to see the flames dancing warmly in its base. She gasped when limbs unfolded from the coals.

Lennox beamed up at her from the fire. "You came! What timing too, since I've finished warming up."

Alora thought they had much different views on warming up, and stammered, "You really are all right?"

"Hard to believe unless you see it yourself, isn't it?" She rose in one graceful motion, lifting onto her toes and raising her hands until her fingertips brushed the highest curved bricks.

Alora's lips parted at Lennox's costume, or lack thereof. Thin straps on her shoulders dipped to a bustier that dangled red and orange beads with bottoms cut extraordinarily high across her pale, freckled thighs. It was more skin than Alora had ever seen on another person in the daytime. She wasn't prudish, but still, she found herself blushing.

"You'll overheat in that cloak; take it off before the fire grows much higher."

"You're going to feed the fire more?" asked Alora, her hands working the clasp at her throat.

Lennox laughed, lifting her leg until it aligned with her ear. "I am."

Alora swung the cloak from her shoulders, baring her arms and cooling her skin. She turned to place it on the nearest divan when William emerged from the shadows. "Allow me," he said, and with an obvious perusal of her form, took the cloak from her. "Enjoy the show."

"Oh," said Alora, reeling somewhat. "You're practicing too?"

"It's an act," said Lennox, now bent fully in half. "And this scene is new. You picked the perfect day to come to Opulence, Alora. How lucky."

Alora palmed her cheeks when William untied his robe and threw it into the fire. She found sudden interest in the walls and the floor, anything to detract from the sight of so much bare skin. Like Lennox, his costume was crimson, satin and snug against his thighs. He wore no shirt.

"Have a seat, Alora!" called Lennox, and Alora shuffled obediently to the nearest divan, crossing her legs and fortifying her breaths.

Only then did she look to the fireplace.

They lay intertwined at the bottom, limbs wrapped around limbs and Lennox's head to William's bare chest, obscured in a wreath of flame. From all around a soft instrument strummed, joined by others in time, until a haunting melody played. Alora soon found her breath would not come. Carefully, unwinding his legs from his partner's, pulling his arm from beneath her body, William stood.

Alora gaped, for where she'd seen just pale skin before, was now bubbled and crisp, charring where he stood, buried in steadily rising flames. She half-stood until he speared her with a glance, smiling devilishly, his body moving with the music. A dance. When the charred bits of skin fell away, new skin appeared, white and unmarked.

He'd said he would heal, and he'd told her true.

Lennox stirred next, crawling through fire, her bare legs leaving trails of flame through the coals. Her skin remained untouched, and when she shifted onto her back, fanning her fiery hair out around her, it didn't catch either, but shimmered like silk against the coal bed. When William lowered a blackened hand toward her, she grasped it with her own.

It was a lover's dance, that much she could see, but one not meant to be. They weren't right for each other, and no matter how each of them tried, it kept cycling back to one of them folded in the coals, burning and burning. Only Lennox couldn't burn, and William couldn't stay that way, and when the dance ended and the flames were snuffed out, Alora found herself standing with tears tracking down her cheeks, clapping until her palms stung.

"Beautiful," said Alora to the pair of them. "Astonishing. The talent you have." She meant it with all of her heart.

"Thank you," said Lennox, and left the fireplace to kiss her quick on the cheek.

Alora beamed brighter, turning to William and finding his skin cleared. She didn't wish to call attention to the fact that he'd told her he could feel the pain of it, so she didn't, though she desperately wanted to know why he'd chosen this, of all things, as a career. She'd been horrorstruck at first, which quickly gave way to fascination, but now that the song had ended and the dance was done, the wrongness of it began to creep back in, dampening her enthusiasm. She forced her smile steady.

"If this is what awaits members of Opulence Mansion, I may utilize my membership after all," Alora said. "Are there more performers here right now?"

"There are," said Lennox. "Though we aren't allowed—"

"It's nearly dusk," interrupted William, retrieving Alora's cloak from a concealed panel in the wall. "You should go."

Another facet of the contract: Alora wasn't to be present during operating hours. And apparently William knew this.

In a quite baffling move, he drew the cloak around her shoulders, working the clasp, his fingers cool at her throat. "I'd tell you to stay, but you look as if you catch fire too easily."

Taken aback, Alora blinked up at him. "What does that mean?"

But William didn't answer, settling instead for dipping his gaze to her mouth and lingering, intention clear. She swallowed.

"Hurry on then, Alora. I don't wish to see you punished! Perhaps we will see each other again soon. I hope so!"

Alora could only offer a hurried goodbye and rushed well-wishes before she was out the door and back onto the landing.

Punished? she wondered. *What an odd choice of word.*

Chapter Eight

The little gold bell chimed her wish to exit at the gate, the small sign above it reading: *Ring If You Wish to Depart.* Alora stepped back as the gate swung toward her.

"Hello!" she said, when the guard was revealed. "I—"

The pinched expression beneath his crimson helm stilled her.

"Pull up your hood, Miss Pennigrim. Hurry! Quicker than that!"

Alora's fingers fumbled with her hood, catching in her hair. She trembled all over merely because of the trembling she heard in his voice. "Whatever is the matter?"

"You're *late.* It's dusk. And if you don't rush away now, I'm frightened you'll never leave."

"Never leave?" The hood drooped low over her eyes, obscuring her vision, but from far down the lane she thought she saw them. Others like her, dressed in golden cloaks.

"Don't let anyone see your face. He'll call you in on breach of contract. Also, thank you for the iced tea. Did you add hibiscus? It was quite nice."

Alora accepted the empty bottle shoved into her hands as easily as she accepted the mild shove to her back. She'd not had a say in either and both were done with before she could say anything at all.

She hurried down the lane.

Dusk had indeed fallen. Shadows draped across the stones, deepening in the thickness of the forest. They brought with them a cool reprieve from the summer's heat, but Alora didn't think the gooseflesh rising on her arms were from any change in temperature.

Golden cloaks neared. Golden cloaks from which extended pairs of arms holding tight to brass lanterns casting circles of swaying light. Six lanterns, so far as she could see, not traveling together but staying apart, though clearly their destinations were the same. How would it look to them, she wondered, to see another dressed the same but without a lantern and going in the opposite direction? Would they question it? Would it even matter?

She allowed herself a glimpse of the man nearing: his fine trousers and pristine loafers, the buttons of his suit jacket reflecting the light of his lantern. But his cowl was pulled nearly as low as her own, and so she didn't see his face—just as she hoped he didn't see hers. She hurried past him, looking down.

The next person she came upon was a woman, taller than her, with black stockings and delicately heeled shoes. She walked slowly, likely because her choice of shoes were difficult to maneuver on the glitter-spewing stones, and Alora quickly ducked her head when she noticed the cowl of the woman's shift in her direction.

The moths were out. They fluttered from the trees, their tufted white wings beating beneath Alora's hood until she batted them away, sending them on. They flocked about the lanterns now, the only brightness in an ever-deepening sky.

Three, four, five, six. The last of the lanterns passed her by, the members of Opulence Mansion moving on without questioning her presence. Alora breathed a sigh of relief—only it caught at its end. Her steps slowed. She squinted. And then her mouth formed a perfect circle as an infernal *sea* of bobbing lanterns came into view.

This wouldn't do. They took up the entire road. If she tried to squeeze through them, would she even manage? She couldn't keep her eyes on her feet and maneuver through a crowd without knocking into at least one person. Why, why, why must she have stayed to watch the dancers' performance?

Alora hesitated for a heartbeat more, staring at the mob of golden-clad members closing in before doing the only thing she thought might save her.

She abandoned the lane.

She disobeyed every flashy sign—and pushed into the woods.

The trees lining the lane to Opulence Mansion had grown tall—taller than anywhere else in Renwick Forest—and the white canopy was thick, blocking almost all light. Flickers of it stuttered across her vision as lanterns passed by where she hid. There were many, many more than she expected, and for the first time, she wondered if there was anyone she knew hidden beneath those draping hoods. Her hand shifted, coming in contact with something like velvet. She pulled it away, thinking it only moss, until a cool light began to glow.

Alora tore her gaze from the lane to examine the trunk of the tree she'd hidden behind. To see a Moonflower now open at her touch.

Its petals were softly pointed, silver and shimmering, and when she touched it again, glittering particles rose from a silver center. She scanned the remainder of the trunk, finding more closed flowers. She brushed the petals of another and pushed back her hood when it unfurled its cold light. One by one, she went, tapping her way along the tree until its bark was no longer shadowed but gleaming, lit from blooms claiming residence along its length.

The most enchanting lane, indeed.

A twig snapped in the dark. Alora glanced over her shoulder at the sound. The lane may have been lantern-lit, and the tree beside her glowing with Moonflowers, but the remainder of the forest hadn't awakened yet. It was still steeped in the coming night.

She squinted into the darkness. Another Moonflower unfurled, this one all its own, deep in the dark. Still, she saw nothing. A stag probably grazed, or an overfed rabbit.

But there were other things that came out in the forests at night, and these were the things she'd been told to fear.

Ms. Merryweather, the stable master, had been the first to inform her. When Alora had purchased George nearly two years ago, she'd warned about them. The shadow beasts—specter wolves—that had moved in from the snow-topped Indigo range some years ago, drawn to the enchantment of Enver. But now she knew it likely wasn't Enver they were attracted to, but Opulence. No other place was so thickly enchanted.

She glanced back to see if the lane was safe yet. It wasn't.

Another twig snapped, this one nearer. And then the gruff exhale of an animal, much bigger than herself. Alora spun toward the noise, eyes scanning wildly. "It's only a stag," she whispered, hoping it was true. The crowd had nearly gone; she only needed to survive a little longer.

But fate played its winning hand against her, and Alora barely managed to imagine a knife in her hand when the black creature stepped within the flowers' glow.

She screamed, stopped, and stumbled back, hands over her heart, the knifepoint somewhere near her ear. It was a horse, only a horse, and hopefully her scream would be mistaken for an owl's screech and not be investigated. She looked up to the dark rider perched atop it.

They drew alongside her, and try as she might, she couldn't make out the face beneath the black hood. Her heartbeat pounded in her ears.

"What are you doing here?" demanded the rider, gruff and rasping. "Renwick isn't safe at night. Or any time for that matter."

A whisper of pain blighted the shell of her ear. Alora lowered the knife. Inwardly, she tried to match the voice to anyone she might know and came up empty.

"The lane was congested," she said, rather lamely, her hand lifting and coming away bloodied. More Moonflowers opened. Soon, the forest was aglow with silver light. Alora watched the rider's hood shift as he glanced up the road.

Masked.

His attention returned to her, and that's when she knew. She'd seen him before. Or, at the very least, someone just like him.

"It isn't now," he said, a clear invitation for her to leave.

One she should have leapt to take but didn't. "You were in Opulence Mansion. Speaking with Master Merridon." A trickle of warmth ran down her neck. If she was wrong, then he could deny it. But she didn't think she was. His build was the same beneath the high-collared coat. Was he also a part of the guard then? A patrol?

Without warning, the rider swung down from his horse. Frightened she'd said something she shouldn't, Alora scurried backward until her back hit the trunk of the tree. It startled her, though not nearly so much as the masked rider stalking toward her. He towered above her when he neared, his leather-clad fingers skating along the length of her neck to her ear. Wincing at the sting, she felt him apply pressure to the small wound.

"What did this?"

Alora made to tuck the knife behind her, but he caught her hand in his, bringing both into the glow.

Silence stretched, one in which she really did hear an owl's screech. Still his hands remained on her, warm on her wrist and pressed to her ear. She desperately tried—and failed—to make out his features behind the mask and beneath the hood, her heart bounding wild.

"A knife is a poor choice if you don't have the skill to wield it. Don't leave the lane again," he said, not verifying in any way he'd recognized her too.

He released her wrist, granting her the courage she needed to step aside, freeing her wound from the pressure of his grip and her body from the nearness of his. She swallowed, relieved he didn't come after her, and lifted her hood.

"I'll make sure to learn the use of it before we meet next," she said, a little bit ominous.

The rider dipped his head, and matching tone for tone, said, "Looking forward to it, Miss Pennigrim."

"So, it was him, after all!" said Alora to Mrs. Flops, relaying all she'd done and seen. "Quite mysterious, isn't it?" She scratched along the creature's soft head while they lounged upon the sofa. She'd eaten dinner, quick and alone, and now she sat, notepad on her lap, creating a list of all she wished to place on order tomorrow. It wasn't that much different from how her nights were usually spent, aside from the discomfiting way she kept checking her notes, the measurements of the room sliding right out of her head from one moment to the next.

She'd never had this happen before, and hoped she wasn't coming down with something.

"But will Miss Sherry have the wallpaper I want? That's the problem, isn't it? Sometimes her patterns are so busy." Another pet for Mrs. Flops. "What do you think he was doing in the woods? Hunting for lurkers?" *And finding one.*

Her eyes strayed to the knife, where she'd placed it on the mantle. She looked hurriedly back. Triple checking, she wrote her notes for the carpenter, then the carpeteer.

"I wonder about the gate guard too. Such a funny fellow. You should have seen how bothered he was by my late departure. *You might never leave,* he said." She scoffed to the rabbit like it was all a big joke, but really, a bitterness filled her insides at the memory of it. And she was old enough to know what it was.

Intuition.

"You don't think..." she trailed. "Those performers. They're allowed to leave. Aren't they?"

The clock hanging against her wall chimed, announcing her bedtime with a whittled bird, a flower in its beak. Alora worried her lip before scooting the rabbit off her lap and heading toward the terrace. She opened the door to the summer air, stepping out until the breeze rustled her hair and the moon touched her skin. Her hand lifted to her ear, clean now and scabbed, unable to avoid the memory of the rider's fingers against it—though, she didn't try very hard.

Alora smelled flowers all around. Because they were all around. In pots, in baskets, and climbing up the handmade trellis. Mrs. Flops had followed her out, already taking advantage of low-hanging berries. Alora had adopted the creature after discovering her doing the same thing—only those bushes had belonged to a furious woman, and those berries had been reserved for pie. Alora did not bake pies.

She stared off toward the west, to where she knew Opulence Mansion to be, and could just make it out if she really tried.

Lennox had seemed well enough, happy even. Surely a prisoner, even a paid one, wouldn't be so joyful? And comments like "remain unseen", "breach of contract", and "never leave" could be interpreted all sorts of ways. Even if she'd done everything wrong: remaining within the mansion during operating hours, allowing everyone to see her face and know her name, what could be the worst thing to happen? She'd lose the account. A blow to her dreams, but certainly not the end of everything. A poor choice of words by a frazzled guard, nothing more.

Alora climbed into bed that night and, after drinking a concoction to cue the indigestion from which she was sure she suffered, smiled contentedly into her pillow. Tonight, she would dream of her very own shop and nothing—*no one*—else.

Chapter Nine

By the end of the week, Alora had placed her orders with both Ms. Sherry, who surprisingly had almost exactly what she'd imagined, the solemn carpenter, and the boisterous carpeteer. In the meantime, she'd celebrate.

Mr. Whitters' grand opening for Confectionary Delights appeared to be an even better attended event than the DeCollier's Spring Has Sprung Ball from three months previous. Alora hadn't gone, but she'd read about it. It appeared Mr. Whitters, already beloved by many, had the entire town's support when it came to the rebuilding of his bakery, the previous one having burned down due to the unfortunate mishap with a faulty stove. But the new one had arrived, if the smell was any indication, and the patrons milling about the entrance—and those tucked shoulder to shoulder inside—seemed to think it up to par with the previous. Endless boxes tied with string emerged from the entrance, as the crowd grew thicker and ever more impatient.

Alora was thankful she wasn't here to purchase anything, as she didn't think there would be anything left by the time she made it to the counter. She hoped Mr. Whitters had hired on help.

She approached the entrance slowly to take in her work. Ignoring the other patrons, she strode nonchalantly to the potted plants, brushing their leaves and testing the soil until she was satisfied. She studied the sign overhead, swinging gently, and felt pride in how well the curling blue letters contrasted with the white background. It looked like a proper place, even better than the one before. Though she'd never tell Mr. Whitters that, obviously.

At the rate of this crowd, she didn't think she'd get the chance to say anything to him at all. For every one person who left, it seemed two joined the line, and the sight of it made Alora's jaw ache. It wasn't as though she held an aversion to people—she worked with people all the time—but so many, and in one small space, was far from ideal. She didn't have great memories of such things. In fact, she had one memory, and it was very, very bad.

"Excuse me, excuse me. Need to feel the sun on my head for just a minute. Oh yes, thank you. Very happy. Very happy, indeed. So blessed." Mr. Whitters wove his way down the steps, taking even longer than usual due to the excessive handshakes and claps on the shoulders. Alora grinned; he deserved every one of them.

She watched his eyes close for a brief moment when he caught the sun, light reflecting from the bald spot at the back of his head. He breathed deep once before swinging his gaze around and finding hers. He beamed.

"Why, Miss Pennigrim! How are you, my dear?" With large hands on either side of her arms, he wobbled her back and forth. "Looking lovely as ever."

Alora smiled, taking in his bright, brown cheeks and even brighter eyes. "I'm well, thanks. But look at you! Look at this! Mister Whitters, it's marvelous."

"Thanks to you. I had to hire Glenda once I realized the opening was marked in the paper. Had people lined up before I even got inside, and I was here at four in the morning!"

Alora chuckled. "And is Glenda going to stay on?"

"No," laughed Mr. Whitters. "She said she signed up to be my wife, not my assistant. We'll see how the week goes. Maybe I'll need to hire someone full time. Someone young, who likes to keep morning hours."

"I think you may," said Alora, eyeing the swelling patrons.

"Are you planning to come inside?"

"I am, but maybe just not yet. I've had the privilege of an entire box of Confectionary Delights all to myself just this week, and I wouldn't want to be greedy."

"Nonsense," chortled Mr. Whitters. "I've been prepping for days. I'll set aside some chocolate creams for you." He rubbed her arm once more, his smile reaching all the way to his eyes and beyond before stepping back. "Thank you for coming." Then turning around, he attempted to make his way back in. "Oh yes, thank you. Very happy. So blessed."

Alora watched until he disappeared beneath the awning. Chuckling to herself, she glanced over the staggered pots lining the walls, to the one near the top that she'd repaired after it nearly smashed her head.

Her smile fixed in memory, its edges drooping. Alora backed away from the store front until she found herself in the alleyway, her recollection shifting from the pot mishap to the mysterious shadow. Mr. Whitters had called them Urchins, a brutish gang who didn't attack often, which meant they likely attacked with purpose. And to leave their victims without memory of them at all... That was a peculiar thing. Alora peered down the lane. What did the victims know? Secrets? Were they defectors? Witnesses? Alora wondered if they'd seen her, if they would have done to her whatever terrible thing they'd exacted upon the other poor soul, if only to keep her quiet.

Come to think of it, she hadn't heard at all of the attack that happened. Not a whisper. Of course, she wasn't very good about reading the paper, and she was quite preoccupied with work. She would buy one on her way home. But perhaps first—

Her feet carried her along the alley.

It couldn't be true that this lane was colder than the others, that the ice frosting her bones was related to the shadows cast by bright-colored buildings. Still, Alora felt these things as she walked, drawing nearer and nearer to where it happened. To the fight she was never meant to hear nor see.

She knew she'd found it by feel alone, her heart cold and fast, goosebumps erupting on every inch of her. Yet, it was only a door, a back entrance stoop, completely unremarkable from the one before and the one after.

Only—

Alora leaned forward, forehead scrunched, eyes narrowed. She reached out with a finger, brushing along the wooden frame until her fingertip was flecked red—as if with dried bits of paint.

Except the door was painted blue.

She knocked, once, twice, three times, and then stepped back.

The door creaked inward.

"Who is it?" the voice demanded.

"Alora Pennigrim, ma'am."

The pause grew heavy. "Do I know you?"

"Perhaps? I think it's too soon to tell." Alora didn't recognize the voice from inside, but she'd seen more faces in her time in Enver than she'd spoken to people. They might have crossed paths.

The door swung in, and the woman standing there was revealed to be as unfamiliar to her as any stranger. She was also crying. "Perhaps?" she managed before reaching out fast as a viper and dragging Alora inside.

They stood in a poorly lit back hall with threadbare jackets on racks and scuffed shoes lined in rows. The woman's fingers hooked into the sensitive skin on the backs of Alora's upper arms as her puddled eyes raked her up and down. "Perhaps I know you?"

Alora couldn't keep up the pretense. "No, I'm sorry. I was mistaken."

"Oh," heaved the woman, her hands falling. "Oh." She shook her head, blonde curls bobbing in time. "Forgive me," she said.

"It was I who barged in on you. Forgive *me*." Alora didn't know what she'd been thinking, pressing herself upon a victim like this. What sort of person was she?

"It's no matter," said the woman, turning away. "I'm all out of sorts these days."

Alora stilled. "What's that there? On your head?"

The woman lifted a hand gingerly to the space just north of her ear, where the hair had been removed, the skin red, black thread puckering the wound. "I was hurt. A few days ago. Though I don't remember it. It's like I— *Do you know what they took?*"

The woman had spun back, eyes suddenly dry and wild. She reached for Alora's arm and missed, as Alora swung it behind her.

"Who?"

"No! What did they *take?*"

Alora, realizing more than ever that some impulses shouldn't be acted upon, backed away. "Who are 'they'?"

"Stupid girl! I don't care about them. What did they take!"

"I don't know. How could I know if you do not?"

It was the wrong thing to say. A keening sound left the woman's mouth then, her hand coming up to the wound on her head and wrenching. Alora cried out, grabbing ahold of her, forcing her to stop. Their fingers both came away bloodied. "Let's bandage this."

"They took it. They *took* it."

"I'll get this fixed up right as rain." Alora exhaled through her nose, the sight of the oozing wound, one stitch pulled free, being quite grotesque. Her arm looped through the woman's; she led them down the hall.

Alora didn't know where she was going, but the home wasn't any larger than her own. She discovered the washroom soon enough, and plunking the woman down upon the vanity stool, set to work wetting a rag and cleaning up the mess she'd caused. She felt absolutely terrible and told the woman as much.

"Why? You didn't do it, did you?"

"No," said Alora. "Did you see a doctor? You must have, I suppose, to close the wound."

"Yes, and they didn't listen either. They stole it from me, from right here!" Again, the woman reached toward her head, though Alora intercepted her before she could cause further damage.

"From your head?" And then she didn't need an answer any longer.

Memories. They'd stolen her memories.

"Look at it! Of course from my head. Hurts something awful, too, and what did I do to deserve it?"

"I don't know," said Alora, horrified. She pressed clean fabric gingerly to the wound. "What did the constable say?"

"That I'd fallen and injured myself. Is that the truth of it then? That 'they' is me and what I've lost are my senses?"

The woman's distress wrenched at Alora; her lips parted, eyes pleading and full of trust though Alora had done nothing to earn it. So she decided to try.

"I saw shadows outside your back door, the day of your attack. Urchins were thought responsible, though I can't say I know anything about them. But I'm told they steal memories. Perhaps that is what you feel is missing?"

The woman nodded, bungling up where Alora tried to tie a bandage in place. "Yes," she said, on a contented sigh. "That's it."

Alora left the house in better shape than she'd found it. After fixing the woman a cold lunch, she'd tidied the sparse kitchen and neglected living space, setting tea outside on the veranda to steep. The flowers in the windows hadn't been watered all week, so those she'd helped as well before paying her respects to her new acquaintance, Ms. Vittabean, and departing. Though the haunted look had remained in her eyes, they'd stayed dry all the while Alora was there, and Ms. Vittabean had even smiled when Alora left, bright beneath the bandage, relieved to know now what was missing even if she hadn't a hope of finding it again.

Alora steered herself in the opposite direction of Mr. Whitters' shop, wanting to avoid crowds for the time being, hunting instead for a newspaper. Could such attacks on Enver's residents really go unreported? And as Ms. Vittabean questioned, what had she done to deserve it?

She circled back home, entering Prints and Papers, the printer's shop below her flat, with a prepared smile. "Today's newspaper, Mister Zanfold. Please and thank you."

"I'll have one as well," said a man's voice from behind her, and Alora swung her head around, unaware anyone had come in after her.

"Good afternoon," said William, grinning.

Alora stumbled over her reply, her theories of prisoners and punishments dashed to a heap with great relief. William was here, in Enver. She found herself scanning for Lennox but came up empty. They were the only two in the shop, aside from Mr. Zanfold.

"Hello," said Alora, uncomfortably breathless. "I was in getting a paper."

"So I'd heard."

Alora hardly managed a sound of protest when William purchased both newspapers from the stoic printer. She'd neighbored this shop for two years, and not once had Mr. Zanfold asked her to call him by his first name or introduce his cat, though she knew it was Hector and the cat was uptight. Still, she smiled at him and the orange tabby that draped lazily over the counter, accepting his quick nod for what it meant: *Have a good day.*

She returned her attention to William and the outstretched paper, taking in his silken shirt and striped trousers and the way they clung nicely to his slim frame. Once reaching his face, she found him smiling still, though it didn't seem to reach his eyes, which were trained upon her intensely, leaving her feeling as if she'd been swallowed.

She took the paper but wasn't sure of what else to do. "Not in a practice today?"

"Not today. I followed an urge to come into town instead. Can't say I've been disappointed."

Alora, having already been swallowed, felt herself sinking further. She made for the door—a path which William eagerly followed. "It's hard to be disappointed in a town like Enver, with all its beauty and magic."

"Do you like it here then?"

Alora glanced at William as he said it, standing outside the printer's shop, steps from her own stairs, but he didn't appear to mean this precise location. After all, how could he know where she lived? "I like it very much," she said. "I hope to open my own shop one day." And then, because she was burning with curiosity, she asked, "Do you like it?"

"The town?"

"The town... What you do." She pretended to examine the paper as she spoke, not at all dying to know what he might say.

"Ah, curious are you?" He leaned in close, and Alora fought the urge to back away. Instead, she counted the freckles on his nose. "To burn is the most exquisite pain; I'll happily burn for the rest of my life." He brushed a strand of hair back from her temple, tucking it behind her ear. "As for the town, I think we may have different definitions of magical." He rolled the newspaper, tucking it under one arm, where it began to drone in a soft, male voice.

"Oh, you've squeezed it. Mister Zanfold's papers are enchanted for those who must—or rather like—listening for their news."

Brow furrowed, William retrieved the paper. He thwacked it against his opposite hand until it silenced. "Come enjoy an early dinner with me."

Alora met his eyes and immediately felt as if she were out to sea, one that was endless and without hope of escape. She thought she might drown—and, with that sensation, the indigestion returned. Or perhaps it really was her intuition this time, warning her away.

Regardless, she really couldn't accept. "I have samples to pick up for a client, I'm afraid. Maybe some other time."

"Don't say 'maybe'. Not to me," said William. With one last perusal of her, he turned away. "Return to us when you can."

Alora frowned after him. Until he disappeared across the street and entered the next. And while she did appreciate the paper, she did *not* appreciate him leaving her mind an uncomfortable jumble.

Chapter Ten

Sometime the following morning, before the sun had fully risen and the world was in the first stages of waking, Alora had a dream. She stood in the room, behind Door Twenty-five, as the walls bled. Each time the walls settled on a color, they liquified, running in thick rivulets down the panels only for another to take its place. The room filled steadily, with paint and paper, chaises and sofas, and beds with chains. Windows would appear and wink out again, leaving holes from which poured in black smoke, and then those would change shape and disappear only for the entire room to change shape too. Alora could make no sense of it, her imagination struggling to get just one thing to stick and hold still. It was as if the room itself didn't exist and so she didn't either, stuck inside it as she was.

When she woke up, she was doused in sweat and her bedroom walls were coated in eight different shades of clashing paints.

"Have you tried Potions and…Potions and—" strained Mr. Pottenbaum when Alora had lost only the tiniest bit of patience after his partner, also Mr. Pottenbaum, spent an entire hour choosing between cerulean and periwinkle curtains.

Alora had only mentioned between mildly clenched teeth how she was struggling in her focus on the particular task. She could have been more forthright, she supposed, but that would have certainly cost her the job. Mr. Pottenbaum's indecision was the problem, and *not* her manifesting nightmares.

"Peculiarities?" she offered, cringing inside.

"That's it! Dingy place, but excellent brews."

"More like the excellent jawline of that proprietor. Talk *him* into some periwinkle curtains."

And so here she stood, outside of Potions and Peculiarities, and noted two things which were very different than before. For one, there was a *Closed* sign hanging crooked and crude in the door. Secondly, there was a yellow flower potted amongst the weeds of the window box. Alora crept up to it and dipped her finger in, surprised to find the soil damp. A cared for flower even. Though that didn't help her problem, not that she quite knew what her problem was. Focus, maybe? Sleep? Memory? Stomach upset?

The thought of discussing any of her personal ailments with the shopkeeper went against her very morals, but still, she couldn't go on like this. She had a few days over two weeks with which to complete the job, and at this rate, it'd take her two months. Which was why, when she heard a voice coming from around the back of the shop, she ceased plucking the weeds from the box and followed it.

The alleyway was slim and devoid of all things green. In fact, it was devoid of all colors at all unless those colors were gray and black. The black walls of the shop faded to the muted gray stones she walked on only to rise up on her opposite side in another black-walled building. It was a little bit like walking between some charred remains of fire, but then she thought of William and pushed that description firmly out of her head.

At the back of the shop, she saw a wagon first, larger than hers, and definitely not considered a cart. It was attached to a mule, much sturdier in the chest than her donkey and with a fouler attitude.

He glared at her in reproach. Last, she saw him, the rude proprietor, and though she'd fixed her lipstick for the occasion, and checked her hair twice, she still dreaded the sight of him. He wore a variation of his usual attire: black trousers, a black vest with silver stitching, though his shirt today boasted shorter sleeves. Sleeves that'd been folded tight over the swell of his upper arms, made more so by the crates he heaved from the wagon to stack by the back door.

Because he didn't notice her, she decided to watch instead. *It would be impolite to interrupt*, she thought.

With the final crate in his arms, he swung his gaze to hers. "And here you've proven you can be quiet. I've lost a bet with myself." At Alora's parted lips, he added, "I sold the barshet, if that's what you wished to know."

"It wasn't, though I'm glad of it," said Alora, and she wasn't lying. She hadn't wanted to step foot inside knowing that creature still wished for her voice.

When she said nothing more, he glanced her over, brushing his hands free of travel dust. "We're closed."

"I saw the sign." Why had she come? Awkwardness pulsed through her. The last time she'd seen the man she'd told him to piss off, for heaven's sake. "And the Zanigold."

"Purchased from a local nursery. Someone there seemed enamored over it, so I thought I'd see if it was worth the attention. So far, it's like any other yellow flower, but maybe it'll reveal some sort of magic soon."

His eyes were like moss over trees, but right now, catching the sun, they seemed to lighten enough to rival the hillsides of her childhood home. It was unbearably attractive. So much so, she realized she'd begun biting at her thumb as he talked. She dropped it from her mouth, scowling. "Alora Pennigrim," she said, hardening her tone. "I'm in need of a potion. I'm told this is the place to go."

The shopkeeper stared at her outstretched hand as if he didn't know what to do with it. Finally, he placed his within, and it was calloused and warm.

"Bash," he said. "What is it you need?"

Alora didn't like he'd not given her his full name. She wasn't used to those she encountered being so secretive. Her fingers twitched where he held them, a current traveling to all corners of her body. She didn't like that either. Not at all.

She pulled her hand free. "I need something for focus. Or to improve memory. My usual aids haven't been working."

Bash crossed his arms over his chest as she spoke, causing Alora to forcibly avert her eyes from the pull of cloth against his skin. "Which aids?"

"Herbal tea. Sleep. A balanced diet."

"And you are prone to distraction?"

Alora, offended, met his gaze. "No. I've told you before, I'm usually very observant."

"Hmm," he said, with an undercurrent of disbelief. He turned toward the door and proceeded to unlock it. "What I have is likely too much for you. I suggest you seek out the town apothecary for some root or weed."

"Please," said Alora, her feet planted. "It is getting worse." She thought of the nightmares, the changes to her home. Of her notebook and how her eyes seemed to slip from the page.

Bash glanced over his shoulder, probably at the thread of panic unwittingly woven into her words. His eyes assessed her quickly before he turned back.

She exhaled in relief when he said, "All right. Come with me."

The back of Potions and Peculiarities didn't surprise Alora at first. There were boxes and crates, shelves lined with assortments of bottles and decanters, and on the countertops were items in various states of unpacking. But then she spotted a crystal skull with eyes made of rubies. She immediately paused to study it.

"Don't look in that." Bash pressed his shoulder between them, forcing a rod to one ruby eye and shoving it away. "Didn't you say you weren't easily distracted?"

"How was I to know you keep so many dangerous artifacts? I was only curious."

"And so nearly became entranced."

"Is that what it does?" Alora couldn't help it. She leaned toward the skull.

"Yes. You'd be entirely at my mercy."

She swung around to him, but he'd moved away, standing before a smaller door and unlocking that one, too. "And I suppose you'd make me accomplish diabolical things for you?" She paused at his back while she waited, unsure why she baited him. Why she couldn't seem to help it.

Because he starts it, she decided.

"I would," he answered. "Beginning with watering my Dirededron."

Alora scoffed, following him through. "Is that all?"

"Would you like there to be more?" A match lit between them, rising, to the lantern hung beside his head.

He watched her as the light grew, the shadows changing shapes across his features, highlighting the edge of his jaw. She thought at once of Mr. Pottenbaum and his, admittedly well-placed, admirations.

Bash made her uncomfortable, she couldn't deny. And he was uncomfortably handsome, which was worse.

"Of course not."

"I didn't think so."

When he turned away, she forcibly swallowed, mouth dry.

She took in the room. Small, with a stove and several burners, a sink and rows of pots. From the cupboard, he pulled out three vials and a well-worn book.

"It's so dark in here." There wasn't a window, the only light from the dim lantern he'd not removed from its hook.

"You dislike the dark?"

"Depends what else is in it with me," said Alora, standing on her toes to better see the shelves. She found some sort of stick there, smooth and thick, and lifted it.

Bash filled a pot with water before setting it atop the stove. "I can make you something to sharpen your memory, though it won't help with the old ones. Anything from the moment you drink and on, so long as you take a little every day."

"So things won't just—" Alora made a motion of water running from her temple.

"Is that what you feel is happening?" He observed her with a frown.

"Sometimes," said Alora, bothered that he was bothered. Her worry deepened. "Why? Have you heard something like it?"

"Maybe," he said, the expression slow to ease from his face. But then his eyes widened, and he lunged toward her. "*Fuck.* Where did you find that?"

Alora froze as the stick was wrenched from her hands. "On the shelf?" She couldn't help but laugh at his obvious distress, which only seemed to fuel it further.

"This baton is one of the most dangerous items in this shop. You're lucky. Keep your hands to yourself from now on, or I'll force you to wait out with the mule, who bites."

Alora's brow dipped. "That little weapon? Why?"

He didn't answer but rather eased the baton into the belt of his trousers, which she observed closer than necessary.

"What did you say you do in Enver?"

"I haven't said." Or had she? "I'm a designer. A decorator. Of buildings, not cakes."

"Not cakes," he echoed, and Alora thought he might have smiled. "And you've suffered from a focus ailment for how long?"

"I should tell you it's being perpetrated by one thing, I think. So you needn't attempt to diagnose me with any ailments. I'm hopeful it will be resolved once it's over."

"Once what is over?"

"My project."

His hands stilled over his brew. "This project brings you distress?"

"No, not really. It brings me hope."

A sound suspiciously similar to a scoff left him. "That *is* distressing."

She shrugged behind his back. "Maybe. But isn't anything worth having a bit of a torment at some point?"

Alora caught his glance this time, the crease is his brow more thoughtful than disturbed over her question. "And what is it? This thing that is worth all your tormented hope."

"You really care to know?"

"I don't ask questions otherwise." He'd taken up stirring again, but when she didn't immediately answer, he turned fully toward her, his expression open and waiting. "You're embarrassed," he finally said.

Her mouth parted in annoyance. "Hardly."

"Shy?"

"No."

"Is it immoral? Are you a secret reprobate?"

Alora felt her cheeks flush at his nettling. She stepped toward him. "A shop of my own, you villain! With walls of my work, samples and storage."

His mouth quirked. "An answer at last. Was it so difficult?"

"You're insufferable."

The concoction on the stove began to whine, stealing the shop-keeper's attention. "It is a good dream." Three vials were funneled with warm, orange liquid. Bash corked each one before placing them in a purse. He added a dropper, a little handwritten note, before he pulled tight the strings. When he handed them to her, she took the bag, reaching into her own larger one for coins.

"Do you have one?"

"One what?" asked Bash. He waited as she counted in her palm. "Ten will do."

"Only?" But she didn't argue. She was comfortable, not flush with money. She held the coins out. "And a dream."

"No."

She watched him turn slightly, tossing the coins into an open vase, where they clinked against others. If he lied, she didn't know him enough to realize; his answer seemed serious enough to her. Maybe he only meant he lived it now, his dream already grasped. Yet the words were out of her mouth before she could help them.

"You don't strike me as a potion-master."

He leaned his hips against the counter, a tight-lipped smile form-ing. "Not a shopkeeper, not a potion-master. What do I strike you as now? Please don't shame me with the pickpocket title again."

Before Alora could think of a reply, because she didn't really know what, a muffled shuffling sounded from somewhere up above. She tipped her face to the ceiling. "Is something up there?"

"Something?"

"Someone?"

Alora focused on Bash, to his smile—curling with something like satisfaction, a wicked gleam in his eyes.

"I've no idea."

Chapter Eleven

Alora felt disappointed by two things that evening. First, the newspaper had absolutely nothing about the attack on the woman living behind Confectionary Delights. Second, the potion created at Potions and Peculiarities tasted like sour, bitter water. She was tired, confused, and terribly scared to sleep.

The walls of her bedroom were green again, but softer and darker than before. Probably because when she'd imagined the color to replace the mess she'd created, she'd thought of certain eyes instead. It soothed her now, though not nearly enough for sleep.

The wallpaper would be ready for Opulence Mansion by tomorrow; she'd need George and the cart to take it all that way. Her stomach twisted at the thought of it, a tight bundle of nerves she couldn't unknot, and thus must ignore instead. William would be there. He was nice, she'd decided, and certainly nice enough to look at—his dancing in minimal clothing would be forever seared into her brain—but there was an intensity in his eyes that gnawed at her. He didn't feel quite safe, and not in a thrilling, unknown sort of way. She thought, guiltily, that at any time he might grow bored of burning alone and so burn her with him too.

What a terrible thought. Of course he wouldn't.

She might see Lennox, though. A bright spot. She wished to talk with her more, to see if they might schedule an outing or three. To see if they could be friends.

Friends. When Alora thought of friends, she thought of children with foul names on their tongues hurling insults in time with their parents. Of a small rabbit, strangely shaped, and oddly eyed. Of Eirian, a town nestled between green hills and endless space to run. A broken leg needing mending. Her memories were all spice, some pleasant but still biting, but maybe these new memories, hopefully more vivid now, would be sweeter.

She glanced down at the potion-master's handwritten instructions, smudged with ink and as messy as his shop.

One dropper-full every day. Preferably in the evening.

Her fingertip traced the postscript.

May you have more good dreams—

Later that night, Alora awoke from a nightmare of melted bones, screaming.

George had never been down Opulence Mansion's lane before, and so Alora told him all about it as they neared. His ears continued to prick forward and back, listening to her prattle.

"Do you notice how thick the forest grows here? At night there are flowers, *Moonflowers*, which glow silver. It's a different light than the moon, more magical, and they smell like—" Alora scrunched up her nose. "You know, I can't remember. But it was lovely."

She wore her cloak even though anyone who had dealings with her would recognize George and her cart should they see her upon the lane—which she didn't see a way around. Master Merridon hadn't told her what she should do with her bigger supplies, and so she'd decided to do what she'd always done.

She glanced back at the rolls of paper and the bucket of glue, all accounted for. "At night, the mansion opens for business, and members walk to it carrying lanterns to light the dark. There are many." A frown creased her features beneath the cowl. "And I'm to be one of them…at the end of this."

Would she use it? She didn't know. She could imagine herself, she supposed, sinking into the curved tub hidden behind Door One, her image reflected back to her from every angle. She could imagine focusing on that singular memory, the one that caused an entire town to shun her, that caused relief to enter her parents' eyes when she'd announced she was leaving at just twenty-two. They'd been happy to see her go, both for her sake and their own. She could allow that memory to siphon away, and then perhaps the shame would follow.

She'd think on it.

George slowed as the gate loomed. She scrambled from the cart when the guard stepped forward, pushing back her hood so he might recognize her.

"Hello, again," she said with a smile, only for it to falter.

Distress showed plainly on the guard's face. "Miss Pennigrim. You've…returned."

"Well, yes. I've a job to do." When the painted guard only looked between her and the donkey with apparent unease, she began to feel uncomfortable herself, reaching into her satchel. "Lemonade today," she said.

The guard took it, and she was thankful. For a moment, she thought he wouldn't. "You are too kind, Miss Pennigrim. You are…" Again his eyes shifted between her and George.

"What is your name? Are you allowed to tell me? You may call me Alora."

Finally, a faint smile. "Reginald."

Alora grinned. "Reginald. I'm sorry if I wasn't supposed to bring the donkey, but I've a large supply of wallpaper and no way of transporting it."

Reginald's smile deteriorated into a grimace. "Yes. The correct thing to have done was to approach Master over the transport."

Alora's face fell to match. "Oh. What should I do?"

The guard appeared torn over her question. He began to say something then stopped, changing course. "Thank you for the lemonade, Miss Alora." Then he turned his back to her, walked to the wall, and bent. Alora watched as he spoke into a gold funnel, piped from the ground. "Just a moment, please," he said, facing her once more.

Alora nodded her appreciation, coming around to pat George on the nose. From the corner of her eye, she noticed Reginald take a sip of lemonade, smacking his lips at its end. "Reginald?"

"Yes?"

"Did you mean what you said the other day? That I might not be allowed to leave should I be too late?"

Opulence Mansion's gate swung in.

Reginald stared at her in silence awhile, his face perfectly, maybe purposefully, blank.

"Yes, I did."

Alora's breath caught at his words. "But—" And then her heart stuck fast as well. For out of the gate came a great wheelbarrow, and pushing that wheelbarrow was the greatest man she'd ever seen.

Alora's eyes refused to blink away the image of those same hairy, muscled arms raking a man bodily into the hedges, though she could see now how he managed it so easily. The giant of a man glanced toward her, his sunburned brow lowered, his lips pressed closed. He had long, gray hair down to his shoulders which were covered in a golden tunic stretched tight. He lumbered over to her and coughed, clearing his throat.

"Mister Macaw is Opulence's groundskeeper. Allow to him to unload the cart and carry it where you need."

Alora swallowed, realizing she'd been staring with her mouth wide. "Thank you, Mister Macaw. I just have these things here."

Mr. Macaw said nothing as he followed her around to the back of the cart. A man of few words, apparently. With two armfuls, he deposited all she had into the oversized wheelbarrow. When he was done, he stood there, watching her. Alora tried for a smile, though it shook.

"What should I do with George while I'm away?"

"Leave him with me, Miss Pennigrim. I'll make sure no harm comes his way."

Alora blinked at the guard, taken aback he'd felt the need to add that last bit. "Thank you." She didn't tack on his given name, taking his lead. Not in front of Mr. Macaw. "Shall we?"

The groundskeeper stared.

"All right, then."

Together, they passed through the gate.

Madam Feebledire appeared apoplectic as she rushed toward them breaching the entrance. "Whatever are you doing!"

Alora thought the woman's coloring matched her crimson vest exact, which didn't bode well. Fighting nerves, Alora smoothed the fabric of her green dress. "I'm papering the walls today, Madam. Mister Macaw kindly offered to assist me."

She didn't need to glance to the large man to know his expression would say nothing of the sort.

"We do not bring *wheelbarrows* into Opulence." A hand to her forehead, Madam Feebledire glanced all around the grand hall, then hissed, "You're lucky Master isn't here to witness this."

Alora frowned at her words as the wheelbarrow wasn't even dirty and opening was hours away yet. Before she could say anything, however, she turned toward the sound of scraping. Mr. Macaw stacked nearly all of what she'd brought along into his arms. Hurrying to help, she grabbed ahold of the bucket of glue and the brush.

"Madam," grunted the man in a voice drawn out and impossibly deep. Then he looked toward Alora, who laughed in surprise.

Following his lead, Alora also said, "Madam Feebledire." Then she inclined her head before walking away.

"You—you cannot simply leave this here!"

"Be back soon," said the groundskeeper staring ahead.

"*Mister Macaw!*"

When the pair entered Door Twenty-five, Alora immediately set to lighting the lamp. She turned back when it was done and found the groundskeeper where she'd left him, standing in the doorway. A deep line had formed between his eyebrows as he perused the newly brightened space.

"I know. I haven't done much to it yet. Nothing actually. But half the work is in the planning, and that I've finished." Smiling like they were old friends, she began to unpack his arms. "Thank you for carrying these all that way. You're so kind." The groundskeeper grunted, depositing what she hadn't taken onto the floor. "Though I'm not sure what Madam Feebledire has against the wheelbarrow. What do you use it for? Carrying dirt? The grounds are very nicely kept." She began to unroll the paper.

"Dirt," agreed Mr. Macaw. "Trimmings. Trespassers."

Alora straightened at that. "Trespassers?" But Mr. Macaw, seeing her work, began to unroll alongside her. "Oh, you needn't do that. I don't want to keep you from your obligations." She swallowed, imagining the darted man hauled away, limbs bent awkward and limp within the wheelbarrow. His work would scar her.

"You're not tall enough."

"Ah—" Alora held up a hand to stop him, but Mr. Macaw wouldn't be deterred.

Taking the glue, he slopped on a generous amount before reaching up higher than she ever could have hoped and pressed the paper on.

She winced.

"That's too much glue," she said, gently, taking the brush from his hand. "It will bulge. Here. I'll paint; you press."

Alora had planned to ask for a stool, or perhaps imagine one if Madam Feebledire proved too prickly, but this would work too. Together they made an efficient team, finishing one wall, then two, in the time it would have taken Alora to do half of one all alone.

"Do you live in Enver, Mister Macaw?" she asked as they began the third wall.

"No," came the low reply.

"Here?"

"Yes."

"Do you enjoy it?"

No response.

"Does the work suit you?"

"I like plants."

"Me too!" said Alora, stretching onto her toes. "I have an entire terrace of them, and I often purchase them for my work, as well. Though not here, I don't think." She glanced around the room.

"No. Not without sun. Not without rain."

"Right." They worked on in silence awhile more. "Mister Macaw," she began carefully, glancing from the corner of her eye. "What happens to trespassers?"

She waited awhile, her breath bated, but no answer came. She sighed in defeat.

"Gone."

"Dead?" Alora paled, spinning toward him.

Mr. Macaw, nonplussed, pressed more paper to the wall. "No. Lost."

"Lost," Alora echoed. "What do you mean?"

But he wasn't given a chance to answer, as a new voice interrupted, "Master Merridon would like to see you, Mister Macaw."

Alora spun with her brush toward the doorway. The groundskeeper, however, didn't seem so easily disturbed and finished with the paper. The large man slowly turned beside her before offering a grunt of acknowledgement, laying down what remained in his hands. He ambled toward the door.

Alora noticed all of this from a faraway place. She only had eyes for the person standing there.

It was *him*. The mysterious man from her first encounter and then again in the forest. Aside from a glimpse of his covered jawline, she could make out nothing beneath his hood. Darkness tumbled in at his back as he faced her.

When the groundskeeper neared, the other man moved aside, letting him pass. Alora offered a feeble smile as Mr. Macaw glanced back toward her. He didn't return it but dipped his head instead. Then he was gone, leaving her all alone with the masked man.

"Is this about the wheelbarrow? Does Master Merridon wish to see me too?"

"No," he replied, before adding in a mildly threatening manner, "Not yet."

His voice was low, almost a growl. Alora wondered if he pitched it that way purposefully to intimidate. It certainly worked on her. She needed to be rid of him. "Well then, if you don't mind, I'm very busy."

"The groundskeeper assisted you?"

Alora squinted, trying to make out his eyes. Between the cowl and the lantern's cast shadows, she was unsuccessful. "I didn't force him."

"I didn't insinuate."

He hadn't, it was true. Except the way he stood there, hidden and watching, made her feel as if she'd done something wrong.

"What is the purpose of this?"

"Excuse me?"

"Are you a messenger for Master Merridon?"

She watched his shoulders stiffen. "Of a kind."

"And you patrol?"

"When necessary."

"And you've been tasked with keeping an eye on me?"

A brief pause. "No, I have not."

"Then I must remind you, again, that I am busy. I don't mean to be rude, but I have a deadline. So please say or do what you will and then allow me to work."

When still, he offered nothing, Alora huffed a breath in disbelief. *Good god, what a dense clod!* She'd ignore him, she decided. Let him stand there and watch her wallpaper the room until he grew bored enough to leave. Served him right.

Though, as she bent to retrieve the paper abandoned by the groundskeeper, she couldn't help wishing she could see beneath his hood. *Just a peek.*

She brushed glue with practiced strokes before taking the paper in her hands, reaching as tall as she could. She landed back on her heels. It was no use. She needed that stool. She needed more height. Alora spun back to the man. If he lacked his own work, perhaps he could fetch her one. But instead of finding him at the door, she turned fully into an unfamiliar chest.

Swathed in black leather, he pressed up against her, and Alora's lips parted as she looked up and up, to his hands stretched above her, dark gloves against ivory paper. He pressed it firm, before sliding them along the edges and down.

She caught the outline of his covered nose, his mouth, the strong shape of his jaw, and her eyes narrowed. "Do I know you?"

"No," he said, stepping back.

Alora felt the loss of his heat like a fever come and gone, which was unsettling. She turned the brush over in her hand. Perhaps it was only the glue making her feel this way.

"But this isn't our first meeting," he added. Plucking the brush from her fingers, he dipped it, applying a thin layer of glue. "The gold is a nice touch. It will please Merridon, which I assume was your intention."

Alora studied the paper as he applied it, appreciating the carefulness he took in aligning the edges. She wondered why he didn't refer to Master Merridon as simply 'Master' with all the rest. "I favor gold in small touches rather than—" She nudged her discarded cloak with her toe.

"It's true, the green suits you better."

Alora canted her head. It was a compliment, maybe. Albeit a poorly delivered one. "As black suits you?"

"All variations of darkness suit me. Enchantments, chocolate, midnights. Hair the color of chestnuts. Hand me more paper, Miss Pennigrim."

Hair the color of—

"It's Alora," she grumbled. Then wondered why she'd told him.

"As you wish. Alora." Her name was a rasp behind the mask. He grabbed ahold of the paper she offered, his gloved hands meeting hers beneath.

"And you are?"

Their hands touched still, the paper partway between, and Alora felt transfixed, dying to know. She waited and wondered, curious why he debated, when he said, "We don't divulge our names, us lowly messengers."

She stopped herself from rolling her eyes at the diversion. "I don't believe there is anything considered 'lowly' about you."

"Don't you, really?"

She could recognize that tone a thousand times over, obvious in every line of his posture. The only thing that might have voided her thinking were his fingers touching hers, seemingly unhurried to move. She huffed, "You're arrogant, aren't you? It wasn't any sort of compliment. But fine, keep your identity secret as I'm sure it works well enough for you." She tipped her head and made a show of examining him, boots to head, and smirked at his hidden mouth. "Or perhaps not. The black on black on black is a bit bland. Almost uninteresting."

"Such barbs, Miss. Are you *quite sure* you are uninterested?"

She could feel the triumph roll off him when she gasped, his fingers enclosing over her own.

"*Quite*," she ground from between her teeth. She forced herself unaffected. Forced her breaths normal. But he was everywhere, eclipsing everything. Even her breath was shared with his they stood so close.

"It is considered impolite to lie."

"You should know best of all."

"It isn't a lie to withhold information."

Which wasn't necessarily wrong. Alora scowled over it, lifting her chin. "I only asked out of decency to begin with. I hardly care."

She waited for him to call *that* for the lie it was. But he didn't. Instead, she felt his attention shift over her features—and wondered what conclusions he'd drawn by the end.

His fingers moved against hers. He cleared his throat, an indecisive sound. "I suppose, for all intents and purposes, that you may know me by my title, if not my true name."

"Your title?" she laughed. "Like a fairytale *lord* or *prince* or—"

"Urchin, Miss Pennigrim."

Alora's hands dropped as quickly as if she'd touched fire. She stumbled back, her heart thudding, fast and painful. "*What* did you say?"

"I'm a messenger, as you assumed."

"You called yourself an Urchin. Those are— They are—"

"What are they?" he said, though now when he fixed his attention on her, Alora felt the darkness threaded in his words. Suddenly the room felt too small, help too far away.

"A gang! Good-for-nothings. Shadows who attack people unprovoked, stealing their memories." She snatched the lamp to her like the flame might keep his evilness at bay.

"Is that what they say?"

"I've witnessed it!"

The words were out of her mouth before she could think. Horrorstruck, Alora clamped her lips closed. She didn't even have a chance to swing the lamp toward him before he was pressed against her, his hand around her wrist.

"What *exactly* have you witnessed?"

"Nothing," she breathed. "Only shadows."

She caught the glimmer of his eyes beneath the hood, though she could neither determine their color nor their exact shape; he held the lamp away from them. "You would be wise to keep such information to yourself. Trust me in this."

"Why?"

His hand flexed atop hers. "Because you put yourself at great risk, and my word only extends so far."

"Your word? Are you their leader?" She made to rip her hand from beneath his, but he held it fast. Disgust roiled through her as she thought of the broken woman. Her bandaged head.

"As a general is. But beneath a king."

"Master Merridon is your 'king'?"

"You're quick. That might pose a problem." He released her at last, though he didn't back from her. "No. It certainly will."

She watched his hand disappear within the folds of his coat with very real terror. It was her turn to be bludgeoned, she knew. Her turn to lose her memories, to wander, asking others what had been stolen. To lose her dream.

Panic seized her.

The Urchin 'general' halted. Tugged. And where he jerked his hand free, his opposite followed. He lifted his hands to the light, the manacles adorning each wrist glinting plain, a short chain taut between. He raised his head to her.

"What"—the growl of his voice thrummed, muffled behind the mask—"is this?"

Alora stepped sideways toward her satchel, toward the door. The Urchin stepped with her. "Shackles?" she offered, stepping again.

"How have shackles appeared on my wrists, Alora?"

"Don't call me by my given name again, you monstrous eel!"

"Miss Pennigrim," he said through gritted teeth, and blocked her bodily. "I think it's time you explained."

"I owe you nothing!"

"You've *bound* me! How?"

"How do you steal people's pasts, Urchin?"

"You'd do better to leave that line of questioning. I mean it."

"Do not tell me what to do as you reach to take my memories."

"I was *not*."

"Then what were you doing? While you search within your coat telling me I will certainly become a problem?" She moved to the opposite side only for him to block her again.

If she must, she'd shackle his legs, too, and run. Though to where she'd run to she didn't know. Enver would never be safe again.

"A pen, Miss Pennigrim."

"What?" she asked in disbelief.

"To write down a location for you. In case you're ever in need of it."

"That sounds like a lie, and even if it wasn't then it sounds like a trap."

"It isn't a lie."

"So it is a trap."

He huffed through his nose. "It is neither."

"You reached for a weapon."

"No. Come and see. I cannot reach deep enough into the pocket on account of these magic manacles conjured from thin air." He awkwardly patted his left breast pocket, hidden beneath the coat.

Alora narrowed her eyes.

"If you harm me, I'll truss you up in chains."

She didn't like that he paused awhile. "Understood."

Alora stepped tentatively nearer, then nearer still, until she could reach out with her fingers and move his coat aside. Beneath was a black shirt with a single pocket. She saw no hint of a pen.

She cried out in surprise when the cool chain met the back of her neck, dragging her in.

"I don't plan to harm you," he said.

But when she looked up beneath the cowl his eyes were black.

Then so was everything.

Chapter Twelve

It was like a starless midnight, a black hole. Alora could see nothing at all, not even an outline. But the shackles were still cold against her neck, the body against her warm and unyielding, and when she clawed at the fabric against her hands, it shifted—real. She had only been plunged into darkness. She was not lost to it. Still, it didn't prevent the cry from leaving her lips.

"You've blinded me!" she cried. Despair echoed in each word.

"We're both in the dark. Reversible. If you only remove the shackles."

This was his plan then.

Her body flushed, cold to hot, her fear giving way to a consuming anger. She struggled against him, attempted to lift her hands, but he only pressed her closer, so tight her breaths turned shallow. She could feel his arms flexed around her; she'd become immobile, the scent of leather all around. She couldn't even raise her leg high enough to stomp on his foot.

"Remove the manacles," he said into her hair.

She seethed against him. "Do you swear you'll stay far from me?"

"As far as I can manage."

"You have to do better than that."

"How far away is enough? I will still need to do my work, and you yours."

Alora could hear his heartbeat, her ear unwillingly pressed to his chest. It beat faster than she expected. Perhaps he was tiring. "I won't finish this job."

"You signed a contract."

"What business is my contract to you?" Pointless as it was, she attempted to break free again. With a grunt of annoyance, the Urchin adjusted his grip on her.

"Master Merridon is not one to take disappointment lightly. Remove the shackles, keep silent, and finish the job. You should be free then."

"Is that meant as a threat?"

"It is meant as a truth. Look at this place. Do you think he's gotten to where he is on goodwill and even better intentions?"

Why, *why* had she signed on to this. She should have known it was all too good to be true. She wilted in his arms. "Fine. I won't say a thing."

"And I will not steal your memories."

Alora laughed in horrific incredulity. What had she gotten herself into? But a deal was a deal, and she couldn't stay buried in this darkness pressed against a demon-souled man forever.

Carefully, she imagined cracks in his manacles—all the way through so that they would fall to the floor. A great clatter marked her success, though she still couldn't see a thing.

Silence ensued. All she could hear were breaths and heartbeats. The Urchin still held her against him, probably to ensure she didn't plan to exact some other punishment, but he needn't have bothered. In place of fear or fury, all that swept through her now was disappointment. All of it in herself.

The darkness lightened. From black to gray to the warm yellow of the lamp beside her. Alora blinked at the change, her eyes pricking as they adjusted. She felt the loss of heat and stability beneath her cheek so profoundly, she stumbled forward. Strong hands enclosed her shoulders.

"It takes a moment," said the Urchin, softly, maybe even apologetic.

She brushed off his grip. "Write what you planned, then leave me be." When he didn't move, she sighed, teeth clenched. "It *was* a lie."

He took the accusation for the fact it was and didn't deny it. "Is there more you can do? Besides conjure iron?"

"Is there more you can do? Besides deceive and trick and force others into the dark?"

"Much more."

Alora shuddered at his tone. "Is that what happened to your latest victim? Could she even see the attack as it came? What did she do to deserve it?"

"She spoke of things she shouldn't." At Alora's returning scowl, he shifted forward, but did not step. "I mean it, Miss Pennigrim. Maintain your silence."

He turned then, his coat clinging to his frame like a shadow. Alora waited until he neared the door before she asked, "Why?"

The Urchin paused, the cowl shifting to align with his shoulder as he focused once more on her. "Why what?"

"Why tell me at all?"

"You wanted the truth. It was something at least." Then he was gone through the door.

She waited a bit to imagine it, and even longer before she called down the darkened hall. "There's something climbing over you."

Silence ensued. Alora didn't breathe. When a strangled curse echoed back to her, she grinned.

He may act fearsome, and maybe in most settings arachnids didn't affect him, but she was hard-pressed to believe there was anyone in existence who wouldn't startle at the surprise appearance of a spider. Especially one as large as their head.

She continued to laugh still, hoarse and a little wicked, as she imagined paper onto the remaining wall. She rolled up what she'd planned to use but now never would—*Lovely. More things to store*—and gripped the glue, slinging it over her shoulder. She stared at the lamp last. It burned just as it had before, and yet it still seemed dimmed, like a permanent shadow had been left behind in reminder. A lingering threat.

Her laughter died as she took it in, bending over the blown glass to see the flame inside. On a steady exhale, she snuffed it, casting herself in gloom.

She might never trust the dark anymore, but she refused to fear it too.

Because unfortunate instances seemed to happen to her in pairs these days, Alora shouldn't have been so surprised when upon making for Opulence Mansion's large front doors, she heard her name called from above. She looked up.

William peered down at her, his face transformed at her attention and pulling into a smile. "Well, well, Miss Pennigrim. I didn't know *you* would be here today."

His voice didn't ring through the grand hall as she would expect, and she found herself puzzling over how that came to be. Sound-proofing was always a tricky business, and never absolute. But this… this *was* absolute. Her expression pinched as she thought it over, and because of it, it took her a rude amount of time to answer.

When she glanced up next, she found William's smile had fallen a bit.

"Door Twenty-five won't design itself," she said, though she softened her annoyance with a small smile. She didn't know if it was even him she was irritated with, or if her feelings were still in an uproar over the Urchin's dark eyes and even darker warnings.

"I was just leaving."

"Oh, don't go just yet," he said, now leaned over the railing.

It was true she'd finished ages earlier than expected, what with the help of the groundskeeper. Well, the groundskeeper and—*him*. The nasty cauldron of emotions he'd invoked had caused her to ignore her own rules, conjuring paper into existence. She'd never been more upset with herself. She only wanted to go home and forget everything she'd learned.

Too bad she'd drank from the potion today.

"I'm afraid I'm very busy." She pulled up her hood.

"That's unfortunate," said William, his mouth turned down in a mock frown. "I'd planned to show you something magical, and now I can't help feeling as if you're avoiding me."

She was avoiding him, but not for the reasons he believed. She pressed her eyes closed beneath the shelter of the cloak. "Magical?"

"Yes," said William, his voice nectar-sweet and coaxing. "You'll be quite in love. It is my favorite door aside from my own."

She tipped her head back at his voice, almost yearning, and found his hopeful smile returned in full force. She couldn't very well leave after seeing it. "All right," she said on a sigh, and walked to the base of the staircase where she began to climb.

Chapter Thirteen

"**D**oor Ten," he said. "Room of Love."

Alora followed in behind him. "When you said I'd be quite in love, I didn't think you meant it literally."

He chuckled, handing her a tumbler of clear liquid. Thirsty and searching for distraction, she swallowed it. "It's more an experience rather than the real thing."

Alora took in the four large beds separated only by thin gauzy curtains, each draped with satin sheets and sleek bed skirts that puddled on the floor. Crimson, of course. "I think I remember Master Merridon saying something similar. That there are no performers here, but an experience for members who are without. But I forget, is it dreams? Or the reliving of old memories?"

"No, you're thinking of Door Eleven. Lennox prefers that one."

Alora watched William remove his shoes, intrigued. "Which is Door Eleven?" She brushed the hood from her head, relishing the feel of the fabric against every strand of her hair as it slid down.

"Room of Happy Days," he supplied, unbuttoning the first few buttons of his shirt. He sat upon the bed, swallowing from the same glass he'd offered her. "Why don't you take off your shoes."

Alora, who found herself unabashedly staring at that revealed triangle of skin, thought: *What a perfect idea.* She bent, unlacing her boots and removing her stockings. She nearly moaned aloud at the feel of her feet in the thick carpet.

"This room is divine." She couldn't fathom she'd thought the colors too overpowering only moments before. When William patted the space beside him, she hurried forward, digging her toes in with every step. She sat down, the mattress giving way pleasantly, shaping to her body. She wanted to cocoon in it.

"May I?" he asked.

Alora glanced down to his hands, extended toward her throat. She lifted her chin in response, and William made quick work of unclasping her cloak and tossing it from the bed. She whimpered where his fingers brushed her skin.

"How do you feel?" he asked, and his hand, where it'd been against her throat, trailed the length of her neck.

"I feel..." she began and broke. Her head tilted, allowing him further access. His fingers were long and smooth, and she moaned. "I feel like I never want you to stop."

"Then I won't," said William and grinned like he'd managed some great triumph. He pushed the straps from her shoulders, and Alora, in response, tangled her fingers in the collar of his shirt.

William moaned in her ear before his lips pressed against the shell of it, his hands stroking her bared shoulders before dipping lower. Alora could hardly breathe from the sensation of it, every nerve coming alive and eager for his touch. She shifted closer, until her body was pressed against his, her hands beginning the task of pulling apart every button of his clothing. She thought of nothing else, nothing but the sensations racketing through her, the heat pooling at her core. She wanted to be free of everything, to lie entirely bare before him, and him bare too. To feel his skin on hers. It didn't matter anymore who he was, what he looked like. That his aftershave was a shade near overpowering. It didn't matter that she barely knew him and what she did left her feeling more than a little uneasy. She'd take him here. She'd take anyone.

William's hand was pressed to her abdomen, his warm mouth on her barely concealed chest, pushing her down, and she made to give in, her eyes fluttering open.

To the darkness pooling under the door.

Can it be so late?

She thought she should care but couldn't, with William's hand more insistent against her and her body molding like clay to the pressure. But the darkness built, leeching the color from the floor. The sight of it caused her chest to hitch beneath William's adamant administrations. Something was happening. Should she be afraid?

She wasn't.

Not even when the door burst open.

William swung around the same moment Alora collapsed back onto her elbows. She couldn't see anything. Nothing but black, black, black, and then suddenly a shape. Not the night, but a man. A man coated in darkness and hooded. A familiar mask.

"*Oh,*" she breathed, and bit her lip against the yearning having overcome her. He was so tall. All of him a mystery to be revealed. Would he join them? It didn't matter that he'd threatened and lied to her only minutes—hours?—before. She'd experienced the strength in his arms, knew what his heartbeat sounded like. He felt danger-ous, but the *good* kind. She'd gladly welcome him in.

She shifted her leg against the other, anything to relieve the ache.

But she didn't think the hooded Urchin looked at her. In fact, she'd bet anything he only spared his wicked black eyes for William. William with his shirt undone, his waistband riding low on his hips. Alora, attention happily diverted, reached for him.

William didn't stop her.

"A knock would have been appreciated, Brother."

Alora thought William's grin appeared taunting and wondered why. Her fingers brushed along his toned abdomen. His eyes fluttered closed, and she was satisfied.

"Get *away* from her."

"Why should I?" he all but groaned.

Yes, why should he?

Alora lifted to nip at William's ear, but her gaze found the Urchin's. "Can I not have you both?"

"For *fuck's sake*, William," he growled, striding in. "She isn't a member."

One moment Alora's hand was dipping into William's strained trousers and the next she found herself hauled to her feet by the wrist, pressed tight within the nook of the Urchin's side. In precise, jerking movements, he pulled the straps of her dress back in place. Alora could have sobbed at the feel of his leather-gloved hands. She wanted them *everywhere*.

She glanced back at William who'd gone quite still. "Close enough," he said, his tone murderous.

"A measure that doesn't exist. Forget your own lack of morals, have you thought of what he'd say?"

"I don't care."

"*You are filth.*" Every word from the Urchin's mouth dripped with venom. Alora pulled back in surprise, though he didn't allow her far. He grabbed her hand. "You're leaving," he said to her, and stared at William, daring him to intervene. When he did not, the Urchin bent, scooping up her shoes and stockings into one arm. "Go." He pointed out the door.

Alora, desperate as she was, did as she was told. She didn't look back.

With the door closing behind her, she glanced at her hand, tucked tight within the Urchin's much larger one. It was an upgrade, certainly—even her heart told her so. She'd ask him to leave the gloves on, she decided. She squeezed harder, flexing her fingers and leaning in.

"Stop that," he said, and pulled his hand from hers. "Put these on."

Alora took the boots from him even as the loss of his touch felt like a chasm ripped open inside her. She pouted immediately. "You won't put them on for me?" The thought of him kneeled at her feet sent her body aching all over again. She nearly pitched forward.

"No, I think you can manage." With a mournful sigh, Alora put on her shoes. Though she stared unabashedly at his bottom half all the while. "Now drink this."

"What is it?" she said, taking the bottle from him.

"Water." He paused while she drank deeply. "Did you know he gave you an enchanted drink?"

"William offered me water too."

"Hardly." The growl was back, and Alora had to grit her teeth to keep from ripping off his mask to feel it against her mouth. "You drank Lust, Miss Pennigrim. It'll wear off with time. Water helps. Though your memories of what happened will be blurry."

"My new normal," said Alora, and licked a droplet from her lips.

"You need to go home."

"*Alone?*" She could think of nothing more tragic.

"I'll take you there, and there you will stay, alone, until you are yourself."

"I am myself!"

"No, you're drugged. High on enchantment. What you're experiencing isn't your natural—"

Either he choked or cleared his throat, but regardless he didn't finish his thought.

"You sound like you're familiar." She didn't know what she meant exactly. With the potion or with herself.

But the Urchin said, "More than I care to admit."

Alora thought she should be bothered that William had offered her Lust without informing her of it first, but she couldn't be bothered right now. How could she think of anything aside from what sort of body, what sort of mouth, she might find beneath those layers of black standing rigid before her now? He looked as if he'd demand everything of her, and *good grief*, she'd give it all and thank him for it.

She knew her assets; she was not delusional. And she'd use them all before their journey ended. Let the lying, conniving 'general' deny her *then*.

Chapter Fourteen

At the gate, the Urchin and Reginald argued.

"You can't take her through the forest with that cart."

"*I* can't accompany her on the road."

Alora lay draped over George's neck, running her fingers through his hair. She wouldn't leave him here. She couldn't. A long-suffering sigh reached her, a loss of some sort.

"Fine. I'll come back for the cart."

A splutter from Reginald. "And how do I explain it in the meantime?"

"Leave that to me."

When the Urchin turned back toward her, the shadow of his gaze drifting over her form, Alora thought she might catch fire. He shifted his head and clicked, and a horse the color of midnight emerged from the trees.

"You'll ride with me. The donkey can follow."

Alora couldn't hide her sly smile as she approached the towering blue-black creature. Nor did she try. She moved slowly, her shoulder shrugging one strap free while her other hand lifted to the horse's nose. He snorted into her palm.

She thought she heard a hissed curse leave the Urchin's mouth at her behavior, but she couldn't be sure. Instead, she moaned as those sinful, gloved hands reached around her waist, gripping her firm. She tried to press back, but he lifted her behind the saddle, leaving her to dig her fingers into the hard leather rather than him. She heard Reginald cough somewhere behind her.

The Urchin swung up in front, and she wasted no time wrapping her arms around his strong torso, burying her face in his coat. She breathed deep. He smelled familiar, she thought. Leather along with a faint woodsy scent, and his tensing didn't faze her in the slightest. She breathed deep again, her lips parting. Her senses were so very heightened in this state, and she couldn't get enough.

"If you've finished," he said. "Hold onto the donkey's reins. Don't let go or he'll be lost to the forest."

She did as she was told, taking the reins from him, though she also used it as an excuse to move her opposite hand, slipping it beneath his coat. There she stayed unmoved, until his tensing eased beneath her fingers, and with a click, urged his horse forward.

She blew a farewell kiss to the guard, who appeared quite mortified to receive it. "What is your horse's name?" she asked.

"Necros."

"Are you serious?"

"Very."

Alora thought it was terrible, but out of politeness didn't say so. Instead, she took to rubbing her cheek against the Urchin's back, sighing at the feel of him. "That's George. I also have a rabbit. Mrs. Flops."

"And you question my choice in names."

"She's the sweetest thing. When we reach home, you might come up and meet her." Alora chewed at her lip while she waited.

"That's not a good idea."

"Why?" Behind his back, she thought she might cry at the injustice of it.

"Because you cannot be trusted."

"I cannot!" But then he shifted against her, and she forgot all about it. Carefully, she pressed her body closer, so that he might feel all of her, aligned to all of him. He stiffened. "You're strong. Stronger than William."

"Do not speak to me of *William*. You'd do well to stay away from him."

"Why should I?" All she could think of were his lips on her neck, on her chest. How much he'd wanted her while the Urchin did not.

"Because he's a performer, and performers are obsessive types."

Alora laughed. "How broad. And you are not?"

"I am not prone to it."

"So you *say*. But I know you for a liar now." She shifted her gaze without lifting her head, studying the pale trees as they passed by, the narrow, secret path they followed. "Are these woods as treacherous as they say?" Not an ounce of fear trickled through her, only curiosity.

"It's exaggerated, but not untrue. Merridon doesn't dispute anything to keep the mystery alive. And the nonmembers away."

Alora could hardly stand it, being so close to him and not being able to get closer. His voice was rough, just as she imagined his hands would be. Her own was held still to the taut plane of his abdomen, but she adjusted it now, slowly down so as not to alarm him. When he stayed silent, she eased it farther still.

"What are you doing?"

"Searching for a pen."

With a grunt of irritation, fingers enclosed around her own, pressing their paired hands tight upon the Urchin's thigh. She couldn't move her hand at all, though she didn't think she wanted to. It was the next best thing. After all, he'd even *laced* them.

"He should have never done this to you. He will regret it soon."

"I don't regret it."

"You will, trust me."

Alora laughed. "Trust an Urchin? I could never. Though, really, I'd do anything to have you for awhile. Are you so sure you can't? I would make it memorable, I swear."

Again, the Urchin hissed a curse, but it was a bit more strangled than before. Perhaps he was crumbling, just a little. To be sure, she pressed herself against him again, hoping to send him into pieces.

Alora yelped in surprise. One moment she was inhaling the Urchin's scent, picturing how his broad back must look unclothed. The next, she found herself draped over his front, her shoulder to his chest and her legs dangling from one side. He ducked his head before she could so much as blink up at him, lashing the donkey's reins to his saddle.

Then a mask was against her ear. "Spread your legs."

Alora, mouth suddenly dry with triumph, did precisely as told. Only for him to grip her about the thigh and drag it over the horse's opposite flank. Her dress rode high up her legs, the saddle horn the only thing protecting her modesty, and it was Alora's turn to swear then. In utter, defeated disappointment.

"You tricked me."

One arm pulled free to drape across her chest, pinning her own in place. "You left me little choice."

Alora, realizing something, grinned. "You were tempted."

"No," said the Urchin.

It was the least convincing 'no' she'd ever heard.

The Urchin blocked Alora's advances at every turn onward. The arch of her back. The tilt of her hips. Aside from his curses and grumblings, she could tell he was affected. His breaths were too quick against her neck, his posture too unyielding. But the journey couldn't continue forever, and at last they were at the edge of the forest where he could be rid of her. He slid down from the saddle before turning and doing the same to her. She gripped his forearms all the while, trying and failing to see what lay beneath his shadowed hood.

She sighed in defeat. "Enver."

"Yes," he said. "I'll leave you here. Can I trust you to make it back on your own?"

"You can trust me." Her lips stuck out in a pout, unbelieving he actually possessed the gall to turn her down. Her hand flexed over George's reins. "Before you leave, I want to know something."

His answering sigh seemed to travel from the depths of him. "What?"

"And I want you to tell me the truth."

"I make no promises."

That rankled her. Still, she took the time to adjust her dress, focusing on some areas more than others. She raised her eyes to his. "Tell me you're attracted to me. Or tell me nothing at all."

Alora watched the Urchin and his unchanging posture. She tucked a wayward strand of her hair, her eyes fluttering over the feel of it. She thought she knew his answer, replaying his fingers wiping her neck of blood, holding pressure to her wounded ear. His assistance with the wallpaper. The firm yet gentle grip of her waist. *Hair the color of chestnuts.* Why, if that didn't describe her coloring perfectly, nothing else could.

The silence ended. "Uncomfortably so."

Alora stepped toward him. "Ha! I knew—" But where she reached there was only darkness, and when she blinked there wasn't even that. He was gone.

"Bastard!" she seethed, and taking a firmer hold of George, stomped from the trees.

Alora shamelessly rapped on the door of Potions and Peculiarities. When the sign remained *Closed*, and the door locked, she dragged poor George around to the back and did the same.

The Urchin had been wrong to trust her.

Bash should be here. It was afternoon, and the shop should be open. At the very least he should be inside, sorting through all his boxes as before. She found him beautiful, so beautiful she might break the door to get to him. Surely, he wouldn't turn her down too. If he did, she thought she might scream.

But no one answered her knocks, and the fire, the ache built up inside her, began to wane. She slumped against the door, sliding down until her knees bent and her bottom hit the stoop. There she began to cry. "No one wants me. A room of love and I am unlovable."

All the while the fire banked, the embers fizzling to nothing. Where she'd felt ecstasy moments ago, she found only acrid puffs of smoke. But she wanted the ecstasy. She *needed* it back. Hell, the world might very well end without it.

When George nudged her hair, she pushed him away. "Leave me. Leave me be," she hiccupped. Curling in on herself, she fell fast asleep.

Chapter Fifteen

"Miss Pennigrim. *Miss Pennigrim.*"

Alora blinked open her eyes to twilight. Twilight and a sculpted mouth. Then sharp cheekbones and forest-like eyes. A knit brow. She swallowed against her parched throat, glancing around in confusion. She was at Potions and Peculiarities, the back door, and her hip throbbed something awful.

"I found your donkey wandering Mugwort Alley, eating every bit of green he could find, including my flower. And here I find you. Why aren't you at home?"

Alora couldn't answer. Why wasn't she at home? She shifted herself to sitting and Bash gave her the space to do so, straightening. Her mind was a rusted wheel, barely pushing forward. She frowned at his bemused look, the wind-tousled hair, at the customary blacks buttoned and zipped upon his broad frame. It was the color that did it for her, finally.

The memories came upon her like an avalanche, bits and pieces, unclear and without order, but still.

She buried her face in her hands on a mortified moan. "*Oh.* I need to die."

A glass of water found her hands. She downed it around a pitiful gasp, half a sob.

"Of course you don't."

"Yes, I do. You've no idea. I've just—" *Goddammit! The Urchin!* She'd propositioned the wicked Urchin on top of everything else. She slumped back to her side, groaning.

Hands reached beneath her arms, hauling her upright. "Are you ill?"

"In my soul," moaned Alora. "I'll never be well again."

A sudden tenseness framed Bash's eyes and hardened his mouth. She both felt and heard his huff of breath. Was he angry at…her?

"Please don't let anything burrow that far, Miss Pennigrim."

"Why are you so formal? My name is *Alora.*" She scowled at him from where she sat, but their eyes were level, and it bothered her. She pushed to her feet, noticing he didn't make space for her to do so as he remained where he was, crouched and quite close. "I need an Urchin."

That sent him reeling upright. "Excuse me?"

"Any one of them you can find. I need my memories of this day purged forever, and I promise I won't miss them."

A bit of the tension eased from Bash's features. "I don't think their work involves philanthropy—"

"And I don't think you realize that I'm dreadfully serious." She moved until they were toe to toe, her face angled up to his as she glared. "Now do you know where I might find one or not?"

They stared at one another. Bash had a calculated look about him, his mouth firm. He appeared as if he wanted to say a million things but could decide on none. Finally, he said, "Keep your memories."

Alora could only grit her teeth, looking away, fighting tears of shame. He would not dismiss her so easily if he knew what had been done. When a pressure met her elbow, she stared at it, remembering another hand, *hands,* in other places. A fury filled her. "I'll kill him."

The present hand tightened on her arm. "Who?"

She ripped herself free. "*William.*"

"William? Did someone—"

She cut him off with a fierce look. "Thank you for retrieving George. I'll replace the flower, though it was in danger of being choked by weeds anyway." She moved around him, to where the donkey stood tethered to a wagon. "You won't tell anyone will you?"

"About what?"

"That you found me as you did."

"Hardly seems a wild enough story for the pub crowd."

Alora sniffed at his flippant comment. "Fine. See you."

"No, Alora. I'm sorry. I should have said I have no one to tell. And even if I did, I would not."

Her lips parted, eyes searching his. But they were as guarded as ever.

"Can I ask why you were here?" he said, slow and needling. "Did you need something more from me?"

Alora paused, staring. Why had she come here? And then it rushed back, blurry and faded as it was, and her cheeks lit bright as apples. "I don't remember."

"Ah," said the shopkeeper, but she knew for certain he didn't believe her. It was plain as day by the tilt of his head.

She stomped to where the donkey had been tethered. "Come along, George. Let's get you back to the stable where you can have a real meal. Hopefully you don't get sick from the nasty weedlings growing on this street. Oh! The cart. How do I get the cart?"

The Urchin had said he would take care of it. What did that mean? She didn't know how she could find out, both because she'd no way of contacting him, and because she was bound and determined to never see him again.

She felt a shift in energy at her back and knew Bash had come up behind her. She pressed her eyes closed, wondering at the feel of it, of why she seemed so drawn to someone she knew quite literally nothing about. Maybe she was just an insufferably shallow creature.

How disappointing.

"I say leave it all alone for tonight. Clearly, you've been through an ordeal. A cart can wait for morning."

Alora spun back toward him. "Thank you, *Bash*, but I've had enough of your vague advice for one day."

"Fine, then. No more advice," he said, and held up his hands in frustration. "At least allow me to walk you home."

Alora's mouth dropped at this uncharacteristic suggestion. She sputtered, "What? Why?"

"Because you seem out of sorts and it's nearly dark."

"I can manage alone."

"My company is better."

"Is it though?"

His answering smile, a full one, not some half-thought smirk, left Alora wondering if this was what it felt like to be struck down by lightning. He'd a dimple in his right cheek. *Good god.*

"Have you been taking the potion?"

"The potion?"

Bash's brows dipped at her confusion. "The one I made for you."

"Oh." Alora shook her head clear. "I did. The once. Though now I wish I hadn't. I wish to forget everything about this day."

In a baffling turn, the shopkeeper appeared to hesitate. Eventually, he said, "I can't promise it'll matter at all...but do you want to talk about it?"

"Oh no. Certainly not." *The idea!* She stumbled away from him, dragging hapless George along. "Goodbye. As you wisely said, everything can be sorted out in the morning." She didn't mean for the dark and threatening edge to tinge her words, and yet so it did.

William, she seethed, picking her way along Mugwort's poorly lit street. He'd regret ever tricking her into those satin-sheeted beds. And the Urchin. *Well, he'd... He would...*

It didn't matter. She'd decide what to do about those conflicting emotions later.

When she arrived home, she found her Opulence-gold cloak folded and set at her door and was immediately sick.

Chapter Sixteen

Alora had vowed long ago to avoid any and all distraction. Yet, she'd never had more to contend with than now. It was the following evening, and the third outfit she'd tried on, when she remembered:

"Brother!"

Mrs. Flops, alarmed, thumped furiously and bounded from the room.

William and the Urchin, *brothers?* They were different in build, it was true, but similar in height, and while one's eyes were dark and the other's light, that didn't mean anything. They both worked for Master Merridan, for one. Did that make William an Urchin as well? He was certainly devious enough for it.

Oh, what a mess!

She'd half a mind to appear at the mansion tomorrow, imagine the room to completion in a moment and be done with the entire thing. But that wouldn't be right. It wouldn't be honest. Hell, at this point it wouldn't be *wise*. Who knew to what lengths the Urchins spied upon Enver, because they must, especially their leader, who could mimic deep shadows and move about unseen. She'd have the shop she'd purchased wallpaper from as an alibi, but no one else, and she'd already let slip she was capable of more than simple, good taste.

She turned in the mirror, eyeing the silver dress from every angle. It was longer than she usually wore, flowing below her knee, the corset bodice free of straps. The hem's stitched flower stems twinkled in the lamplight. *This will do*, she thought, and began the quick process of twisting the hair from her face. The rest she left long and draping down her back.

She fixed gems in her ears and red to her lips. She puckered them in the mirror and frowned immediately after. Maybe she'd made a mistake. Maybe she should cancel—

The knock on her door told her that line of thinking had come far too late.

Alora slipped on her shoes, blue, with a thin strap slid over her heel, and hurried from the bedroom.

"Hello," she said, only a little breathless.

The stable hand grinned in reply. "Hello."

Alora didn't find Timothy Lofte near as beautiful as Bash nor as mysterious as the Urchin nor as devious as William—all of which made him ideal. A fine dinner date. And if she used the situation to learn more of what the 'young people' of Enver gossiped about in regard to the Urchins and their dealings, it would take a fine date and elevate it to perfect.

Or so she told herself.

She also told herself she wasn't using him. That Timothy must offer saucy winks to more than just her, and likely with good results—he *was* handsome. And a date was a *date*. Good grief, she didn't agree to marry the boy.

"You're right on time," said Alora, and smiled her perfected smile.

"Always. You look beautiful; are you ready?"

He sounded so damned sincere. So *nice*. A part of her cringed away, withering. *Oh no*. Perhaps she was using him. His hair was the color of golden sand, thick with waves that continuously desired to flop over one umber-colored eye. She felt no wish to push it back in place—a fact she noted with dismay, as she frequently fought the urge to rifle her hands through Bash's ink-dark hair like some unfettered breeze.

"Thank you, and I am ready. Did you choose a place then?" She traded her satchel for a small purse, snapping it closed over lipstick and her key.

He stepped back to allow her through. "I thought Delight and Truffle. Have you been before?"

"I've passed it by, I think. On Foxglove Lane?" She led them down the stairs.

"The same. It's quiet but not overly, and the sauces are some of the best I've had in the country. The service is unmatched. Also, they use barrels of Wilderwood for their aged whiskey, and serve it in these small—"

Alora tried to listen, for she wasn't often purposefully rude, but despite her best effort, her attention wandered. She'd the distinct impression Mr. Lofte went on many first dates without making time for many seconds, and Delight and Truffle would recognize him on sight. Not to mention the golden cloak now returned to her closet, the need for her to rearrange her entire bedroom after waking to ten wall-length mirrors imagined to existence then shattered, William's hands on her, *Bash's* hands on her, the Urchin's voice behind the mask demanding, *"Spread your legs"*—

"—your cart returning this morning. Miss Merryweather parked it in its usual—" Timothy startled and glanced at his forearm where Alora gripped it like a falcon.

"My cart is returned?"

He frowned beneath the flop of his hair. "Should it not have been?"

At his obvious discomfort, Alora released him at once. "Yes. Yes, it should have been. I'm only pleasantly surprised; the person I'd asked to return it isn't exactly…"

"Pleasantly surprised?" interjected Timothy between the break of her thoughts. He rubbed at his arm, and Alora knew in that instant, she'd not be asked out a second time, even if she wished it.

They arrived at Delight and Truffle without further incident if not relative silence. It wasn't until the door was opened and the hostess seated them—after a familiar smile for Mr. Lofte—that Alora attempted to salvage what she could.

"Tell me more of this whiskey. I'll admit I'm a complete novice in terms of its process, but I'd like to try some."

Timothy, in a surprisingly forgiving turn, smiled hugely at her. "Would you, really? So it begins with—"

As she was prone to do, Alora took notice of the room. Square and dimly lit, it was quiet despite more than half the tables being occupied, and it smelled of wood, liquor, and roasted meat. At the back were barrels, stacked on their sides and stamped, a barman picking his way amongst them, and to the side was a fireplace with cushioned seating before it. A single person sat there, a glass in his hand and eyes trained on the flames.

When their server approached, uniform starched and impeccably white, Alora inclined her head at Timothy's order for two house whiskeys, served neat. When he went away, Timothy returned his attention to her, and like that day in the stable, winked boldly.

It did not do to her what Bash's had done.

"We will see what you make of it," he said, as if knowing what her opinion would be.

Alora pasted a smile to her lips but said nothing else of it. Instead, she asked, "What do you do when you're not occupied in the stables, Mister Lofte?"

"No, *Mister Lofte*, please. Makes me feel like we're conducting a business meeting instead of getting to know one another." When Alora only smiled her agreement, he continued, "I do this, mostly.

Not dates! Well, not always. But I explore local pubs and distilleries, cataloguing which I like best and why. It's good fun."

Alora, preferring the taste of flowers and grapes over wheat and barley, said, "How invigorating. Perhaps you will start your own one day."

"What a thought!" said Timothy, beaming like it was a good one. "But this is too competitive of a market for the likes of me. I've not got any special talent to speak of."

The whiskeys arrived on a curved, wooden platter, the glasses heavy crystal. Timothy offered one to her first before taking the other for himself. He sniffed it deeply, sighing. Alora studied him, at how he fit. Her gaze drifted above him, to the carved beams beneath the ceiling, and below, to the legs of the table chiseled until they resembled living trees with leaves and roots and textured bark. She glanced at the fireplace, empty of admirers now.

"It isn't always about the product, though that is important, and I'm sure you'd do a fine job. But the ambiance as well. Everything in this room works toward its purpose. I'm sure you could replicate it while still maintaining originality." When Timothy only stared at her, bemused with a touch of humor, she asked, "What?"

"Did you grow up here?"

Alora felt her face warm. Through no fault of the whiskey, which she hadn't yet touched. "No. Did you?"

"I did. And while I appreciate your faith in me—like it a great deal, in fact—Enver isn't like anywhere else. Wilderwood trees didn't even exist until the great-grandfather of the current owner grew them from Indigo Mountain stream stones in his greenhouse. To this day, none but his descendants have access to the grove outside of town. Myrtle Merryweather is my aunt. She can soothe anything that grazes. If I've got anything in me, it's a touch of that, nothing more. I tried to brew my own ale awhile back and it tasted like pasture and piss. Excuse my language. Maybe in most places hard work can get you by, but in Enver, if you can't add a touch of enchantment, you might as well give up before you've begun."

Alora wasn't sure what to say. How could she say anything to that? She couldn't imagine possessing an affinity for something she held no passion for, and now she felt like a dolt for bringing it up to begin with. This was why she avoided dates; she was not good at them.

She swallowed a sip of whiskey and tried not to let the distaste show plainly on her face. If he described his own ale so poorly, she didn't want to imagine how terribly it had tasted. The liquor burned a bitter trail down her throat. "I suppose there is still much I've yet to learn about the way of everything."

"It's a lot for any outsider, pardon my use of the word. It's why most are visitors. Or traders. That way they can leave when their minds grow too overwhelmed, returning to the classic 'normal'. But you've been here for some time now."

Alora recognized the leading statement for what it was and side-stepped it gracefully. "Two years. I will say I've become used to the surprising, but I wasn't anticipating the shocking." Timothy continued to watch her openly, his whiskey nearly finished. Emboldened, she leaned forward, her voice dropping. "I recently learned of a gang underfoot."

Her date, having waved for a second tumbler, pushed the piece of obstinate hair from his eye. "Ah, you mean the Urchins."

Alora's lungs squeezed. "Yes, that's the name! What a dreadful business. I'm appalled nothing is being done." The next sip she took of the whiskey was fake.

Timothy polished off what remained in his as the second was delivered, and with it, a cart was wheeled. The server lifted the lids from the trays in a practiced flourish.

"Your choices this evening," the server said, and looked to Alora first. The meats were piled high and the vegetables steaming.

The cheeses were as plentiful as they were diverse, and the renowned sauces bubbled in their boats. She made her choices quickly and without much thought. Timothy spent more time deciding, enough that Alora had to physically place a hand on her knee so she would not tap her foot. When the server left them at last, he took to sampling each thing in turn.

"I'm sorry, what were we speaking of?"

"I'm shocked nothing is being done about the Urchins," rushed Alora.

"Oh." Another swallow of whiskey. "Well, they tried. Before. Now they don't bother with it anymore."

"How can that be? How can attacks go unpunished?"

Timothy's cheeks were flushed, having nearly finished his second pour, and his eyes were bright. "They've never been caught, for one. Some say it's like laying a trap for a ghost. Or the wind. Rumor is nearly all the less savory trading is overseen by them, the darker side of Enver's enchantment. That they usher in all manner of cursed and monstrous things from the forgotten corners of the world."

Alora could think of one street where such dealings would happen.

In fact, she could think of one shop in particular.

It felt hard to swallow.

No, surely not.

She said mostly to herself, "And anyone who speaks out is silenced."

Timothy shrugged, bold in his drink.

"Depends on what you say. I can say they're filthy criminals, cowards hiding in the dark, and nothing will probably happen. But see something you shouldn't"—he pressed a finger to the side of his nose—"heaven help you. Because no one else will."

Chapter Seventeen

The date ended rather abruptly. One moment, Timothy was bidding her goodnight with a kiss she avoided at the last moment, glancing across her cheek, and the next she met an oddly familiar face peering at her from across the street.

She gasped, pulling back, and Timothy, apologizing profusely, shuffled away. She spared him a glance. "No, not you," she found herself saying. She really was the worst at this. "Thank you, Mister Lofte. I enjoyed the night. I'll likely see you tomorrow, I think. Goodbye!" Then she ran in the direction she'd last seen the strange man staring back at her.

It was the trespasser. The man darted in the neck on Opulence's grounds. She was as sure of it as she was in her newfound hatred of whiskey. The moonlight offered a brief glimpse of a torn brown shirt turning the corner, and she rounded it at an outright run, her heels clacking alarmingly on the cobblestones.

"Wait!" she called.

She never once considered he'd obey. A mistake, for as she turned the corner, she smacked straight into him, sending them both stumbling. The man nearly went down, while Alora twisted her ankle with a muted cry. Righting herself, she breathed through clenched teeth, willing the pain into submission.

"I'm so sorry," she hissed at the man.

"You told me to wait," he said simply, and stood there in his tattered clothes.

He looked utterly lost.

He was middle-aged, judging from the hint of wrinkles and sparse peppering of gray hair, but it was his eyes she focused on. Eyes that were once so intense in his intent as he ran past her that day but were now dark and empty.

"Do I know you?" he asked, in a hopeless tone.

Alora felt a sudden surge of discomfort, same as she did while in the presence of the Urchin's victim. "No. But I've seen you before."

"Oh," said the man and sighed. "I do not remember 'before.'"

"None of it?" She shifted her weight to her opposite foot, the pain ebbing and flowing like waves.

Suddenly his eyes were no longer empty but filled to the brim with unshed tears. "None of it. I don't even know my name. I keep wandering, wondering, waiting for someone to recognize me, but so far no one has. Aside from you. I'm starting to believe I was never meant to be here."

Alora's heart clenched. "Perhaps you're not from Enver."

"How would I ever know?"

She'd no answer, other than loading him up in her cart and taking him from one town to the next herself. Though that would require a good deal of time she didn't have, what with the deadline encroaching. Not to mention the impossibility of her ever returning to Eirian, the town that disowned her.

"What do you know of Opulence Mansion?" Alora glanced around as she said it, pitching her voice low.

"Nearly nothing," he replied, not near so quiet as herself. "Only that it's a place of great enchantment, and open to members rich enough or desperate enough to scrounge the coin. Or that is what I've heard."

She didn't know what to do. Clearly, the dart had contained something which stole his memories, and at a much larger scale than whatever the Urchins utilized. But no doctor could help him, and she'd heard several times now the constable was useless in this. It made her incredibly furious when she thought it through.

"I saw you once when you knew yourself. Your memories were stolen from you." She reached out with the coin she had and imagined a bit more into her palm. "Hire a driver to take you to the nearby towns. I never met you properly, but you hadn't looked like you traveled far; no horse or carriage brought you to the mansion's gates. Maybe you'll find someone who remembers. Worst case you find some honest work. I'm told Enver can be a difficult place to make your way."

The man stared into his palm in confused wonder. When he said nothing at all, she thought maybe she'd overstepped. "Or you could stay. I know a baker looking for help."

When he finally looked up, Alora was warmed. The man looked to be overfull of gratitude—a sight which made what happened next all the more shocking. His eyes rounded alongside his mouth, and he began backing slowly away. "Run," he said. "Run!"

Alora heard several coins plink upon the stones as she whipped around best she could, her ankle sending a searing pain up her calf. She was met with darkness.

And not the sort that happens in the night.

"*You*," she seethed, and lunged inside it.

She couldn't see. Whether she blinked or not, the darkness was the same. And then she could, her ankle giving way beneath her, and her hands reaching out to grip the wall, everything lit by the pale light of the moon. She stood there, braced and heaving, angry and hurting. Had she imagined it?

No. That man saw it too.

A shadow played over the stones. A regular one, caused by clouds and moonlight, and yet her fingers drifted toward it anyway.

"Reaching for me?"

Alora cried out at the voice in her ear, at first in alarm and then in pain, as she spun once more on her injured foot. Her back met the wall in a jarring thud. One moment she saw a bottomless dark, and the next, a man. The Urchin towered above her.

His hand found her arm, steadying. A twisted sort of comfort. She wanted to toss him off but couldn't afford the imbalance, which only angered her further.

"Do not *touch* me."

The Urchin released her at once, but he didn't step away. "You're angry with me. That's well enough. I'm angry with you too."

"Pardon me?" she said, shocked over this more than anything come before.

"No, I will not. What is the one thing I asked of you, Miss Pennigrim?"

"Nothing. You've never once *asked* me anything at all!"

The Urchin hissed a breath. "Do not speak of what you've witnessed. That is what I needed from you, and now I overhear far worse than I could have imagined. You've also been present at a trespassing?"

Apparently, Alora's refusal to admit anything fueled his fury. She could feel the uncontrolled energy encircling them both the longer she kept her lips pressed tight. The Urchin bent forward, his masked mouth unbearably near her own.

"*Answer me.*"

"Fine," Alora snapped. "I was there, and the trespasser is now lost, just as Mister Macaw said."

"Mister Macaw said? He should not be speaking of it to you at all!"

The incredulity she felt over where her dream's path had brought her was unmatched. She laughed, biting and hysterical.

"What is this madness? Opulence Mansion and its exclusivity, harboring some festered secret society full of black-market dealings and muscled goons. I can't hardly stand it! This is Enver, city of enchantment and dreams. I came here to escape, not be pulled down again to a pit of wolves."

She should be careful; her laugh was well on its way to becoming a sob. She'd so much hope for the road ahead, only now there was a wall of darkness standing in her way. Quite literally. She wanted to pound against it, scale it, anything but remain here like another helpless victim of Opulence. And she would have. She would have tried anything. But unfortunately for her, her ankle abruptly decided itself unfit to endure what little weight she pressed upon it—and buckled.

The Urchin's arms were swift to catch her, his grip hard around her waist. How quickly he'd forgotten she'd told him not to touch her.

How slow she was at reminding him.

Alora felt his hood brush her hair as he bent nearer. "Are you injured or unwell?"

"Injured," she told him, honestly. Because while he'd certainly hurt others, he hadn't hurt her. Not yet.

At the least, she expected his hands to remain where they were until she regained her footing enough that he could interrogate her further. At most, she thought he might offer a shoulder to assist her in hobbling home. What she did not expect was for the Urchin to sink onto one knee. Alora stared at the top of his covered head in blatant shock, her mouth wide. A memory, albeit a distorted one, niggled at her mind. Of her once wishing for exactly this—and why she wished it. Her cheeks burned.

One gloved hand remained at her waist while the other skimmed her side, down the curve of her hip and thigh, all the way to her pulsing ankle. She gasped at his prodding, and not all of it pain.

"It isn't broken," he told her.

"I didn't think it was."

"But it's swollen. You will need to be off your feet for some time unless it's mended now."

His thumb brushed over her joint like a caress, and Alora felt the uptick in her heartbeat. When she thought it impossible to beat any faster.

She swallowed. "The doctor's then."

"Inefficient places," he scoffed, and rose to his feet.

"Do you have a better suggestion? Are you also a gifted healer as well as capable of casting out light?" She tried to add bite to her words, but his hand remained at her waist, searing her to distraction.

"Cast out light? What do you think I do? Play with the paltry shadows?" He loomed over her then, mask reflecting moonlight, eyes a pool of black. The air pulsed. "I take light and break it, Miss Pennigrim. And there's no escape from me unless I wish it."

The darkness threatened to consume her. *He* threatened it.

She'd been subjected to the former before and it terrified her. But a part—a small, incredibly unwise part—twinged with curiosity over the latter. *What might it be like?*

"Tell me, Miss Pennigrim. When did you forget to fear me?"

I honestly can't say.

Instead, she glared up at him. And she continued to do so, even when the darkness grew, and the black overtook them both.

Chapter Eighteen

The darkness receded, black to gray, gray to dim lamplight. A room materialized, large and furnished with supple leather sofas and high-backed chairs. Alora blinked slowly against the change, forcing her breaths deep rather than shallow. Both were recommended to her by the Urchin releasing her now.

But she didn't, couldn't have, accounted for his hands to move. To slip the strap from her ankle and remove her shoe with a gentleness so at odds with the look of him. She bit at the inside of her cheek as she studied his profile.

"These are the shoes you chose when digging for secrets in the dark?"

Alora scowled at his shadowed hood when it turned toward her. "I was *not* digging. It was happenstance. I was at the end of a date when I saw that man."

"A date?"

His voice changed around the word. She didn't imagine it. The pitch of it caused her eyes to narrow at his form. "You'll not seek him out. He has nothing to do with any of this."

"Protective of him, are you? It must have gone well." Bitterness? From her kidnapper? *Let him think whatever he likes.* So long as he left Mr. Lofte alone. Alora couldn't imagine facing down his aunt should anything happen to him because of her.

"Where have you brought me?"

"Somewhere safe. As I said."

She'd argued with him well over half their journey. Berated, rather. At least at first. For him to put her down, to tell her what he planned. To give her back the light he'd broken. But he'd ignored every demand, scoffed at every threat. He'd told her he wouldn't hurt her. That he was only taking her somewhere secret. Somewhere safe. And she'd believed him. Just as she believed him now.

What a fool she was, to believe someone she didn't trust.

There were two windows, each blocked by heavy, black curtains. No fireplace warmed the space. Instead, there were lamps, two of which were lit upon the end tables that bracketed the sofa. She didn't recognize any of it.

"At least tell me we're still in Enver."

"Considering I cannot manipulate time and space, yes. We're not so far from your home."

"How would you know where my home is?" At first, she frowned up at him, where he draped a blanket over her legs, propping her swollen ankle onto a pillow. Then her expression melted into one of realization. "You've been there. It was you who brought my cloak back."

The Urchin's fingers stilled where they cupped her heel. "Your Opulence cloak was missing?"

"Yes. I'd left it behind. In the Room of—"

"Love?"

If his hand weren't so tender on her skin, she might have leapt back at the danger in his voice. As it was, she merely stiffened. And nodded.

The Urchin replaced her heel with care, but Alora could see the shift in his form. How every muscle beneath his dark clothing seemed to vibrate with tension.

"If you didn't return it—" she began and faltered.

"I did not."

A stone settled in her stomach. "William?"

"Most likely."

She thought she'd feel terror. That William would have not only tricked her back at Opulence but now sought her out. Knew where she lived, and where she slept. But she didn't. Instead, white fury seared through her. "How dare he!"

She could feel the Urchin's attention on her face, on her fingers gripping the sofa beneath her until they blanched. *How dare he.* Imaginings coursed through her. Of the punishments she wished to exact. Appendages she yearned to remove.

"I should have choked the light from him."

Alora stuttered over her thinking. Slowly, she surfaced from her many inspirations, enough that she watched the Urchin move to another lamp and snap the matchstick before it reached its destination. He tossed it away with a growl.

Another strike. Another broken match.

"Maybe you should leave it," Alora suggested.

"Leave it? I can't *leave* it. William has always toyed with boundaries, crossed several, but he has dropped over the edge with this. Merridon will hear of it, and he will intervene. You won't be punished; I won't allow it. You will finish your project, quick as you can, and leave Opulence be."

"I meant the match."

"What?"

Her eyes widened at his full attention, body turned toward her, towering above. "I meant to leave the match. There's enough lamplight."

A loud exhale left the Urchin then, the tension in his shoulders easing some. A breathless laugh echoed between them, a sound she'd never heard. "Leave the match…" She startled when the box clattered onto the table. "Miss Pennigrim—" he began.

Alora, she corrected inside.

They both turned toward the door when it swung in.

"What is it now, Mer—" The stranger ceased speaking at seeing Alora sprawled upon the sofa. Another Urchin. Another black cowl and masked jaw, though this one's hands were uncovered.

Alora ceased thinking at all. All except for one thought. *I've made another grave mistake.*

"Well. If this isn't a first," droned the new arrival.

She pushed to the heels of her palms and flinched when the grip of a hand found her bare shoulder. She couldn't help glancing down at it. "He's a healer," said the man beside her.

A healer. An *Urchin* healer.

"The best there is. It will be effortless, painless—"

"Some effort, I'd say. I did have to get out of bed," said the second Urchin, and he moved farther into the room, enough to latch the door closed. His voice, too, was rasping.

A singular moment flashed in Alora's mind from back in the street. *"When did you forget to fear me?"*

She certainly remembered now. Her heart sped, her palms slick. She didn't want to give away any more of herself than she already had, but if she needed to in order to protect herself, she'd do what she must. If she imagined them asleep, would they fall to dreams? They might never wake would be the problem. Or perhaps the solution?

The Urchin must have become alerted to her stress, because his fingers pressed deeper into her shoulder. "You won't be harmed."

"Where have you brought me?" she whispered, as the healer moved to pour himself a drink from a cart against the far wall.

"A meeting place."

"Of Urchins."

"Yes."

His hand hadn't moved, like he was worried she'd bolt. Which she wouldn't. Not until she ensured they couldn't follow.

"What is the damage then?" said the healer. He remained turned from her as to pull down his mask and drain his glass.

"Ankle sprain. Fairly certain it isn't broken."

"It isn't," said Alora in a near shout. A ball of panic began to grow in her chest. She didn't want him to touch her. Didn't want him to mend the bones. What if he made a mistake? What if he caused them to disappear entirely? There was no cure for that. Bones could not be regrown.

She would know.

"Let's see, shall we?" The healer rubbed his hands together.

Distantly, Alora thought perhaps it was to warm them before he placed them against her skin. Directly in front of her though, it appeared a gleeful gesture. Like he couldn't wait to dig around inside her with his ability. Her stare riveted on the rings adorning his thumbs.

"No."

"Miss Pennigrim, please. That ankle requires attention."

Alora tracked up the arm holding her, to the masked mouth, as it was all she could see. "I said I would go to the doctor."

"They won't heal you so well as him."

"You can't know that for sure."

"Yes, I can."

Her breaths were rapid. She could see the girl's face, plain as the masked men in front of her now. Eirian's square. A strange-shaped rabbit. The pothole. The blacksmith's daughter sprawled between the two, her leg twisted beneath her. The surging crowds.

Alora had panicked, tried to imagine it whole. And had removed every bone within it instead. Nothing else to be done. Permanent ruination. And Alora would never forget her face.

"Please—"

"*Alora*—"

"No! I said no." The Urchin healer moved one step closer, and the ball of panic burst. It engulfed her fully. "*Stop.*"

He stopped. Every part of him. His muscles, his breath. Maybe even his heart. The Urchin stood like a statue, frozen before her.

Her mouth fell wide. *Damn!* What had she done?

She swung her gaze to the Urchin beside her, and for a hellish moment thought she'd frozen him too. But the seconds passed, and he turned toward her, achingly slow.

"I think you'd better explain to me *exactly* what you can do." His words were clipped. Angry.

Alora shrank into the cushions.

His hand abandoned her shoulder for the armrest beneath her. His opposite went to the back of the sofa, caging her in. "What are you capable of, Miss Pennigrim?"

"I won't tell you."

She could see his chest rise and fall above her, furious.

"He would not have touched you without your permission."

"Just as every other victim of yours?"

Abruptly, the breaths she watched ceased. In one swift motion, the Urchin pushed from where he leaned above her. "That is not the same."

"It is the same! You asked when I'd forgotten to fear you, and I haven't. You can't be trusted."

"I won't argue with you over what must be done. Now can you reverse it or not?"

Can you regrow her bones or not?

The answer had turned out to be 'no' back then. She didn't know how to imagine the girl's leg whole without knowing what was missing. She was young, unpracticed, and scared. She was already a strange commodity because of her ever-present rabbit. It was such a terrible mistake. A shame she carried to this day.

Move, she imagined, and the healer stumbled forward.

"My apologies," he stammered. "My leg must have fallen asleep. And my…arms." He rubbed at his limbs.

Alora refused to look at the man beside her. Instead, she tossed off the blanket, uncaring that her dress was rucked up above her knees, and sat up.

"You're a healer?"

"I am…" Except now he sounded uncertain.

"Thank you for coming. I'm sure it isn't how you wanted to spend your night. But please, do not mend any bone without speaking of it to me first. I've a particularly bad memory I'd not like repeated."

"Simple enough," he said. And this time, when the healer rubbed his hands, Alora didn't sense anything gleeful about it at all.

His palms were still cool against her skin, but not cold, and he held the joint as gently as the Urchin before. Seconds passed without comment. Not from her or from him, and certainly not from the unmoving pillar at her side.

"Sprained, as you thought. No need to mend any bones tonight."

Alora exhaled in relief. "Thank you."

"Anytime." A tingling sensation swept through her ankle like a gust of wind, but before she could so much as twitch, it was done. The Urchin healer stretched to his full height and glanced around the room. "Anything else?"

"No," said the man at her side. "I appreciate your quick response."

"Captain." The healer nodded toward him, a slight bow to his upper body, and then he was gone through the door.

Alora didn't move. She continued to stare in an unseeing haze at the closed door, disbelieving she'd shown even more of herself to the Urchin she so distrusted and feared. Because she did, didn't she? Distrusted and feared him so much?

She came back to herself when leather gloves enclosed the backs of her knees, shifting her until she faced the front. Her feet met the floor. She glanced up to the dark shape of the Urchin captain's eyes before he dropped his head. Her shoe was slipped back onto her foot, simple and painless.

"I'll take you home."

Alora could see nothing. Less than nothing, if that were possible. But she could feel *everything*. Cobblestones clacked beneath her heels, uneven and familiar. Cool, night air brushed her skin. Her hair fell down her back, strands of it brushing her face with the push in the breeze. And her hand. Her *hand*. She twitched her fingers to be sure it wasn't a dream. Or a nightmare.

The Urchin tightened his grip upon them.

He'd held her hand once before, just like this. She couldn't remember where exactly, or at which point in their meeting, but she remembered this feeling. Her heart must have fallen out of rhythm. It was the only plausible explanation for the sensation in her chest now.

"Are you managing?"

"Yes," said Alora, the word clipped. He'd tried to carry her again. *Her*. With two perfectly adequate feet.

There was so much to say. Of what he'd witnessed between her and the lost man. Of why he'd been there to begin with. What he planned to do about her after all, if anything. She wanted to confront him over Timothy Lofte's allegations, and William's actions. She wanted to confront him over so many things.

"Could you—"

"Is William—"

They both sucked in a breath.

"After you," said the Urchin.

Alora exhaled, then began again. "Is William truly your brother?"

She'd counted to thirty before he answered. "I'd forgotten he called me that in front of you, I was so furious. Stupid of him."

"So it's true?"

"It is. In name over blood, but brothers all the same."

"He was adopted?"

"We both were."

"Both? Goodness. And you were raised together as children?"

"Are we questioning my past now or his?"

Alora ignored him. "Is he an Urchin as well?"

"No. He's a performer, as I've said."

Adopted brothers. "Do your adoptive parents live nearby?"

"Near enough."

Alora could feel it, the tension building and now rolling off him. His fingers flexed around her own, and it was a warning to her even if he didn't mean it as such. "What did you wish to ask me?"

Alora nearly began her counting again when she felt him inhale.

"Could you manage to forget everything you've seen? Everything you've heard?"

"Are you asking me to pretend? To go on as I've always done?"

"Yes."

Alora thought about it. Of the lost man, and the injured woman. Of Mr. Whitters and his resigned worry. William and his terrible choices, and the impossible darkness she now walked inside. *Pretend? How could I?*

"No, I don't think so."

"I assumed as much."

"Are you going to bludgeon me now?"

A resigned sigh. "No. I don't think so."

They walked in silence for some time, Alora's footsteps the only sound. She opened her mouth and closed it again; once, then twice.

"I can feel you practically vibrating beside me. What is it?"

Alora scrunched her nose. "Is it true you deal in dark artifacts? That you channel wicked enchantments in and out of Enver?"

"*Wicked* is a subjective term. What makes an enchantment wicked, do you think?"

Alora rolled her eyes.

"I can see you, you'll remember."

Her expression quickly hardened into a scowl, and she felt the Urchin's humor more than heard him. But she needed to know.

And she couldn't tell him why. "There's a shop that deals in questionable objects. Creatures too. I'm curious if you supply it."

"And I would tell you something like this, why?"

She didn't have an answer for that. By all rights, he *shouldn't* tell her. The hand beneath hers tugged, and she followed.

"Uneven stone," he said. Then, "Which shop?"

"Potions and Peculiarities."

The Urchin scoffed. "That place is a pitiful mess. And its owner? An idiot."

Chapter Nineteen

The Urchin took her straight to her front door, confirming he knew precisely where she lived. Light returned as he released it, and Alora blinked up at the moon trending lower in the sky. She pressed the back of her hand to her mouth to stifle the yawn.

"About the healing…"

Alora's brow raised when he paused. "Yes?"

"I didn't recognize your reaction for what it was. I'm sorry."

"I feel foolish over it now."

"Don't. And don't think to go to the constable about me, Miss Pennigrim. They're all in Merridon's pocket. Good night."

"Wait." The word was out of her mouth before she thought why she wished it. Before she'd processed even a sliver of what he meant by the constable and Master Merridon's seemingly endless pockets. She imagined his eyebrow arched as he turned back toward her, tried to picture what color it would be. *Dark, I suppose.*

"What would happen if I didn't complete the contract?"

"Those are scenarios I would not put into your head before bedtime."

Alora swallowed. "So bad?"

"Either you run very, very far and very fast," he said, steadfast as ever. "Or you finish what you began."

What in the godforsaken earth?

Her first breath drew shaky, but her next steadied her. *One week,* she thought. *One week, and after that we'll see what can be done about these bludgeoning Urchins.* Because she did love Enver. She adored the people who said good morning to strangers and singing while atop her terrace. She loved the flowers and shops and variety of enchantments. But this contract. This *contract.*

"I've already run away once. I won't do it again. Goodnight." Then she closed the door and imagined three locks after it.

Let William try anything now.

She'd not slept well.

Alora yawned though the hour crept toward noon only to lose it partway. A letter slipped through the slot. She walked toward it slowly as the envelope hinted at what it was—the gold lettering, the gold embossing at the corners.

She bent and lifted it, her heart somewhere near her toes.

Miss Alora Pennigrim, 126 Eldergrove Avenue, Enver.

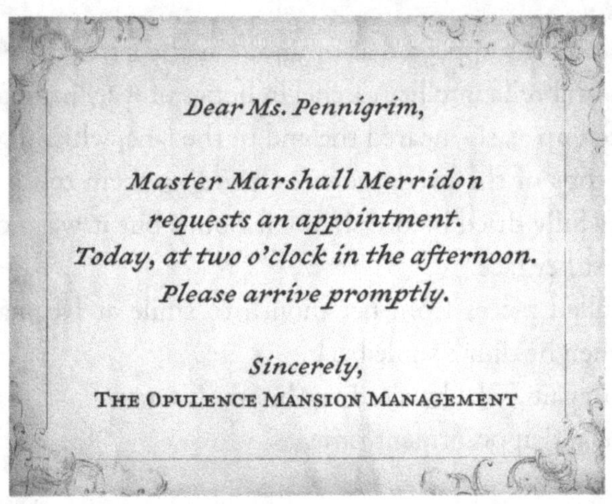

Dear Ms. Pennigrim,

Master Marshall Merridon
requests an appointment.
Today, at two o'clock in the afternoon.
Please arrive promptly.

Sincerely,
THE OPULENCE MANSION MANAGEMENT

She slipped her finger inside, unfolded it, and read it quick. Then she read it again.

She swallowed the distinct taste of bile. Fear squeezed her like a snake. She'd been all bravery and bravado last night, but now the thought of running very, very far and very fast didn't sound so bad an idea. Of course, it didn't help that she'd nearly scorched her entire home with nightmarish imaginings. She'd woken to black marks charred onto her walls in the distinct shape of flames; William had haunted her, managing past her locks and into her dreams, and she loathed him for it.

And now she must meet with Master Merridon. Master Merridon, who would surely have something to say over how she'd only a week remaining and all she'd managed was wallpaper. Well, if his Urchins and his performers would only leave her and Enver be, she might have been done days ago. As it were—

"Mrs. Flops! Forage on the terrace today. I've an appointment with my early demise which can't be missed."

Then she ran and leapt into the tub.

The afternoon sky appeared as ominous as the letter felt. Alora had packed an umbrella into her satchel in hopes of warding it away. The wind picked up as she neared the end of the lane, whistling through the white tops of the overlarge trees, bending them to its will. Her hair hadn't fully dried before she'd left home, but it was now, whipping against her face.

She pulled pieces from her mouth to smile at Reginald. Then faltered when he didn't smile back.

"Hello, again." She lowered her hood. "It's me—"

"Name and appointment time."

Alora startled. Because the voice wasn't Reginald's at all, but deeper and more exacting. She braved a step to peer beneath his helm. Narrowed hazel eyes stared back at her, not coppery brown. Cold eyes. A hard-set mouth. His uniform was the same down to the curling shoes and gold paint, but that was where the similarities ended. This guard did not want to make friends.

Her fingers retreated from her satchel where they'd begun to enclose a bottle of Winnowillow juice. "Alora Pennigrim," she said. "Two o'clock."

When he held out a hand, she didn't place her own within it, but the letter. The guard scanned it before brusquely handing it back. A reach behind him and the gate swung in. No instruction. No warnings. The guard faced forward once more and didn't so much as glance her way when she stepped past him and onto Opulence's grounds.

Where has Reginald gone? She wanted to ask but was scared for the answer. She only hoped he had a day off to himself, a vacation to somewhere cool and temperate with no gold paint in sight. She hoped it, but the ominous feeling only grew. Same as the thunderclouds in the east.

Something was wrong.

The grounds were still; even the wind had vanished. Alora picked her way tensely down the lane. Aside from the darkening sky, she could neither hear nor see anything out of the ordinary. Maybe—

Snip. Snip, snip, snip.

At the end of the path, upon a ladder wide enough to support his large frame, perched Mr. Macaw. In the groundkeeper's hands was an enormous pair of sheers, which he used with expert precision as he sliced and snipped a new topiary into submission. Alora stared awhile, transfixed, as the glinting blades maneuvered through the greenery. She couldn't yet tell what it was meant to be.

"Good afternoon, Mister Macaw."

Snip. Snip.

She frowned. *He must not have heard me. The storm is loud.*

"I didn't know you were such an artist!" There. He couldn't have missed that. She'd practically shouted.

But aside from a brief pause in his work, the groundskeeper continued on. Alora was more than a little offended now, wondering what she could have done to earn his ire. Until she remembered their parting. His meeting with Master Merridon and the wheelbarrow. Perhaps she'd gotten him into some trouble with management. Discarding her feelings, she hurried down the pebbled path, far enough that she came upon his opposite side.

"Mister Macaw. Have I caused you trouble?"

She thought he would continue snipping and slashing forever when he didn't immediately turn around, and she made to leave on a defeated sigh, when he shifted at last. His long gray hair lay lank around his head as he held a finger to his lips. A single gesture and no words.

Alora could only nod her understanding.

Yes, something was *very* wrong.

Madam Feebledire answered at the end of her third knock, and the crease between the woman's eyes became a canyon upon seeing Alora standing there.

"Miss Pennigrim."

"Madam."

"Well, hurry in. You're nearly late, which would be a horrible offense, considering."

Alora could take it no more. "Considering what? Where is Reg— the usual guard?"

A scoff burst from Madam Feebledire. "*Reginald,* is it? Do you ignore all warning and instruction, Miss Pennigrim, or only when it suits you?"

Alora's eyes widened, taken aback. "What do you mean?"

"I *mean*— Nevermind. You'll find out soon enough. Door Zero. Good luck."

Alora briefly contemplated yelling out for Madam Feebledire not to abandon her, but the woman was already far away. It was just as well. She would have only scowled at Alora in disgust over her raised voice and abandoned her anyway.

You are a professional, Alora, she reminded herself. *Business meetings are a part of the work. As are disgruntled clients.*

If disgruntled was even what he was. Oh, she should have run when she had the chance. Damn her stubbornness!

Alora knocked three times.

The door swung in.

"Ah, Miss Pennigrim. Two o'clock, exactly. I do enjoy your promptness."

"Master Merridon." Alora inclined her head as she stepped in, noting with a practiced air that the owner of Opulence sat rather rigid in his seat. He wore a golden jacket today, finer than when she'd first met him, and his smile, though still meant to charm, seemed fixed. "You wished a meeting with me?"

"I did. Care for some refreshment?"

The sight of the crystal bottle of clear liquid upon his desk along with matching tumblers brought back unwanted memories. Alora shook her head. "No, thank you."

"Then let us jump straight into it then. Sit, please. How do you feel your progress on our project is coming along?"

Ugh. She hated questions worded in such a way. It left her feeling like a trap was being carefully assembled at her feet. And she did not want to be trapped by a man like Merridon. She sat.

"It is, perhaps, moving a little slower than I'm accustomed to, but part of that is the distance. I still have a clear idea of what I intend for it, and I've not missed a deadline yet. I won't in this project either." She offered him her most polished smile.

"It is a rather bare considering the month's end is encroaching. I'll admit I'm growing worried."

"Please allow me to appease that." Good grief, how she hated simpering before such a man. Every time she looked at him all she could see were lost eyes and nothing to be done about them. "The carpenter has what I've ordered ready for pickup, same as the carpeteer, and every detail after that will be no problem in acquiring."

"And how do you plan on delivering your larger purchases?"

Alora fixed her smile same as his. He tested her, the hardness of his eyes at odds with the pull of his lips. "I'd planned to inquire after transport options with Madam Feebledire."

"As is appropriate. Good to hear, Miss Pennigrim. Our establishment abides by rules which, if not followed, can embark catastrophic consequences. One cannot hope to maintain so much enchantment without them." Beneath the desk, Alora clenched her hands to fists. "To the next matter. I'm told of a most unfortunate incident involving you and one of my performers."

Alora flushed scarlet. She could feel it like a dousing. Same as she could feel the phantom press of William's lips to her neck.

"I don't mean to cause you discomfort, but I think it's best if we lay out this rule clearly for you. You are not, no matter the circumstances, to go beyond any door besides Door Twenty-five until you've acquired your membership. After that, by all means, enjoy what Door Ten, Door Eighteen, and all others have to offer. As for the performer in question, he has since been reprimanded." Master Merridon's face pinched. "Both in a professional and…unprofessional manner. But I digress."

The Urchin's words came back to her. "*I should have choked the light from him.*"

Oh god. Had he?

"You will not engage with any employees unless you need to do so in a strictly work-related practice, which I can't imagine you would require outside of management. You are certainly *not* to engage any performers. Do we understand one another?"

"Yes, Master Merridon."

"Good. Now are you sure you wouldn't like some refreshment? Water? I also have iced tea. And fresh lemonade."

Trap, warned Alora's intuition. *A horrid little trap.* Poor Reginald. She didn't think he was on vacation after all.

"No." Her teeth clenched around the word, not allowing even a forced polite 'thank you' to follow it.

"Suit yourself," said Merridon, and abruptly his smile turned real. "Do enjoy the remainder of your day. I look forward to what the end of the week brings."

Minutes later, Alora stood outside Door Zero, her hand on the knob and unable to let go. Inside her, fury bubbled away. At herself, for putting Reginald in danger by her continued interactions. For ignoring her intuition when it came to William and following him behind that door. And at everyone else in this horrible place, spewing their evil across Enver like some foul-smelling infection.

She knew with one-thousand-percent certainty, she'd never use that membership. In fact, she might burn it at her contract's end. Perhaps even in front of Merridon.

One by one, her fingers eased from the knob. *Calm yourself,* she admonished. She did need to find Madam Feebledire and schedule transportation for the trim she'd ordered. But how? She scanned the length of the hall and found no one. The woman had gone that way though after abandoning her and so must be somewhere.

Adjusting her satchel, Alora stepped past Door Zero and continued on through the depths of Opulence.

Chapter Twenty

Alora didn't notice a sound aside from her own footsteps on the marble floor until she caught sight of Door Eighteen. From there she heard crying.

They were quiet cries, muffled. The kind where one doesn't mean for them to escape but they manage somehow. Alora held all the fresh warnings and instructions close to heart, and she couldn't afford more mistakes. But she glanced in all directions and followed the cries anyway. They led her up a spiral staircase and revealed themselves outside the Room of Fire.

"Lennox?"

"Alora?" Lennox leaned against her closed door, her made-up eyes now trailing black down her cheeks. She swiped at them in a hurry, smudging them further. "Dammit. I didn't know you'd be here today."

"I didn't know either, to be honest. Whatever is the matter?" She hurried forward, gripping the girl's hands before she could make more fruitless attempts at her cheeks.

"It's William! They've punished him. Punished me! I'm to perform alone until he's recovered, and I've not practiced a solo routine in ages."

Alora's heart sank. "How long until he's recovered?"

"I don't know. His face is all a mess I've heard."

"Master Merridon had him beaten?"

"No," said Lennox, and sniffed. "No, he only was to have certain privileges revoked awhile. It's those blasted—" Her anger spouted and died in the next breath. She glanced hurriedly around. "He was attacked by someone else."

The so-called captain of the Urchins no doubt.

"Can't he be seen by a healer?" Alora's ankle was in perfect condition. Surely that Urchin could fix a swollen eye.

"Master is allowing it to heal naturally. I could be performing alone for a week or more!"

Alora stared into Lennox's puddled eyes and couldn't bear it. "I'm afraid this is all because of me. He asked me to enter Door Ten with him and gave me something to drink. I was…not myself. We were discovered there."

"William took you into Door Ten?"

Lennox's eyes were large and vivid green with emotion. Alora couldn't tell if she was hurt or shocked or on the verge of a fit of rage.

"It was a huge mistake. I should have questioned what I was being offered. I'm sorry."

"And William just— What an *ass*. Don't you dare blame yourself at all; he should know better! And to not even explain it all to you first? Why, I—I'd punch him myself if I could get to him!"

"Please don't! Not on my account." Alora already had her hands full with one person acting out for transgressions against her.

"I couldn't even if I wanted to. His room, or *rooms*, is separate from ours." She swiped at her nose and then her eyes. "Be honest with me, Alora. How ruined is my face?"

"Fairly ruined."

"I thought so. Well, I suppose it must be redone. Come along." Alora's feet didn't move, not even as Lennox moved around her and tugged at her hand. She glanced back, brow furrowed. "Oh, I forget you don't keep the same hours. Are you working?"

"No, not exactly. Though I do need to ask Madam Feebledire a question."

"Ask her afterward, please. I could use the company. We don't get much of it; not of the sort I want."

Alora worried her lip. "Isn't it against the rules?"

"Um. Yes, probably."

"I've just come from a meeting with Master Merridon. He made it quite clear I was not to break, or even bend, any rules." At the downfall in Lennox's face, she couldn't help adding, "And it seems he has eyes nearly everywhere."

"He does seem to. Oh, I wish we could be made invisible. Just for a while."

Alora squeezed her hand. "I wish that too."

"Shh, Alora. You're not as quiet as you think!"

Alora adjusted where she placed weight on her feet, hoping for less sound as she and Lennox followed the path around Opulence. They'd passed two signs already.

Employees Only.

And the second. *No Members Beyond This Point.*

The topiaries were gone behind them, replaced by more uniformed shrubbery, trimmed into round, bulbous shapes. Thunder cracked all around, and the lightning was fierce. Alora adjusted the coat, ensuring all of her remained tucked inside.

"Can you see my shoes?"

Lennox squinted back at her. "A little, but it's like a trick of the light or shadows. I would never guess there was a whole person attached." Alora had imagined a coat which would make her invisible, and it had worked. She couldn't hardly believe it. "No more talking now. There are bound to be other performers out and about at this time of day."

"Even in the storm?"

"Shh!"

Alora obeyed, continuing silently along the mansion's massive side. She was thankful for the bouts of thunder and even the whistling wind, though it was somehow kept outside the grounds. She would have been far more nervous in the utter stillness of the Opulence she was used to. As it were, she was still very, very nervous.

The silver coat itched where its hood met her forehead and swished about her feet. She'd not given much thought to craftsman-ship over functionality, her haste and doubt in the possibility of its creation affecting the outcome. But she'd done it. Brought a thing of enchantment into reality. If she weren't so frightened over breaking another set of rules, she might have made the time to awe over what she'd managed. Still, she allowed one prideful thought.

She could create extraordinary things, and clearly, she'd stifled herself with fear for far too long.

The hidden grounds behind Opulence Mansion were dotted with more bulbous hedges and golden, square buildings. The struc-tures ranged in sizing, and were topped with crimson, slanted roofs. None, she noticed, possessed window boxes. In fact, there were no windows in these structures at all, but tacked on framing to create the illusion. Certainly, there were no flowers.

She made to ask Lennox about them but held the question for later. Right now, a stranger had exited one of the buildings. Short and curvaceous with black hair braided down to her thighs, she was middle-aged, if Alora had to guess. She wore a red, latex suit hugging every curve, revealing an expansive amount of flesh across her chest. Her boots met the ends of her hair. She was beautiful. And intimi-dating—a whip lay tucked in her hand.

"Lennox," she said, without stopping.

"Noelnina."

Alora glanced once more at her shoes just to be sure she wasn't revealing an ankle. She was not. Noelnina passed them by.

The pebbled path branched now from house to house. Alora guessed the buildings couldn't be anything else, as it was made clear early on that most of Opulence's employees and performers lived on the grounds. She followed Lennox dutifully, jolting now and then at a particularly loud crack of thunder. It'd not yet started to rain, which she was thankful for.

She stopped when Lennox did, before a rather small building with only two fake windows and one small hedge. She said nothing as the other woman reached out and turned the knob, pushing the door in. When Lennox moved inside and gripped the door's edge, making a show of looking out over the landscaping, Alora took that as her cue to rush inside.

She flung off her coat as the door closed.

"Welcome to my room!"

And it was. A single room.

Alora took in the details with a quick, assessing eye. The unmade bed. The chaos of a desk. Paintings of flowers and fire. Two chairs and a small table were covered in outfits she guessed were used for performances, and a mug drained to dregs. She turned to Lennox and smiled.

"It's very nice."

"It's a mess, is what it is."

Lennox sat at the desk and immediately began the process of removing her makeup before the small mirror. "But it's nicer than some. Bigger than the ground's employees are given." She scrubbed aggressively at her cheeks with a cloth.

"And William lives here, too?"

"He has to. Not near me though, so don't worry."

"It's a requirement? What if you wished to live in town and commute?"

"Non-negotiable per the contract. Maybe someday I'll get to see it. Did you know that I've been here nearly three years and I've yet to see Enver?" She giggled about it, swiping charcoal onto her lids, but Alora noted something else behind it.

Longing.

A terrible taste filled her mouth as a realization encroached. "Lennox, can you not leave?"

Vivid eyes met her own through the glass, and Alora knew at once. "Non-negotiable."

"But I've seen William in Enver! He was at the print shop."

"Well, of course he was. William has special privileges, remember? The perks of being Master's son." Lennox frowned through the mirror. A choked sound had emanated from Alora before she could help it. "You didn't know?" Alora could only shake her head. "Well, he is. Though that doesn't excuse his behavior. If anything, I think it makes it worse."

Lennox puckered her lips at the glass. Then she rose with a flourish. Striding to the mess of a table, she flung garments aside until she reached wood. There, she extracted a cigarillo from a now-revealed box and lit it. The scent of cloves filled the room.

Alora noted all of this distantly, as the only thought barraging through her head now was the idea that William and the Urchin were not only brothers but brothers belonging to Master Merridon.

He might have told me who his adoptive father was!

"Are you all right?"

Alora released a breath. "I'm quite shocked, to be honest."

Lennox shrugged, having apparently come to terms with the fact long ago. "I'll tell you I'm not all right. I can't believe you have the ability to bring coats into reality. Not to mention invisibility ones!"

Breath stilled in her chest. Alora waited for one of the several reactions she expected, but when they didn't come, and Lennox continued to look at her with awe, she finally released it. And then she did more than that. "I can bring about more than coats."

"Can you really?"

"Whatever I'm capable of imagining. Though it doesn't always turn out as I would hope, especially not with complex things."

"Ah. Like clocks?"

"No, I think I could bring about a clock fine, though I haven't tried. I meant living things. More specifically, things with souls."

Lennox's eyes grew wide. "People?"

"People. Animals. I…I've not told anyone this."

"Oh, I won't tell anyone."

Alora reached out and Lennox obliged, placing the cigarillo between her fingers. Alora dragged in a breath against its end, her mouth filling with sweet smoke. She coughed, a plume rising between them. Lennox grinned.

"I brought a rabbit into the world once, as a girl," said Alora, eyes streaming. "But I didn't pay close enough attention. He had too large of teeth and these empty white eyes. When I peered into them, I couldn't see anything staring back at me. It was…disconcerting. But I was his mistress, and he followed me everywhere. Mindless, I realized too late. People talked about it—all through the town I grew up in. Some said I summoned a demon. Some said I tortured a living creature into what it had become. They were very cruel, to both of us. Then he bit a girl, and she fell." Alora breathed in a second time from the cigarillo, on the off chance the first coughing fit was a fluke. It was not.

When she could speak again, she handed it back to Lennox with a shake of her head. Smoking, it seemed, was not for her. "Anyway, I can't ever go back there."

"You can never return, and I can never leave. What a pair we are," said Lennox. This time there was no false laughter. Lennox stared down at her shoes, her mouth slightly parted and breaths shallow.

Alora thought she'd the better situation herself but didn't say so. Lennox didn't need to hear it; likely she already knew. Alora wondered how long her contract extended. Then she asked.

"Twenty years," Lennox said, smiling sadly when Alora gasped outright. "By then, they'll find someone younger I would assume."

"Lennox, I'm—"

But Lennox shook her head. "I went all on my own. I read the contract. I've only myself to blame."

"But you can't have been much more than a child!"

"Seventeen." She shrugged. "I didn't have much. Not much to me besides this ability. And when I was approached to work at Opulence, I thought it was a blessing. In some ways, it is. I'm fed and housed and clothed. Some people could say far less."

Approached. Alora thought she might be sick. "You're still trapped. What Merridon is doing is still wrong, even if he feeds you."

"As I said: I've only myself to blame."

"That's not—"

All at once, Lennox was done with the conversation. She stuffed the cigarillo into her bodice and gripped Alora's shoulders after. "I need the Room of Happy Days. Right now. Come with me?"

Alora had broken so many rules, but she could see something worse was near shattering in Lennox. Really, what was one more? She nodded.

"Perfect. Maybe we can sneak a look at what Mister Macaw is working on. It's the new topiary to represent Door Twenty-five, and I'm dying to know who, if anyone, is going inside it."

<h1 style="text-align:center">Chapter Twenty-One</h1>

Alora stood inside the ground floor's Door Eleven surrounded by bathing suits of all sizes. Lennox selected one for herself and tossed another toward her. Alora caught it, staring at the crimson garment like she'd never seen one. Meanwhile, Lennox decided to forgo the changing rooms and stripped to nothing beside her.

"You might want to rush. Dusk isn't far off."

Quickly, Alora kicked off her shoes, loosening her skirt, and slipping the straps of her top from her shoulders. She was all skittering nerves, her heart bounding away after her previous experience in one of Opulence's many rooms. She tried to remember what Door Eleven entailed and couldn't. Damn her failing mind.

She shimmied into the suit alongside Lennox, the garment the snuggest thing she'd ever worn. A robe appeared in her line of vision, and then slippers for her feet.

"Don't forget the coat," said Lennox.

Together, they left the room for the spiral stairs.

"Are there performers here?" Alora whispered, when they were at the top and yet to see anyone else.

"No. At least not of the kind you think. I wouldn't endanger you like that, Alora, you're my only friend!"

A warm feeling bloomed in her chest at those words, and a smile stretched her cheeks. "As are you."

Lennox grinned back at her, though her gaze was somewhat off from Alora's person, as she still wore her coat. Her hand rested upon the knob. "Ready to feel better?"

Am I ever. "Yes, please."

The door swung in.

The floor was tiled in gold, the walls glittering beneath the sconces lining them. In the center of the extravagance was nestled the pool. The water rippled, a deep, dark blue. Iridescent steps led down into the depths.

"There's a mermaid in here," said Lennox, and finally Alora remembered. "Normally, they'd be dangerous, but Master has this one muzzled. Did you know their faces look different to every person? It's like a lure, so they might bring you in and feast on your bones."

"This isn't making me feel better at all," said Alora, horrified.

"Well, that part doesn't," agreed Lennox. "But mermaids are also capable of making you relive your happiest moments. I think so you're distracted in your death. Sort of a kindness, isn't it?"

"Sort of," replied Alora, clutching her robe tighter.

Lennox tossed her slippers and her robe, ignoring the hooks and cubbies supplied for just that purpose. Alora watched her step into the water. "It's warm. If that's what is worrying you."

Alora didn't say that the temperature was the farthest thing from her mind in that moment. Instead, she hung up her coat and the borrowed robe. She took off her slippers and tucked them away. The tile was warm on her bare feet. "You've done this before?"

"Every day," said Lennox, and with a deep inhale, dropped below the surface.

"Every day," murmured Alora.

Then she, too, stepped into the pool.

It was warm. Not luxuriantly warm, but comfortable, and Alora braved another step down. The water bubbled and rippled where Lennox had disappeared, and she waited and waited. Lennox surfaced. Her eyes were shining, her grin wider than Alora had ever seen.

"Don't be scared."

A deep breath, a final nod, and Alora stepped off the final stair and fell beneath the water. She opened her eyes without preamble, wanting to see what swam in the depths with her. She was surprised to find they didn't sting in the slightest, and that Lennox had dropped in beside her, blinking at her and pointing.

Alora followed the gesture.

The mermaid floated placidly in the corner. The creature was only half her size, the bottom half consisting of great fins in a pinkish hue the color of coral. Its top half was a mixture of pale skin and turquoise scales, with arms similar to a human's but with nails more akin to claws. Alora couldn't tell the creature's sex from the body alone, but the mermaid's hair was long and yellow, mouth a perfect rosebud red and eyes silver like a winter moon. A face only she could see. But a golden cage broke up the mermaid's features, bars over plump lips. A flare of compassion overwhelmed Alora then.

Like most everyone else in Opulence Mansion, this creature was obviously entrapped.

Then the mermaid bared fangs of a kind she'd never seen, all bone-white needles, and she immediately shrieked a slurry of bubbles and flew to the surface.

Lennox sputtered beside her a second later. "Sorry! I should have warned you what they're like. But don't worry, the mermaid can't bite you."

"What is Merridon thinking! Capturing a creature like that?"

Lennox lifted a shoulder above the water. "Probably that it would add to the enchantment of the mansion."

Alora kicked her feet beneath the water, hoping to deter the mermaid from latching on. "And nobody has ever been drowned?"

Lennox shook her head. "That isn't their way." She must have noticed Alora's continued distrust, because she reached out and gripped her arm. "You don't have to stay if you don't want. I just thought it would help. You only need to get a little closer to feel it."

Alora released a shuddering breath. "You're a brave thing, aren't you? Fine. I'll try."

Lennox beamed and nodded, and she didn't wait before sinking beneath once more.

This time, Alora followed her.

The muzzled mermaid remained in the corner, watching. The creature turned its attention to Lennox first as she approached, but when Alora swam near, those silver eyes shifted to focus on her. Alora swallowed, drawn in despite herself, and once the creature ensnared her within that wintry gaze, that was all it took. Alora felt herself drifting, drifting, and then, quite impossibly, leaving the pool behind.

She laid now upon a sun-soaked, green hilltop covered in wild-flowers and bees, and she recognized it at once. The hill behind her childhood home. She'd returned to Eirian, when she never thought she could. The sky was an impossible blue, wisps of clouds and a warm yellow sun to her right. She felt it on the side of her face and smiled. She spread her arms and was met with something shifting. She turned her head to look. It was the doll, the one she'd imagined so long ago, and it nestled in the crook of her arm. An arm that was child sized. Alora lifted her fingers to the sky, marveling at them.

She'd returned to her childhood.

Carefully, she picked up the doll around its waist and held it above her too. The features were everything she'd wanted. Yellow hair and silver eyes. Red lips. The doll wore a blue dress and little brown shoes, and her hair was braided and tied with ribbon. Pride enveloped her. Pride and amazement and all of it in herself. She'd done something extraordinary. She had an ability greater than anything she could have thought possible. A giggle escaped her, and she hugged the doll to her chest until she thought she might burst. She'd keep the toy forever and use her enchantment freely. Anything anyone wanted, she'd give them. It would be simple and wonderful, and all would love her for it. A butterfly landed on her arm, and she smiled in utter contentment before her eyes closed.

Alora blinked open her eyes to water and twin orbs like the moon. The mermaid studied her still, but there was no drawing sensation as before. Instead, the creature lifted its arms. The mermaid gripped the mask on either side, pulling at it with such force, Alora thought for sure it'd give way. But it didn't. It held, and one by one the mermaid's fingers released until its arms hung, almost limply, at its side.

She knew what the creature wanted. Of course she did. And she could imagine it easily, the muzzle falling to the pool's bottom. But even if she waited until Lennox was gone and herself safe at the pool's edge, what would happen to the next person who stepped in?

An instant meal, she was sure.

She couldn't do it. She couldn't condemn someone innocent just to assuage the feeling coursing through her now. She shook her head at the mermaid, hoping her eyes conveyed what she yearned to say.

I'm sorry. Not yet.

Chapter Twenty-Two

The deluge threatened to begin. Alora pulled the hood of her Opulence cloak lower on her head, the invisibility coat draped over her arm, as she rushed for the gate. She couldn't waste time on umbrellas.

Madam Feebledire had been shocked to see her still within the grounds, which Alora had smoothed by saying she'd been kept busy with more measurements. A horse and wagon would arrive at the carpenter's tomorrow morning. That rule, at least, she'd followed.

She rang the bell, bouncing on her toes as she waited for the gate to swing in. When it did, she hurried out into an abrupt downpour without bothering to say goodbye to the ill-tempered guard, though she did glance at him, and noted his paint ran in rivulets down his face. It reminded her of Reginald, and sorrow filled her.

Thunder cracked and lightning zipped across the sky in an aggressive display that mimicked her feelings. She couldn't see far ahead due to the rain, and it left her with a sense of isolation she couldn't shake. She didn't know what to do.

Her thoughts tumbled over one another so relentlessly, she felt like she'd been tossed into the ocean, but near the shore. One with cliffs and very large rocks. She couldn't escape them. Briefly, she contemplated setting the entire mansion on fire. But how many would be lost to the blaze? The mermaid for certain, and who knew how well all that stone would burn anyway. The frame would likely only end up scorched and be rebuilt, the arson traced to her.

She'd grown up hearing stories about the spectacular enchantments of Opulence Mansion; she could have never imagined it to be so corrupt. For its contracts to be akin to shackles, and its dealings built on a foundation of greed. And it had managed to leech into Enver. Beautiful Enver, which she loved so much. Kind Ellie Turkens and strong Ms. Merryweather. Eager Mr. Whitters and Hector Zanfold, her curmudgeonly neighbor. None of them deserved to live in the gilded, poisoned shadow which Merridon created. He needed to be stopped and held accountable. Him and every Urchin he employed.

But how?

How could one person topple such a scheme? Especially one anchored in gold?

Her cowl drooped, muddling her vision. She entered the cobbled streets of Enver and ripped it off, shoving the blasted thing in her satchel. She didn't care if it wrinkled or mildewed. She was so upset, she could have stomped it into the puddled road, damn anyone who witnessed her.

Lennox had thought to make her day better, and Alora hoped, at least for her friend's sake, that it had worked for her. But it had done the opposite for Alora. That childhood memory was one of the purest she had, when her heart was full of pride and possibilities. It had ended tragically for her. For her and the blacksmith's daughter, and even for the rabbit.

Her enchantment did not, in fact, make anyone love her.

Mugwort Alley was the shortest route home, and she took it. The dark sky and endless rain made the lane of gray and black buildings even more dreadful in appearance, but for once, she didn't scoff at how the town could allow it. Instead, she thought of how it matched her mood. Maybe she should move here. Give up her flowers and terrace and become a witch who resided in the muck, growing mushrooms to sicken those who stared at her too long.

Lightning lit the sky, brighter than any she'd seen yet, and she halted at once in the middle of the street. The subsequent thunder rattled windows all around, but she didn't pay it any attention. She'd become distracted. Unashamedly so. Relievedly so. It gave her... ideas.

Bash lowered a bag filled to the brim with who knew what onto the soaked porch of Potions and Peculiarities, a hand deep in his pocket. She'd not seen him since the evening she'd woken on his back stoop, when he'd offered her all sorts of unsolicited advice before, bafflingly, requesting to see her home. He hadn't noticed her yet. Or maybe he had and pretended not to.

What brings him out into the storm? He must have been caught in the rain at least as long as her, considering his hair was curled and clinging to his forehead, and his shirt was soaked through and practically adhered to his skin. She could see every dip and swell of him. He rolled up his shirtsleeves upon swinging the door in, revealing quite nice forearms.

Goodness.

Bash bent to retrieve the bag he'd discarded. She was near enough to notice rain dripped from his nose and from his chin. She watched it run down his cheekbone and was jealous. It was all the push she needed. Alora started toward him.

"Excuse me, sir! I'd like to purchase a Dirededron. Do you have one lurking about?"

"Miss Pennigrim?" Bash straightened, the bag slung once more over his shoulder. "What are you doing out here?"

"Same as usual. Weathering another storm." She'd meant to make her tone mysterious, or at least brave. But it came out as neither, and her voice broke at the end.

"What's happened?"

"Nothing," she managed. Then, with her voice turned falsely bright, she said, "And everything. I'm in over my head, I think. But that isn't what I wished to discuss with you now."

His eyes narrowed at her. They were so deeply green, like everything after the rain. Her glance strayed from them to follow along the angles of his face. Callous and distant, his emotions probably never freed, she thought he looked precisely the type who'd be up for what she wanted. How could he not be?

"Well, get under the awning at least," he replied. She did as he told her, climbing the step until they were nearly touching beneath the overhang, both spared from the storm. "Do you not own an umbrella?"

"Don't you?" She scoffed at him, but not too seriously. She couldn't have him mad at her. Or, on second thought, maybe she could? His brow remained furrowed, and she decided she liked it when he looked at her that way—as if she were something he wanted to desperately understand, annoyed that he couldn't.

"Where have you come from then?" she asked.

The mingling scents of dust and sage leaked from the exposed room beyond them. Bash stepped firmly into the doorway, the bag plunking down at his feet with a disturbing jangle. "Is that what you wished to discuss with me? I didn't know you to be concerned over my whereabouts."

"I wasn't. I'm *not*."

His lips curved, another one-sided smirk, and Alora scowled. This was not how she pictured things would go. His arm lifted to lean against the doorframe, and she stopped herself before she asked after the scrape across his knuckles. He'd only leap upon that, too, thinking she was worried over him.

"It's growing late. Out with it, Miss Pennigrim."

Dammit. Never mind, she couldn't do it. Maybe if they'd not started as they had, now to the point of arguing. Alora stepped back down, into the rain. "It was nothing."

"Good grief," he groaned. "Come on." Before she could protest, his hand reached to encircle her wrist. He dragged her back up the step until she stood in the doorway with him, barely room at all to move. "What has you bothered?"

She snatched her arm away. "*That* I don't care to talk about right now. Actually, I can't even if I wanted to. I only thought…" She trailed off, her eyes on their boots. Bash's were muddied, with bits of moss clinging to the sides.

"Thought?" he coaxed.

Alora felt her body flush when she glanced up at him. At how his dark hair lay dripping and tousled to one side, his eyes wide and impatient—kohl-smeared from his time in the storm. "I only wanted a sort of…distraction." She squeezed her eyes shut briefly, disbelieving she'd actually said the words aloud.

"A distraction," he said. When her cheeks flushed the same as the rest of her, he seemed to finally maneuver through her maze of a meaning. He angled his head, though, as if he wasn't sure how to react over what he'd found. "And you thought to find that distraction *here?*"

"Actually, no. I beg you to forget this happened." Alora meant to back away, but jolted when her back met the doorframe, unable to move farther. She pasted on her best smile. "Have a good evening with…whatever you've foraged for."

Bash's arm stopped her where she would have bolted down the step and away. She stared at his fingertips digging into the wood before tracking his arm all the way up, again to his eyes.

"Why do you do that?" he asked.

"Do what?"

"That smile. I know you aren't happy. So why do it?"

Alora opened her mouth to defend herself, but no explanation came. Instead, she felt herself deflate. Her shoulder sagged into his arm, and still he didn't remove it. "I don't know," she said at last. "An old reaction that became habit, I suppose."

He nodded as if this, at least, he could understand. "So what are you, then, if not happy?"

Alora laughed humorlessly, her fingers rising to tick off her emotions. "Oh, hmm, where to begin… Angry, I suppose. No, furious, really. Frustrated beyond comprehension. Scared. And still a little hopeful, despite it all. I just feel like I need—"

"A distraction."

"Yes."

"To what extent?"

Alora felt her entire body must be cherry-red, imagining all she could ask for. "Nothing so great. Just something to pull me out of my own head a little bit."

He nodded slowly. "A kiss, then."

"Oh!" *Did he have to come right out and say it?* "I mean…"

"Just ask for what you want already, Miss Pennigrim."

Alora huffed a frustrated breath. "I already told you. My name is *Alora.*"

"Is that what you'd have me call you?"

"Well, yes. I wouldn't have told you otherwi—"

"Done."

His rude interruption infuriated her, her embarrassment forgotten because of it. "And yes, Bash! I'd like a kiss so perfect that I forget about everything else for a little while. Can you manage that? Or should I proposition someone else?"

Bash's eyes darkened. A trick of the waning light, surely, and his hand left the doorframe. A heartbeat later, it brushed her cheek, his fingers tangling in the dripping mass of her hair. He pulled her head back, effectively angling her chin up to him, and she gasped. "Alora. Are you trying to discover if I've a jealous streak?"

Alora shook her head. A difficult thing to do, entrapped as it was. "How could I?"

"Easier than you might think." His thumb traced her chin, his other hand coming round to meet the frame at her opposite side. His voice deepened, quieter now that he'd closed her in. "You've put a lot of pressure on me. I can't say I've been this anxious over a kiss in a long time."

"Done a lot of mindless kissing, have you?" Alora felt breathless and her voice mirrored it.

"Be quiet. You're making it worse."

She smiled then, and it was completely real.

Bash's thumb paused at the point of her chin. He stared at her, at the pull of her lips, but Alora didn't have a chance to ask what had flabbergasted him so completely before he bit out, "Goddammit. I shouldn't be doing this," and the pressure of his mouth fell against hers.

Of course, she'd dreamt of this while alone. Either in bed, or on the sofa—sometimes on the terrace overlooking the town. *Heaven help me, this is so much better.* She couldn't place how he tasted, only that she wanted to taste more. Which she did at her next opportunity. Her bravery earned her a groan from him, which she absorbed against her lips and greedily wished for again. She bit his lower lip and was rewarded. If this was mindless kissing on his part, a pity favor granted, she couldn't dare imagine how he might be with someone he was passionate about.

His jaw scraped her chin, one hand tangled in her hair, the other wrapped around her back, fingertips digging possessively into her ribs. She returned what she could, her own fingers finally doing as they'd wished, knotting in his hair. She relished that it felt just as she imagined it would, soft and thick. Every other part of him, though, was solid and unyielding—which she could tell with certainty, being as his hips were pressed flush against hers.

Kissing was nice. She'd always liked it. And she'd kissed enough to have an opinion, both boys and, later, men. But she'd never felt quite like this. That at any moment, she might burst into a million pieces of light. This distraction was proving to be more than she bargained for. Everything *ached*. If she hadn't known for certain she'd not drunk anything, she might have worried she'd been overcome with Lust again. Her need was outrageous. She *needed* to *stop*.

"*Bash*," she said, but her body was traitorous, and his name fell like a sigh between them. She shoved against his chest, meaning to push him away. But when he stepped backward, she didn't pull back as intended, following him relentlessly. Her foot snagged. She tripped, and a scattering clatter sent her blinking upright.

"I'm sorry," she breathed, and turned to the mess she'd made.

Her mind emptied. Her heart stuttered once, twice, then galloped ahead.

Bones.

Bones on the floor. Bones by her feet. The bag had been overfilled with them, large and wet and starkly white. She was never any good at matching bones with bodies; she only hoped they came from an animal—and one that was found already dead. She felt Bash's stare and met it.

His eyes were bright; his shirt rumpled from her hands. His hair was mussed from her dragging her fingers through it. If there'd been a bed behind him, she would have pushed him onto it.

She grimaced instead.

"Alora—"

"Is it an animal?"

"Yes, of course."

A small relief, but a relief all the same. "Why?"

"Peculiarities, darling. Business is relentless."

She scoffed at the thoughtless endearment, over his lighthearted tone. Though, this close, she couldn't help but note the way his eyes clouded by the smallest fraction. "How cryptic you are, especially when considering I'm standing on top of them."

"Cryptic? Shall we trade truth for truth then? Where have you come from? With that strange, silver coat in the middle of summer in your satchel?" He arched a brow at her, expectant.

Alora bristled. "I really can't say."

He made a low sound, deep in his throat, and she scowled after it. His jaw set at her expression. "Don't glower at me when you are just as secretive."

Alora dug the heels of her palms into her eyes. "You *imbecile*," she groaned. "Do you think I want to be?"

She felt his hands wrap around her own, pulling them away. "You could tell me."

Her eyes drifted over his face. He'd a pale scar above his left eyebrow. She could see the barest indent where his dimple would be. He'd not shaved in some days—like he couldn't be bothered to take even a moment for himself. All of this, and still she barely knew what made him. "I couldn't."

"Why?"

"Because I hardly know you."

"Yes, you do."

She shifted at his words, at the way he seemed determined to stare into the depths of her. *Because I'm frightened*, she said only to herself, but she wondered if he could see it. She cast her gaze down. "Also, because those are the rules. I'm nothing but a doting follower of rules."

His answering huff was pure disbelief. Still, he reached between them, and Alora shivered when his fingers met her temple, brushing a lock of hair away. His fingertip traced the tip of her ear. "Maybe I'm an obsessive type, after all."

She frowned, the words needling somewhere between her eyes. "What do you mean by that?"

"Nothing." He stepped into the dank dark of the shop, careful of bones. "The storm is moving on. You should go. I'm sorry the kiss wasn't helpful."

"Oh." Alora stepped back, caught off guard. "Right, well, you did say you were nervous."

"I did."

His eyes were dark with purpose. Alora wondered what he planned to do once she'd gone. She couldn't ask, though, not without giving him something secret in return. She turned away so he might not see that his dismissal wounded her, because it shouldn't have. He'd given her all she'd come for, after all.

"No matter what anyone else might say to you, you could never be trapped. Not someone like you."

Alora turned back to him, her eyebrows meeting over his parting remark. "What makes you say that to me?"

"You had a cornered look about you when you came upon me tonight. You have it still."

"Anyone can be trapped, Bash. I'm hardly special."

"*I* think you might be the most special person I've ever met. Goodnight, Alora."

The door closed between them. The finality of it mimicked the last distant bout of thunder, and when a heavy quiet descended over Mugwort Alley, it was punctured only by dripping gutters and her own breaths. A neighbor's second story curtain shifted. A cat meowed from an alleyway.

And Alora pressed her hand over her heart and sighed like she'd lost some great battle, sure she'd been hollowed out.

Chapter Twenty-Three

Alora folded herself into the cushioned chair at El's Books and Nibbles. Her head collapsed into her palms. She rubbed circles at her temples as she listened to the quiet sounds of pages turning and tea being sipped. There were no bees today, but Lucille and Loretta shuffled along the beams, nosy and judging. When Loretta dropped to the back of the chair opposite her, Alora didn't startle, but imagined a shadow-mouse scurrying off into the corner. The owl abandoned her at once.

She wanted to be alone.

"Tea, dear?"

Alora lifted heavy eyes to the soft countenance of Ellie Turkens and couldn't even bring about a smile. "Strong as you can make it, please."

A brief pat to the head, and the old woman returned her nose to its novel and was gone.

There was a tornado inside her brain, moths eating holes in her thoughts. Alora couldn't pin down any singular idea.

Merridon and his bribery.

Merridon and his contracts.

The Urchins' shuttling of dark artifacts and captive creatures.

The Urchins and their stealing of memories.

The collective gag on Enver's mouth.

The gag on her own.

China clinked in front of her, and Alora reached toward it, unseeing. "Ellie..."

"What is it, dear?"

"What do you know about the owner of Opulence?"

When she could focus again, she noticed Ellie's eyes darting in all directions before landing upon the twin owls in the rafters. She waggled a finger at them.

"Sorry. They like to gossip. As for your question, I know some. What are you looking for?"

"All of it. Everything."

Ellie Turkens must have noticed the desperation in her eyes because she did something then that she'd never done before. She sat down. Her book closed and settled on her lap. "Alora. You're not thinking of a membership, are you?"

"Why do you ask that?"

Ellie pursed magenta lips. "There are far more worthwhile things to spend your hard-earned money on."

"Yes, I—"

"I've seen people grow wild trying to scrounge enough for a year's worth, and I've never seen anyone better for it."

"You haven't?"

"Goodness, no! You don't need to get close to feel the wrongness pulsing about that place." She made a choked little sound then, lowering her voice. "We should be careful. There are eyes and ears at attention for such talk, and I don't mean the owls."

The bookshop was dimly lit against the encroaching night. Shadows were everywhere. But none were absolute—as if the very light had been swallowed. Goosebumps rose to Alora's arms, and not all because of her wet clothing. She didn't think they were being watched, but how could someone ever be sure?

Ellie Turkens leaned in until her forehead nearly brushed Alora's own across the small table.

"Mister Marshall Merridon is a con man."

Alora was about to say she knew this when Ellie rushed on, as if the more quickly she spewed the information, the less likely she'd find herself in trouble over it. "He isn't from Enver to begin with, and I remember when he showed up on our streets, not much older than you. He had a fancy cart which he'd open up, and inside would be rows and rows of vials, and a sign that said something along the lines of 'Memory Oil: Massage Your Troubles Away'. Now traders come all the time, that wasn't the unique part. No, the uniqueness to Marshall Merridon was in the way he seemed to draw people. He was skilled in bartering, skilled in that smile of his. Sometimes, he didn't even accept money, but other things. It was like blinking. One moment a cart, and the next, a mansion. I don't think anyone here today knows quite how he managed it."

"I've seen this oil at work," said Alora between her teeth. She knew now what was in Reginald's darts and the Urchins' bludgeoning weapons. Likely there was a smaller concentration dripping out from one of the several faucets hidden behind Door One.

"No you haven't," said Ellie, tapping the side of her nose.

Right.

"If it's only the curiosity driving you, fine; you wouldn't be the first to be intrigued over the mansion's mysteries. But if it's something else, then let me warn you now. Marshall Merridon is like a specter wolf. The more enchantment fed to him, the bigger he grows. Don't give him an ounce of you."

Soft hands encased Alora's cheeks for a brief moment before Ellie Turkens rose from the table. Alora watched her weave through the others until she disappeared among the stacks at the back of the shop.

A little bit sick, Alora sipped her tea, and it was deliciously strong.

She wondered if the owner of Books and Nibbles guessed more about her than she thought. She also wondered what Merridon would look like with pure white eyes and a snout full of teeth. Eventually, though, she was too tired to wonder anything at all.

When only a swirl of leaves remained at the bottom, Alora pushed from her seat. It was night now, and even though she knew nightmares awaited her, she yearned for her bed. Few people remained aside from her, and all had their noses buried, oblivious to anything around them. She yearned so badly for that sort of detachment, her chest ached. She turned to leave.

"Miss Pennigrim."

Alora stilled. She glanced to the remaining patrons, but all seemed unbothered and none looked at her. Tentatively, she lifted her gaze to the rafters.

"Alora."

Lucille and Loretta stared over their backs at her in a sniping, unblinking fashion; they knew the mouse had been a trick and wouldn't forgive easily. But no, they didn't speak.

She squinted into the shadows and caught her breath when a hand beckoned her in. She hesitated for several heartbeats before making for it. Surely, someone wouldn't launch an attack in a bookstore?

At the first set of shelves, she lifted the lantern free of its hook and peered within.

A man stood there. He was fairly tall, with deep brown skin and patches of gray at his temples. She held the lantern between them like a shield, though he was the one backed into a corner and not her. Shadows danced away from the shifting light, the scent of paper all around.

"There you are," he said, his voice no longer a hissed whisper. "I'd hoped to find you safe."

At once, Alora recognized his voice and raised the lantern higher. Yes, copper eyes. Just as she thought.

"Reginald?"

Before he could answer, she'd thrown her arms around him.

Warm hands came around her back slowly, almost disbelieving. She felt several brief pats between her shoulder blades. "Mortimer now. I answer to my middle name."

Alora pulled back at last, setting the lantern at their feet. She noted his sensible brown shoes. No longer did he wear the curled, golden boots belonging to a guard. "I looked for you today! What happened? I hoped maybe a vacation, but after speaking with Master Merridon, I thought something worse."

"Don't speak of him," said Reginald. *No—Mortimer.* His eyes darted beyond her head. "It isn't safe to do so, for you most of all."

"For me?"

But Mortimer chose to answer her earlier questions instead. "I'm not on holiday. Wouldn't know what to do with myself if I were. No, I've been fired from my post."

Alora gasped, even though she wondered as much. "Why? Because of me?"

Mortimer winced. Alora couldn't get over how different he looked without all his gold paint and armor. And she dreaded his answer.

"Our interactions were reported. They were deemed inappropriate by management."

Madam Feebledire. Alora yearned to wrap her hands around the woman's skinny neck and throttle her. "I'm endlessly sorry, Reg—ah, Mortimer. I shouldn't have pushed when you declined those times."

"It isn't your fault."

"But it is! If only I had some weight, that I could beg for your job back."

Mortimer shook his head. "Oh no, I wouldn't want it back. You've helped me, Alora."

She blinked up at him, unsure she'd heard correctly. "Helped you?"

"I was just another contract without end. I had a few more privileges than some, considering my role, but not many. I was just as chained to the grounds."

Alora didn't know how to ask without sounding indelicate. Maybe there wasn't a way. She worried her lip a moment before giving in and saying, "I'm thrilled you've kept your memories. I would be horrified if they'd stolen them from you. If you didn't remember me."

At that, Mortimer gripped her elbow, and Alora followed him deeper, until they were all in shadow. He whispered, "They meant to take them from me."

"They did?" Alora lowered her voice to match, her voice breathless with horror. "How did you escape?"

"When they made me turn, to dart me in the back, I knew my time was at an end. No more Reginald Mortimer Nortsen. I knew too many of their secrets to lose just a little. But at the last moment, when I'd closed my eyes and dreamt of wintry days, I was pulled free."

Alora stared up at him transfixed. "By whom?"

"The young captain. He told them some story of his own personal vendetta against me and his desire to exact revenge, but I knew it was all a hoax because I've never gotten into a scuffle with any of them save one, and that boy deserved it back then. Then he hauled me off by the collar into the woods, and the next thing I knew I was in Enver, sense of self intact."

Alora's mouth fell wide. "Why would he do that?"

Mortimer stared at her. "I asked him the same. He said I was important to someone important to him, and to not make him regret his decision. And if I did, then losing my memory should become the least of my fears. Quite dramatic, if you ask me, but I promised him all the same; I was so full of gratitude. And now I'm here to warn you."

Alora could hardly keep up. "Warn me of what?"

"There's never been a contract like yours. Not in all the years I've been employed, and I've been employed a long time. He doesn't just allow people to come and go as they please. Not outside of members during operating hours. I'm worried over what he has planned. I'm worried for you. Don't go back."

"Don't— But what of the contract?"

"Hang the contract!" exclaimed Mortimer, and Alora recoiled at the sudden rise in volume. He noticed and softened right after. "Do you have nowhere else to go? Nowhere else you'd like to be?"

"My dream is here," she replied, quiet.

Mortimer must have noticed her forlorn look, because he reached out and gripped her shoulders. "What dream is there to be had if you lose to him?"

His words were a catalyst to an eruption long simmering beneath the surface. It soon spewed a fury that scorched everything inside. Alora reached up to grip the backs of Mortimer's hands where they held onto her and felt that feeling harden to stone. Her eyes burned into his.

"I *won't* lose."

Alora rolled the vial of tonic purchased from Potions and Peculiarities between her fingers. It shimmered a ghastly orange under the lamplight, and she shuddered as she brought the dropper to her lips. Bash could do with some tweaking of his recipes.

Mrs. Flops leapt onto the bed and stretched alongside her, a yawn revealing overlarge front teeth. Alora gave her head a scratch, thinking aloud. "It tastes terrible, but I think it's working, Mrs. Flops.

I suppose I should be grateful for that. It's just so strange, isn't it? A mansion built upon memory oil, and I'm the one struggling to maintain mine. Maybe it's another way for my body to tell me that something isn't right, along with the alarm in my stomach and in my heart."

She examined her room, the moss-green walls, an arched bookcase, and the newly purchased mirror. She'd fixed the scratches in the flooring where the shattering in her dreams had harmed it. She'd fixed where the walls had burned.

"I probably should have listened to it from the beginning, but that's hope for you. I wanted my own shop too much." Alora reached to dim the lamp—she couldn't bring herself to douse it completely—and yawned. "The Urchin captain saved Reginald, who is now Mortimer. Because he was important to someone important to him. Who would an Urchin care for?"

But she'd seen the way Mortimer had stared at her. She'd be a fool to misunderstand.

"He's a bad sort, though. Look at what he's done. Look at who he commands! It's probably him that enforces the rule that keeps Lennox and all the others locked away. For all I know, he's out bludgeoning innocents right now. And he lied to me, remember? That once. No, I could *never*." Suddenly too hot, she tossed off the blankets. Because she couldn't tell the rabbit how their sparring made her heart quicken, or that his touch made her skin flush with want.

What sort of person have I become?

It was a thought that segued aggressively into another.

"Bash is hiding something from me, Mrs. Flops. What do you think it is?"

Alora fell fast asleep waiting on the answer, though she thought it might have brushed her fingertips just as dreams carried her away.

Chapter Twenty-Four

Alora couldn't help peering beneath the rim of the driver's wide-brimmed hat. The man was an Urchin. He must be.

His face was unmasked, however, revealing a large mustache and a narrow jaw, and his nose appeared as if it'd been broken and reset more than once. He stared back at Alora in a challenge, his eyes light and cold. He wasn't the captain; she was sure of it. The desire to prove himself rolled off him in waves she'd not felt while in the other Urchin's presence.

He turned his head away to scowl once more at the lane, and she thought, *Fetching wood and rugs isn't helping his ego any.*

Her fingers knotted beneath the hem of the golden cloak, and she used the jostling of the fine wagon to put a little more distance between herself and the driver. She didn't know whether he'd do anything if she bumped into him, but she certainly knew he wouldn't appreciate it.

She settled back with a sigh. It hadn't crossed her mind to add cushions to her own cart, as she never took it any great distance, but the gold cushions in the otherwise white wagon were comfortable enough that she made a mental note to commission some at her next opportunity. But the horses she would forgo, never mind they were fine and white and looked to have been carved from the same mold.

Master Merridon and his appearances.

She rolled her eyes skyward.

"I'm sure this isn't how you wanted to spend your morning, but thank you all the same."

A brief scoff stirred the air beside her. "Please, Miss Pennigrim, don't speak to me."

Alora's mouth fell wide as she twisted her torso to stare at him. *Of all the rude—*

The thought disintegrated to dust. Alora peered into the silver-edged ferns lining Opulence's lane and thought surely, *surely*, they weren't staring back.

"Specter wolf," she murmured.

A large body, gray and silver, with eyes like pale orbs, tracked them through the shadows. The morning was cool yet, but nowhere near cold enough to cause the chills racing along her spine. When the creature focused on her, teeth bared, Alora lost her breath. Without thinking, she reached out to grip the driver's arm, her opposite pointing across his chest and into the wood beyond.

"There's a wolf following us!"

A flash of indignation crossed the man's face as he shook himself free of her. "Save your hysterics. It's daylight."

Which only meant this specter wolf was especially powerful.

Or hungry.

Or both.

Alora would know; she'd finished the entire book of *Rare Creatures of the West.*

"Quit your arguing, Urchin, and *look!*"

Alora wasn't sure if it was her furious desperation or the fact she'd let slip she knew his true occupation, but the Urchin narrowed his gaze at her before doing as she bid and glancing into the trees. Only then did she feel him tense beside her. "What in the blistering hell is that thing doing so close to the lane?"

He called the creature a *thing* like doing so might make it lesser, but Alora could feel the fear rolling off him in abundance. Despite the man's attempt at an ample mustache, he was clearly younger than her. And he obviously knew nothing of specter wolves.

"They are drawn to enchantment."

"But I've not got much to speak of. I can sense emotions, that's all." When the quiet grew weighted, the Urchin fixed her with a glare. "Unless *you*—no, this makes much more sense to me now."

The wolf weaved among the ferns, disappearing from view now and then to reappear later. All the while, it watched her.

"What does?"

"I'd been given strict orders to see you safe to the gate."

"By Merridon?"

He sneered at her as if she were a burden he'd rather toss off. "One of them."

Alora emitted an incredulous sound at his admission. "Will they attack the horses?"

"They can't sense the horses."

Had she read that? Fine, perhaps he knew a little more than she thought.

Her pulse thrummed, and she yearned to stifle it. To squash the enchantment churning in her blood before the creature decided it would no longer wait to make a feast of it. "Should we increase our pace?"

"*Would you*— I don't know, all right? Just quit prattling a moment so I can think!"

Alora glared at him, thinking about how much she'd like to add another bump to his nose, when he said, "They were supposed to be exterminated. What is it doing here?"

Exterminated?

As far as Enver was aware, the entire forest crawled with them.

A brief flash of memory, of the Urchin captain telling her the threat of the woods was exaggerated, and she realized there likely hadn't been a specter wolf sighted in a long time.

A break in the foliage revealed the true size of the creature and Alora gasped. "It's fed on a lot of enchantment."

A pitiful sound left the Urchin when his eyes found what hers did. The wolf rivaled the height of George. "Increase our pace, it is." With a snap of the reins, the horses leapt into a run.

Alora's back met the cushions with a jolt, and she hung onto the side of the wagon with all her strength. The trees blurred past her, the horses' ears flattened to their skulls, and she wondered, somewhere in the background of her desperate thoughts of survival, if they would lose all the lovely wood trim she'd commissioned from the carpenter. She wouldn't have time to get more.

"Nearly there," said the Urchin like a prayer, at the same moment Alora said, "Oh my heavens, there are *two* of them."

"What!"

"There's another on my side. Not as big, I don't think, but I can't be sure with how fast we're moving."

"You better be hanging on, because I won't come back for you."

Alora believed him completely as he snapped the reins again, and the horses hurtled faster yet. She could hear, and feel, the trim bouncing all around, and knew for certain that most would be cracked if they made it through at all.

A clattering thud drew her attention as a shorter piece was flung from the wagon. If she weren't so frightened of dying, she would have shouted in dismay.

They rounded the corner, the wagon pulling up onto two wheels before smacking down, and she saw it, the gate, and could have wept in relief. The Urchin saw it, too, and leapt from his seat, standing and waving as he shouted, "Open it! Open the gate!"

But it didn't open. It remained closed, and the horses were careening toward it, snorting and wild. And Alora saw that it couldn't be opened—because there was no guard.

"Stop!" she screamed.

"I CAN'T!"

The Urchin dragged on the reins, the horses fighting the momentum carrying them forward, but it was too much. She could see it plain as day, her skull fracturing on the gold-wrought gate, her blood spilling as a feast for the wolves hurtling alongside them.

Alora squeezed her eyes closed and covered her head. She fiercely imagined a branch breaking from the boughs above, swinging down at just the right angle to meet the lever, shoving it forward. A sharp crack rent the air, dragging a curse from the man beside her, and then a shout of surprise.

Alora peeked open her eyes to find topiaries on either side.

They'd made it. They were on Opulence's grounds.

She was flung forward as the horses skidded to a halt, their sides heaving and slick with sweat, and she spun in her seat to the gate, her mouth gaping when she found it wide open. Just outside it, two specter wolves prowled forward along the lane, hackles raised.

No! she almost cried. *I'm supposed to be safe.*

"Where is the guard?" she shouted instead and flung herself from the wagon.

The Urchin didn't answer, and when she looked back, she cried aloud, as she saw he'd been tossed into the front of the wagon and was unconscious. *Idiot! You should have hung on!*

She'd two choices. Run to the mansion or run to the gate, and neither were ideal. But one subjected every enchanted performer— and the helpless Urchin—to the wolves, and the other subjected only her so really she chose what only made sense. She raced for the gate.

The wolves seemed to hesitate, seeing their prey barreling toward them, her teeth bared like theirs, but once they remembered they outnumbered her two to one, they growled a challenge. With measured steps, they stalked toward her.

Alora made it to the gate before they did, gripping the bars and wrenching. But all that seemed to dislodge were her joints from their sockets. The gate didn't budge. She swore beneath her breath, realizing she would need to release the lever. But when she managed to locate it beneath the branch she'd broken, it looked mangled beyond repair.

A choked sound emerged from her throat, because she saw him then. The guard. Or at least his boots. Those curled, golden toes pointed to the sky from amongst the ferns. The wolves had gotten to him first.

She would need to imagine it repaired. She would need to imagine the branch burned away and then—

A low growl huffed against the side of her face.

Alora froze. Not even her lungs moved. Perhaps her heart even stopped beating. She couldn't feel it anymore.

The wolves were upon her.

One on either side, they stared at her, their orb-like eyes drinking her in, their nostrils flaring at her scent. They wanted her terribly; she could feel their yearning hunger, but it was no basic sort of need. This kind fed on enchantment with a boundless greed, and they'd done this many times before. Specter wolves didn't grow so powerfully brave otherwise.

Terrified tears tracked down her cheeks, and she did the only thing she could think of, even if it might reveal her and damn her, all in one moment. *You are stone*, she thought.

The wolves shuddered and halted. Where growls and breaths had ruffled her hair, there was now silence. Alora stared upon their faces and felt fresh tears fall against her own. Their stone forms had kept every detail, down to singular strands of fur, but she knew if she were to press hard enough, they'd break apart in her hand like needles.

She reached out, her fingers trailing along one overlarge canine, and realized she'd have to destroy them. They must be dust before anyone saw. Her mind began its imaginings when she heard something in the woods.

Alora squinted beyond the fallen guard's boots and into the shadows. She feared it was another wolf until she saw him walk from the trees.

No, *stumble*.

The Urchin was hooded and masked, one gloved hand hanging limp at his side, with a wickedly long knife gleaming wet and dripping silver. The other was pressed beneath his cowl, hidden from her. He tripped over the bough she'd toppled and nearly went down, which must have been when he saw her.

"Alora," he rasped, sinking to his knees.

She saw then that his coat was shredded in places, and the shirt beneath too, as she could see skin, weeping red. She rushed toward him, statues forgotten. She dropped onto her knees before him, gripping his shoulders when he slumped.

"What's happened? Where are you hurt?"

He still hadn't removed his hand, and she worried about what he held pressure to. The cuts on his chest, at least, appeared shallow, but he didn't act as if he were giving into a fit of terror, relieved in his escape.

He acted as if he were bleeding out.

He didn't answer her but instead leaned forward. She could feel the press of his forehead against her shoulder, his breath shallow and warm against her neck. If he gave up supporting himself entirely, she'd fall beneath him, she knew. She pushed against his shoulders.

"Urchin—" she began.

"Don't call me that." His voice was muffled and ragged, more so because his mouth, already masked, was now buried against her.

She huffed, annoyed in spite of his attempts at dying, because what else was she supposed to call him? "Was it the wolves? Did they overpower you?"

"Six," he breathed. "All dead."

Six? Her eyes were wide as moons. "What wound are you hiding?"

"My…neck."

He slumped further against her, and Alora grunted at the added weight. "How do I help you? Whom should I fetch?"

"No one. Just…stay here."

His voice had grown softer, almost distant. Alarm rang throughout her body. All she could smell was his blood. "You are not dying today, Urchin. Drudge up what strength you have left." Then she released one shoulder to find where his grip had slipped between them. She felt about blindly until tattered skin and a warm wetness met her fingertips. She fought a gag, holding tight to the wound.

"If you die against me, I will be endlessly traumatized."

A wheeze of a laugh met her ears.

"I will do my best…to avoid it." But more of his weight added to her own.

"Urchin!"

"Don't…" he sighed.

Shouts rang out behind them, and Alora released a cry in relief. Help had come.

In seconds, the Urchin captain was hauled off her, his body carried away by more hooded and masked men and several others dressed in the gold and crimson of Opulence. Alora tried to see where they took him, to see what they did, but he was lost to the sudden swell of people.

"His neck is wounded!" was all she managed to shout before he was gone from her sight, and only then did she realize she was crying.

"Miss Pennigrim," said a familiar voice. It was slow and deep, and Alora turned to find the groundskeeper at her elbow, eyeing her front. "Are you hurt?"

"No, Mister Macaw. It's the poor captain's blood."

He nodded, and glanced beyond her, spying the golden boots from amongst the ferns. "Talk little," he said to her, then lumbered off toward the body.

Talk little…

"Miss Pennigrim!"

Alora twisted away from the body being hauled from the brush to find Merridon making quick strides toward her. Madam Feebledire followed behind with a pinched expression, and when their eyes met, Alora scowled so deeply her vision blurred. That heinous woman tried to take *everything* from Reginald.

Madam Feebledire blinked in shock back at her, but she said nothing, glancing instead to Merridon when he stopped in front of her.

"My dear, you are covered in blood!"

"It isn't mine," she said, already tiring.

"Thank the heavens for that. Patrice, fetch her a new cloak." He spared a glance for the guard's body as it was carried past him, but only that. No hint of emotion entered his eyes aside from maybe a flare of irritation.

Alora hurriedly wiped her cheeks. "Has the driver awakened?"

"Yes, yes, he has. Specter wolves. It's as I've said, the swath of forest separating Opulence and Enver is treacherous. I've the signage for good reason."

Few workers remained behind, already attentive to cleaning the stones and removing the branch from the lever. A sight which

Merridon observed for a moment before his arm snaked around her shoulders.

"Tell me what's happened. Tell me everything." When he turned them both, they were face to face with the stone wolves.

A warning rippled through her. Alora cleared her throat and fidgeted, scrounging for time, but the hand on her was unyielding. He wouldn't allow her to go without his answers.

"They came upon us on the lane. One at first, then two. We raced for the gate. The driver was knocked unconscious when we halted, and I rushed to close the wolves out from the grounds, but the guard must have fallen to them. I tried to reach the lever when the wolves surrounded me. I'd given up on being saved when they became *this*."

Truth and lies and many holes. Alora tried to be conscious of how quickly she breathed but didn't know how good a job she did. Merridon remained unmoved beside her, silent. Then all at once he released her. Contemplative, he stepped forward, enough that his hand came to rest on the wolf.

"Such a marvelous beast. And the largest I've seen. Do you know much about them, Miss Pennigrim?"

Breaths, Alora. Your godforsaken breaths!

"A little."

"Ah. Well, you may or may not know then, that the largest of specter wolves, like these here before us, are only drawn to the most powerful of enchantments."

"Like those that reside within Opulence."

Merridon hummed a non-committal sound. "Also, they cannot see what is not enchanted."

His son might be dying, and a guard is dead! And yet we've time for a lesson?

"The driver mentioned his gift."

"Did he? How well and good." Merridon's pursed lips said differently. He moved to stroke the second stone creature. "It is strange, isn't it? How their eyes appear."

Alora nodded. "Like moons."

"Quite right. And none can see them, unless they are enchanted themselves."

It took longer than it should have for what Merridon said to sink in. When it did, she swung her gaze to his, and found him watching her, a look like triumph playing across his features. He waited, yearning for her to fold before him, and she could now see the resemblance that Ellie Turkens had mentioned. Between him and a powerful wolf.

He fed on Opulence. On all those locked inside. And he wanted her secrets.

Run away! screamed her instincts.

But she couldn't. She had goals and dreams and friends to save.

"It's better to see your attacker for what it is, I suppose. No conscience and a soul forged in greed." She'd torn her gaze from Merridon before she spoke, choosing instead to imitate him, running her fingers along the stone wolf's snout.

"Indeed." The word seemed to edge around his teeth. She jumped when his voice suddenly rose between them, "Mister Macaw! Do bring these magnificent statues to the front doors. I'd like them situated at either side."

The groundskeeper inclined his head in acknowledgment as he made his way toward them. Alora noticed he avoided her gaze, just as she noticed his hands were now empty.

To her, Marshall Merridon said, "Thank you, Miss Pennigrim, for your continued dedication in making Opulence beautiful. I can scarcely wait for what else you have to show me." Then he patted the wolf farewell and left her.

Chapter Twenty-Five

He knew. Because of course he *knew*. But—did it matter? What harm was it really, that he guessed she'd turned the beasts to stone?

Alora did not ask for help, nor did she get any, as she unloaded what trim remained from their frantic journey. It was just as well, being as how she needed to imagine nearly every piece whole again. Cracks and splinters abounded, and one piece was missing entirely. She knew the one and discreetly checked her measurements before bringing another into existence. What else could anyone have done?

Mr. Macaw met her eyes briefly but didn't return her wan smile, his face reddened with exertion as he hauled the first specter wolf into place. Alora hated that the creatures responsible for killing a man and gravely wounding another would be immortalized before the mansion's front doors. Because that's all the Urchin was: wounded. Not dead.

He couldn't be dead.

Alora stacked as many pieces of trim as she could comfortably handle before making her way up the steps. She spared a glance for the new topiary. It was still unfinished, as Mr. Macaw was now busy with other things, but the bottom half looked nearly complete. There were all manner of objects along the base, and they seemed to be trickling down from something, but that something was yet incomplete, and so she couldn't be sure what it would eventually be. Nothing, if she didn't finish the room.

Except her mind was far from her project. She'd told the Urchin captain she'd become traumatized if he died in her arms, but in truth, she'd become traumatized already. She could think of nothing aside from what she'd done and how he'd felt, his body slumping to unconsciousness against her. She supposed they would have taken him out the back. He must have rooms similar to William. She hoped they'd found the healer who'd helped her.

Of course they will have.

She was being foolish. He was too young—too important—to let die. He was Master Merridon's son, after all, though she couldn't help but think of what little regard the man had seemed to spare for him. What if help had come too late?

Dammit, she shouldn't care! He wasn't a good person. How could he be? Good people didn't skulk about bludgeoning others and spying for wicked men. They certainly didn't command others to do so.

Except—

He'd saved her once, had helped her more than that. He'd saved Reginald. And he'd kept her secrets. All of them.

The trim was heavy, as quality wood often was. Alora was out of breath by the time she reached the darkened hall, and her arms were afire. Yet she refused herself a reprieve. She also refused to shuffle what she held in order to retrieve her lantern. She knew the way now regardless of light.

She regretted the latter choice a moment later.

"Miss Pennigrim."

Alora stilled in the dark. "Who's there?"

"I'm wounded you don't recognize my voice." She felt movement to her right and swung toward it, her eyes adjusting enough to make out the human shape. "Easy with those. I've enough bruises to contend with because of you."

William.

Alora didn't know it was possible to be both equal parts furious and frightened. Her voice dripped with vitriol. "How long have you been down here?"

"You're angry I didn't come to you sooner? I tried. You weren't at home."

Her entire body spasmed at his words. She yearned to lash at him until he was nothing more than pulp. Her leap to such imaginings scared even her, enough that she came back to herself.

"That is not why I'm angry, and you very well know it! What were you thinking, coming to me after what you did? What you meant to further do?" She reached out blindly and murmured a blessing in relief when she found the knob. She swung the door in.

She could feel William follow her inside.

"Do you want an apology? Forgive me then, Alora. For not realizing you didn't want things to progress between us. But need I remind how differently you behaved that day? The rules you disregarded. How you begged against my throat?"

"You drugged me with Lust!" She tossed the trim down and found the lamp. She felt like the Urchin captain, striking and breaking matches in her rage. At last, one caught and flared between them.

She gasped at what she saw.

"Ghastly, isn't it?" William traced the split in his lower lip, though it was his eye that had apparently suffered the most. "The captain thinks he is quite the enforcer of expectation, but I think we all know his true motivation, don't we?"

Alora turned up the lamp with shaking fingers. "I don't know what you mean."

"I *hate* feigned ignorance."

She looked up in time to see his eyes harden, his lips pressed tight. *"Feigned ignorance?* As you stand here and spout about your confusion in my behavior? You gave me an enchanted drink, William. Yes, I did not ask, but I should not have had to. You're manipulative and entitled and I want nothing to do with you, not even a friendship."

"Such harsh words! It seems I need to convince you otherwise." His hand shot out to grip her wrist, and he tugged, meaning to pull her in.

But Alora leaned back and dug in her heels. "Let *go.*"

"What is it? Is it because I am not my brother?" William's lips lifted into a sneer, his eyes narrowed and flashing. "Should I pull on a hood and an atrocious leather coat to claim you?"

"Of course not. It isn't that. That *Urchin*—"

"Urchin? So, he's divulged the secrets of his associations to you and still you want him? My, you are more devious than your innocent look claims." He smiled then, though it didn't reach his eyes. Instead, a fire seemed to build inside him. "It is lucky for you that I enjoy those traits even more."

The next time he pulled her, she didn't have a hope of stopping him.

Her chest met his in a rush of air.

"Enough of this, William! I will go to Master Merridon."

"Master Merridon?" His laugh was dark and lasted so long, goosebumps erupted all over her skin. "By all means, please do. And I will follow you after and tell him of all you know but shouldn't. Do you realize what sort of weapon your beloved Urchins use?" His opposite hand left her arm to caress her temple. "I would hate to see you bleed over it."

"What have I done to make you believe I wanted you this way? I'm not interested in anything between us. This obsession you have needs to end."

"*Obsession?*"

Alora cried out as his grip turned crushing on her wrist. "William," she whimpered.

"I loathe that word. And I know precisely who's given it to you to use. Did you know, Miss Pennigrim, that he is dead? Good riddance, if you ask me."

Alora felt as if the ground crumbled beneath her feet, the earth falling away. "What?"

"They couldn't save him in time. He lost too much blood. Oh, fucking hell. Look at your face. And here you tried to convince me you harbored no feelings." He reached to her cheek, his thumb wiping the tears beginning to fall. His gaze softened to something mimicking tenderness. "Forget about him, Alora. Forget all the past ugliness between us. Let's start anew."

"It can't be true."

"Oh, but it is. You might think I am manipulative and whatever else, but I've never lied to you."

His hand moved along her jaw, tangling almost painfully in her hair. Alora cringed at the feel of it, her entire body recoiling. "Please. Stop."

"Never," said William, and bent his head to hers.

Alora pressed her eyes closed as William bellowed, stumbling backward when his hands fell away. He cupped his face, groaning. Blood trickled through his fingers. "My nose! You've broken my nose!"

Alora gripped the trim she'd imagined into her hand like a lifeline. "I asked you to stop."

At her quiet words, William ceased his moaning. When he lowered his hands, it took all her fortitude not to run.

William's eyes were a nasty web of broken capillaries, his nose bruised and crooked, running red over his lips and chin. When he bared his teeth, they were stained with blood. He looked murderous, and she'd no doubt at all that he would follow through on those feelings. He stepped toward her.

"Do not come near me. Not another step."

In answer, William spat a stream of crimson onto the floor.

"*William—*"

He lunged.

Tripped.

And Alora wasted no time swinging again, wood meeting his skull with a horrid crack that rattled the room. Master Merridon's second son slumped to the floor.

Alora's breaths were coming too fast to be useful. She put a hand to her forehead to fend off the dizziness threatening to consume her. A pool of blood formed beneath William's head, the floorboards returning as they once were, no longer warped and protruding, but flat and straight. She'd done that—tripped him up when he would have tackled her to the ground, and she'd bludgeoned him. Like some kind of Urchin.

She almost vomited right then, but somehow her body managed to hold out.

She didn't know what to do. Who to turn to. Who could she trust in this place?

Or maybe that was the wrong question.

"Madam Feebledire," she said, her gaze still focused on William and his shallow breaths.

"MADAM FEEBLEDIRE!"

Chapter Twenty-Six

Outside of the mansion, Alora hurried to keep up with the swift pace of Opulence's head of management. Some distance ahead of them, William was being carried by several painted employees clad in crimson and gold. No black cloaks were to be found.

"He attempted an attack then," Alora continued, holding out her reddened wrist that was sure to bruise. "I honestly thought he might kill me. And all the while he kept accusing me of cavorting with Urchins, though I know nothing of them and never wish to. What should I do, Madam Feebledire? Should I relay all this to Master Merridon?"

At the mention of Merridon's name, Madam Feebledire seemed to come to herself. She stopped at the back of Opulence in a sudden motion, as if only now realizing how far they'd come—and who she'd come with. "No. You were right to come to me. I will bring all of this before Master and allow him to decide how best to proceed. We don't often have trouble like this, but we do have it." She tracked the distancing outline of William for a moment. "You shouldn't be back here. I don't know why I allowed it from the start. Go. Now, Miss Pennigrim. Finish your work if you must before you depart."

But Alora heard nothing of what she said as her attention had become transfixed on a cart being pulled through.

It came from one of the larger buildings at the back. Maybe an infirmary. Or perhaps a home with multiple rooms; a home large enough to represent an Urchin captain. A black horse pulled it, though she couldn't tell at this distance if it was the one called Necros, and inside was the distinct outline of a body draped with a white sheet.

Who is that? Alora wanted to say but couldn't.

What she did manage was: "Is that the fallen guard?"

"No," said Madam Feebledire, and pursed her lips. "No, it's not."

A roaring filled Alora's ears, her eyes straining to see. She both wanted and didn't want it confirmed. She didn't know what would be better. Then she decided neither would be, that nothing could make this better. When a swath of black fabric fell from the edge, it took all her strength to remain standing. She couldn't fall to pieces. Not in front of Madam Feebledire.

Still, her next breath was loud and ragged. Enough that the older woman turned upon her with fierce eyes. "Go."

Alora did. Ran, in fact. By the time she reached the stairs, she was sobbing like her heart had shattered, her hand reaching out to steady herself on anything and finding the textured stone of a specter wolf. She recoiled with a choked cry, stumbling and nearly falling away from it. But it was the shock she needed.

Her sobs quieted behind clenched teeth, the sun drying tears against her cheeks, only to be replaced by new ones. Opulence Mansion, this *place*, advertised itself as a creation of wonder and dreams. Alora could see its truth behind the façade now. Its wonder was an illusion, hiding a toxic tincture that would keep you coming back, day after day, year after year. And its dreams were only prettily disguised nightmares, ones that would leap and devour you the moment you didn't look at them directly. There was no escape from Opulence, not once you'd had a taste.

Poor Lennox, drowning herself every evening in a happy memory because she didn't see a hope of making more. The poor Urchin captain, dying in a fight forced upon him by a father who'd never cared for him. Even William, as diabolical as his choices were now, was forged by the hand of Opulence and its creator.

Lonely Reginald. Sad Mr. Macaw.

The halls didn't echo in Opulence, and the wind never ruffled the hedges. She'd once thought of the mansion as something that defied natural existence—and it was. Marshall Merridon had created something unnatural. But unlike her rabbit, he'd done it purposefully, and he'd done it for all the wrong reasons.

She retrieved the rug from the abandoned wagon, her grip fierce and unyielding. Then she brought the wind.

It was an oddly satisfying accomplishment, watching the hundreds of candles snuff out. Gaudy chandelier by gaudy chandelier, Alora allowed the wind to whistle and howl in her wake, until Opulence Mansion, likely for the first time in its existence, was cast into shadow. She could hear doors being opened, investigating footsteps and confused voices, but she didn't pause in her steps. She continued on through the dark hall, oblivious to the burning in her arms and the ache in her heart. She'd finish this blasted room if it killed her.

Door Twenty-five's lamp burst to light upon her entrance. She took in the scattered trim, the extra piece she'd conjured, and the blood on the floor. She thought she might crack her teeth, her jaw clenched so hard. She'd brought nails to attach the trim and glue for the rug; she didn't use them now. Instead, she spun in a slow circle.

She inhaled deep, shaking out her hands all the while. Her head rolled, stretching her neck. "Don't lose focus now. You can't afford it."

Merridon expects it. She cleaned the floor. She pounded the trim. She smoothed the rug. And all the while, she wondered what Opulence would look like reduced to a pile of rubble.

Several hours later, Alora emerged from the Room of Desire, but she did so invisible. She'd forgotten her original creation, so she fashioned herself a new one, though she spent more time on this garment than she had the one before. The cuffs were silken, the trimmings the same, so that they brushed gently against her skin and didn't itch. The only downfall was she didn't have Lennox here to tell her if its enchantment worked; she'd have to step out and hope for the best.

The hall had become overrun. Ladders extended impossibly high, from the floor to each chandelier, and atop each was perched a crimson-clad employee of Opulence with an overlarge matchstick. One by one, the candles were relit.

Alora listened for the wind, watched for its flicker in the flames, but it was gone, shut out by the front doors latched tight against it. If she were in higher spirits, she might have smirked over what she'd done, but as it was, her heart felt so sick and her insides so filled with fury, that she couldn't manage anything other than breathing.

She stepped out into the light.

Nobody glanced her way. Either she was deemed inconsequential, or she was truly invisible. She hoped desperately for the second. If she weren't and did happen to run into another soul wishing to speak with her, she thought her own would wither and die. It barely hung on even now.

She weaved among the ladders, noting their rungs were coated in gold and they'd only two feet on the floor. How they remained upright without any support was a mysterious enchantment in itself; they weren't supported by anything at the top.

She had two days left. Two days in which to gather everything she needed to furnish the room and complete her contract. She knew she could do it. Really, though, she had no other choice. She needed to supply Merridon with her receipts for reimbursement, and she couldn't very well do that if she imagined them all into existence.

It would be a very long night, and a very long day tomorrow. So much would need transported—*oh*.

"Damn it *all*." Alora, realizing her mistake, slapped her palm against her mouth. She'd not meant to speak aloud. She glanced around, but everyone was too high and too concentrated to pay her unattached voice any mind. For the first time, she was thankful for the strange corridor and its inability to echo.

She would need the irritable horses and the blasted, stupid wagon, and a driver for it all. Damn Merridon and his cumbersome rules! Now she must search out the crotchety Madam Feebledire again and have yet another joyous interaction where she'd be made to feel like an insect being swatted.

Alora headed toward the nearest door hidden beneath stairs, Door Three, to remove her coat, when she saw the subject of her chagrin step from the shadow. Madam Feebledire appeared more resigned than usual, her fierce countenance replaced with something more akin to weariness. She moved toward the mansion's entrance, where Alora thought she would leave. However, the head of management paused there, and with a deep sigh, pivoted to her right. Madam Feebledire knocked three times upon Door Zero.

The door swung in, and Alora heard, "Marshall. I think we need to speak of your son."

Chapter Twenty-Seven

Alora only just managed to maneuver her way into Door Zero before the door closed with a resounding *click*. For all the world, it felt like a padlock had been secured from the outside. She tried not to dwell on it.

Her heart beat wild as a hummingbird's, and she tried to keep her breaths silent. Still, she thought surely they could hear both. Merridon sat at his customary place behind the desk, his legs stretched out before him, and his head leaned back. He spared one glance toward the door, where Alora now stood, and away again. His eyes trained upon the ceiling, he threw a weathered ball into the air and caught it. Over and over again.

"Which son, Patrice?"

Alora's eyes welled before she could quell it.

"Don't take that long-suffering tone with me, Brother. You don't seem to remember most of the time that it is due to my responsibilities that Opulence runs so smoothly." When Merridon only scoffed, she continued, "It's William. And another transgression against Miss Pennigrim, I've come to find out."

The ball fell to the floor, and Merridon swung upright. "Against Miss Pennigrim? What has he done now?"

Alora's mouth fell wider than it had already been since Madam Feebledire's use of the word 'brother'. There was concern in her tone, and it sounded genuine. *What in the world?*

"He attacked her while she was working behind Door Twenty-five. It seems as though he held certain aspirations for the two of them, which she didn't reciprocate. Anyway, she struck him. He has a nasty head wound to go along with what his brother bestowed upon him, and his nose is cracked."

"Did he now…" Merridon trailed off, his thumb and finger tracing the curve of his mustache. The silence stretched, one in which Alora didn't dare breathe, certain they'd hear her. "Send the healer to him."

"He's already been."

Merridon curled his lip as if offended by her forthright thinking, but he didn't admonish her for it. "Fine. I will speak to him once he's rested. Miss Pennigrim is without a doubt a strong, young woman, and quite a burgeoning success. I hope she is well. See to it that she understands no further harm shall come to her while upon Opulence's grounds. Even though they're far more temperamental as of late. How that god-awful wind happened, I'd love to know."

Even Madam Feebledire appeared caught off guard by Merridon's praise. She blinked at him slowly, the wrinkle between her eyes growing more pronounced with time. "I will see to it," she said, at last. "As for the wind, the old man is probably dead now. That one who enchanted the estate. We will have to find another to fix the problem or adjust." Madam Feebledire turned toward the door, which Alora panicked over and immediately lurched away from. But the older woman turned back.

"Marshall," she began. "About Miss Pennigrim—"

"That's *enough*, Patrice," spat Merridon, with a fierceness that startled Madam Feebledire and Alora, both. "See that it's done. All of it."

Madam Feebledire allowed herself a loud huff, but nothing more, as she spun back toward the door and threw it open. Alora had chosen the wrong side and was nearly struck by it. She rushed to catch up with the head of management when she swept through the doorway. The door closed all on its own at their backs.

"That insufferable man," muttered Madam Feebledire. "He thinks he can manage me like a lowly employee? I am his elder by *six years*. I used to change his soiled drawers. And now I am the one ordered about like a child? I think *not*." She paused in the great hall, turning first one way and then the other. "Where has that girl gotten to? I swear, if I have to search the place for her... If I so much as find her with a toe outside of where it should..."

A cold sweat formed on Alora's palms. She ran to the front door, and while Madam Feebledire made to continue down into the depths of the corridor, Alora opened it, closed it, and took off her coat, all in a breath.

"Madam Feebledire," she said. "I've a request."

The woman jolted before turning on her heel. "Devil take me, girl. Where did you come from?"

Alora's brow dipped in false befuddlement. "From just outside, of course. I've finished for the day and was only making sure I had everything accounted for. But I require transportation again. Tomorrow, in fact."

Madam Feebledire nodded at this, her mind clearly occupied by other things. "Fine. I'll arrange it. Leave me the name of the shop outside of which to meet you."

"Thank you."

"Another thing, Miss Pennigrim."

"Yes?"

"I would like to formally apologize on behalf of Opulence Mansion for what has transpired between you and William. Master, specifically, would like it known that you are quite respected by him, and that no further harm shall come to you while upon our illustrious grounds."

Alora had heard it all before, of course, but still, a breath of relief rushed past her lips. Madam Feebledire, for all her prickliness, seemed sincere. "Thank you, Madam Feebledire."

The older woman said nothing more, waiting while Alora dug through her satchel until her fingers enclosed around an imagined card. She handed it over, the calligraphy reading *Ichibald's Fanciful Furnishings* with an address printed in bold beneath. "This is the place."

Madam Feebledire sniffed her understanding, and tucking the card into her vest pocket, said, "I don't care if you can turn things to stone, Miss Pennigrim. *Don't* stray from the lane."

So Opulence management and its owner were both convinced of her enchantment. Oh well. It wasn't as if Merridon would find any use for it, and even if he could, she was bound and determined to refuse anything else he might offer her. She'd never work for him again. Hell, if she got her way in the end, the whole of Enver would never see him again.

The wind whispered through the hedges like a heartfelt sigh, gusting overtop the topiaries. Alora wondered what Merridon planned to do about it. If he was sincerely angry over nature taking back control from what he'd commandeered for himself or not. She allowed the breeze to play against her hair, closing her eyes to feel it better against her skin. She hadn't realized how stale the air had become within the grounds until it wasn't. For the first time, she wondered if the grass was even real.

She blinked open her eyes again upon nearing the bell. She reached up and rang it.

The gilded gate swung in, but not by any mechanism. Instead, it was pushed open by a guard. His painted face was strained against the effort, and he scowled at her when she only stood there. "Hurry up now! This gate isn't made of twigs!"

Alora rushed through, and the gate shuddered closed behind her with a resonating ring. She glanced at the lever, still bent in an unusable angle, and the metalsmiths at work over it. The branch had been cleared away.

She pondered over whether she should fix it herself—it was her fault it was broken to start—but decided against it. She'd made too many attention-acquiring choices today and couldn't afford another one. She pulled the hood of her Opulence cloak over her hair and continued on.

Around the bend in the lane, she came upon the first enchanted sign. One that would stay alight no matter the time or weather, warning passerby with a jaunty script and bright display. She paused before it, examining the silver-tipped ferns beyond, and the white trees beyond those. Her fingers tapped a quick rhythm against her thighs.

She searched for eyes. For specter wolves. The Urchin captain had said he'd killed six of the creatures and she'd turned two to stone, though she didn't know whether they would return to the world alive or dead should she wish them as they were. She squinted harder, but nothing stared back at her.

Somewhere inside Renwick was a path. A shortcut between Opulence and Enver, and a way for Urchins to come and go and patrol as required. Who said, aside from this sign and Madam Feebledire, that she could not use it too? Her hand came up to brush against her ear, the scar left there from a mistake in her choice of weapons. Or perhaps that night came about as it was meant to. As fine as the Urchin captain might have looked as stone, she much preferred him alive and breathing against her, his fingers holding pressure to her wound. None of which would have happened if she'd turned him into a rock.

Of course, he wouldn't have been mauled by wolves then.

Her chest hitched at the memory of his weight, his voice against her neck. "You didn't try very hard to live, did you? You didn't listen to me." But that was unfair. He'd lost so much blood.

She tugged off the ugly cloak and tucked it away. In its place, she shrugged on her lovely enchanted coat; it was a more breathable fabric than the last creation. She studied the sign serving as a reminder that, while the forest was by no means private property, it was still controlled by Opulence. Well, to hell with that.

Your rules protect none but yourselves. She glowered, and in the next breath imagined the sign dismantled. It fell to the forest floor in a pile of gilded wood chippings. There, now she disobeyed nothing.

She walked overtop them and into the trees.

The path created in the woods wasn't wide, but it was well-used. Alora didn't find so much as a root as she weaved through the white forest. She thought over when she was last here, or attempted to, her memory from that day blurry and faded with the concoction William had fed her. Mostly, what she remembered was a feeling, one that if not satisfied, she'd thought would surely kill her. The devastation had been so real, the desire to feel the high again so pronounced, it was little wonder members returned every night to chase it.

Did Merridon relay all these side effects to every patron at the door? She sincerely doubted his honor.

A butterfly flitted past her nose, and Alora paused to see what it wished from her. When it landed on her shoulder, folding its wings in a contented sort of way, she felt the tiniest beginnings of a smile. "You don't fear the forest, do you? Merridon is a con man, indeed."

Still, specter wolves were a very real thing, and she kept her eyes alert for any sign of a moon-white gaze.

Dusk neared; she could sense its creeping feel as she'd become trained to fear its encroachment toward Opulence. She also hadn't eaten a thing since breakfast. Her stomach protested this development loudly now, though everything else within her wanted nothing less. She contained too much inside her to make room for a meal. If only she could slit her veins, a bloodletting that would sieve the poison that was the mansion and all its secrets from her insides. Her body felt abuzz with it. She could feel the vibration in her chest, blooming outward until it reached her toes and fingertips. She glanced down at herself, wondering if she could see it. Sure she could hear it.

Wait.

She *could.*

Alora spun a circle, eyes darting amongst the trees. She could see nothing but foliage and shadow on the forest floor, nothing but stark bark in line with her vision, but then she lifted her gaze and stilled. Nests of white paper lined the high boughs. They were cone-shaped, and larger than her head, and from inside, a buzzing so incessant that it resounded within her.

"Did you know there were bees here?" she asked the butterfly. The creature only twitched its antennae in reply, unperturbed.

She couldn't remember them, couldn't recall feeling their buzzing inside her when taking this path once before. But she'd been drugged and distracted, and it made sense she'd not noticed it then. She'd almost missed it now. It was a relaxed sort of buzzing, she thought. A note that didn't sound especially loud or aggressive. She glanced to the opposite side of the path, scanning the boughs there until she discovered more. A small rustle drew her attention to the forest floor and a chipmunk bounded along a fallen limb.

"Bees and butterflies and chipmunks. What a treacherous place," she mused with healthy sarcasm.

She wondered if this was where Bash had ventured to collect his bones. If he wandered out here, donned in black from head to foot, cloaked in shadow to mimic the dark. If his face would be covered to hide from whoever might witness him, even if those things were only chipmunks. If he would move silently so as not to alert his prey.

Alora imagined it all and faltered.

No.

She doubled over, retching. Through watering eyes and a tender throat, she wheezed, "No. No, it can't *be.*"

"And you are not?"

"I am not prone to it."

The memory returned, skipping and repeating like some broken record before it finally transformed from blurred remembrance to a new one, plain as the present.

"Maybe I'm an obsessive type, after all."

The sudden despair caught and swept her up, a dizzying maelstrom that drained the contents from her stomach and from her head until only one thought remained. It pounded away like a malevolent tumor. She trembled all over.

It wouldn't be true. She'd hurry to Potions and Peculiarities, and she'd find it open. She'd find Bash at the worn counter dallying over ledgers, or she'd find him at the back boiling some foul-tasting elixir for his cabinet. She wouldn't find it closed. She wouldn't find him gone.

"Hold tight," she whispered to the butterfly.

She didn't think of it until later, that it could see her.

Chapter Twenty-Eight

Closed. The sign may as well have said something else. It may as well have said exactly what she feared. *Dead.* But hope could sometimes be a brutal thing, gripping tight even when it was in the best interest of the mind to let go. It didn't let Alora go now, its claws digging as deep as a witch's fingers. She rattled the latch with all her strength. It didn't give; it was locked. She ran to the back.

Mugwort Alley was the least popular place in Enver. Its location next to Renwick Forest made it not only dangerous, or so they were led to believe, but also overshadowed. The canopy blocked the sun by early afternoon. It was a place for dark things. Quite a convenient location for Urchins.

The wagon was there. The mule was not. Alora hurried to the back door and once again pushed against the latch. It didn't budge.

If it weren't for the ice built up inside her, the sick-sweat coating her skin, she would have thought he was only out. He did that, she knew. After all, she'd come upon him once after an afternoon gathering of bones. She'd come upon him in the nursery buying up Forget-Me-Nots. But somehow, she knew he was doing none of those things.

She slumped against his door, sinking until her bottom met the stoop. She'd done this once before, sat like this, but

when she'd awoken, he'd been there, his hands coming around her to lift her up. She didn't think that would happen this time. She didn't know how any tears could be left inside her, but there were. Her shoulders heaved against her cries, her head buried in her knees.

Voices came from the street. She ignored them. But when they sounded nearer, on that colorless, narrow lane between buildings, she couldn't any longer and scrambled to stand. Her sobs caught and quieted.

A moment later, four men appeared around the corner.

From the safety of her enchanted coat, Alora focused on each in turn, not recognizing any of them—until she reached the last and gasped aloud. The sound drew attention. She pressed her lips closed as four pairs of eyes turned toward her general direction. Four bodies grew rigid as they waited. They assessed for a threat, she thought, which was understandable, considering they must all be Urchins.

She stared the hardest at the crooked-nosed man, his light mustache and blue eyes revealing him as the Urchin who had driven her only that morning. The one who had been knocked unconscious within Opulence's grounds. He looked no worse for wear. They must have healed the bump he surely should have sprouted on his forehead.

"What's the matter with that butterfly?" said one.

Oh no! Fly away! Alora panicked and shrugged, and the creature obeyed, lifting from her shoulder.

When nothing else shifted or made any further noise, they resumed their conversation. Slowly at first, and then more confident. One produced a key from his pocket and opened the door. They were going inside.

The door was left wide, and Alora wasted no thought in hurrying in after the last. She moved to a corner out of the way when the final Urchin turned and closed them in. A screeching announced the deadbolt had slid home.

"Tell us the rest of it then, Salvoy. What happened after you saw the second wolf?"

It was apparent the young Urchin enjoyed the attention he was receiving over that terrible moment as he smiled hugely, his mustache rising at the corners. "Well," he said, "I looked over at the girl, and she was all in hysterics, crying and shouting, and I thought: This is the last person I'd want to be eaten by wolves with. So I beat the horses into the fastest gallop imaginable, hoping to outrun them."

The four men left the backroom in a single file, making for the main room of the shop. Alora followed them in a rage, wishing beyond anything that she could reveal herself as that hysterical girl and rip the bedraggled caterpillar from Mr. Salvoy's thin upper lip. She imagined it would come off all at once—how satisfying. Rather than continuing past the counter, the Urchins turned and headed up the stairs.

"I heard the guard was already dead by the time you reached the gate. How did you manage past it?"

"I heard the lever is still being repaired. Did you run it over?"

"I was there after it happened. There was a branch broken across it."

"No," said Salvoy, and for the first time, Alora heard the uncertainty in his voice. She wondered if the others did. If they guessed that the Urchin embellished for his own sake. "No, I didn't run it over. It's true a branch fell at the exact moment we would have smashed into the gate. It happened to land upon the lever, which was obviously a stroke of good luck."

Finally, a bit of truth from him. The door atop the stairs swung in, and the Urchins moved through it.

"Do you think it was her? Can she control the wind? It's been unchecked over the grounds ever since, and the captain must have thought she was worth some trouble to send you with her rather than a guard."

Another laughed. "Worth so much that he blackened the eye of that skin-burning prat over her too."

"Did he, really? I hadn't heard that one yet. What's gotten into him?"

Salvoy snorted. "More like how long has she been letting him get into her?"

Alora's fist clenched so hard, she thought surely her nails had punctured the skin of her palms. She should have punched him when she'd had the chance, there in that wagon.

"Easy. Don't go there, Salvoy." The oldest Urchin frowned at him before striking a match. The lamp lit a moment later.

Alora stilled on the threshold. She absorbed the room with new eyes. The black-curtained windows. The lack of fireplace. The twin chairs, the end tables, and the sofa. That *sofa.*

She'd been here before. She'd lain on that couch. The cushion the Urchin captain had propped her foot upon sat crooked at its corner. This was the room above Potions and Peculiarities. A secret meeting place for Urchins.

She held her hand out to the doorframe to steady herself.

The same Urchin as before ordered the rest about, "Get dressed. We've work to do."

Together, the four of them moved to the wall.

The closets were hidden in the panels, and Alora could only stare blankly as one by one they were pushed open. Black coats. Black boots. Black masks. Black gloves.

"It's a terrible shame about Ezra. He was one of the best. I can't think of how he would have been overcome unless there were many of them."

Ezra, Alora thought. Was this the Urchin captain's true name? *Bash's* true name?

"There were. Eight in total, I think, including the two turned to stone."

Alora swung her attention toward the rasping voice. It wasn't the captain's voice, but the rough quality was the same. The Urchin was dressed, all but for his gloves, which he donned now. His mouth was masked and hidden from her.

"Do we know how that could have happened? How the beasts were petrified?" The oldest Urchin spoke again, except now his voice was changed, too: the same rasping quality as the last. A mask also covered the lower portion of his face.

One by one, all four donned their garb, and one by one, their true voices fell away.

The masks are enchanted.

The captain hadn't pitched his voice to purposefully frighten her. The mask had done that for him. She shook her head at her folly. At the secrets she still uncovered.

"If anyone knows, they're keeping quiet about it." This Urchin reached back into the shadows, and when his arm retracted, Alora gaped at what she saw held in his hand.

The baton was smooth and thick, the wood dark. It was a replica of what she'd found tucked away on the shelf that day Bash brewed a potion to assist her memory. An object that the Potions and Peculiarities proprietor deemed the most dangerous item in his shop. For all her struggles in her focus lately, she could still picture him clearly. The way the soft light of the lantern had skipped across the hollows and settled instead on the angular cut of his jaw and cheekbones. How it'd lit his eyes a forest green as he'd threatened to send her out to the mule.

How he'd baited her into sharing her dream…

The core of her had warmed with want even as he'd admonished and teased her, and she should have known.

They had always affected her the same.

Only she could have sworn the Urchin captain's eyes were black. She must have been mistaken.

The tide of her grief receded enough that Alora began to fit pieces together. Of every interaction she'd had with both Bash, the shopkeeper, and Ezra, the captain.

Water helps, said the captain. Bash handing her a glass.

The dark head she'd briefly seen staring into the fire while at dinner with Timothy Lofte. The Urchin finding her in the street that night.

"I don't even know you", she'd said.

"Yes, you do."

He'd played her well enough, she thought. What with calling the owner of the shop an idiot. Of pretending he'd no idea who William was. But the bones, the flowers. Were they all ingredients then? Was Bash behind the creation of the memory oil? Had his father trusted him with the process?

So many answers she wished for and could never ask.

Just like that, the tide returned, and Alora fell against the wall beneath the pain of it. She hardly heard the Urchins' continued conversation. Not until one of them began to speak of what they planned for next.

"Here are the names. I've written down the addresses on the backs."

It must have been the oldest of them yet. Alora could recognize the slight difference to his voice now that she'd heard it transform from one to the next. He handed out the small cards.

"Merridon never writes them in case they would be dropped."

"Well, considering Salvoy set himself against the wrong man last week, forgive me for doing one thing different than the captain would."

"Fuck. I didn't—"

Another Urchin clapped his hand on the younger's shoulder, effectively silencing him.

"It's happened before. Just don't let it happen again."

Alora could hear the disdainful scoff even through the mask, and then Salvoy said, "Ellie Turkens?" He turned over the card. "I've been here before, I think. Isn't this an old woman?"

Alora froze, her entire body doused in fear. She didn't dare move, or breathe, or even think.

"Does it matter? Get it done."

Chapter Twenty-Nine

Alora didn't wait for the Urchins to depart ahead of her. Instead, she ran. The deadbolt sounded an alarmed screech against her hand that she hoped they didn't hear but knew couldn't be helped if they did. She must reach Ellie Turkens before they did. She couldn't allow any other future.

My fault, she cried in her head. *It's my fault*. When would she ever learn? She'd harmed the newly named Mortimer the same way. By asking questions when she'd known it to be dangerous. By encouraging interactions when she'd known they were unwise. If any harm were to come to Ellie because of her, she'd never forgive herself for as long as she lived. And so she ran. Down the entirety of Mugwort Alley. Across Slumber Lane, through Thistledown Square, and along the length of Rune Street until she skidded to a halt before the yellow outside of Books and Nibbles. The violet shutters were thrown open, the windows and door, too. Alora bent at the waist to regain her breath and used precious seconds to step between buildings and remove her coat. She couldn't surprise Ellie in such a way. It wouldn't do to stop her heart for the sake of saving her memories.

When she was as presentable as she could make herself, though she knew there was sweat dampening her hair yet, Alora straightened her shoulders and walked through the entrance.

She found the bookshop's owner as she often did, her nose in a story and delivering a cup of tea.

"Sugar, dear? Yes, it's right here."

Alora skirted around the table of two young women until she planted herself right in Ellie's way. The old woman's book pressed into Alora's chest before she noticed anyone in her path. Hooded blue eyes flicked across the top of its pages to find hers.

"Alora! What are you doing? Oh my, whatever is the matter?"

"Mrs. Turkens, I—" A shadow passed by the window, and on instinct she reached for Ellie's wrists. "I must speak with you."

Urging Ellie Turkens after her required more effort than she wished. The old woman seemed convinced she could only go at one pace, and that pace was slow. Alora might have felt badly over how she pushed the bookshop owner, but she'd seen Ellie in a rush, and knew her capable of some speed yet.

"Dear, I must protest this rough grip."

"I'm sorry," said Alora, and released her at once. They were near the back of the shop now, not far from the kitchen. "Have I hurt you?"

"No, you haven't. But can you say the same? Your energy is all out of sorts." Ellie made a smoothing motion on either side of her head, close to touching, but not quite.

"Physically, I am well. Mrs. Turkens, I'm afraid for you. I've just come from Mugwort Alley." Alora cut off abruptly, realizing how loudly she spoke in her rush to get it all out of her before they arrived. "I overheard something I wasn't meant to. Ellie, the Urchins are coming for you."

Ellie Turkens blinked at her in a fair imitation of her owls. Then her plum lips pursed. "Over what we discussed? Oh, that odious man." She spun away from Alora and marched off, revealing she did indeed have quite more agility than most other eighty-something-year-olds Alora knew. Alora followed her into the kitchen.

"It's that fragile ego. It has grown so big and bloated over the years that one little prick of a word sends it tooting away like a popped balloon. *Well*, just let one of his shadowy underlings come and find me here."

Alora watched with wide eyes as Ellie set three kettles to boiling atop the stove. Her gaze lifted to the violet wall across, to the amassed group of teacups hung from little hooks. They began at the ceiling and trailed all the way down to the floor. "What should we do?"

Ellie turned toward her, her expression softening. "Don't worry about me, dearest. You should get out of here while you can. Go home and drink green tea with a dollop of pumpkin and cream. Sprinkle on a smidgeon of cayenne, if you can stomach it, to zap the zest back into you."

"What? No, Mrs. Turkens. I won't leave you to fight with an Urchin alone. I've seen their weapons, and I've seen what damage they can do."

Ellie shook her head at her as if she could dispel the image. "Shh. *Shh*, Alora. What are you doing saying such things out loud? Do you wish to be next?"

Alora groaned in frustration. "I don't care about myself! And even so, I'm starting to think I'm under some protection. At least as far as the next couple days are concerned. It's you I'm worried for!"

The kettles took to whistling, which earned them a grin from their owner. "As I've said, you needn't worry over me."

Twilight had given in to night, and still there was only one lamp burning along the wall. It bathed the kitchen in soft light that didn't extend beyond the doorway. Alora focused on those shadows, waiting for what she knew would come.

And it did.

Between one blink and the next, an Urchin stood there. Alora startled and Ellie hissed a breath. A heartbeat later, the old woman held a kettle between them and him.

"Your kind aren't welcome here, Urchin."

A rasping snort of disbelief left the masked man. Alora watched his attention travel between her and Ellie Turkens, his hood shifting. "Miss Pennigrim," he said, tipping his head. "I didn't expect to find another here. Least of all, you."

That earned her a sideways glance from Ellie, which Alora promptly ignored. Instead, she glowered. She knew precisely who was behind this disguise. "It seems you cannot help but continue making mistakes, Urchin. Perhaps you should leave."

He made a threatening noise, the effect of which was quite terrifying beneath the mask and stepped farther into the room. "I can smell your fear. Your agitation."

"I am *agitated* because you will not leave my bookstore," said Ellie, and scowled fiercer than Alora had ever seen. If there was any fear to be smelled, she was sure it didn't come from Ellie Turkens.

In response, the Urchin drew the baton from his belt. "If I have to dispense with the both of you, I will."

"And when Master Merridon learns of why I cannot finish my contract? What will you say to him?"

Another pointed look from Ellie was all the reaction she received for her admission. An admission she contractually shouldn't have made, but she needed to call the Urchin's bluff before he did something drastic. Fragile egos, as Ellie Turkens explained, were something to be wary of.

The Urchin seemed to hesitate, his hand shifting along the edge of the baton. "I would only need to tell him that you interfered with an important assignment. That you knew and witnessed more than you should. He would understand."

"And whose fault is it that I'm here as witness at all? If you were as skilled as your cohorts, you'd have waited until Mrs. Turkens was alone. Instead, you burst through at the first stroke of night without a care for your surroundings. I don't believe he would be so under-standing."

A hiss sounded from behind the Urchin's shadowed hood. "It is a good thing then, that you won't remember it all to relay it."

He took another step into the room and raised his weapon, and Alora realized in that moment there would be no talking him out of what he planned. Three things happened in the following seconds, and they seemed to happen all at once:

A figure leapt through the doorway.

Ellie Turkens tossed a boiling kettle of water.

And Alora imagined the baton into a snake, but a fangless one, of course.

The figure turned out to be Mortimer, and in his raised hands was held a giant tome. He smacked it over the head of the Urchin with such force that the younger man went down to his knees. It was there that Ellie's boiling water met him, and the screech emanating from behind the mask was otherworldly due to its enchantment. The baton dropped from his hand to slither dazedly away, curling around Alora's ankle, soulless and knowing only she commanded it.

Alora opened her mouth to demand the Urchin never return or else face something much worse, but it seemed Mortimer hit him harder than she thought. The Urchin swayed back and forth a mo-ment before he toppled forward onto the floor. He didn't move again.

They all stared down at him in silence, watching for his contin-ued breaths.

"*The Encyclopedia of Continental Flora.* My apologies, madam. I'll pay for it."

"Don't worry yourself over it. Nobody likes books that heavy; it's been gathering dust for a decade."

Alora crouched enough to see that Mr. Salvoy breathed still and drew a breath of her own in relief. Her hand met the snake's head absently, where she brushed her fingers along it before they came away, carrying a piece of string. She tucked it into her satchel.

"What should we do with him?" she said, pulling back his hood. His hair was left in disarray from the cowl, the skin on his forehead red and promising to blister. Otherwise, he appeared as if he could be sleeping.

"Send for the captain is what we should do. I know for fact that he wouldn't agree with what this boy attempted. Attacking a second person without order, and that person, specifically, being you."

"There will be no more of these ruffians in my shop," said Ellie, her voice quaking but final. She returned the empty kettle to the stove, where she gripped another. With a practiced hand, she poured three cups of tea.

Alora took hers without comment, her mind far away. When it returned to the kitchen, she said in a flat voice, "The captain is dead anyway."

Mortimer gasped. "No. Surely not."

"He was brought down by specter wolves."

"Specter wolves! Where?"

"Renwick. Not far from the mansion's gate." Her voice was toneless and quiet. Still, it sounded loud in the kitchen.

"I've not seen a specter wolf in… Why, it must be six or seven years, at least. Even then, it wasn't a large one. It only came out at night." When no one else spoke, Mortimer stepped over the unconscious Urchin until he stood before Alora. His voice grew soft with sympathy. "I'm sorry, Miss Pennigrim."

"Whatever for? I hardly knew him."

"Sometimes that doesn't matter." He said it as if he understood firsthand, and the grip on her shoulder told her she had a friend to come to, should she need him.

She found it hard to breathe.

"Leave the Urchin with me," said Ellie.

"With you?" questioned Mortimer, his brow raised. "But what about when he wakes?"

"I've not read thousands of stories for nothing. And I know a lot of people, specifically merchants. If one leaves tomorrow with a trussed-up sack of grain after making his deliveries, no one will suspect a thing. Even if it is squawking." Taking a long sip of tea, she studied Alora over the rim. The steam wafted around the old woman's nose, iridescent tendrils in the shape of moth wings. "I'm not sure how you managed to get so mixed up in all this, my dear, but be certain that your humors are not at all thrilled with what you've put yourself through. Go home this minute and leave these young men to me."

Mortimer turned a finger on himself, looking one way then the other.

"Yes, you. I'll have your help. Your humors, at least, appear quite fine."

"Oh. Well. Thank you, madam."

Ellie Turkens nodded as curtly as a king. When Alora handed over her teacup, the old woman took it and Alora's hand all in one grasp. Quietly, so as not to be overheard, she said, "I'm not some cracked mug. I've played with the dangers of handsome devils, too, back in my day. But be assured, darling, though he might smile like one, Marshall Merridon is no devil. He's pond scum. He should be lying belly up in a swamp. I don't know what sort of contract you have with him, but find a way out of it fast as you can. That mansion is like quicksand." She planted a kiss on Alora's forehead, swift and soft. "Trust your instincts. They're good ones."

Chapter Thirty

Mrs. Flops was not at all thrilled to have been left alone for the entire day. Alora attempted to appease the disgruntled rabbit with an enormous salad, but she could tell from the reproachful stare it would be some days yet before she was forgiven.

"Maybe Mister Zanfold will take pity on me, and you. I've another long day tomorrow. I'm not sure when I'll return. Perhaps he'll come up and visit. I'll ask him in the morning."

Alora said all this while she combed her hair. The air was cool outside, blowing through the open doors of her terrace and finding its way into her bedroom. She'd changed into a nightgown, but one that hardly brushed her knees. She didn't enjoy being over warm, and she'd felt feverish for nearly the entire day. Ever since—

Her wrist paused at her shoulder. She dreaded what the following morning would bring. Of being subjected to the scrutiny of yet another Urchin or guard or whatever else Madam Feebledire deemed to send her way. Of using prancing horses over George. She dreaded seeing Opulence again. Of all the memories it would bring that she'd rather not have.

Another bout of sweats came upon her. She sank to the edge of the bed and took in the room—the color of the walls. That *green*. She couldn't bear it. She'd never be able to look at the shade again; it would have to go. Only, what if she never found it again? What if she forgot it forever? Was that better? Would it be better to accept Merridon's membership for a single night? To take advantage of Door One and allow just a trickle of that enchanted water to coat her skin, seep inside and steal all of what transpired between her and Bash—both versions of him—away? The pain was horrid, but it was also hers.

She pressed the heels of her hands to her eyes with a sigh. It was too soon to decide. About all of it. She would leave the walls alone—for now.

Her palms lowered to cup her cheeks. "Enough of this nonsense, Alora. Go fix your goddamned drink."

It'd taken her entirely too long still, but at last Alora had made it into the kitchen. A sprinkle of cayenne settled atop her tea in a red flurry, and she watched it drift and sink, dreading the moment when she'd be forced to choke it down. But she trusted Ellie Turkens. If the old woman said it would restore her to a semblance of her former self, well, it was worth a sip at least.

She blew across the surface, her nose wrinkling in discomfited anticipation, when a gust of wind rustled past the terrace doors. It whistled across the mantle, dislodging a painting and sending something heavy clattering to the floor. Alora grumbled in annoyance—she didn't know if she could gather the courage to sip the tea a second time—and abandoned her cup to see what it was.

Sunk into the floorboards in front of the fireplace, wobbled a knife. Alora bent, her fingers enclosing around the hilt, its blade thin and sharp and glinting in the soft lamplight.

She remembered the sting of it. A phantom throb in her ear reminded her more succinctly, and she straightened from her crouch, reaching up to the small scar before her hand covered her mouth, her eyes pressed tight. If it'd been only lust she had felt, she didn't think she should still be so affected.

The dreadful William had been correct in his accusation. There were true feelings there. How long would they stay, muddying her emotions?

She'd come to trust him. Bash. The Urchin captain. Not in that he wouldn't hurt anyone, but in that he wouldn't hurt her. Did that make her a bad person? That she might have turned a blind eye to his past and present? But what if his future had looked the same?

Hypotheticals, really. It didn't matter now. Yanking free the blade, she strode to the terrace doors with purpose. She didn't need the wind reminding her of what she'd lost. She grabbed ahold of the handles, but when she would have muscled them shut against the elements, she froze instead.

Because there should have been light outside.

Not lights on the terrace because she'd never bothered with any, but light beyond it. Streetlights. Starlight. She could feel the moon above her, but directly ahead there was nothing. Only darkness. And it was absolute.

Goosebumps littered Alora's skin. She held the knife in front of her like a warning. What the devil was this conjuring? Was her mind finally on the verge of collapse?

But the darkness didn't waver. Nor did it make any move against her. As the seconds stretched, she began to feel less threatened and more wary. Confused.

"Are you smoke?" she asked of it, moving nearer. "A shadow?"

The dark didn't shift with the wind, and there was nothing to cast a shadow. Alora held the knife out farther and stepped closer, until only the smallest fraction of movement would push it through. "It can't be," she murmured to herself.

She shoved the knife inside.

She couldn't see the blade, nor her arm, as it was swallowed, and she pressed farther, sure that any moment, she'd feel the point scrape against the terrace's stone edge. When it did meet resistance, however, it was more forgiving, and from somewhere she couldn't see, came a noise.

Like a hissed intake of breath.

"I can tell by the grip alone you've not listened to me and learned to use it."

She jolted, faltering, and when the feel of a gloved hand enclosed her wrist, she allowed the blade to clatter to the stones.

"*Bash?*"

In the next heartbeat Alora found herself tugged inside the dark.

Both her wrists were captured. In the pitch black, it was all she could sense. She squirmed against her constraints, the broken light leaving her disoriented and overwhelmed. Or maybe that was the feel of her hands now, pressed against a leather-clad chest. A familiar current traveled all through her, warm and electrifying, and her breath shuddered with ragged gasps. She felt like she'd run for miles.

"Bash, is it?"

His teasing was gentle, but still Alora hesitated. "Am I dreaming? I'm not sure I like it if I am." His voice was a perfect, rasping replica of what it was in life. *Heaven help me if this is a dream.*

"No, this isn't a dream. Though now I'm interested to know what you *do* dream of."

Which was exactly something she thought a dream would say. With her free hand, she reached up, feeling her way, along the fabric of his shirt and the leather of his coat, up to his neck. She reached beneath his hood. She could feel the hitch in his breath against her chest as her fingertips brushed across the raised row of scars.

Then her hand crept higher.

She found the edge of his mask and soon discovered the clasp at the back of his head. It loosened with one quick movement, and Alora tugged it the remainder of the way until it hung around his neck. "I thought you'd *died*," she whispered, full of relief and pain and, mortifyingly, something a lot like *longing*.

"You told me not to," he said, and it was *his* voice. Bash's voice. The rough, low pitch remained. The rasp was gone.

She pressed her forehead to his chest then, a sob breaking free from her lips. And only once he pulled his coat aside, wrapping her up against the thin shirt beneath, did she realize he smelled of something she knew. Had grown to crave. Of vetiver. She breathed that scent in now like it was her only air. She felt him curve around her, and her fingers stayed tangled in the folds of his shirt. Some wary part of her thought he might not yet be real.

"You've kept so many secrets," she said, an edge creeping into her voice.

"I know."

"Don't I deserve to know them?"

"I think so."

She scrunched her eyes closed, thinking of all Ellie Turkens had said, of her warnings and advice. "Are you really a devil then? Have I chosen wrong?"

She refused to cry anymore, though her breaths remained unsteady. She sniffed against him, and he tucked her in further. "Not with you, Alora."

He didn't answer either question, she noticed. *Damn.* Perhaps she was a bad person after all, because in that moment, it sounded like enough to her.

She angled her chin, though she couldn't see even his outline. "Can you fly?"

She felt his huffed breath against her nose. "No?"

"Then how are you on my terrace?"

"I walked the ledge."

"That's hardly wide enough for a cat!"

His hands left her back to skim down her hips, only to return to her arms, neck, and lastly cupping her face. "I was motivated."

She wondered how her eyes looked to him now. Wide? Her pupils dilated until their color was more black than gray? And then she remembered. "I thought the Urchin captain's eyes were dark, with a rasping voice and a certain unfavorable opinion about a Potions and Peculiarities shopkeeper."

"You're not incorrect about my eyes. As far as the voice, the mask is enchanted, another facet of disguise. And I stand by my opinion of the shopkeeper. He can be an idiot. Like not telling you how he felt the moment you'd come to his doorstep, politely demanding a distraction."

Alora's cheeks warmed over how forward she'd been. But it was nothing compared to the heat she felt everywhere else inside her now. "That *was* rather idiotic of him," she teased.

His nose met the tip of hers. "Please say you'll come to me and only me if you ever need another."

"I suppose so. I can't imagine anyone doing it better," she said, and her breath caught when his lips met her temple. He hummed his approval there. He moved to her cheek. When she breathed again at last, it was jagged. She couldn't believe how easily affected she was. It was not ever like this. Not with anyone else. She stammered, "Is your name really Bash?"

"Bash Merridon. I don't suppose I properly introduced myself the first time." His lips settled upon her opposite cheek. "I'm sorry," he said, against her skin.

Her mouth turned toward his, a pull she couldn't ignore. "I thought it might be Ezra."

"Ezra? Why?"

"The Urchins said he had died. And I'd seen the body behind Opulence, and William said it was you."

Because her hands had found themselves gripping his waist, Alora felt the moment Bash stiffened beneath her fingers. He had to have been built of nothing but muscle, to become so rigid. She frowned. "Did I—"

"*William* spoke to you?"

Alora almost reached to his mouth again, sure the mask must have somehow been replaced. His voice rasped with barely contained fury, the cold of it raking across her skin. She shivered.

"He found me outside the Room of Desire."

"For what purpose?"

She knew he could feel her hesitation, sure as she could sense everything rising inside him. And she wasn't frightened of him, precisely, but more the chain of events she might ignite next. "He told me you were dead. Then he tried to—" The Urchin captain's grip tightened upon her arms until they almost hurt, then they dropped away. She felt him move back. "Bash…"

Suddenly, her wrist was in his hand again, though this time she could feel his gloved fingers roving across the skin. Too late, she realized it must have bruised. She'd guessed it would.

"He did this?"

Alora winced at the whisper of death in his words. "I hit him over the head right after."

She'd thought that would appease him. She was wrong.

"Is he dead?"

"No, of course not!"

"Then it isn't enough."

"Surely you wouldn't! Merridon said I shouldn't be worried over him anymore. That no further harm would come to me while on Opulence's grounds." She clung to his arm, desperate, but felt him slipping through her fingers.

"And what about outside them?"

"Outside them?"

She could see again. A gradual change. Black to gray to the soft light of the moon. When she was reoriented at last, she found the night densest at the ledge and ran toward it. "*Bash*," she hissed.

He didn't respond. Instead, she heard something unexpected. The soft rattle of a latch. A scraping of metal against metal.

The angle was all wrong to see her front door, so she sprinted from the terrace and through the flat, nearly crashing into the door as the rug bunched beneath her feet. She opened the peephole—

To a leather fist meeting a clean-shaven jaw.

Chapter Thirty-One

Alora caught a glimpse of auburn hair before it jerked away from view, a visceral grunt of pain the only sound. *William is here?*

There had been no knock. No calling of her name. Instead, she'd heard the doorknob rattle. She'd heard scraping. *Like a lock being picked.*

Alora's body flushed white hot. Then she flung open the door.

Bash had given up his fracturing of light. His dark hood hung until it caressed William's face, his glove around the other man's throat, squeezing. She didn't know if he'd replaced his mask or if he was simply that angry, but his voice scraped up his throat as he said, "I should have done this from the beginning."

William choked, a gurgling sound escaping his mouth that made Alora's stomach twist. He folded backward, his back touching the stoop's edge, his head and shoulders open to the free air on the opposite side. Beneath the lamplight spilling from behind her, his sea-glass gaze caught hers and held.

Once, she'd thought that if William grew bored enough, he'd set her afire alongside him. She'd brushed it off as an unwelcome thought, without meaning. But she looked into his eyes now, and she saw the truth of it.

If he were to go down, he would bring her right with him.

"Alora," he gasped.

"Do not *speak to her.*"

William's eyes shuttered. A heartbeat later, his knee came up. He risked toppling over the side, but it was one he took, and when it connected with Bash's middle, a rush of air burst from Alora at the same moment a grunt of pain escaped the Urchin captain. His grip faltered.

William slipped free like an eel, sinking to a crouch to avoid the swipe of Bash's fist. When he surged upward again, it was with a blow of his own, the sound excruciating as it connected with the Urchin's jaw. William bled from a new cut on his cheekbone and his lower lip. The rest of him was clear and without so much as a bruise; he'd been seen by a healer, and a good one at that. It angered her that she carried the marks of his fingers on her wrist, but he showed nothing from her.

As awful as William's punch had sounded, Bash didn't falter. In seconds, he swept his brother up about the middle, sending him crashing to the white stone in a lung-crushing fall. This time, William's knees were useless, as the Urchin straddled his hips and pressed a black-clad forearm to his windpipe.

"Did he...tell you," ground out William. "That he...used to douse...me...with oil...and set it...alight?"

However it was possible, Bash pressed harder. A gurgle left William, saliva running from the corner of his mouth. He tried turning to the side, but Bash followed him, relentless. Alora was sure she'd vomit over the horror of it.

"Bash..." she whispered.

For the second time, William's eyes fluttered closed.

"Bash!"

A hiss of pain, of surprise, echoed from beneath Bash's hood. A moment later, and he was rolling away, his hand pressed to his side.

William coughed and spluttered, curling into a fetal position as his hands encircled his throat. When Bash staggered back, Alora caught a glimpse of a handle. Or a hilt.

It protruded from his side, embedded fully.

White noise built inside her head.

William jerked when rope lashed his ankles together—his wrists too. He stared down at them in disbelief before his gaze sought hers. She didn't allow him a glance. Instead, she rushed toward Bash, to where he stood, his hand reaching to grip the blade. With a curse, he yanked it free. The knife was wicked, serrated, and long. A blade meant for killing. It clattered to the stones.

Alora immediately added her hand to his to stem the flow from the wound.

"I don't think it's healthy to bleed so much in a single day," he murmured.

"It isn't," said Alora, panicked. "Where is the Urchin healer?"

"Likely at Opulence."

He pressed his opposite hand atop hers, sandwiching her fingers between. She stacked her opposite, too, for good measure. Even so, she could feel wet against her palms. His blood, again.

She should be thankful he was still standing, she supposed.

But then again, *no*, she wasn't thankful at all. She pulled her hands free, which the Urchin grunted at. "Bring up your shirt."

"Are you going to stitch me closed?"

Alora shuddered at the idea. "Absolutely not. You need someone to heal whatever is cut apart internally. But I can bind it at least. Our hands seem to be useless."

"As useless as they may be, I don't think I can release it."

"Fine," said Alora. "I'll do it then." Reaching beneath his coat, she hauled at his shirt. When it came free from his trousers, she imagined every button undone.

"A trick I'd like to see under different circumstances," whispered Bash, and cleared his throat weakly.

"Stop it." She scowled as she pushed the fabric aside. In her hands were now stacked bandages and wrappings. She folded them quickly. "I'm ready. Let go."

He did as told, his hands coming free to fall at his side. Alora finished pulling the cloth from his skin, though it came away slow and sticking. Her mouth filled with saliva, but she swallowed it down. She was too proud to empty her stomach in front of William.

When the wound was at last revealed to her, it was deceptively small. Blood pulsed from its opening, not far above his hip, coloring his pale skin red. "Hold this all away from your waist so I can wrap it. If you can," she added, gentler than before.

"Anything for you," said Bash, but she could hear the difference in his voice; it was tight with pain.

Still, he hauled up the fabric, his coat and shirt knotted in his grip until his entire torso was revealed to her. Alora pressed the bandages to the wound at once. His muscles bunched just beneath the surface as he hissed over the discomfort she'd unfortunately caused. "Just a moment more," she said quietly so as to bely her terror.

While holding the bandage in place, she worked the wrapping around his back. She had to press up against him to reach, and his smooth skin was warm where it touched her. Her fingers brushed against his back, side, then abdomen, and her gaze dipped to his low-slung trousers before making another pass. She cleared her throat.

With the bandage tied off and secure, Alora stepped back. He released his clothing immediately, but being as it was no longer buttoned, his shirt hung open on either side. He made no move to fix it, and his sculpted chest showed thin, white lines now. She grimaced in remembering the specter wolves' bloodied marks.

"You need a doctor. Stay here. I'll call for one," she said, meaning to hurry away down the steps.

"No." Bash reached to stop her as she passed by him, his arm corralling her about the waist. "Necros is below. I'll ride to Opulence."

"You really think you can make it all that way? The doctor will be closer."

"With this bandage, I could probably make Eirian."

His tone was light, but Alora couldn't suppress the involuntary shudder at the mere mention of the name.

"What is it?" he asked.

"Nothing. Only I don't appreciate you making a mockery over nearly dying again. For all I know, you could pass out from blood loss on the road, and nobody would find you until morning."

"Necros won't allow me to fall."

"I hate that name," muttered Alora.

Bash ignored her opinion, choosing instead to make quick work of his shirt's buttons. His breaths were labored by the time he was through, his hand coming up to press against his side. His sigh was long-suffering as he reached inside his coat. Alora gasped at what he removed.

It was Mortimer's weapon. Or one just like it. Bash pushed a dart into the chamber.

"What are you doing?" she said, and her voice shook.

Was this what he planned to reveal to me that day? Obviously it was not a pen, but it would certainly have relayed a message. It was so much worse than a baton, its own sort of death.

The Urchin captain paused, taking the time to scan her face. She could see his eyes beneath the hood, and they were narrowed. "Taking care of William, once and for all. What? Did you think I would use this on you?"

"I…"

Bash's expression fell to darkness before he turned from her.

William hadn't spoken since he'd been on the verge of suffocation. But now, seeing his brother step over him, he attempted again.

His voice was rough as gravel dirt, grating up his throat. Alora winced in hearing it, certain the activity must hurt even worse than it sounded. *He heals quicker than all of us*, she reminded herself, lest she get too upset.

"You can't do this," pleaded William. "I'm as much his son as you are."

"As in you are as useful to him as I am? Don't tell me you believe he harbors some affection for you? If he does, it's kept well hidden. The only thing he'll miss is the draw you brought to Door Eighteen. Nothing more."

They were such harsh parting words. Alora covered her mouth, though it wasn't enough to hide her sharp intake of air. The Urchin's hood shifted toward her a fraction before turning back.

"I'm not a *fool*. I know what we were traded for."

Bash knelt beside him. "Then be thankful I'm releasing you from this prison at last. And who knows, Brother. Perhaps I'll follow you out afterward."

Alora only managed one step forward before the dart met William's neck. He didn't release even a grunt of pain before his eyes closed. For all appearances, he might have been sleeping. The silence stretched on. From a street away, she could make out the sound of carriage wheels. From beyond that, she heard a nightingale. It all sounded so *ordinary*. Still, Bash knelt unmoving beside William.

Alora sniffed, and it was loud in the quiet. "Are you well?"

"Well enough," he replied. With a groan, he pushed to his feet, then bent. His arms made to lift beneath William's.

"No, don't do that." She hurried forward and pressed against Bash's shoulder. "I'll help." A stretcher materialized beneath the performer. She reached to grab hold at his feet. "Where do we go?"

"Down the steps, to start."

Alora nodded as Bash gripped the handles near William's head. Together, they lifted, and William was light as a feather between them. She'd gone above what she would have normally done; the imagined stretcher gave lightness to whatever was inside it. Bash huffed an incredulous breath.

At the bottom of the stairs, in a shadowed alleyway, they found Necros waiting. He stared at them with a calculating expression, so much so that Alora wondered if perhaps he wasn't like other horses. She lifted as high as she could and observed Bash ease his brother onto the horse's back so that William draped sideways across the animal. The stretcher clattered to the ground when it was done, Alora dropping it without care.

"You're taking him to Opulence? Won't everyone have questions?"

"You forget what I am." With a moan grinding behind his teeth, Bash lifted into the saddle. When his breathing steadied after some moments, she felt the shift of his attention to her. "You told me once that this project brings you hope. Is your dream worth seeing it through?"

Alora frowned up at him. "Are you asking me to abandon it?"

"No," he said. "But it's still a question I would like the answer to. I know you well enough now to realize your choices aren't unwise."

She snorted. "Truly? All of them?"

His tone turned grave. "Perhaps not. You did choose to associate with me, after all."

"*That* was hardly a choice," Alora said, wanting to diffuse the darkness rising between them. But it didn't seem to work. She wished she could see his expression behind the silence, but as it was the shadows were deep in the alley, where the moon couldn't reach, and his hood eclipsed even those. "No, the project isn't worth the money for my shop. Not at all. But I'll see it through anyway, as my reasons have changed."

Necros shifted beneath the stagnant weight. She could tell the creature yearned to move on. Bash took up the reins. "I won't tell you to run and abandon it then, even if I'd feel infinitely better if you decided to do so. I will say, at least, don't allow him to sign you to another contract."

"I won't," said Alora, shaking her head vehemently. If she got her way in the end, Merridon would never be allowed to offer another contract to anyone ever again.

Necros was granted several steps forward before he was halted a second time. At the toss of his head, she shuffled backward, wondering if Bash had ever been bitten. "I would never hurt you, Alora. I want you to realize."

Her mind immediately went to the weapon concealed somewhere on his person. *I know*, she nearly said. What she did say was, "Even if you thought I would be helped in the end?"

"Even then."

She stared down at her bare feet, every part of her body suddenly weighed down and impossibly heavy. She bit at her lip. "Hurry on now, before your bandage gives way."

"I have the utmost faith in it." His head dipped and Necros sidestepped, eager to be off. "Really, I have the utmost faith in you."

The shadows deepened, the light breaking, and all Alora could make out was a vast darkness before it was gone.

Chapter Thirty-Two

That night, Alora stood between them—Bash and William—in a nightmare. Bash's eyes had grown black. So did the air. It pulsed around him, circling like a tornado, and then he was gone within it, and he took William too.

It lasted for only a heartbeat.

When the dark disappeared, William lay on the ground. His skin was blackened, bubbled with blisters, his mouth open in a scream no one could hear, and his eyes were wide and blue and tormented.

Bash stood beside him, a torch extinguished. Laughing.

Alora awoke; she breathed in nothing but smoke.

"Who is your friend there?" questioned Mr. Ichibald.

Alora braced herself against a wardrobe, her breath rife with relief as she was at last able to maneuver herself away from her hovering escort. He was an Urchin she'd seen before at Potions and Peculiarities. Middle-aged, if she were to guess, with blonde hair and slashing dark eyebrows. He was the only one of the four who'd questioned her enchantment. The only one to admonish Mr. Salvoy. His gaze, whenever she noticed it upon her, was uncomfortably scrutinizing. He was an observant sort, hunting for secrets.

"Oh. That's my driver, being as I have so much to transport. George doesn't do well with excessive loads, and my cart is too small. Thank you for opening early for me, by the way." She smiled at Mr. Ichibald with charm.

The proprietor promptly returned it. He was a portly fellow at age fifty and worked closer with traders and merchants than anyone she knew. Also, he dressed in a spectacular way, like one foot remained instore, but the other was halfway to a show.

He spent a moment adjusting his yellow cravat, considering the driver making for them. "It's no problem. Not for one of my best customers. Have you chosen which you like better then?"

"Yes. I think this chaise will do perfectly."

"You there!" Mr. Ichibald hollered to the Urchin, which earned him a flat look in return. Alora doubted he'd ever been addressed as such in his adult life. "You look like a brawny fellow. Between you and Percy, I'm sure you'll be able to manage loading Miss Pennigrim's purchase."

Her assigned driver worked his jaw but eventually offered a curt nod. When Mr. Ichibald's assistant emerged from the back, cobwebs all in his hair, the Urchin waited for the other man to bend first. Only then did he reach down himself. With hardly a strain, the pair made off with Door Twenty-five's newest furniture.

"Bit uppity for a driver," murmured Mr. Ichibald.

Alora ignored him. The man was also a horrific gossip.

"I'm also in need of four sconces, two lamps, an end table, and an ottoman."

"Any art?"

"No, thank you." She'd decided a while ago that nothing would hang on the walls. She didn't want anything to distract or transport the visitor away. If they came to the Room of Desire, they should remain firmly planted in the dream that led them.

"Well enough." Mr. Ichibald strode away. "If you'll follow me, I've just gotten this lamp in yesterday. Perhaps you'll—"

Alora followed only to be brought up short. A tapestry hung against the wall. It was tall and wide, a statement piece to be sure, its borders stitched in silver. She stepped closer to it, and noticed the more she studied it, the more grounded she felt. How calm. Her heart, for the first time all morning, beat at a usual pace.

It depicted a singular cloud at the forefront, near the top. One that was gray and white and puffy without being overly so. The background had been saturated a deep blue. When she closed her eyes, she could see it still, and a small smile tugged at her lips.

It was the exact opposite of everything Marshall Merridon adored.

"Miss Pennigrim? Have you changed your mind?"

She glanced over to the store's proprietor, to the lamp held fast in his hand. "Yes, Mister Ichibald. I'd like this tapestry."

"Right away."

Gone from the shop, and not long later, Alora noticed she didn't feel well. Not at all. If she didn't know better, she would have guessed she'd eaten something poor for breakfast. As it were, she'd not been able to stomach breakfast at all. She massaged at the growing discomfort pressing upon her insides with a wince, her gaze cast to the early morning routines of her fellow townsfolk.

The Urchin maneuvered the streets with ease, though the wagon took up nearly the entire thing. He didn't try to speak to her, same as Mr. Salvoy, but he also didn't seem angered at his assignment as Mr. Salvoy had been. She wanted to ask if Bash had assigned him to her, but that would be unwise. For one, she didn't think she'd be able to stop herself from following up with, *And how is he? All healed? Where is William? Locked up or wandering, lost?*

Have any Urchins gone missing lately? Or been recently found?

No, it was best to keep quiet.

She covered her mouth against a yawn, her eyes fluttering closed. She knew she looked a fright with her hair pulled back messily and not a stitch of color to her cheeks. Purple crescents swelled beneath her eyes, so pronounced they mimicked bruises. She'd not fallen asleep until near-dawn, and from there, that godawful nightmare had found her.

They turned onto Rune Street. Alora tried to remain rigid, but her stomach was too heavy and sick, and her mind too tired. Not even the fresh flower scents and the wafting bread smells were enough to entice her upright. She slumped in her seat.

Books and Nibbles neared. She could see the closed shutters and shifting sign. She pressed her lips tight, her arms encircling her waist. *Please be all right*, she thought out into the universe. Then the door opened.

A pink slipper preceded a stockinged ankle, which was then followed by a skirt patterned with owls and a violet top. Ellie Turkens stepped onto the porch with a broom only to turn her back to them. The sign flipped from *End* to *Begin*.

Alora lurched to sitting before she could think better of it, staring intently at the back of Ellie's gray head—at the stark bandage wrapped around it. *Surely it can't be.* Alora didn't dare look at the Urchin beside her, the one who had issued the names, and thus the order, to have Ellie Turken's memories removed, but she could feel his attention shift toward the bookshop's owner all the same.

Ellie spotted them herself a heartbeat later. At first, Alora thought perhaps her eyes narrowed, but then she winced, her hand coming up to the side of her skull as if it pained her. As if there really were sutures hidden under there, tethering a new wound closed.

"Such a frail state, isn't it? Being old," said the Urchin. "You'd think the people of Enver would retire at a respectable age."

Alora's fingers dug into the fabric of her Opulence-gold cloak. She didn't know if Ellie knew who she was beneath it. Her voice came out harder than she meant, the material pinching between her hands. She wanted to shred it. "She makes the strongest tea and the best tomato and cheese sandwiches. Also, I think she knows every book ever written."

Ellie continued to watch them as they ambled by, her lips pursed all the while.

"I hate tomato and cheese sandwiches."

Alora could only shake her head, sick to death over these people with whom she was forced to keep company. They'd only caused her heartache, illness, and injury. Truly, there was nothing she could be thankful for.

Her hand came up to press over her heart. Maybe if she squeezed hard enough, she'd purge herself of whatever anchoring barbs the Urchin captain had implanted there. They must be poisonous, whatever they were. That must be the only plausible explanation for how one moment she felt she'd die if she didn't feel the jolt of his touch again, and the next she wished to draw inspiration from his name and bash his head apart for the harm he'd caused. She refused to acknowledge that it was much more the former rather than the latter now—a matter of self preservation.

Hearts were fickle things. She'd read that once. One more day and the contract would be over. She'd let Bash go then. She'd have to, being as how she planned to destroy them all.

"Let us hope our journey is less adventuresome than your last, Miss Pennigrim."

Alora glanced at the Urchin out of the corner of her eye before shifting her attention forward again. "Yes, well, so long as specter wolves aren't vengeful creatures." Her words were clipped clean from her teeth. She wanted no part in any conversation. Her stomach twisted, and she gripped it harder.

They left town by means of the little-used western road. Another fork, and they'd turn onto Opulence Mansion's enchanted lane.

Go home, pulsed her stomach. *Drink something warm, cuddle your rabbit. Lock your door and soak in the bath for hours.*

She wished she could listen.

"I wouldn't know," continued the Urchin, oblivious to her discomfort. "Though I'm relieved to think that should we encounter them again, I am in your company. I heard you saved the day."

Alora clenched her jaw. Because she knew exactly what he'd heard, and it wasn't that. "I hardly saved anything."

"You didn't manage to open the gate?"

"No."

The Urchin hummed beside her. Annoyed or amused, she couldn't tell. She didn't look at him. "I also heard you assigned quite the title to your driver that day."

At this, Alora swung to him, confused. Her body protested the sudden movement with a bout of nausea. She breathed it away. "What in the devil are you talking about?"

His eyebrows slashed even further. It was an impressive effect. She felt almost frightened. "You called him an Urchin. Now, I wonder, why would you do that?"

Alora swallowed, drumming up what time she could to think of a reply. "Maybe I called him an urchin. As in a wretch, a miscreant. He wouldn't listen to me about the specter wolves."

"Don't you realize that's an unfortunate choice of word, especially here in Enver?" The present Urchin worked his hand beneath his coat, grasping at something she couldn't see, though she could guess at what it was.

"You're about to hear a slew of unfortunate words if you don't get me to Opulence quickly. I've a heap of work to do for Master Merridon, and he's made it crystal clear he's counting on me to see it through." The stare she angled at the driver was pure venom, daring him to intervene in his master's plans.

She smiled, triumphant, when he backed down, his eyebrows easing to their normal position.

"I would be wary if I were you, Miss Pennigrim."

She couldn't help but laugh, though it pained her immensely to do so. She looped her arms tight about her middle. *Threats on threats. Is that all men are good for?* But no, not all men. Mr. Whitters was a notable exception.

The Urchin, bewildered by her response, flicked the reins. Their pace quickened until the sound of the horses' shoes clipping on the lane eclipsed everything else.

Chapter Thirty-Three

A pleasant breeze rustled the perfectly trimmed topiaries of Opulence Mansion. Alora made for the stairs as the sound washed over her, a strange shushing through clipped leaves, and when it nestled in her chest thereafter, she felt herself thrum as if she were a part of it. She'd done that somehow—broken whatever barrier Merridon had forged overtop the grounds—but only trepidation greeted her now, not pride.

The Urchin had disappeared, abandoning her without asking if she would require help. Probably off reporting to the surly management and leaving her without hope of assistance. Alora cursed him and all the rest as her stomach continued to beg retreat. She lifted the wagon's latch, lowering the back.

The new topiary called to her curiosity, covered now by a white sheet, and staked firmly into the ground. Had Mr. Macaw finished it then? She wondered if it would be revealed tomorrow, at her contract's end. She tried to dredge up the excitement such a reveal warranted for someone as kind as Mr. Macaw, and almost succeeded.

She trudged up the stairs, her shoulders curved inward.

Madam Feebledire answered her knocks.

"Back again, are we?"

Alora wanted to scowl and gnash out a scathing 'obviously', but she could not. Instead, she forced an almost pretty smile. "The final pieces. If all goes smoothly, I'll be done a day early. Today might be the last you see of me."

"Oh, I doubt that," said Madam Feebledire with a quirk of her lips, but her tone said she was anything but amused.

Alora yearned to pinch the woman's long nose. "Is Mister Macaw available, perchance? I've got quite a lot that requires muscle."

Madam Feebledire's lips settled back into their comfortable frown. "I'm afraid Mister Macaw is no longer employed at Opulence Mansion."

Alora blinked at her, stunned to silence. She watched as Madam Feebledire removed a small notebook and an equally tiny pencil from her form-fitting vest. Though the woman's attention seemed diverted by the checklist, Alora could sense her reaction wasn't entirely missed. Eventually, Alora cleared her throat.

"Did something…" she trailed off, then straightened her shoulders. "I hope under mutual circumstances."

"Hardly," said Madam Feebledire, her pencil light and quick. *Check, check, check.*

Alora's mouth worked around words she didn't have the power to say. What could she ask that Madam Feebledire would answer? She glanced over her shoulder to the topiary standing firm beneath the breeze. She could see the vague outline beneath. A human shape.

"That's finished, at least," Madam Feebledire said, noticing Alora's shifted attention. As if Alora must only care that the man completed his work before departing. "As for the unloading of the wagon, I'll send someone to you. Be patient."

Alora was left without a chance to respond. The door closed on her open mouth, an inch from her nose. She breathed harshly against it.

Bash had managed to save Mortimer back then, but she doubted he could manage it a second time. Which meant he hadn't known about Mr. Macaw when he'd come to her, or he'd chosen not to tell her purposefully. But he was the Urchin captain—surely, he must have known?

The idea of the strong and shy Mr. Macaw out there alone at this very moment, wandering lost without even his name to guide him, sent a wave of dizziness through Alora that she couldn't fight. Her hands came up to the doors, grounding her. She stayed that way until a throat cleared.

The woman beside the wagon was of medium height and broad—a perfect stranger. She wore her hair tied back in a severe knot, and her arms were corded with muscle beneath her crimson vest. She pushed a dolly ahead of her, and when her eyes met Alora's they reminded her of the new guard. *Don't speak to me*, warned her expression, and Alora wilted a little more upon seeing it.

The new groundskeeper waited at the back of the wagon as Alora carefully stacked the crates, then pushed off without a backward glance.

Alora remained behind, her hands enclosed over the packaged tapestry. She felt the whip of the topiary's sheeting against her skin, a lash with every snap of the fabric. When she could take it no more, she sent a furious thought out, snapping the tethers between it and the stakes, sending the fabric flying free. It took three gusts of the breeze to lift it fully, each one revealing a little more than the last. But finally, Alora could see it—all of it—and it was indeed finished, detailed beyond any of the other twenty-four behind.

It depicted a person, as she'd suspected. Their head was tipped to the sky, one hand pressed to their temple as if in quiet rumination. The other arm, however, was bent at the elbow, palm out, and below it spilled all manner of objects: books, coin, a heart. They pooled into nondescript shapes at the base, causing Alora to wish to step closer and discover each one.

The Room of Desire had a token angel, for that is what the figure reminded her of. An angel, a goddess, something otherworldly.

It was beautifully crafted; a true work of art. Mr. Macaw had certainly outdone himself in his craftsmanship.

That thought sobered her. She pulled her gaze away. Hefting the package into her hands, she made for the stairs again. This time, she would continue all the way through to Door Twenty-five and finally be done with this entire thing.

Alora held the original lamp in her hands, lit for the last time within this room. It was an ugly thing by Opulence's standards, a bulky and scratched copper. It leaked. She hadn't realized it until now, that it dripped from a crack in the base, oil seeping into the pads of her fingers. She hurriedly wiped them clean.

The project was done, and it was lovely. The oversized chaise atop an ivory rug. The maple accents of the ottoman, the end tables, and the trim. No single piece shouted for attention, but together, the room demanded it. For a visitor to sit and think and dream. Alora worried for a moment that the tapestry might not fit the space, but it did, somehow, breathing light into a room built in the dark. If she didn't have lamp oil all over her fingers, she might lay down and use her final, remaining time in the Room of Desire to imagine a world without Opulence. How would that be? Just to scrub it from existence?

A slow clap had her spinning on her heels.

"Bravo, Miss Pennigrim. Bravo."

Alora steadied herself against the presence of Marshall Merridon. The man was dressed as any other day, though the glow of the lamplight flickered against the gold of his buttons and turned his eyes molten. His smile dripped charm, pressing upon her until she thought in the back of her head of sinking to the floor.

"Thank you, Master Merridon," she managed. "It's finished."

"And a day early too. Sensational."

She fought against revealing how his incredulity irked her. Even so, her jaw throbbed. She tracked his perusal of the room as he bent to every piece she'd picked, how he examined the pattern on the walls.

"Your attention to detail is astonishing. Why, this might be my new favorite room." He stepped over the spot of William's attack, the one now scrubbed clean of his blood. "Did you always know you possessed such a talent?"

She should be blushing prettily by now, but all Alora could manage were two angry blotches of color in her cheeks. "Not always, but fairly young."

"Yes. I suppose that is how it often works, isn't it?"

She didn't bother with a reply. Instead, she studied him as he studied the tapestry, his posture straight, hands clasped behind his back. It was the only piece he might take issue with, and a part of her did want him to rip it down. Really, it didn't belong here in Opulence. It was too free.

But he surprised her by saying nothing. Instead, he turned back around, and this time, rather than studying the art, he studied *her*.

Alora fidgeted under his scrutiny. "If you're satisfied with things as they are then I'm happy to call this project completed within the specified timeframe. Thank you for this…incomparable opportunity, Master Merridon."

Marshall Merridon eased once more into his charming smile, and Alora saw it for what it was: a mask. His smile was the same as hers, honed and perfected, and often entirely without merit. Alora didn't understand why she suddenly felt upended into an ice bath. "You're quite welcome, Miss Pennigrim, though I should say *thank you* just the same. I do have one little change, though, if I may?"

"By all means." Alora moved from his way as he walked around the room to step into the hall. He returned a moment later with a crate, smaller than any she'd brought.

The door clicked closed as he worked the lid. "I thought this would be a charming addition. Something to mark the room."

He motioned her closer, and she took the smallest step forward. A flicker of something entered his gaze and was gone as he bridged the gap between them instead. Alora couldn't help but peer into the crate as he lifted an intriguing crystal skull free.

She frowned, sure she'd seen it before.

But where had she encountered it? Her memories were blurry, slopping around in her head.

Somewhere dark and uninviting. And something else. Something about eyes…perhaps?

But the only eyes she could conjure were ones of mossy green. Then where—? It was in that moment of puzzlement that the ruby orbs of the skull ensnared her own. They swirled, enticing, down there in the depths. She stepped closer to inspect it better, to find the source of the maelstrom. Was that a pinprick of fire at the center? She wanted to see.

Merridon's voice seemed very far away from where she was, surrounded by crimson waves. Still, his words permeated her mind.

"Alora Pennigrim, cheers to your completed contract. As promised, 100,000 evergolds. And a membership for one year, paid in full. Take them."

As if a tether had roped itself around her arm, Alora reached for the proffered envelope, and it was thick with her fulfilled hopes. A sturdy, golden card was tied to the front, pretty and official, with her name embossed upon it.

Alora Pennigrim

Member of Opulence Mansion

"Now, I want you to sit."

Alora promptly sat on the floor, her legs folding in front of her, the envelope pressed to her chest. Merridon cursed. "Not on the *floor*, on the chaise."

Alora rose from the floor to sit on the chaise. She settled back until she grew comfortable. *No,* she thought, suddenly. *What are you doing, you idiot! You need to run!*

But her limbs were no longer hers to command. She tucked her ankles back.

"You've pleased me with your talent. Impressed me, rather more. I've witnessed what you are capable of, and so I've decided to present you with a new contract." From the inner pocket of his jacket, he produced a folded bit of paper and a pen. "Read it aloud."

Smack it away!

Alora took the page from him, and began to read, "*I, Alora Pennigrim, the undersigned, do agree to a lifetime commitment to Opulence Mansion and its owner, Marshall Merridon. I agree to fulfill, to the best of my ability, any imagined desire hereby brought forth by a paying member of Opulence or its management, with the exception of those that might harm the grounds, the employees, Marshall Merridon, or cause incapacitation to myself. I declare that my enchantment may not be utilized otherwise. I declare I will not travel between my accommodations and Door Twenty-five without an Opulence escort. Lastly, I agree, I will abide by all further rules set forth by management as they pertain to Opulence Mansion performers as a whole.*"

"Wonderful," crooned Master Merridon. "Now sign."

Alora screamed inside as she accepted the pen from Marshall Merridon, as she signed her name with a practiced flourish.

"You will refer to me as 'Master' from this moment on." He plucked the pen and paper from her fingers, returning them to his jacket pocket, and laughed so self-assuredly that Alora yearned to wring his head from his neck. "Thanks to you, I'm about to raise my prices. Just think, anything you can imagine, yours for the keeping; word should spread quick. What. A. Gift." At that, he chucked her under the chin. Only he stepped forward right after, gripping her jaw and turning her face to the lamplight. "You look a bit worse for wear though, don't you? Hardly a goddess of gift-bringing and desire. Never matter, we'll have you fixed up properly."

The skull was gone, returned to its crate, but she could still see its eyes, the swirl of red wishing for her silence, to not ask questions. She somehow managed one, though it burned up her throat.

"Why?"

"Why? *Why?* Because I can! What other reason do I need? Fine, I'll tell you, and only you, because I know you can keep a secret. I discovered you some time ago in Enver. Do you know how? Because I'm enchanted myself, Miss Pennigrim. But my enchantment is unique in that I can sense *others'* enchantment. I knew what you were and what you were capable of long before you stepped foot on Opulence ground. How's that for a twist? I knew of every performer here, sometimes the moment I met them, sometimes before then. Young Miss Lennox Flowers, Miss Noelnina Dynasti, Mister Gilbert Velfoy...it's a scent in the air which I follow like a map, leading straight to you. Even my own sons, raggedy street urchins I exchanged for a thimble of memory oil each. A light-breaker and a regenerator? Their minder was a colossal dunce for not knowing what he had. And no one knows the truth. No one knows the truth of it but you and me, and you cannot tell. What an empire you will help me build, Miss Pennigrim. Why, even your topiary out front is magnificent. Now sit tight. I'll send someone for you."

He managed two strides to the door before he spun with a snap of his fingers.

"Ah, another thing. Should any member try to steal you away for themselves, imagine them maimed, and yourself as well. Also, if anyone should recognize you from your life before, you are to tell them you dreamt of performing at Opulence since you were a child. Heaven knows I'm only here to make dreams come true."

A quick check on the crystal skull, from which Alora recoiled, then Merridon replaced the lid with a dooming creak. He surveyed the room a final time, and Alora could see his smile, one of a monster fully sated and satisfied. His attention landed on the copper lamp in the corner, burning away.

"I wish for that lamp to disappear. Do that for me, my Goddess of Desire."

The wish pushed against her like a pressure in her mind. She'd no choice but to see it done. The lamp winked out of existence.

For the second time in her life, she'd caused something to vanish. For the first time, it was purposeful. She'd never allowed herself to practice it, worried over what might happen. When she couldn't make her childhood rabbit disappear, the blacksmith had broken its neck in revenge instead. She'd buried the creature in her backyard.

Marshall Merridon's grin widened as he peered at her, his thumb and forefinger rubbing against one another, as if some substance lay between them.

"Memory oil is how I started. I stole the recipe along with many others, all written in a book, from a merchant capable of concocting marvelous potions. Things you wouldn't think you could drink and then do. He's dead now, of course. Dried Forget-Me-Not blooms. Did you know if they're hung upside down, they manage the opposite? Week-old bones. Honey made by pepper-powder bees, which only make their nests in the Whitehorn trees of Renwick. It burns just like regular lamp oil too. Much too precious to do on the day to day. Don't repeat any of this, by the way." He tucked the crate beneath his arm and opened the door. "I must say, it is nice to have someone to talk to after all these years. There are some things one's own family wouldn't even understand." Merridon traced the line of the doorframe, lost to himself for a moment.

"You're a charlatan." The words scraped against her teeth.

He didn't even bother with a look back.

"No, darling girl. I'm a genius. Now, don't say another bad word against me, or I'll be forced to have you turn your impressive imagination against that tongue of yours."

The door closed behind him, effectively sealing her inside the Room of Desire all alone.

Chapter Thirty-Four

Alora tested her binding. She moved her arms first, and they obeyed. She tried to throw the envelope with all her strength, and they refused.

She hissed a slew of obscenities.

She was able to swing her legs forward and back but wasn't able to stand. Marshall Merridon, the bloated, old toad, had told her to sit and remain. He'd told her to take the envelope and keep it.

She could feel something there, at the back of her head, some memory she couldn't grasp that related to the ruby-eyed skull. It aggravated her further the more she tried. She wiped her fingers across the cloak she wore until she thought she'd shed a layer of skin, but still her head didn't right itself. The oil she'd inadvertently touched had already seeped inside and done its damage. Could it ever be fixed?

She knew she forgot things. Important things. If she focused on a singular spot in the room, she could see each one shifting in front of her eyes. But pay attention to one too long and it scuttled away, sifting through her fingers like sand. It infuriated her to no end!

She wanted to tear the room apart, destroy everything she'd managed for that odious man, but she couldn't so much as rake her nails across the fabric.

She wasn't allowed to destroy any portion of Opulence. Merridon had effectively restrained her, locking her inside her own head.

But she thought there might be people who could help her here. Though she couldn't remember their names. Merridon had mentioned someone, she thought. Someone she might know. A brief flash of red came and went, a memory floating just out of reach. She touched the edge of it but couldn't...quite...pin...it...

A young Miss Lennox Flowers!

Yes, Alora knew her! A contented feeling drifted through her then. *This must mean something. Something positive.*

She'd an inkling there were others too. Her mind, however it managed, wanted to fight what had been done. Perhaps her brain was stronger than Merridon expected. Or maybe it was all the black tea she drank day to day. Or something else she drank...

He'd mentioned sons. How could someone like that procreate? Who allowed such a thing?

At once, her mind whirled with the direction of her thoughts. Like she'd chosen the wrong path, and it wished to cast her upon the correct one. However well-meaning, it was disorienting, and Alora cursed and spat, trying with everything in her to grip onto any particular memory and pin it like she'd done with Lennox. She was gifted with eyes.

Merridon, she thought. *Merridon. Merridon. Merridon.*

"*Bash,*" she breathed, and slumped in relief. She knew him, Marshall Merridon's son. But how well? The sensation his name brought upon her wasn't so much contentment, but an excitable warmth, a vague agitation. Whatever that meant. Would he help her?

The doorknob across the room began to turn. Alora swung her head toward it as a tall figure, dressed in black, stepped into the room.

She stiffened. Her contracted mind recognized this person as an employee of Opulence and thus unable to be harmed. The stuttering of her memories revealed she'd seen others like this before, even if she couldn't recall any singular one with clarity. She thought she might have had very bad experiences with such people. But then she thought she might have had very good ones too.

How terribly confusing. She felt on the verge of tears.

"Miss Pennigrim," began the figure, the voice distinctly male and rasping. "I've come to escort you to your new accommodations."

An unwinding sensation occurred across her thighs. Alora rushed to stand so quickly, her vision blurred. She reached out to steady herself against the chaise at the same moment a gloved hand encircled her elbow.

Alora ripped her arm from his grasp. Her vision righted. "Where?"

"On the grounds. Same as us all. Come with me."

She had to obey. It had been right there in the contract. Alora stared at her feet as they moved one in front of the other. It was a strange sensation, having no control.

"Do I know you?" She stared up into a masked face, the rest of him shadowed by the drape of his hood. *Please. Let me know you.*

But the figure shook his head, and Alora wilted. Embarrassingly, her eyes welled. She looked away.

Tears dripped from her downturned nose. She'd had a plan once, she thought. Something to be rid of this evil place. Or at least to discredit it. But she couldn't remember any of it now. She knew who she was at least. She knew she had a rabbit at home that would need feeding, a donkey in a stable who would miss her visits. She knew from where she'd come from. That she loved tea and tomato and cheese sandwiches, an old baker and even older bookshop owner.

She followed the broad figure down the hall, now lit with gold sconces. Their flames enticed, the newly laid carpet beneath her feet crimson and plush and lined with twinkling lights. It made her want to turn back and see how it led to Door Twenty-five. But she'd been told to follow and so she did.

They stepped into the great hall, and the sight sent every memory Alora held of it into a flurry. She tried to grab at one, but it was as futile as catching a flake in a blizzard and just as dizzying. She exhaled long and slow.

The sound drew the attention of the masked man, who turned back to her briefly. But he did not stop, and so she didn't either.

Then a woman marched toward them.

She had a deep groove between her eyebrows and a fierce downturn to her mouth. Her shoes clipped against the veined marble but did not echo. Alora thought she knew her. If nothing else, the uptick of scurrying memories in her head hinted at it. She focused on that. It was a clue, at least, toward something forgotten.

"Madam Feebledire," rasped the man ahead of her. He stopped, meaning Alora did too.

But then he surprised her by stepping back. Alora glanced at her shoulder, now pressed against his arm. A shock rattled through her, pleasant and light. She didn't move away. It was familiar to her, a hint of something more. Intense memories whirled around her. A tornado of fear and anger, relief and desire.

But he'd said he didn't know her.

Madam Feebledire echoed in her head, demanding her attention.

"I know you," whispered Alora.

The arm against her stiffened. His pinky finger brushed her own.

"I'll take her the remainder of the way. Master wishes to speak with you about an urgent matter."

Her escort remained solid at her side. Alora glanced up at him, his attention riveted on the woman in front of them. She could see the line of his masked jaw and could feel indecision rolling off him like waves. *Why does he hesitate?*

It took the deepening of the groove between Madam Feebledire's brows for him to finally step away. She moved toward Alora, pausing only when she passed near him.

"Be wary of which road you choose, Captain."

The woman voiced the warning quietly and through her teeth, but Alora heard it anyway. She would not succumb to this strange entrapment of Merridon's. She would take any clue she could until something was able to be made from them. This woman was a part of Opulence. Of management, Alora thought, considering she could command her escort with ease.

Alora knew her. She'd had many interactions with this woman before.

"Madam Feebledire," she said, stepping forward to meet her. "I hear I'm to be made presentable. Where to next?"

Madam Feebledire's lip lifted into a sneer. *Yes*, thought Alora. *I remember that face.*

"Only the best for our newest performer, I hear," said the older woman, as if she'd just been made aware of the fact and didn't enjoy the last-minute knowledge. She crooked a finger, and Alora had no real choice but to give into the motion. As much as she wanted to snub it. Or bite it.

Alora bothered with another look at the enshrouded man, standing stoic and oh-so-mysterious as he watched the pair of them make for the front of the mansion. She found herself wishing she could see beneath his hood.

Just a peek.

The doors opened without touch, and Alora blinked against the sunshine. There was a nip in the air that hadn't been there before; autumn rode close, almost upon them. She followed Madam Feebledire down the stairs. A topiary at their end drew her attention. It was of a woman, pouring out desires. The topiary meant to represent Door Twenty-five. Meant to represent her. Alora peered over her shoulder, as Madam Feebledire would not be stopped, and thought, *It does look like me a little.* The resemblance was there, in the slope of the nose, the point of the chin. It had been sculpted by someone gifted, to be sure; someone who knew her perhaps? Someone she had known?

Memories barreled behind her eyes. *Okay. Someone I've met more than once.*

A breeze swept the grounds as Alora followed Opulence Mansion's management around the side of the building. It lifted Madam Feebledire's hair, pulling more pieces from the tight bun at the top of her head.

"Damn this blasted *wind.* What has become of this place?"

Alora said nothing while Madam Feebledire patted her hair back into shape.

"Once we reach your accommodations, you'll be seen to by one of our employees. Now, don't start thinking of yourself as some sort of commodity because of it. It is only a temporary assignment. Once you've learned the routine, you'll be in charge of your own appearance. And you mustn't allow it to lapse. Our performers are held to the highest standards of beauty. You are meant to engage, entice—to cause members to wish for return night after night. Do you understand?"

Alora thought she might vomit all over her shoes. "Yes, Madam Feebledire."

"Apparently you're to be escorted to all shifts," said the older woman, like the idea was distasteful and unnecessary. "I can only imagine it is because of your unique abilities. Abilities managed to be kept from me until you decided membership didn't suit you so much as becoming a performer yourself." She arched an eyebrow at Alora, clearly hankering for answers.

These truths Alora would have happily given had she not been entrapped by an entrancing skull. A terribly dark artifact if she'd ever seen one. Where did someone find something wicked like that? Surely not in Enver.

An obscure chirp permeated her mutilated memories. The scent of vetiver. Those blasted, lovely eyes. *Again.*

It was maddening, but Alora took solace in one thing: Madam Feebledire didn't enjoy the idea of Alora and Merridon in cahoots behind her back. Even realizing the depths of Alora's enchantment now, she clearly did not know of all that he had done. Of all the details of the contract, nor the trickery currently at play.

Alora didn't know for certain that Madam Feebledire would care even if she were made aware how different it all really was. But it was worth a try. She said, "My contract is as unique as I am. You should read it."

Madam Feebledire didn't pause in her walk down the glittered path. "Why would I do that? I'm not in the business of contracts."

Alora couldn't say more. The ideas wouldn't even form in her head, so thick was the entrancement placed upon her. But she thought she caught a waft of curiosity about Madam Feebledire at the suggestion. It would have to be enough.

Memories fluttered as she neared the dwellings at the back of the property. Alora knew she had been here before, and seeing as how the only performer's name she recognized from Marshall Merridon's mouth had been Lennox Flowers, she thought that must be why. She must have visited once or twice. She thought maybe she could have visited Bash Merridon here, but for some reason, she just couldn't believe he was a performer. It didn't feel right.

"I take light and break it, Miss Pennigrim."

Alora stumbled in her steps. "Good *god,*" she breathed beneath the wind.

The memory was only that. Only words. But the voice behind them had been deep and rasping. A voice the same as the hooded, masked figure who fetched her from behind Door Twenty-five.

"Captain", Madam Feebledire had called him. A title the hidden man once called himself.

To her.

He lied about not knowing me!

Which meant he must be in Merridon's confidences. He wished to keep her buried in the confusing dark of lost memories. The sudden urge to enact terrible things upon him, upon Marshall Merridon, too, overcame her, but her imagination wasn't there to greet it. She could go no further than the feeling of it. These new inadequacies infuriated her. Alora fairly vibrated in her rage. Because she could do nothing but dutifully follow Madam Feebledire, she sank her teeth into her lip instead, setting it to bleeding. Her nails, too, dug so deep into her palms they threatened to puncture skin. She didn't want to hurt herself; she didn't deserve it, but it was all she had.

They passed by smaller dwellings, with fake windows and bulbous bushes. Alora wondered about the windows, confused by them. She quickened her pace to near Madam Feebledire. "Why tack on fake windows to these buildings? It looks strange."

The older woman tipped her head in their direction. "What do you have against illusions, Miss Pennigrim?"

"Nothing, if they serve a purpose."

"And so these do."

They didn't though. Except perhaps to create the illusion of a real home. But Alora had a real home. With real windows and a real terrace and many plants, and not a single one bulbous or dangerously close to an over-trimming. How *dare* they try to take it all from her? A lifetime of servitude, relaxing prettily, dumping desires into the world? Once upon a time, her dream had been to make everyone else's come true. But not like this. *Never* like this.

Behind the rows of smaller buildings rose larger ones. Now these could almost be deemed acceptable. Though there still weren't any actual windows, at least they seemed to have more than one cramped room. The houses rose two stories, and the hedges were no longer bulbous but coned. Madam Feebledire made for one at their right, on the far edge.

"You'll find your accommodations already furnished with everything you should need, including a bath. You're lucky you're deemed so special. Most other performers have to use a communal." At the white door, Madam Feebledire produced a key from her bodice and fitted it to the lock. "Someone will be by shortly to assist you in readying yourself. Dinner will be delivered at six. Afterward, you'll be escorted to your door."

Alora remained on the strange house's threshold. "To my door? Tonight? But I've only just finished it."

For the first time Madam Feebledire seemed to really look at her. At the circles that must have assuredly deepened, the unkempt hair, and her swollen eyes. "Master is a very ambitious man. Once he decides on a course, he does not take it at a walk. You'll do well to remember that."

"But—"

Madam Feebledire held up a hand. "I won't hear an argument. You signed the contract of your own volition, Miss Pennigrim. If Master has decided on surprising the public with an early opening of the Room of Desire, then that is his prerogative. Opulence Mansion belongs solely to him, after all."

Alora noted the sneering quality of Madam Feebledire's last words even as the rest of what she said left her knees quaking. *Tonight? It is already late afternoon!* "How am I to know what to do?"

Madam Feebledire sent her a side-eye full of meaning. "Figure it out, Miss Imagination." Opulence's management skirted around her and pushed through the door. She laid the key upon the entryway table. "Good luck."

The door latched closed behind her.

Chapter Thirty-Five

Alora stared at the key. At how it gleamed beneath the sconce on the wall. Real and probably heavy and shining new, and yet it had no purpose in her life. Madam Feebledire hadn't used it to lock her in. The bolt on the inside meant she didn't need it against anyone wishing her harm. So what would she do? Lock up the house every night she left? For what? To deter trespassers?

She spun within the space. The bottom level contained four rooms, the doorways arched and opened in a way that she could move from one to the other and still see them all at once, even the washroom. She had a dining table with two chairs, a sitting room with a sofa. There was a kitchen which couldn't really be considered as such since she had no stove and no oven, and in the washroom sat a vanity, a tub, and the largest full-length mirror she'd ever owned.

She looked away before she could see herself within it.

A spiral stair speared upward from the house's center, winding around and around to a loft. Alora didn't need to go up there to know there'd be no terrace. There would be no dried flowers on a nightstand, salvaged from her favorite blooms. There would be no wardrobe filled with silvers and blues. The vanity wouldn't have her new favorite shade of lipstick, and certainly not her embroidered towels, and the sitting room most definitely wouldn't have a knife hidden upon the mantle. There would be no dishes for Mrs. Flops in the kitchen.

There would be no rabbit at all…

Let them come. Anyone who wants. Let them take whatever they can carry.

She didn't care. None of it was hers.

Alora marched toward the key, scooped it up, and in the next breath, flung open the door. She froze mid-throw, her hand behind her ear.

A woman cowered on the stoop. When no object met her face, she lowered her gold-painted hands with caution. Her eyes were wide and brown behind them, and Alora's memories remained still. She'd never met this person.

"May I help you?" demanded Alora with more hostility than she meant.

The middle-aged woman tittered in response. She wore the same nondescript uniform as the rest of the mansion's employees, crimson and gold, her skin painted to match, but her hair was done up rather nicely, with soft waves framing her face and cascading behind.

Is this what I'm meant to learn? She'd curling tongs at home. She didn't want for instruction.

"Forgive me, but I'm told to assist in readying you for the evening."

"Who told you?"

"Madam"—the employee swallowed rather loudly—"Feebledire."

What could this woman possibly do? Aside from watch Alora bathe and ensure she made up her eyes as sultry as a siren's? No. The entrancement held no power in this instance, and in turn, it fed Alora's own. She turned up her nose.

"No, thank you."

A hand smacked against the door with surprising force where Alora meant to close it between them.

Alora stared at the woman, her mouth parted in surprise. "*Excuse—*"

"You don't understand. They are *watching.*"

Alora flung her attention from the desperate appearance of the Opulence employee in order to scan the quiet grounds. All she could see were perfect, little houses, traced from the same pattern. She squinted, searching for shadows, but those were few and far between and didn't bear any human shape. "Who is watching?" she eventually asked.

"The *mansion.*"

"The building itself now cares whether I'm properly cleaned and manicured before the evening?"

"Madam Feebledire does, and she told me Master does. And Master is the mansion. There is nothing that goes on that they do not see. Let me in. *Please.*"

Alora found her hand dropping limply to her side before she realized it. The woman pushed past her as if chased by an ogre, breaths heavy in the silence. Alora didn't glance back at her but lifted her gaze to Opulence once more. It didn't look so impressive from the back, she didn't think. There were no windows and no doors. No monstrous wolf statues. But it was tall and gold and impenetrable. Like a fortress. She scanned the rooftop for spies and found nothing.

"Who told you you're always being watched?" Alora's eyes settled on the fluttering crimson flags atop the turrets. Memories attempted to resurface again. *I've broken rules here before.*

"Everyone. Management and others like me."

"Hmm," hummed Alora. "It could be true, I suppose." She closed the door and turned to face the house's interior. "Or they could be lying to keep you in line."

"Is it worth the risk to find out? What if we're caught?"

Alora stared at the woman like she'd sprouted another head. "I would think we already are."

Chapter Thirty-Six

Alora floated amongst sweet-scented bubbles. Across the room and behind her, she could hear Harriet, the skittish Opulence employee, pulling open the vanity drawers, assembling what she assumed to be costume makeup. Something befitting a 'Goddess of Desire'. Alora gagged at the idea. Gracious, even the name left her sickened. The fact Merridon had used it in all seriousness was enough to make her screech.

"Master enjoys a heavy eye and a bold lip," Harriet had explained before she'd begun.

Of course he does, thought Alora. "Yes, I've seen his office," she'd said, startling seconds later.

She'd remembered!

The memory was blurred and faded, but it was there. Gold on gold, the furniture too big. But there'd been no response to any of it from the mousy woman, neither her comments nor her sloshing.

Alora watched the sconces on the wall now as she stewed, her hair hanging heavy over the tub's lip, slick with oil. Harriet's gem-be-decked comb tugged at her scalp. Alora wondered over if she could somehow get around the rule of going to and from Door Twenty-five and nowhere else, if she could jog her memory in other ways. She'd managed it with Lennox, with Bash, and even that rogue captain, vague as they still were in her brain. Now she'd done it again with Merridon's office. It was a relief that her memories were only hidden, rather than having been entirely taken from her. If she could manage a bending of the rules, surely she could excavate them fully?

"I'll go and ready your costume now. Wash out the excess oil but not all of it, and wait for me at the vanity, if you would. I must finish with you before dinner."

"Whatever you say," called Alora, feeling a child again, and dunked her head below the surface.

Not long later, she'd managed the final instruction. Alora sat at the vanity in a crimson robe, uncaring that it was oversized and slipping down one shoulder. She picked up palettes and brushes and lipsticks in turn and shook her head at it all. When she could avoid it no more, she chewed at her lip. Slowly, so slowly it pained her, she looked into the mirror.

Her eyes were no longer puffy; it'd been some hours now since she'd cried. But the circles were still there, purple and blooming, as well as the dead, gray cast to her eyes. Her hair hung heavy and wet down her back, lank pieces framing her face. She looked like she'd been a prisoner for months instead of a single afternoon. So very pathetic.

She glared into the glass. "No. You are not this *weak*."

She continued to glare, her teeth scraping against the others, a muscle feathering in her jaw, until the dead in her eyes came alive again, but this time with a cold, silver rage. Nevermind the robe was crimson and did nothing for her coloring. Alora's eyes were ice through and through, and they couldn't be tamped. *God help you, Marshall Merridon, when I'm freed from your invisible bonds.*

She would—

Well, she *could*—

The sconce moved in the mirror. At first, Alora didn't pay it any mind as she was too busy in her vast failure of attempts in imagining revenge. But when the light eased across the wall as if being breathed in, she froze in her seat. Her scowl fell from her face. She tilted her body. But no matter the angle, it was the same.

The light was leaving. And then it was gone.

"Good god! Harriet!" The darkness was absolute, a black hole. Alora stretched out her fingers tentatively, and knew by the sudden flurry in her head, *This has happened to me before.*

But why?

And then she remembered—only a little—but she remembered. A dream of masks and hoods and leather gloves.

"I take light and break it, Miss Pennigrim."

"A light-breaker and a regenerator."

Captain.

Bash.

Oh. Oh no.

Bash *fucking* Merridon.

So much for a potential ally; they were the same man! Alora felt a rising presence behind her, the sensation skittering across her skin before diving further in. She smelled leather and *guilt*, and it filled her nostrils until nothing else remained. Her fingers found the only thing available to her—a hair pin. *Hideous gold*, she thought.

"You lied to me," she whispered, and wondered why the idea of it hurt so much. Of what memory she couldn't yet find.

"Alora," said the presence, apologetic. Leather-clad fingers enclosed her own.

If she'd her full capabilities, she would have imagined him maimed, but as it was, she couldn't even conjure the thought. So, instead, she did the next best thing and spun in her seat. Straight into his waiting chest, she stabbed.

The light returned in an instant. Alora crushed her hands to her temples to avoid falling off the stool. It was disorienting to be catapulted from an impenetrable dark, and she nearly swooned.

"Son of a fucking hellhound," hissed the voice from somewhere in front. "Can I not go more than a day without being stabbed?"

Alora blinked slowly at the ground, taking in black boots, the hairpin now clattering to the tile, its end coated scarlet. The cold fury she'd seen in the mirror disappeared as she stared at that hairpin, replaced instead with something hot and fierce. She'd been deceived. By someone she cared about. She was so angry, spots danced in her vision. She rose from the stool.

"Again, I'll ask, do I *know you?*" Alora took advantage of the captain's preoccupation with finding the puncture wound on his chest. She shoved him.

His hood shifted as he stumbled, focusing on her. "Easy, Alora. I can explain."

"Please do," she said, marching forward until her bare feet toed his boots. "You lied to me. I'd love to know why. Is it because I can hardly remember and so you wished to take advantage of that fact? Well, I'll tell you, I haven't forgotten everything, and I certainly won't forget this."

"We were being watched."

"Oh, I've heard that line before."

"I'm telling you the truth. We were not alone in that hall. The fairy lights—"

"And we're alone now? My chaperone is just upstairs!"

"She never made it that far. I sent her away."

"Did you now? Well, that is just...*perfect.*" Alora pulsed with anger. And she didn't want to keep it locked in. For once, she wanted to act rashly. To show how she felt inside on the out.

She knew precisely how Bash stood and precisely where she wanted him to fall. She kicked at his knee, and when it buckled, she didn't reach to steady him but pushed instead.

Bash Merridon, the master's dutiful son, toppled into her cold bathwater with a splash that soaked the room.

Silence. Alora could hear nothing besides her own breaths in the aftermath, and that quiet felt charged, prepared to explode. *Oh, he is angry.* But that suited her just fine; she was angry too. As the captain climbed from the water by slow, exacting measures, his shirt clinging to his skin beneath his coat, Alora backed away. He looked like a grim reaper like this, which was an unpleasant comparison to make when she was incapable of running farther than the front door. He ripped the hood from his head. He stripped the gloves away. The coat he shed without difficulty, pulling it from his arms.

When he lifted his gaze to her, she stilled. Above the mask, his eyes were green but veined by black. Even as she watched, darkness writhed within the whites of them, like it wished to take over and destroy every modicum of light within the room. She swallowed, trying and failing to imagine what he might do to her.

I've not thought this through.

He reached for the topmost button of his shirt, undoing it. When he finished, he moved onto the next. It wasn't until the fourth button that Alora finally found her voice again.

"What are you doing?"

His fingertips stilled for only a heartbeat. "Reminding you."

Then his shirt was shrugged from his shoulders and dropped to the puddle of water formed on the floor.

Alora cleared her throat. It was all she could manage while drinking in the sight of every sculpted part of him. "Of what?" If he took off his trousers, she'd faint dead away, she knew.

Bash made several purposeful strides toward her, which Alora only realized belatedly, backing away too late. Her bottom met the vanity, the makeup scattering. His chest made up her view. Her gaze flicked to the wound she inflicted upon him. As it wept slowly, already beginning to clot.

But that wasn't where she was meant to look. Two fingers pressed beneath her chin forcing her attention upward. She allowed him this, her eyes skimming over his chest and shoulder, the skin smooth and lightly marked, and she wondered if what he planned for her would really be so bad, after all. What did it mean that a flutter of anticipation built inside her now?

Except her eyes landed on a disruption in his flesh, there where his shoulder met his neck, snuffing any eagerness dead. Four long scars, purpled and raised. Her abrupt intake of air had him asking, "Do you remember that day?"

Alora shook her head. "No. What happened?"

"Specter wolves. You turned two to stone. The very same that now adorn Opulence's entrance. I nearly died that day."

Brief flashes of feeling and images came for her. Of blood and panic, of the captain's weight slumped against her. *Oh.* She'd been terrified.

"And this." He released her chin to duck his own, and her gaze drifted to follow. A small red line marked the flesh just above his hip. "I was stabbed by my brother. On your front stoop, no less. A less dramatic moment than the wolves."

Alora blinked as she recalled the feel of him beneath her fingertips, a dressing tied into place. There'd been no small dose of horror that day, too, though she couldn't drudge up the particulars. And relief. She'd been so relieved, she could have perished.

Her finger reached to trace the fresh scar. His hand clenched beside it.

"So you've come to inform me that all our interactions before were of you nearly dying in my company?"

His kohl-rimmed eyes creased by the smallest measure. "No. You've had your fair share of unfortunate experiences too."

"What? Why would I ever—" Alora stopped and pressed her eyes closed. It didn't make sense to her, that she would spend so much time with someone who barely outran death. What sort of dangerous situations had she gotten into because of him? It didn't sound like her at all.

But then his hand covered hers, there on his hip, and she knew.

Oh god, she *knew*. She didn't only tolerate this person. Or like him some. She must either be a little bit obsessed or a little bit in love. And that was why nothing sounded like her—because she'd never felt like this before.

What a *tragedy*. Her nails clawed at the vanity wood. "Is this all I can hope for? Bits and pieces to return but nothing whole?"

"It depends. I need to know what he did to you. It can't be the darts. They're the most concentrated, entering the bloodstream. The batons are less, mixing with the wounds they leave behind, but I see no marks on you."

She couldn't tell him everything, the entrancement forbade it. But she could say, "I touched the lamp."

"The oil?"

She nodded, teeth ruining her cheek as she stared at the water coating the floor. "You had no part in this? Truly?"

"Goddammit," he growled, dragging her face back to his. "Alora, look at me. I would *never*."

She focused on his masked mouth, something else returning to her as she took in the stretch of leather. "You're an Urchin, aren't you? I remember Mister Whitters warning me away from you."

"That is only part of who I am."

But she couldn't help it, this distrustful emotion. "What did"— she swallowed, fighting it—"*Master*...wish from you?" Her voice was hard, even as she fairly choked on the word.

"We're still in search of Mister Macaw, the groundskeeper who eloped just this morning. You've met him before. Rumor is he realized whom he sculpted upon that topiary and fled in disappointment. I think it's more likely he fled in protest; he did seem to like you quite a lot. And then he asked after William. He hasn't been seen all day."

William. Mister Macaw. Alora knew those names, one invoking much more pleasant feelings than the other. Her brow furrowed as she tried to rein in every memory that bombarded her brain. *Mister Macaw protested my joining Opulence?*

"Alora."

"Yes?" She scrunched her eyes closed.

"I will save you from this."

She shook her head. "You don't know what he's done."

"I think I do," he said, and above the mask, his eyes turned pained. The darkness in them had gone.

She frowned over it, tracking his fingers as they reached behind his head. He tossed the mask to the floor, which Alora hardly noticed as she stared instead at his mouth. "You do?" she said, full of disbelief. Merridon had led her to believe only the pair of them knew what had been done. "How?"

"The topiary," he said.

Oh god. His voice was *everything.* Deep still, and rough, but no longer rasping. She yearned to drink it in.

He continued like she wasn't becoming undone before him. "That was my first concern. And when I'd been informed you'd arrived, I had planned to intercept you, to remind you of your promise in not entering into another contract. To make sure you were all right. But I was detained over business. An Urchin, missing."

"And then?"

"I confronted management, who didn't seem keen to give me any information. I said some things she will no doubt report me for, but it hardly matters; she isn't so above me as she thinks. After, I found an employee waiting to act as escort for the new performer, he said. I told him I was to take his place."

"You eavesdropped?"

"He was already making his final demands, and I knew I'd come too late. That you were bespelled. In that moment, I'll admit, I went almost blind with rage. But my bursting in would have done nothing for either of us."

"So you waited."

"I waited. Did I do the wrong thing?"

Alora thought over his question. At what chain of events would have begun had Marshall Merridon's own son, the captain of his dreadful Urchins, betrayed him so openly. Her instincts told her she would have survived it, bound in her head as she was now, but Bash would not. Merridon didn't appear to tolerate liabilities, no matter how close they were to him. After that, she really would have been all alone. Alora shook her head.

"No, I don't think you did."

Except her words didn't seem to relieve whatever bothered him. "There is something else," he began, swallowing. "Something I want to admit to you, but I know you'll hate me for it. God knows I hate myself." Alora stiffened, preparing herself for another betrayal. Bash noticed, and his hand came forward to cup her face. "I only wish you would remember me first. Remember everything that happened before."

A new sensation fell upon her suddenly at his earnest request. Like a clearing of clouds or dawn over night. Or maybe it was better described as a passageway, opening straight into her mind. Bash's wish was his and not her own and he'd spoken it to her to fulfill. He *desired* for her to remember.

The smile that stretched her face was hopeful and luminous with triumph. "If that is what you desire," she said.

And set her memories free.

Chapter Thirty-Seven

"It was *yours*." If Bash hadn't blocked her, he would have been stuck like a pincushion. As it were, he gripped her wrist. The hairpins clattered onto the tile.

"Alora! Stop! What the hell has come over you?" He gripped her opposite wrist now, too, worried she'd slap him. Which she'd been about to; his anticipation was infuriating.

"Let me go!"

"That doesn't seem a safe choice for either of us. Are you ill?"

Alora gritted her teeth. "No, you cretin. I *remember*. You said Madam Feebledire is not above you? You're right! Your *management* of your evil Urchins gave you power over me. Your little desire called straight into my enchantment! And thank you! Thank you for reminding me of what your true nature is. Wicked artifacts are subjective, are they? Well! I don't think that ruby-eyed"—her tongue stuck to the roof of her mouth—"*thing* is subjectively evil. I'd say it definitely is!" A gray cast stole into Bash's complexion. A damning if there ever was one. She could have sobbed. "You gave it to him. How could you?"

"I'm so sorry, Alora. I'll never quit being sorry. He'd sent me out to retrieve it months ago. An old crone was rumored to have entranced her entire family, including her great-grandchildren, into spending every minute of the day with her. Even to follow her along in death. They put up quite a fight." He touched the scar on his eyebrow. "I'd no idea he'd ever think to use it on you. I'd no idea you were to become the performer behind Door Twenty-five. Fuck, I didn't know all you were capable of! That you could even deliver what he wanted. I told you once before—I would never do anything to hurt you."

When she ripped her wrists from him this time, he allowed it. Her eyes welled, which infuriated her further. "Then why do I feel like my chest is carved open?"

"I'm—"

"Stop. I thought I could look away from it, your past, even your present, leaning into how much I've come to care, but I can't. You have hurt the people of Enver and beyond time and time again, and if you didn't do it directly, you commanded it done. Maybe they haven't all been innocent, maybe you've saved a few, but it isn't enough to condone every other evil. *Bash*," His name broke her last thread of control. She felt the warm wet of tears on her cheeks. "You went from a child who hurt another to a man who leads a vindictive mob. Do you even understand what you've become?"

His eyes were wide and pleading as he closed her in. His hands came to rest on either side of her hips, his face level with her own. "Yes, Alora. I know *exactly* what I've become. Believe me when I say I am not proud of it. That I wish to change *it*." His forehead pressed to hers, and Alora couldn't help but close her eyes at the feel of him. She shivered.

"Please," he murmured, and his voice broke. "You are my tormented dream."

This isn't fair. Her breaths mingled with his, tortuous. She whispered, "I need to be free. From it all."

The pressure abandoned her as Bash pulled away. Alora opened her eyes to his, in time to see the veins of black as they returned, snaking across his irises, blatant anguish in his expression. "I told you I'd see it done. If you believe nothing else of me, believe that."

"Do it then. Desire me out of this."

"Of entrancement?"

"Yes, why not? You brought back my memories when I'd lost them. I'm bespelled; desire me free."

She avoided focusing too much on the hope blooming inside her. Or on Bash's hands, coming away from the vanity to rest against her thighs. But his touch was a sweet agony; she could never ignore it in a hundred years.

"I desire for the entrancement upon you to end."

Alora held still with bated breath, but seconds passed, and no feeling of opening returned. Her mind remained shut away, dark and contained. She couldn't access it. Her shoulders slumped.

"It didn't work?"

"No. My contract… There's a portion in there. It must prevent it." Apparently, to drag her from entrancement was to harm her. At least in Marshall Merridon's eyes. She swiped at her cheeks, where the tears had begun to dry, pulling at her skin. "I'll have to think of some other way."

"Maybe if it was against your own will. What if I bound you? Tied you to Necros and kidnapped you from the grounds?"

The imagery bombarded her.

At once, a sharp pain twisted inside her abdomen. Alora gasped, hunching over. In some faraway distance, she could feel Bash's hand on her bare upper back, the robe having slipped farther. Felt him drop to a knee in front of her.

"Alora! What's happened?"

She righted herself, albeit slowly and shaking.

She sniffed as the pain ebbed. "No. I think it would kill me."

"That goddamned *bastard*," he seethed. "We'll think of something else."

He adjusted the robe on her shoulders, and Alora, despite everything, relished the feel of his touch. Though it didn't stop her from shrugging it off. His nearness distracted her still, but not enough to prevent a seed of an idea from beginning to grow.

Maybe it could work.

More than maybe, even.

Her eyes found his, determined and sure. "I'm allowed to move through the grounds with an Opulence escort. Escort me then, and right now. I need to find Lennox Flowers."

Chapter Thirty-Eight

Poor Lennox looked as if she'd either seen a ghost or passed away herself. Her darted glances between Alora and the Urchin captain might have been comical under different circumstances, with the cigarillo having fallen from her lips to smoke between her bare feet. Meanwhile, Alora couldn't be more thrilled that she stood at her friend's front door. The fire performer's cottage was technically on the way to the mansion; she'd not broken any contract rules. Yet.

"Can we come in?" she asked.

"Oh! Yes!" Lennox backed from the doorway to allow them room, closing it quickly behind her when they filled the small space. The bolt slid through. When she turned back around, it was only to stare at them in a daze once more. Until she scooped up her burning cigarillo and said in a stage whisper, "You're with the captain, Alora. You're not wearing your invisibility coat."

"I know. I don't have it with me," said Alora. "I—" She faltered. She didn't even know where to begin. Or how to work around the entrancement. But Lennox continued to stare at her, open and waiting, and so she finally said, "I'm the performer behind the Room of Desire." At Lennox's cry of surprise, she hurriedly tried to say, "But not by—"

Except, once again, her disobedient tongue adhered itself to the roof of her mouth.

Alora scowled as she attempted to dislodge it.

"But not by choice. Is what I think she meant to say," rasped Bash.

His mask was firmly in place, his clothing dried. Alora had told him to desire them dried and mended, and it'd worked. She couldn't do anything of her own volition, but at least she could persuade others into making their own demands. Another loophole.

"Right," said Alora. "My contract was presented in an…unusual way."

"She's bespelled," explained Bash.

"With some exceptions in clients, I must grant desires to anyone who wishes."

"I don't understand," cut in Lennox, when Bash looked about to say more. "Bespelled? What does that even mean? What could force you to do something you didn't want to?"

At that, Alora's face pinched, and she looked to Bash, waiting for him to explain the situation he'd unwittingly placed them in. She could all but feel his resolve weaken, even knowing he was about to infuriate a second woman with his past choices. "I run an operation of dark artifacts out of Enver, mostly at the behest of Merridon. I'd acquired a skull capable of entrancement. Then I gave that skull to him."

Lennox's eyebrows snapped together. "What in the godforsaken earth possessed you to do *that?*"

"I would have found some way out of it if I'd thought he'd use it against her."

But Lennox wasn't listening as she'd come instead to stand beside Alora, wrapping an arm possessively around her shoulders. "Sure, gift the madman a new tool to control people. What could go wrong?" Her scowl was so fierce, Alora hoped to never be on the receiving end of it.

As *he* was on the receiving end, Bash held up his hands. "I made a mistake. I won't make further excuses for myself."

"Good," said Alora and Lennox in unison.

"I realize," he began, lowering his hood, "you both have every right to be angry. But know that no one is angrier with me than myself. Now—" He paused, waiting for them to interject. When Alora remained quiet and so did Lennox, he continued, "We need your help, Miss Flowers."

"My help? What can I do?"

"A distraction. We need to get past Door Zero."

"And I need your help in zipping up this dress. I'll not have *him* do it." Alora held out the golden gown in her arms as Bash scowled.

"Your makeup, too, I would think. Goodness, Alora, when was the last time you've slept?"

"It's been awhile," she admitted.

Lennox stared at the gown, at Alora's purple-rimmed eyes, and at the Urchin captain watching them both from a safe distance. "I take it we're stealing back a skull?"

"That is the plan," said Alora, and smiled as best she could.

Lennox nodded, continuing to do so as she looked around her mess of a room. "All right. Well, hop behind the partition then, Alora. Let's make you the most dangerous performer Opulence has ever seen."

Alora couldn't have been more thankful it was Lennox and not tittering Harriet who took control of her makeup. Her eyes were lined by a dramatic upsweep, her lids unadorned otherwise, and while her lips were red, they were the color of blood rather than true crimson. She thought it fit her mood.

There wasn't anything to be done about the dress, however. The color couldn't be anything other than gold or Merridon would become suspicious should he see her. Still, she had Bash wish for the gown to be a tad less revealing in the chest, the extravagant neckline diminished. He'd blushed at the sight of her in the original. And he'd flushed all over when she made him say his desire aloud.

She couldn't deny she enjoyed it immensely.

Not long later, Alora pulled on her new invisibility coat along with Lennox, both desired by Bash for the heist, and checked herself over in the mirror. Lennox, she thought, moved nearby. She couldn't see her.

"Flawless, Alora! And so comfy!"

Bash, needing nothing besides his own enchantment, stood at the door. "I'll wait for you at the entrance. I can't take as direct a route in daylight."

He would stick to the lengthening shadows, acting as scout and bodyguard both. Meanwhile, Alora would keep Lennox at her side. At least for a while.

"After you," Alora said, and Bash inclined his head. The light vanished around him. She couldn't make out his form.

From the dark, he said, "Should anyone discover you, Miss Flowers, shout to me so that I can desire Alora to have them stopped. She's managed it before, the poor fellow."

His request came with a note of teasing that Alora found inappropriate and she glowered in his direction. Lennox said, "I'm sure he deserved it."

"He didn't. He was actually very kind, and I'm sure you would have liked him." Alora took her friend's arm. "Go on, Bash. Being a menace isn't coaxing me into forgiving you."

In reply, the dark disappeared.

"Thank you, Lennox. For helping me."

Lennox squeezed the arm she held.

"Don't mention it, Alora. I know you'd do the same for me if I'd ever looked into a cursed skull's eyes."

Yes, she certainly would.

Chapter Thirty-Nine

"**M**aster!" wailed Lennox. "Master, *please*. I need your help!" Alora hardly breathed as she watched from beside the darkness that was Bash. Far enough away that Merridon hopefully wouldn't sense any specific enchantment, the pair of them were pressed against the shadowed wall, waiting for the horrid man to grow sick of Lennox's cries and come to her aid. Which he finally did, some moments later.

Door Zero flung wide, and Lennox stumbled back at the suddenness of it. But she recovered quickly, her conjured tears welling. Alora thought her quite an impressive actress.

"What is the meaning of this, Miss Flowers? I don't appreciate hysterics, especially not at this hour."

Lennox moved back several steps, prompting Merridon to follow. Only then did she lunge forward, draping her arms around him on a sob fit for the theater.

"Where is *William-m-m?*"

Merridon appeared stunned at the contact, rigid as a tree. He attempted to extract himself from Lennox's limbs. "I've told you that you might be performing for a time without him."

"But I haven't even seen him! How can I dance if I don't know if he's okay?"

"I assure you he will be fine. And you'll dance regardless of partner. It's *your* contract, not a dual one between the two of you."

At last, he maneuvered free of Lennox's grip, just in time for her to drag him away into further grievances and for Door Zero to seemingly close all its own and shut them all out.

Alora wasted no time in rushing to Marshall Merridon's desk drawers.

"Don't you think we should focus on the skull first?" said Bash. He'd become visible again while Alora did not. Though she did lower her hood.

"You find the skull! It's in a crate. Probably the same one you packaged it in. I want my contract." She tore open the larger drawer at the base, rummaging through the files. None of them were contracts. "Dammit."

"Have a care, would you? He'll notice more than you think."

Alora's frustration compounded with her fear. She lashed out. "Maybe if you'd *look* in that cabinet instead of looking at *me*, half our mission would be complete!" She spared him a glance in time to watch his eyes widen at her temper. But he said nothing else and turned to the cabinet. Soon, the only sounds were the further shuffling of papers and the telltale sounds of lock-picking.

Not a pickpocket, but a lockpick. Alora shook her head as she searched, bewildered at the secrets continuing to spill from the man with whom she'd chosen to break every rule. She couldn't deny it was useful though—under the current circumstances.

Alora opened the large drawer at the opposite side, when Bash said, "I've got it."

She looked up to him holding the familiar crate. The feel of watchful ruby eyes immediately stole over her, and she shuddered. "I still haven't found my contract. There's—"

Lennox Flowers.

Alora pulled the parchment free. Behind it were more contracts. More names she didn't recognize. She held onto Lennox's, searching for her own, until:

Bash Merridon (Syntaine).

Then:

William Merridon (Halvard).

She grabbed them both, and one in either hand, read them through. With every sentence, her heart dropped, until it landed somewhere so distant, she couldn't even feel its beat. She'd gone numb. "Lifetime commitments. Both of you."

"What's that?" Bash came around behind the desk, the crate tucked beneath his arm. "Have you found it?"

Alora lifted her eyes to his. She didn't answer him, and when it went on long enough, his brow lowered, turning instead to what she held. His expression hardened.

"Bash. Why didn't you tell me all he's forced on you?"

"Believe it or not, there hasn't been a lot of quiet moments since I've met you. And now isn't one of them either."

"But I never would have—"

"Alora," he warned.

Alora could feel a sob thickening her throat, but he was correct. They didn't have much time. Adding the papers to Lennox's contract, she searched through the rest. It was luckless. Hers wasn't here. She shoved the drawer closed and stood.

"What are you doing with those?" Bash stood over her, his chest pressed to her shoulder.

"Taking them, of course."

"Don't. He might not notice one, but he'll certainly notice three. Take Lennox's if you must take someone's."

"He doesn't deserve any of them!"

"Alora…" Bash rubbed at his eyes, clear exasperation on his features. "At this rate, we're never going to get out of here undiscovered."

"Yes, we will." She shoved the pages into her coat. Then she surveyed the room a final time, gaze lingering on the desk last.

She'd seen one like this before now that she thought about it. In Ichibald's shop no less. He'd boasted about its many drawers and writing compartments. About its secret latch—

Alora dropped to her knees in a sudden movement that had Bash rushing to catch her elbow like she'd fainted. She didn't bother to speak or shrug him off, intent on reaching beneath the desk until her fingers found the small ring. A drawer popped open, nearly smashing her atop the head. She scrambled backward and let out a hushed squeal of triumph.

Her contract stared back at her.

Alora Pennigrim.

She snatched it to her as Bash said, "Perfect, let's go."

At the same moment, the knob of Door Zero began to turn.

"Fuck," he hissed, the rasp in her ear making her lurch. A heartbeat later, she was plunged into darkness.

Alora felt it—the moment the page slipped through her startled fingers. She couldn't see to lunge and grab it, and she couldn't dare speak being as she could hear the door had opened, footsteps entering the room. Bash held her against him in the dark. Where in Merridon's office she'd been dragged to, she wasn't sure. She knew she was standing, his arm tight across her front. She knew the quarters were tight.

How could I have dropped it!

She turned her face into the captain's chest to quiet her harsh breathing. She could hear Bash's heartbeat bounding away. He was nervous, same as she was. Honestly, in that moment she didn't know which was better. To see what happened next or remain blind to it all.

Either way, if it was Marshall Merridon behind the noise, the game was up.

The footsteps drew closer, and Alora stiffened. She pressed her eyes closed, though it hardly mattered. She heard the crack of aged joints, the rustle of parchment, and then, at last, a voice.

"*Marshall.* What in the world are you thinking?"

Madam Feebledire.

Merridon's elder sister had also crept into his office while it was unoccupied. What a snoop! Alora's eyes widened in the black that was Bash's enchantment, wondering if it had all been because of her cryptic remark concerning her contract's contents. She felt Bash's arm shift against her own, until his hand gripped the back of her neck, applying enough pressure that she bowed—then knelt. Her fingers grabbed ahold of his bicep when he crouched beside her.

But he pulled her hand from him and placed it on the floor. Her opposite went lower still. And she realized—they were in tight quarters because they were in Merridon's *cabinet.*

Alora's mouth pinched. *He wants me to crawl…while he can see everything, and I can't?* He nudged her forward, and she couldn't ignore him. Madam Feebledire would surely notice a densely black cloud moving across the walls if they remained upright. Alora bit back a huffed breath—and crawled forward.

Door Zero was quiet, hardly creaking as it opened. But at its closing, she heard the head of management demand, "Who's there? Marshall Matthew Merridon, is that you? We have something to discuss!"

The latch clicked closed.

Chapter Forty

Alora could breathe. She knew they were in the main hall purely by the sensation of space around her, but she didn't dare ask Bash what he planned next. She didn't want to risk anyone hearing her. The captain's pace quickened, his hand laced with hers, and Alora soon felt the change around them. The coolness, the slight downturn, the enclosed feel. They were headed down the hall, straight for Door Twenty-five.

Minus the monumental loss of her contract, at least everything else seemed to be going according to plan. Alora heard another knob being turned, another door quietly creaking inward. A frightened, "H-h-hello?"

"It's only us, Miss Flowers," said Bash and eased them from the darkness. The slow transition was all for her sake, she knew. He'd told her once that his plunging and returning from enchantment didn't disorient him in the slightest.

She wished she could say the same. She blinked tears from her eyes, the dim lamplight feeling like the summer sun at high noon. When she could once again see the room she'd created, she didn't notice another soul inside it. "Lennox?"

At her name, Lennox shrugged off her coat. She sat on the chaise, her fingers forming a trail against the velvet fabric.

"I love the seating in here. I want one for myself. Where did you find it?"

"Ichibald's Fanciful Furnishings, a shop in Thistledown Square. I'll take you there, when this is all over."

Lennox smiled at the idea of it, though Alora sensed a shadow about her. Like she wouldn't allow the hope to delve further than her expression. She was draped in melancholy, the hour growing late and minutes away from opening, and it made Alora say, "You weren't able to go to Door Eleven this afternoon."

Her friend shook her head, her smile drooping. "It's all right, Alora. This is much more important."

Alora wanted to reach out and hug her. Tell her that soon, she wouldn't have to worry over a pool with a muzzled mermaid to bring her a happy memory because she would be out in the world making new ones all for herself. But the time never came as a horrific crack rent the room.

Alora sucked in a breath and Lennox yelped, both turning to Bash and the skull he held, the box in pieces on the floor. "Apologies," he said. His hood shifted as he bent to examine the artifact, careful to keep the rubies from their line of sight. "He'd nailed it shut."

Lennox rose from the chaise. "Okay, Alora. Are you ready?"

Alora took her friend's place on the chair and shed her own coat. "Ready."

Bash handed the skull to Lennox with care. Alora wished she could see his expression, to see if it bothered him at all that she'd chosen Lennox rather than him as the one to entrance her. He'd acted fine about it when they'd come up with the idea, but she knew him well enough now to understand when he hid some emotion from her. Only, she didn't know what it was—hurt or something else? The truth was that she couldn't even placate him even if he were upset.

At the base of it, she realized she cared for him—quite a lot—but he'd done so many things, held so many secrets, and a small part of her didn't know for certain that he would choose her at the end of everything. That was it. Unfair or not, that was her truth.

Lennox's face twisted. "Gracious, it even *feels* evil."

Alora scowled and swung her gaze to Bash, only for him to shake his head at her. She *knew* it.

"We're running out of time," he said.

"Yes. All right. Well, look into it, I guess." Then she shoved the ruby eyes straight in front of Alora's gray ones.

The sensation was the same as before, of diving into an enchanted red sea. She yearned to be there, to see the very depths of it. To never leave. In the far away distance, she heard a male voice say, "That's enough. Command her to do something."

The eyes disappeared. Alora almost protested, but then Lennox was there, standing in front of her instead, demanding, "Stand on one leg. Please."

Alora promptly did as told, wobbling in her golden gown. "It's worked!"

"It should have erased every command from before," said Bash. "Picture me stealing you away now. Does it hurt?"

Alora didn't need to obey him, but she did anyway, imagining herself on horseback, her arms around Bash's middle, rushing through the gate. "Nothing," she said, and grinned.

She could visibly see the tension leave them both. She felt it leak from her too. "Lennox? My leg is tired."

"Oh! Stand on both legs, please."

Alora sighed in relief at having both feet planted again. "All right. Should we give it a go?"

Lennox nodded an enthusiastic agreement, hugging the skull to her. She said, "Alora, I command you to be disentranced."

Alora closed her eyes, breathing deeply. She didn't exactly feel the same unwinding sensation as she'd felt from the physical commands, but she'd had other commands forced upon her by Merridon, too, that she'd not felt. It might not mean anything.

She blinked her eyes open.

"Well?"

"I don't know," said Alora. "Try to have me stand on one leg again."

Lennox obliged, and Alora immediately returned to her awkward pose. Her abdominals strained and her thigh burned. Her eyes filled, and no matter how hard she blinked them away, they wouldn't recede. A tear trickled down her cheek. "That's that, then."

Bash lowered his hood, his expression tormented. He took a single step forward before stopping.

"No," said Lennox. "I refuse to just *give up*. Alora, I command you not to listen to me."

The world immediately quieted to silence. Alora, properly horrified, observed Lennox's mouth moving, and said, "I can't hear a thing!" She didn't know for sure if the words had even left her mouth at all, but both Lennox and Bash startled, and then Lennox's mouth was moving again.

Alora's hearing returned. "Well. That was terrifying."

"Sorry," said Lennox, visibly shaking. "I didn't think it would be so literal. How about, I command you to disobey me."

Alora stood still.

Lennox frowned. "You're still on one leg."

"Don't I know it," groaned Alora.

"Stand normal, please."

The foot held aloft, unwound. Alora slowly lowered it to the floor. "It won't work. It won't let me escape it."

"What if I break it?" said Lennox.

"I've tried," said Bash, his eyes no less distressed above the mask. "At the coast. I tried smashing it against the rocks. It broke the stones apart and didn't so much as scratch the skull."

"You didn't want to bring it back?"

"I thought it would release the family from their entrancement and rid the world of it all at once. It did neither."

"So they are still beholden to their frightening witch of a grandmother?" Alora shuddered at the idea of someone wishing her into an early death.

"No. In holding it out and demanding they not obey the old woman, I transferred that power. They're beholden to me. But I've no plans to ever see them again. To ever issue out any command they would need to follow. They're as safe as I can make them."

Alora couldn't help but turn to Lennox, as the realization dawned upon her the same moment it did herself. *Never see them again.* "But…"

Lennox's mouth opened and closed, a protest she couldn't voice. Then determination hardened her. "Destroy the skull, Alora."

She tried. She tried everything. She set flames to it, imagined it melted. Turned it freezing, willing it to shatter. She even tried to imagine it vanished. Whomever had created the skull to begin with had been thorough. Just as the clause in her contract, she could cause no harm to what mastered her. She growled in frustration.

"Alora."

Her gaze met Bash's, and he moved toward her until their chests nearly brushed. His scent enveloped her, and she breathed deeper without meaning.

"Let me do it. Burn my contract and allow me free. I promise to stay at the opposite end of the world to give you your own will."

"Bash…" But Lennox was already obeying his outstretched hands, his gloves enclosing the skull.

"Burn them. Make them disappear. Whatever you can or want."

Her hands, shaking, pulled free the pages. The enchanted ink shimmered, black to red to gold, warning her. She fanned the trio of contracts in her hands and knew her second contract wasn't at all like her first. Her first had been plain ink and paper. Her second would keep her chained for eternity. *Burn to ashes*, she thought and imagined, and when she blinked next, they were gone, dusting from her fingers.

"I feel different," whispered Lennox. "Lighter, almost."

Bash said nothing, staring directly at Alora. He waited for her decision. And beyond him—the only sound to ever echo throughout Opulence—rang a bell.

Lennox paled, swinging around to the closed door. "Opening," she said.

"Time's up," said Bash. "Which is it to be, Alora?"

But Alora could only shake her head. "Don't. I can't. I can't make that choice."

"Yes, you can."

"Nobody will be making any choices soon enough if we're caught," hissed Lennox.

"Alora—"

"Bash! I said I can't! Aren't you listening? I *will not choose!* I will have you both or nothing!" A stunned silence settled over the Room of Desire. "I've not had a true friend since I was a child, and I won't give Lennox up. And I haven't felt like—well, I'm not sure how to describe what I'm feeling when I'm—" Alora felt herself blushing. *Always at the worst of times.* "Once, you said that if you were a betting man, you'd say I smile at everyone. You're right. I do. And I think it was easy then because I knew that was as close with someone as I'd ever allow myself to be. But that's not what *I* desire. I won't give you up, either. I've been told to abandon this project, to run, to hide, to do this and that and to *choose*, and I'm sick to death of it. I want to *win*. I want to beat Marshall Merridon, that old pond scum, at his own twisted game. Now, kindly allow me to move, Lennox. I have things to do."

"O-oh," stumbled Lennox. "Well, let's… Goodness, hold on! How about…Alora, I command you to move about the mansion at will."

"And the grounds."

"And the grounds."

"Thank you. I would go and pack your things," said Alora, and then she flung open the door.

Chapter Forty-One

Alora Pennigrim had realized some time ago that Marshall Merridon played a game. A long one, where he'd rigged the rules from the start so that he would always come out on top. She didn't realize until this moment, though, quite how intricate those riggings were.

It began with the grounds themselves. *"Mind your step"*, she'd been told. But why? What would happen to her if she didn't? What secrets might she uncover? Because that's all those warnings were good for. Keeping secrets.

The special bees in Renwick Forest.

The windowless dwellings of Opulence employees.

The oversized rake and wheelbarrow of the groundskeeper.

Outside, Alora and Bash stepped off the white-pebbled front lane and into the shadows of gargantuan topiaries. There, her hand reached out, visible from fingertips to wrist, the rest of her unable to be seen. By all but Merridon and his enchantment.

Alora crouched, where she ran her fingers through a lawn that'd always looked too green.

"Care to elaborate on the specifics of your plan here, Miss Pennigrim?"

"I'm still thinking of new specifics, Captain. Since I wasn't able to burn my contract, I'm a little limited right now."

She'd not come out here on a whim, though. This was where it'd all began. With glittered lanes and shadowed hedges and grass she could not touch. Alora sank fully onto her knees, ripping up the oddly textured greenery. She eyed the fistful from every angle. "This grass doesn't feel like any I've touched before."

"It's synthetic."

"Fake?" She peered around a topiary, eyeing the arrival of patrons, noticing the hoods being lowered, the cloaks being folded and handed away. She startled when she recognized both Mr. Pottenbaums.

Twin torches burned at the matching bases of the specter wolves, lighting their stone fangs and intriguing more than one member enough to circle them. An ill feeling settled over Alora at their delighted perusal. To distract herself, she reached out for the nearest topiary.

"Fake also," he said.

Alora dropped her hand away. "I suppose that explains why no rain or wind was allowed in. There wasn't a need."

Opulence Mansion had been kept in a petrified perfection. Another veil with which to hide its rotted insides. Alora studied its front from where she was obscured—every golden stacked stone. Something niggled at her. Something not right. She shrugged off her coat.

The Urchin captain made a sound of protest beside her, and Alora turned toward him. He was covered still, completely obscured in his dark coat and hood, so she couldn't read him at all. She raised an eyebrow.

"I'm tired of hiding. Aren't you?"

The golden gown she wore hugged every curve, heavy and resplendent. She couldn't tell if Bash cared for it at all, or if he hated it as much as she did.

"Is this your plan then? Reveal yourself to Opulence?"

Alora surveyed all she could see. The lawn and topiaries, the stone walkway and flame-washed stairs. "I think so. Merridon has done a lot of work painting over his secrets. I think the best place to start is by washing some of them clean. Could you wish for rain?"

Bash did, and the skies rumbled in answer. Seconds later, the downpour began. Alora felt badly over the shouts of protest from the elegantly dressed as they rushed inside, but not so badly that she thought about stopping. The rain pummeled the grounds, splattering the path in fat drops that sent bursts of glitter into the air with their velocity.

Alora watched as the white lane began to run with gold, the mansion's walls losing their luster moment by moment. Gray stone lay beneath, plain as a mountain. She watched as the topiaries wilted, too, beneath the onslaught. In a matter of seconds, they were no longer green but taupe—fake and plain. She stepped backward, the lawn protected where her shoes had been, and saw the blades quickly fade as the rain found them too.

She glanced at Bash last.

He'd lowered his hood, his face upturned to the sky. She glanced over his covered jawline, his mouth and nose, and when he pulled off his coat, she smiled that he wore a black vest, vining with silver leaves. A 'mending' he'd allowed.

"I prefer you dressed like a shopkeeper," she said.

His gaze found hers.

He reached backward, unclasping the mask, until he could pull it free, stuffing it into the pocket of his trousers. He held out a hand, thought better of it, and removed the gloves first. Then his bare palm was there, waiting to be grasped by hers, as he said, "Bash Syntaine. Enchanted with the ability to both destroy and restore light. I own a shop called Potions and Peculiarities that I'd be interested in selling to the right buyer. I've traveled widely, almost never by my own choice, and have hurt a lot of people, most against my own will.

I could have fought harder against it, but I stopped quite some time ago. Until now."

Alora put to rest the lonely look of his stranded hand and slid her own within it. "Alora Pennigrim. Enchanted with a too-vivid imagination. I would love to buy your shop—for the right price. I've hardly traveled at all, except from Eirian, which I abandoned when I hurt someone very badly under rather good intentions and couldn't fix it. I also haven't fought very hard, until now."

They stared at one another awhile, the rain soaking them through. Veins of black snaked across the whites of Bash's eyes, and Alora wondered what that meant.

He said, "How's that for revealing myself?"

Alora smiled, and it wasn't at all perfect nor practiced. "A good start." His eyes cleared to that familiar, deep green at her statement, and she knew then what had brought upon the darkness, because she felt that vulnerability the same.

She didn't want to be free of him. Not at all.

He stepped nearer, the fake topiary standing stark and ugly behind him, and she couldn't deny anymore that she'd more than one dream now. That hers was the same as his and just as much of a worthwhile torment. Her breath hitched when his hand came around the back of her head.

His mouth dropped near hers. "Tell me what to wish for and when to wish it. I'll see this place fall for us both."

Alora did, her new plan tumbling from her lips in a rush—all for it to be dashed to a heap at Lennox's scream.

Chapter Forty-Two

Marshall Merridon had slapped Lennox Flowers straight across the cheek, and he'd grabbed ahold of her before she could fall beneath the aggression of it; there upon the front steps of the mansion.

Alora's vision blurred in her rage.

It nearly caused her to miss Bash's leaving.

"Enough!"

The malevolence of Bash's shout jolted her, enough that her eyes cleared, and she found him rushing through the rain with long-legged strides. He'd made it to the stairs before Alora could even step on the path, his hand enclosing Lennox's wrist, hauling her behind him.

Alora ran, missing the beginnings of their exchange due to the harsh rain, and stopped at the first stair. Marshall Merridon loomed over his adopted son in a threatening manner. When his hands came up to shove Bash backward, Bash smacked them away. Hard enough that Merridon stumbled, and Alora gasped.

This wasn't *at all* going according to plan.

"You dare put your hands on me? I am the Master of Opulence! I own you all!"

"You do not *own* me," said the Urchin captain and fisted his hand around Merridon's sopping crimson tie.

"Me neither," said Lennox, from behind Bash's back. Her cheek was red as cherries, but her eyes were vivid and angry.

"Or me," said Alora, but much quieter.

Still, it drew attention. Merridon turned toward her, his hands attempting to find purchase on Bash's wrists and failing. His eyes widened as he took her in.

"Miss Pennigrim? Get back to the Room of Desire this *instant*." When Alora didn't so much as twitch, he appeared overcome, his features an apoplectic purple. "What has happened? Obey me!"

At last, he jerked his front free of Bash, only for his arm to be captured as he managed one step down, nearer to her. Marshall Merridon stopped, a single rigid movement, tracking the grip up to the arm and then the figure holding him. A shocked, incomprehensible look came over his features as if he couldn't believe his son had the audacity to halt him a second time.

Or maybe it was simply the scorching look of loathing his captain directed at him.

"You are not to defy me! In *anything*. It's right there in your contract."

"A pity it no longer exists."

"Marshall! There you are! I've been—"

The front doors of Opulence were at once flooded with light and dashed in shadow in a single breath when Madam Feebledire slammed the doors shut at her back. "*What is going on here?*" she whispered on a strangled cry. "We are *open!*"

She focused on each of them in turn. Alora in her sagging, golden gown, Lennox and her handprinted cheek in a plain travel dress, and Bash in none of his usual attire, looking less and less like their devoted Urchin captain and more like an avenging devil, his eyes entirely consumed.

It was Merridon who spoke first. "Shut up, Patrice. This is a father-son matter." And then he pulled back his free arm and punched Bash square in the jaw.

"Oh my heavens!" screeched Madam Feebledire a moment before the light broke.

Alora was left outside it, as were Lennox and Madam Feebledire, but only for a few seconds. With a slew of improper curses, Madam Feebledire tossed aside the paper she carried and leapt into the void. Alora lunged for the parchment. Hope was a painful beat in her chest, and it dissolved to relief at finding her contract safe in her hands.

She didn't waste another second, hurrying to where the torches guttered weak beneath the rain. She shoved the contract inside the flame, waiting for an agonizing amount of time as it slowly ate up the damp paper. The moment the last corner disintegrated to ash, Alora felt it. A stiffness had left her, her body no longer draped in chains. She stopped the rain at once. It'd done more than enough in revealing the wonderland Merridon touted as the fake show it really was.

"Marshall Matthew Merridon! You have extensive explaining to do."

Alora eased around the disembodied voice of Madam Feebledire until she stood beside Lennox.

"What should we do?" whispered her friend.

"I'm not sure," said Alora. "I won't be able to see either if I go in with them."

They were saved from further indecision when the light returned. It wasn't gradual, but sudden. One moment there was a black void and the next, she saw all three.

Bash knelt upon one knee. In front of him, sprawled Merridon, his back to Bash's chest and his neck encircled by Bash's arm. Merridon fought against the hold, his fingers digging into the Urchin captain's forearm without avail. Meanwhile, Madam Feebledire crouched, pulling at her brother's gold-buckled boot. She was even less successful at freeing him than Merridon was himself.

"Bash Merridon, release him at once! He has to answer for what he's done."

Bash glared at his aunt, muscles straining in his neck, another feathering in his jaw. "That's precisely what he's doing."

"With words! Not with death!" Her hands slipped on her brother's wet boot, sending her sprawling onto her backside.

With a growl, Bash flung his father away. "Fine. Have your interrogation. But we get to bear witness."

Merridon knelt on the slick stairs, wheezing. One hand remained on the step as the other massaged his throat. Alora squinted in the dim light as his hand moved lower, traveling into his waistcoat.

"Wait. What are you—" she choked.

In a single bound, Marshall Merridon was turning on his feet. In his hand was a weapon—a blowgun. A dart stuck in its end. He pointed it straight at Bash, his mouth at its opposite end, and Alora thought she would pass out from the panic overcoming her.

"No!" she screamed, just as Merridon blew with all his strength.

They were all stunned in the aftermath. Alora swayed on her feet, and Lennox gripped her elbow, steadying her.

"It's all right," her friend whispered in her ear.

But it was not all right.

Because Marshall Merridon was looking at her as if he would kill her.

He blew into the paper tube again to be sure, but same as before, it unrolled, a horn-like noise sounding from its end.

A child's party favor. She'd loved them growing up.

"You meddling bitch," hissed Marshall Merridon, and flung the toy at her. "How have you used your enchantment without my wishing?"

"I burned my contract while you were fumbling in the dark."

"Your contract! How did you have it?"

"I brought it, Marshall. I've been trying to find you to ask after its wording." Madam Feebledire brushed off her skirt, stepping back when her brother stepped forward. "Did you mean to make it sound like you entrapped the girl?"

"Of course I did!" Merridon's temples pulsed with his rage. "I command you back to your door!"

Alora only continued to stare at him with wide eyes. "No, thank you."

At that, Marshall Merridon howled in fury. He swung to Bash, lifting a finger between them. "That skull was meant to entrance indefinitely!"

"It must be broken. My apologies." Bash's grin was pure malice. He crossed his arms, the wet fabric a second skin.

"Marshall! What is this about entrapment and entrancing? It's one thing to do to simple creatures, but to *people?*"

Alora pursed her lips. There was nothing simple about mermaids, but she remained silent, waiting for what he might say.

"I said shut *up*, Patrice! Look at this! Look at what they've done. The wind. The *rain*. My expensive grounds. My extraordinary mansion! The members can't witness this. Lock the gate! Let no one else inside."

As if in response, a large crack rent the air, the wolves split down the middle by lightning.

An animalistic sound tore from Merridon's throat. He spun on his heel, meaning to spring toward Alora and likely detach her head from her neck, but Bash was there first, and a second crack shocked the air—as a memory baton met the temple of Opulence Mansion's owner. Marshall Merridon slumped to his knees, then to his front. Blessedly unconscious.

"Why. *Why…*" moaned Madam Feebledire from behind her hands.

Bash wiped blood from the baton, returning it again to his belt. "Any suggestions?"

"I say we feed him to the mermaid," said Lennox, her eyes hard and a little bit hungry.

"The mermaid doesn't deserve a first real meal this unappetizing," said Alora. "I have an idea, I think. Only allow me to do something quick. We shouldn't strain ourselves over him."

She grabbed ahold of his boots.

"Absolutely *not.*"

Alora stared at Madam Feebledire. At how she'd splayed herself in front of Opulence Mansion's carved front doors, her normally coifed hair unfurling around her ears in frizzy tendrils.

"Madam Feebledire, please move. Or I'll be tempted to add a monument to replace the broken wolves."

Opulence's head of management appeared caught off guard at that, her lips parting into a silent circle. She came to with a shrug of her shoulders, though Alora could see she'd paled.

"Don't threaten me, girl. If not for me, you'd still be beholden to that enchanted contract you made the mistake in signing."

"It wasn't a mistake! I was forced!"

Madam Feebledire shook her head like this detail was of little consequence. "I can't let you harm him."

"Who said we would harm him?" said Bash, who probably wasn't the best one to say it considering there were bruises quickly forming on Merridon's throat that matched his own fingertips and blood dripping yet from the man's temple.

"Putting him inside that tub *would* be harming him!"

"Ha!" said Alora and gritted her teeth at Madam Feebledire's baffled expression. "At last, someone admits it!"

The head of management spluttered. "Now wait a minute. *Wait.* I didn't mean it harms all. But it would harm *him.*"

Lennox's stare narrowed. "Why?"

"She's lying," said Alora. "See how she fidgets?"

Madam Feebledire stood still at once. "Fine, perhaps it does some harm to everyone. Maybe the tub itself is an enchanted artifact. Maybe, when combined with the oil, it does sever your worst memories but leaves a crack instead that crumbles its way into an eventual void in your person. Maybe it does. But to some, that's *worth it!*"

"It should be the Room of Severed Memories then, not the room of *forgotten* ones! And I suppose members are made aware of this future effect?" Alora said it with a healthy lathering of sarcasm. She didn't doubt in the slightest that Opulence Mansion was untruthful.

"Well..." Madam Feebledire shifted again and caught herself. "I can't speak for everyone..."

"Patrice?" Four heads swiveled down toward another. To Merridon shifting on his conjured stretcher, his hand to his head. "What's happened? Why am I outside? On the ground no less." No one uttered a word. "Bash? Miss Flowers? Miss—"

Alora's breath stilled in her lungs. She waited for Merridon to recognize her, his expression pinched and assessing. But then they widened, and he was scrambling until he could stand before her, his hand outstretched. "My dear. My *dear.* What is your name?"

Alora swallowed against the bile threatening to rise inside her. Merridon looked as if he'd not eaten in days and here she was, a feast brought before him. Blood matted in his hair, drying on his cheek, his neck red and swollen—surely it all must hurt, but he appeared oblivious, concerned only with her. With what his enchantment sensed in her blood.

Such a nasty specter wolf.

"Germania Jones," said Alora, ignoring Bash's smothered cough to her left.

She didn't have a hope of pulling her arm back fast enough to avoid Master Merridon's grip. He held her hand firm. "I'm Master Marshall Merridon, the owner of Opulence Mansion. Would you be open to a meeting? I have a particularly enticing opportunity I think you were born to inherit."

"Perhaps." Alora heard Lennox's murmur of surprise behind her and smiled picture perfect. "If it includes a tour."

Chapter Forty-Three

A melody filled the grand hall, coaxing and a little bit wild. Upon entering it, the sound immediately set Alora's heartbeat to a faster pace and her head to muddling. Suddenly, she wanted to *experience* things. Exotic things, tempting things, dangerous things.

Gone were the golden cloaks, checked at the door. Without them, the members of Opulence Mansion were dressed in all sorts of finery. From silken trousers and laced cuffs to satin skirts and glittering bodices. Everything she could see, clothing and jewelry and eager eyes, were set to further brilliance by the yellow glow of endless gilded chandeliers. The scent, too, had changed. Alora smelled hints of wine and wax, cinnamon, amber and vanilla. It was an intoxicating blend to be sure, and everything and everyone so very *beautiful*. She breathed heartily, her lip caught between her teeth.

Don't be tricked, she reminded herself. *Don't be swayed by this place.*

Doors clicked quietly near her: Door One and Door Two. A woman with a luxurious golden robe rounded the spiral staircase to her left, up and up until Alora knew with certainty she would sail into the Room of Forgotten Memories and bathe away her deepest regrets. What changes would she undergo by its end? An unfair one no matter what, considering what she didn't understand. A handsome employee dressed in Opulence crimson and painted in Opulence gold met her there, turning the knob and beckoning her in. A soft smile exchanged. Alora shuddered and looked away.

She found instead Door Two, remembering above it waited the Room of Reward, a place of gambling and vice. She startled upon meeting the equally startled expression of Mr. Pottenbaum. A sheepish wave was all he offered her, along with a parting study of the man beside her, until he, too, made for the stairs.

He thinks I'm like them. A member.

Bash set a steadying hand on her wrist. At first, she did not know why. Then a disoriented and disgruntled Marshall Merridon spun toward them.

"We're *open*," he said, scathingly, accusatory eyes spearing his head of management.

"Of course we are. It's passed dusk," huffed Madam Feebledire. "Mar—ahh, Master. Shall you begin the tour with your office? You have a little—" Madam Feebledire motioned to her own temple, pausing when her brother's scowl deepened.

"No! We're open and Miss Flowers is *right here*. And my captain is wearing...*silver*." Merridon's throat worked as if he fought back a gag. "*Get to your door—*"

Alora's mouth parted at the hostile words directed at Lennox. Merridon, noting this, halted at once, easing into a false, rich laugh. "I'm sorry, Miss Flowers. I have quite the headache all of a sudden. But your partner is likely waiting on you, as are our many *well-paying* patrons. Let's not disappoint them! After all, that is not Opulence's way."

Lennox looked down at her dress; while not unsightly, it was decidedly drab in the changed environment. Not to mention there would be no partner awaiting her, either, should she obey. "Erm..."

"Thank you for helping me out of the rain, Miss Flowers. I won't forget your assistance in righting my skirt. Perhaps I will see you again." Alora stared pointedly at Lennox and then down the hall.

"What rain?" said Merridon with a scoff of disbelief. "*Outside?*"

Lennox chose to ignore him. Alora had dried them each and he didn't need the insight. "My deepest apologies, Master. I'll perform beyond perfection to make up for my tardiness." Her quick curtsy transformed into a scurrying walk, and soon she was lost to the hall's expanse.

All at once Merridon was at Bash's ear. She heard the words "change" and "immediately" before he turned toward Alora with affected cheer. "Miss Jones, you seem to have caught us at a rare— nay—I'll say *singular* moment in which we aren't quite at our best. But you are dressed exquisitely. May I say again how fated I feel this meeting is?"

Alora could see it writhing inside him, that greed. It was what stilled his tongue, she thought, over questions as to how she came to be here to begin with. "You may," she said.

Merridon chuckled at that. "What a wit. I admit this is going to be a shade more difficult, touring with a full house, but if you insist—"

"I do."

"Well, we will become inventive then." His dark gaze left hers for the man beside her. "Captain. I thought you had to be *elsewhere?*"

"I do not, actually. But here you are. All the silver I possess."

Alora watched him shrug the patterned vest from his broad shoulders much the same way Marshall Merridon had watched her on the front steps. With unabashed *want.* She couldn't even pull her gaze away to see what look might have been exchanged between father and son.

Instead, Bash's gaze landed on her, cool with warning.

Right. We are in the thick of it, you loon.

She made to grant her attention back to Merridon, only to have it stolen from her.

"You there! What need do you have of me?"

Alora saw the man jump at Merridon's voice, his fist prepared to gift another knock upon Door Zero. He hurried over toward them, his skin gold and shining beneath the abundant candlelight, and slid to a halt.

"My apologies, Master. I didn't see you."

The silence stretched. "*And—?*"

The employee had taken to examining Merridon's head wound with obvious distaste and equal confusion. At his master's sharp word, however, he glanced over Alora, his painted face creased with worry. Whatever information he had, he clearly didn't want to part with it in front of her. "May I speak with you in private?"

Merridon's mask began to crack. He bared his teeth, his fist clenching around Bash's discarded vest. "If you must."

The man backed away, and Merridon, incensed though he was, immediately followed.

"What do you think you're about?" whispered Madam Feebledire in a harsh voice. "Fine if you want to rid him of the summer's decisions. What is done is done, and heaven knows what he did to Miss Pennigrim was wrong on several levels of morality, but a *tour?* For what reason?"

"Apologies, *again*," said Marshall Merridon, shocking his sister into leaping away from Alora and Bash. "My employee was under the impression we've a Door Twenty-five opening tonight. Not tonight, I told him, but hopefully soon." He looked at Alora with meaning. "Shall we begin there in our grand tour?"

"In an unfinished room?" said Alora, her voice wavering. True, Lennox had the skull hidden away, and Alora's contract was burned, but knowing that didn't halt the bout of nerves come upon her at remembering that long corridor and windowless room.

"Unfinished though it may be, it is soon to be the greatest offering of Opulence: the Room of Desire." Merridon's features turned wolf-like. "You remind me of someone. Someone I noticed some time ago in Enver. You have the same—"

Scent? thought Alora.

But Master Merridon struggled. His eyebrows dipped, and he rubbed at his bearded chin. "Hmm. Anyway, what do you do for work, Miss Jones?"

Alora cleared her throat, fighting a glance at Bash. "A decorator… of cakes."

"How nice," said Master Merridon. "Have you tried your mind at anything else?" With two fingers he motioned Bash to him. When the Urchin captain neared, he said, "Fetch that latest crystal artifact. I'd like to show our guest."

"No, I haven't," said Alora, her blood boiling away.

Not even a false contract and a month of work this time!

Marshall Merridon could remember his plan for Door Twenty-five and he remembered Alora, or at least the feel of her enchantment. She'd apparently been the one to trigger the room's planning and purpose, however long ago. And here she was, about to replace herself with Germania Jones.

"Would you like to?" said Merridon to her. To Bash, he hissed a whispered, "And cover your face!"

Bash obeyed, his eyes so flat Alora thought it must be purposeful, hiding away his rage. From the pocket of his trousers, he removed his mask. He pressed it over the lower half of his face, clasping it at the back.

"Better?" he rasped.

The owner of Opulence was less careful at concealing his anger. His eyes sparked, his lip curling. He glanced between Bash and Alora, at how she watched his masking, heard his voice change with its enchantment. "For now," he ground out.

For now. Until he was left alone with him.

"Master," said Madam Feebledire. "I really must insist on—"

"*Patrice,*" spat Merridon. "Leave us."

"But—"

"See to your duty! There are people milling about the front doors. Why is that? Go away, *now,* and find out." Madam Feebledire cast a wounded look toward her brother, but it was only a flash, one that quickly solidified into something more. Her face hardened as she spun away, her heels clicking soft on the marble.

"Now then," said Merridon with a shake of his head. "Captain, fetch what I asked. You may meet us at Door Twenty-five when it is done." With a charming smile, he turned to Alora and proffered an arm. "Shall we?"

Alora watched as Bash melded with the bodies behind him, his eyes on her, wholly black above the fabric. He inclined his head by the smallest fraction moments before she lost him, but she understood. He'd disappear, would follow them, and beneath her breath, where no one could have a hope of hearing, she whispered, "I trust you entirely."

And oh, how good that felt.

Chapter Forty-Four

The music came from a gramophone. One so overlarge and gilded that Alora wondered how she'd not seen it rising up from the middle of the hall. It rested on a lacquered table, curved upward and carved, while Doors Eleven and Twelve winked at her on either side. The sound spun itself all around her.

Drink, it sang. *Partake.*

On either side of the gramophone were two cascading fountains: one red and one gold. The liquid streamed steadily from the fanciful stone, ready for one of the many flutes to be placed beneath it and filled. Merridon paused near them.

"Wine, Miss Jones? Champagne?"

Alora could smell its potency across the distance. She'd not eaten any dinner; one glass would surely send her stumbling, useless in her endeavor. She waved a hand. "Oh, no. Thank you."

"Suit yourself," he said, but she noticed he didn't partake either.

Expose the rot. That was her grand plan. Well, she'd already stripped the grounds of gold, but what did anyone really care about that so long as the attractions remained the same? So long as the music kept them eager, the drink euphoric, and the magical doors unlocked?

She thought over the song, at how it worked at her mind. It urged her to dance. To drink, be frivolous and impulsive, to find a pretty someone and a shadowed alcove. Alora buried her instincts—as surely, this was another of Merridon's shuttled dark artifacts—and let the music soak into the very depths of her. It permeated her veins, lit her nerves with sensation. At once, she felt carefree, but also care*less*.

No, thank you. She'd been subjected to a much worse version than this once, and she didn't enjoy the reminder. Alora cast an appreciative look around the expansive space, all for show. Then she changed the tune.

It was the same song, anyone would say so, but it also was decidedly *not*. The enchantment of the gramophone was stripped, so quick it would have been impossible to see even if you did not blink. She'd replaced its horn with a new one, her own imagining conjured.

All at once, she did not feel like dancing or drinking. Though she couldn't deny that if a *certain* handsome someone invited her into a shadowed alcove, she would absolutely trip in her haste. She eyed Merridon from the edge of her vision. As of yet, he didn't notice. His attention had been diverted, it seemed, by whatever transpired at the front door. She snatched at the opportunity.

The wine was a red so deep it was almost purple. With a simple thought, it became only grape juice, sweet and smooth, safe enough for a child to enjoy. The champagne would be trickier; it frothed up a fuss as it tumbled. Winnowillow juice was a similar color, though not bubbly naturally. That was fine, for what was one more detail? She would create bubbles.

She waited a moment, another sidelong glance revealing Merridon still preoccupied by the discussion at the front entrance where one door was left wide, and sniffed the air. No more cloying scent of alcohol lingered. Nothing but sugar and fruit.

"Master Merridon? Are you all right?"

At her question, Marshall Merridon turned around.

He appeared irritated, and Alora had to smother a smile over why. She could well imagine what caused a commotion at the front entrance as the late arrivals were likely experiencing the grounds for the first time without its gilded glory. The strange, cracked wolves. But then he seemed to catch hold of her enchantment again, breathing deep, his pupils dilating with insatiable hunger. He wanted her for his mansion in a terrible way.

How tragic for him, that she would never be trapped again.

"Miss Jones…" He looked torn, his attention shifting between the fuss at the door and her. "My sincerest apologies, but might we continue our tour once my captain has returned? Here." He scooped up a flute and filled it with grape juice. "Enjoy a glass of wine. Finest vintage from the southern coast." Then he strode quickly away.

Alora sipped at her juice. *This will not end well,* she thought. But for whom? That she didn't know. She *hoped,* but she didn't know.

She drained her glass, setting it onto a tray being whisked about by a gold-faced employee. "I would abandon your shift early," she whispered.

The woman's eyes widened at her remark. "Why is that?"

"Because Master Merridon is about to lose his composure, and I think we would all benefit from being far away when it vanishes."

The employee turned toward the front entrance with alarm, in time to catch Merridon throwing the doors wide. They were too far away to see any great detail, however.

"I don't understand." She glanced back to Alora, her forehead wrinkling now in suspicion. "What's happened?"

"Secrets of the mansion are being revealed. And unfortunately, they're far less pretty than the lies. Please, just consider it."

Alora filled a flute with winnowillow juice next, glancing around for a shadow denser than all the rest. She didn't find one. She did find more than one melancholic face, however. The employees of Opulence were steadily losing hold of their golden smiles. Even the patrons seemed to have lost a little of the luster in their eyes. Still, the gramophone sang on.

"I suppose I'll just continue the tour on my own then," she said to no one in particular.

Alora then strode down the corridor, her chin high, for all the world like she was meant to be there. She hummed along with the song.

Chapter Forty-Five

Noelnina Dynasti. That was her name. And Door Twenty-four was hers. Room of Ribbons. Alora offered a smile to the employee who had turned the doorknob for her, which he returned, but wanly. She stepped into the dark.

It was an intriguing dark, not at all absolute, as the ceiling was covered in twinkling lights mimicking stars. And from it hung the room's namesake: ribbons. Many of them, in rich blues and reds, coiled much like the staircase she'd taken to lead her here. Twisting among them, in a hugging suit of crimson and black, was Noelnina, the performer she'd encountered once but never met.

Her body moved decadently, mesmerizing everyone in the room. Members sat in plush seating or leaned against the wall, nearly all with flutes in their hands and enraptured looks upon their faces. Alora couldn't blame them. It was an impressive display of talent.

One of the ribbons lifted all on its own. Drawn upward as though attracted to the performer, it snaked around Noelnina's ankle. Alora noted the woman notice its ascent, thinking she'd grasp hold and swing. Instead, Alora's eyes widened, as the performer pulled a whip from between her breasts and thwacked the ribbon smartly.

It dropped away, chastised.

And she saw then that this ribbon possessed odd little fangs. But no. Not only this ribbon. Alora moved along the wall, apologizing to those whose view she momentarily blocked, until she was sure she could say every ribbon in the Room of Ribbons was fanged.

Were they alive? Or enchanted artifacts?

Slitted, yellow eyes, there in the dark. *Alive, then.*

Had Bash collected these unique serpents? What corner of the world had he gone to find them? She'd never seen a snake with a body so flat it could be mistaken for a ribbon. Staring at Noelnina twisting about their lengths made her insides do the same. *How awful.*

Alora took note of the sconces on the walls, burning so low, they were nearly extinguished. Her jaw set as she burned them bright. At once, there were cries of protest around her, though none was as loud as Noelnina's, who cried aloud as she lost her grip in her surprise. Before Alora could think of conjuring something to catch her, the performer caught herself at the last moment, the ribbon-snake's fangs in line with her nose and hissing.

The woman touched her boots to the floor and swept the room with quick assessment. A disgruntled few abandoned the show soon after. "Nevermind, ladies and gentlemen," the performer proclaimed. "It is all part of the entertainment. A new routine! Debuted tonight and only for your illustrious selves."

This seemed to placate what remained of her audience, a look of intrigue appearing on more than one face. Alora could almost feel the relief emanating from Miss Dynasti. She wished that it could last.

But Alora had seen what transpired at the ceiling. At how the rafters crisscrossed, the ribbon-snakes' tails tied in knots. It wasn't Noelnina's fault; she didn't harvest these snakes from their home. Still, she couldn't dance with them any longer either.

When Noelnina reached to pull upon the serpent's body, it toppled on her head instead. The performer's cry was more akin to a shriek as the snake slithered on the floor, its eyes—and fangs—

focused solely on her. Members startled to standing, some screaming and climbing on their chairs while others pushed for the door. One by one, the ribbons fell from the ceiling until the floor was a mix of red and blue and yellow eyes. Alora saw the employee who'd let her in for a single second before he fled.

She needed to work quickly.

"Miss Dynasti!"

Noelnina diverted her attention to Alora a moment before smacking a snake across the face with her whip.

"What do you want?"

"Come out of there!"

The performer seemed torn, her lips parted, hesitation in every line of her dark features. This was her job, her *contract*.

"Miss Dynasti, the snakes look bent on revenge. Please come!"

There was considerable truth to Alora's words. Every snake—and there were a *lot*—had turned upon the performer, raising their strange flat heads and baring their fangs. None paid the slightest mind to anyone else in the room.

With a pained expression, Noelnina abandoned where she stood, leaping over the blue body of a serpent to land before Alora.

"Who are you? How do you know my name?"

"Alora Pennigrim. I was forced into a contract by Master Merridon to occupy Door Twenty-five, but I've burned it now. I'll burn yours, too, if you'd like?"

Noelnina's lip curled, her eyebrows lowered. "You set my ribbons free."

"The *snakes* free."

As if responding to their discussion over them, more hissing sounded from the room, moving closer.

"You burned your contract? You're free?"

"I am." *Mostly.*

A hardness settled in Noelnina Dynasti's amber eyes. "Do the same for me. Or I'll string you up from the rafters and twirl around you instead."

Alora wobbled, a bit dumbfounded over the vivid imagery for a moment. But eventually, she nodded.

"Good luck," said the performer, and rushed through the door.

Alora stared into the bright room, at the mass of snakes now come upon her. She was alone, her back to the door.

"Please don't bite. It was me who untied your ends. I'll leave the door open. See that you find your way outside?"

Snakes were not usually simple creatures. These snakes weren't either. At her remarks, their heads swayed in unison, to the door behind the ridiculously dressed woman talking to them. Two to three at a time, they slithered past. Not one attempted a bite of her. She mimicked Noelnina when the last slipped through.

"Good luck."

The chaos of disrupted rooms leeched throughout all of Opulence.

By the time Alora gripped the doorknob belonging to Room of Happy Days, she knew chaos no longer fit the description. It was disaster.

The staff were scrambling, taking their orders from a pale Madam Feebledire and a red-faced Merridon. None were posted at the doors any longer, making Alora's work simpler, her demure smiles unnecessary. And the members—well, from what she could see there weren't many left. Alora had released snakes upon them, dismantled nearly half the mansion's enchantments, and whoever still remained inside were either clueless behind closed doors she'd yet to disrupt or desperate.

So far, she'd promised eight burned contracts. So far, every performer had accepted. Though none were as colorful in their acceptance as Noelnina had been.

She glanced over her shoulder to observe Bash's enchantment roll over the floor. Beginning with Door Twenty-four, he'd waited until she'd gone from a room before breaking the light. Half of Opulence was now swallowed like some evil had come upon them, dragging them slowly down to the deepest pit of hell. It must have been a truly frightening sight for everyone who did not understand him.

But she did. Alora stared into the void a moment and thought only about him inside it. Her skin immediately flushed hot. "You are an obsessive type, too, aren't you." She'd wondered before, but here it was, confirmed.

She slipped into Door Eleven.

Chapter Forty-Six

The Room of Happy Days was empty. Of people, at least. Alora hurried to the edge. "Mermaid," she hissed. When nothing stirred, she said, louder, "Mermaid! I've come to set you free."

She waited for what felt like many minutes—but was likely only seconds—before gritting her teeth and grumbling, working at the zipper of her gown. She'd only managed an inch before she remembered she needn't bother fussing with it, and imagined the entire thing unzipped. It dropped to the floor with more noise than a gown had any business creating. Why Merridon thought to put her in such a heavy thing made no sense; she couldn't have run beneath his entrancement anyway.

Her shift beneath was thin and ivory, covered only by a crimson corset that pulled her waist in and pushed her breasts to ungodly heights. But she'd not waste time imagining anything more. She shucked her shoes and promptly dove into the pool.

It wasn't cold, but still the change in environment shocked her. She'd gone in so slowly last time. Alora opened her eyes before the bubbles managed to settle and felt struck by how lovely it really was beneath the surface. She'd not been swimming in ages.

She paddled forward.

The mermaid waited for her. In a nearly identical position as before, it studied her approach, and Alora recognized the expression. Resignation, but haunted. Haunted by a bare flickering of hope.

Alora gestured when she neared, careful not to get lost within the mermaid's gaze lest she be swept away into a memory. *Up,* she pointed. *Free,* she mimed, pulling at her face.

The mermaid angled its head, clawed fingers raising to the barred mask.

Yes, Alora nodded.

But the mermaid made no further movement. It remained in the corner, iridescent tail swaying in the pool's depths, waiting. Alora, however, could not wait. She was unpracticed and decidedly out of air. She kicked to the surface.

Her nose broke through the water the same moment Marshall Merridon burst through the door.

The startled cry never made it passed her teeth. Alora only managed a small breath before dropping below the surface as Merridon filled the doorway. It was nowhere near enough air to hold herself down for long; she only hoped the water was dim enough, the sconces kept low enough, that he would not see her and leave.

So much for that.

What precious air she kept left in a flurry of bubbles when a rough grip encircled her arm. Alora screamed in the pool, flailing, managing only a glimpse of the mermaid watching oh-so-carefully through the disrupted water.

Fine, you do not trust me? she thought, and focused on the picture of the creature in its horrid mask, before imagining the straps severed through. *There you are!*

Not a second later, and she was hauled up and over the ledge.

Coughing and sputtering, water pouring from her nose and mouth, Alora flipped to her hands and knees, begging for breaths that burned. But Marshall Merridon wouldn't be deterred by the pathetic picture she made. Frazzled to a frenzy, his hand encircled her throat this time and hauled her to her feet.

"What have you done to my mansion, Miss Smith? Or I should I say…Miss Pennigrim!"

Alora must have appeared as taken aback as she felt, because Merridon huffed a humorless laugh, his opposite hand coming up to his wounded head. "Betrayal. *Betrayed* by those I thought most loyal to me. My performers. My *son*. My *sister*. It took her until just minutes ago to explain to me that I'd been bludgeoned. Even longer to be *persuaded* into being more forthcoming with the details. You wench! I catalogue my contracts twice a day! Did you think I wouldn't notice what was missing?"

Alora choked as his thumb pressed to that delicate point. His forefinger, too. Good god, would she really die in the Room of Happy Days? What luckless irony.

She attempted to alleviate the pressure against her arteries, but her toes hardly touched the floor anymore.

"Lucky for you, little liar, that I want you."

That he *needed* her, more like. But leave it to Marshall Merridon to stroke his own ego even with his mansion collapsing around him. His grip eased by the smallest fraction, Alora finding her footing again.

"Now, you will tell me everything you've done. Spare nothing. If you do, I might rethink using this and start over fresh." At that, he waved a blowgun, newly loaded.

Alora mentally shook her head. Did he think her that much of an idiot? He would dart her anyway—she knew it for fact—only now he'd have her answers first. It would be an inconvenience to him, of course. He'd have to convince her of her enchantment, of how to wield it, and there would likely be many mistakes. But for a loyal performer capable of granting any desire? Any hiccups could be considered minor.

But Merridon had forgotten her previous trick, and with the oxygen once more returned to her brain, Alora imagined the needled end into one of rubber. He didn't notice at all.

Nor did he notice the mermaid swimming carefully below the surface toward them, its silver eyes and long, yellow hair the only features visible. He also didn't notice the impenetrable dark sweeping along the floor, taking the sconce light and casting them deeper in shadow. Alora did, though, because she was a designer, and she liked details.

Three things happened then, and they seemed to happen all at once:

Bash emerged from the dark, and her throat was released at the same moment Marshall Merridon's was captured.

The mermaid broke the surface and sank its claws into its former master's ankles until he screamed.

And Alora imagined a gag in the conman's mouth so he could listen for once and not speak.

"How *dare* you touch her," said Bash, a rasping growl that sent Alora's teeth into her lip.

He didn't tower over his father; in truth, he was not taller than him, but in this moment, the Urchin captain seemed to loom high above, ready to exact retribution.

A slew of muffled words came from Marshall Merridon's mouth.

"Shut *up*." Bash shook him hard enough that the rubber dart and blowgun tumbled into the water with a splash.

But Master Marshall Merridon, owner of Opulence Mansion, did not take kindly to hearing his own favorite command turned upon him. He made to kick out, only to scream anew, as his captured ankles tore and bled freely. He tried then to swing at Bash, but Alora had been forthright in her thinking after seeing his kick. Like what had once adorned Bash's wrists, shackles lashed themselves to

Marshall Merridon's. Bash's had been iron, though. Master Merridon's were gold to match his outfit—and very heavy.

Expensive, thought Alora.

Not that she'd ever sell them. Heavens knew there were enough dark artifacts in the world without adding accursed shackles to the mix. And after adorning Marshall Merridon's wrists, that's what they would assuredly be: cursed.

Bash dragged his father in close. "You have taken advantage of every soul who's ever made the mistake of trusting you. Me included. Your intentions have always been self-serving, your greed limitless, and you've not cared a whit for all you've hurt in the process. I'll have no part of you anymore, and I wish that every part of you now regrets the day you traded for me, the sad child who had all the hope for a family."

Whatever he saw in Bash's eyes seemed to mesmerize Merridon; he didn't attempt to strike or speak. Perhaps it was the resolve there. He must have known he wouldn't ever walk free.

Seconds pulsed in the air until Marshall Merridon attempted a single word.

"Please?" Bash laughed aloud, an inhumane sound behind the mask, humorless and deadened. "No."

Alora wasn't sure what he would have done then, darted him or stabbed him, but she supposed it didn't matter, as Lennox burst through the door, panting and wild, her dress scorched.

"There you...are. Ran. Must stop...smoking." She closed the door behind her, where she leaned against it. "Good news! I burned all the contracts. Learned this is one of my old dresses and not fireproofed. Bad news! There are about two dozen Urchins below stairs, and they've rounded up all the performers."

"Fucking hell," swore Bash, then shook Merridon when he grinned behind the gag.

"*Give him to me.*"

At once, the three of them looked to the mermaid. Even Merridon attempted a sidelong glance.

The creature had come above the water until Alora could see its entire face along with the graceful curve of its neck. The mermaid's features still appeared similar to the face she'd imagined for her childhood doll, though much more menacing considering she could see every needlepoint of many teeth. Scars lined both cheeks, a wicked reminder of Marshall Merridon's cruelty.

"Give him to me. I have been so hungry for fresh meat. So many years. Many years and only scraps of burnt ends."

"Are you sure you want him? He's pure evil. Pond scum, some would say." Alora pursed her lips at Merridon's form.

"Evil or good, it does not matter. Give him to me." Claws retracted only to dig into the generous calves hidden beneath Merridon's trousers. Not even the gag could tamp his shriek.

Alora moved closer to Bash, until his eyes met hers, shifting green to black. "It's up to you. He's your—"

"My father died when I was a boy. He is nothing to me."

Bash spared Marshall Merridon another glance, but in the end, nothing more was said. Instead, he pushed out lightly with the hand encircling his adoptive father's throat. Merridon lost his balance. Bound hands waved uselessly above his head before he toppled backward into the water with a spraying splash.

Alora scanned the surface, though she could see little. Even when the water turned red, a crimson so beloved by Opulence's owner, she didn't move away. Aside from the initial splash, hardly a disturbance marked Master Marshall Merridon's passing into the afterlife. Lennox must have been correct in a mermaid's capabilities in transfixing its prey to a peaceful death.

"That's that, then," murmured Lennox from the door.

"Aside from Feebledire and two dozen Urchins and all the stories spreading about Enver by panicked members as we speak, sure.

That's that." If Bash meant his remarks as sarcastic, they weren't. They'd only come out flat.

Alora stepped beside him, her hand folding into his. She wasn't satisfied until he squeezed it back. "This has been a terrible business. From day one."

"It has," Bash agreed, and looked down at her. He blinked, pulled back, then *looked*. From her bare feet to her head, kohl undoubtedly smeared down her cheeks.

If he hadn't seen her before, he finally saw her now, and she could tell even beneath the mask that his jaw had fallen, color creeping up his collar.

"I couldn't swim in that dress!"

"Alora. You're—"

"Devastating," said Lennox. "Yes, she knows. You know, I know, gods above and devils below know. The Urchins, remember? The *Urchins*."

Alora flushed at Lennox's obvious frustration. Or was it Bash's staring? Either way, she felt hot all over, no matter she was wearing next to nothing, and that it was sopping wet.

"One moment," murmured Alora, embarrassed, and swapped her clothing for a simple dress. Simple for *her*, at least. It still cinched her waist and flared at her hip, and there were an assortment of butter-flies and bees stitched at the waist. Blue, her favorite color.

"Ah, so light. Let's go."

Chapter Forty-Seven

The dark hadn't receded from half of Opulence, and it only made what remained in the light that much brighter. Kneeling in a huddled mass by the shut front doors was a mixture of performers and employees. Surrounding them were many men, hooded and masked, with batons held out or at their sides, menacing and ready for disruption. Madam Feebledire paced beside them.

Her normally severe plait had come undone. Alora thought she looked younger—kinder, too. But at their approach, her eyebrows met, and Alora knew then that while Madam Feebledire might have a better heart than her brother, she still had a sour disposition. Maybe she always would.

Twenty-two Urchins straightened at their approach. Two were missing: one dead and one impersonating a sack of grain thanks to Ellie Turkens. *Twenty-five Urchins. Twenty-five rooms.* Perhaps Marshall Merridon had liked his details even more than Alora first thought.

She slowed into step with Lennox, allowing Bash to walk ahead.

"Put away your weapons. These people are free to go."

Hoods shifted, Urchins glancing to one another. A few obeyed at once. More did not.

"We were ordered by Master Merridon to ensure no one left the building," rasped an Urchin.

"We were told you'd turned on us as well," said another, and his cowl shifted, nodding at the darkness grown behind them.

"A lie crafted to cover another. I did not betray you."

"Where is Marshall?" said Madam Feebledire, exasperated from holding the question in so long.

"He's dead," Bash replied, without any regard. "The mermaid freed itself at last; I always warned him of the chance, and he was too close to the pool's edge."

"That monstrous beast!" wailed Madam Feebledire.

"That *monstrous beast* was only acting on instinct. The mermaid would be eagerly eating fresh fish over anything else, had you bothered to treat it humanely!" Alora fumed, almost wanting the woman to argue with her, but Madam Feebledire had turned away, crying noisily into her shirtsleeves. A pang of regret rattled in her chest. But only in that Madam Feebledire was so upset over her brother's passing.

"As the only present son to Master Merridon, I am the rightful authority on Opulence Mansion. Not to mention I am still your captain. These people are free to go." His final words permitted no argument. This time, the majority returned their batons to their belts.

"And so are you all. The Urchins are hereby disbanded. Opulence has faced irreparable damage, its performers no longer obligated to work. We will be closing—effective immediately."

Alarmed gasps sounded by several Urchins and employees alike. But most, Alora noticed, did not. In fact, more employees appeared relieved over anything, as did every single performer.

Slowly, and without interference, they rose.

"Turn over your batons and masks to me."

A line of twenty-two people formed.

"Wait just a minute!" Madam Feebledire had spun around as the Urchins piled their discarded things, her tear-streaked face pinched.

"You can't just throw us out onto the street! This has been many of our homes for *years*. What authority do you have that I do not? No, I refuse!"

Bash regarded his aunt awhile, and Alora could see him forming a plan so easily now that she knew him. She stepped against his back, folding an imagined piece of paper into his pocket. He reached inside and pulled it free. His chin tucked against his shoulder, where he caught her eye—and grinned.

"I've a copy of his will right here, Aunt. Read it over later if you'd like." Then his voice rose. "Naturally, I'll provide the promised payouts and severance pay for every Urchin, employee, and performer. Also—whatever gold you can carry is yours. *Only* gold. You all have one hour."

At first, Bash's remarks were met with stunned silence. But when he restored the light he'd broken, and Madam Feebledire took off like a dart, everyone followed suit. Soon the sounds of hammering and smashing could be heard, the dismantling of Opulence Mansion's many staircases rattling in Alora's head. The cracking of marble filled her ears until she thought they might bleed.

"The ankle hold up all right?"

Alora whirled to the unfamiliar voice. To a tall man in Urchin black with close-cropped hair a similar shade to her own and the kindest eyes of her favorite shade of blue. Her nose wrinkled at his glance to her foot. Then she recognized his hands. Those rings on his thumbs—she'd seen them before. They matched the rings in his ears, and she realized she stood before the rather renowned Urchin healer.

Alora's forehead smoothed. Her lips lifted in a grin. "Perfectly. You're very talented."

"I'm in good company," he replied, and unclasped his mask before smiling himself.

Alora noticed his canines to be particularly pointed, but his smile was as kind as his eyes.

She felt Bash's chest press against her back. She bit at her cheek.

"Not enticed by the gold, Morley?" Bash's voice vibrated deep against her, and Alora leaned her weight back. He accepted it, his gloved hand coming to rest on her hip.

The healer pursed his lips, surveying the great hall. "Not my style," he said. "Miss Pennigrim, correct? Our Captain Merridon's manners have always been poor. Maybe consider the value of your loyalties." He snatched her hand from where it'd settled overtop Bash's, his lips brushing warm over her knuckles. "Durant Morley. If you're ever in need of mending, be sure to find me." He winked boldly, and Bash's fingers tightened against her. Alora blushed.

Oh, he is a shameless flirt.

"Thank you for mending him each time," she said, willing her cheeks to pale.

Beneath his breath, she heard Bash mutter, "*He's* about to be in need of mending."

"You're welcome," replied the healer and grinned at Bash as if he'd heard the threat and found it wildly entertaining. Then his glance slid sideways. "Lennox."

"Durant."

Alora looked at her friend and blinked, taken aback that Lennox kept her gaze upturned to the ceiling. *Hmm.* What history did she not know?

Alora could hardly wait to ask.

"Well, being as it's gone suddenly cold in here, I should take my talent outside and see if I can put it to any use." His bow caught Alora off her guard, and she laughed. A laugh she then cut at noting Lennox's sneer.

When he'd gone, Alora said, "What did he do to you?"

"I'll tell you later," Lennox replied, staring after him.

Which was fine; Alora could be patient. She stepped out of Bash's grip to slip her arm around Lennox's shoulders. "I'd best see to the rest of the rooms. Retrieve the mermaid from the pool before I have nothing left to climb."

"Let me help you," said Bash. He pulled the mask from his mouth and made to toss it onto the pile formed beside his boots.

"Wait," rushed Alora. She blushed. "Keep it."

"Keep…" Bash looked from the mask to her, his eyes narrowed and so deeply green. Slowly, he shook his head, but he didn't toss the mask as he'd meant, tucking it into his pocket instead. "As you wish."

Red as apples now, Alora looked to Lennox, meaning to ask if she'd want to stay with Alora now that she was free. But her friend had eyes only for what happened behind them, at the pieces of gold being hauled away. "I'll help you chip off a step, if you'd like."

At that, Lennox sniffed, returning her attention to Alora. "It's not that, though maybe. Now that you're offering," she said, her smile unsteady. "It just doesn't seem real. That not a day ago, I was in the middle of another night of another routine, and now I am free. Oh, don't look at me. I'm a mess."

At once, Alora's eyes snapped away.

Oh hell.

Alora had forgotten she was still entranced.

Chapter Forty-Eight

A new moon rose over deep-blue ocean waters that night. How fitting. Alora lifted the latch of the glass enclosure from where it rested in the sand. These were not like the beaches she'd read about in other places of the world: all black cliffs and black sands, rugged and dangerous, the water cold. These beaches were white and yellow sands, warm and soft and inviting.

And there were flowers. All colors, growing from cracked logs and creeping over dunes. It looked so well together, the delicate and vast, that Alora knew she would come back to visit often, now that she didn't fear for her and others' lives.

The mermaid climbed from the enclosure, its eyes closed, nose upturned to the salt on the breeze and starlight. Alora watched the deep inhales and prolonged exhales of the creature's chest, her own tight.

She swung the lantern in her grip. "I'm sorry it took me so long to come back for you after we first met."

"I understand."

"Will you be all right on your own?"

"I am home. I will be well." Alora nodded. She'd not been gone a full day and already she yearned for home. How must it have been for the mermaid, entrapped for nearly two decades? For once, she could not imagine.

A particularly large wave crashed across the beach, its pull reaching the mermaid and grasping hold. A sound much like relief left the creature's lips. It didn't fight the water's retreat but leaned into the drag.

"*Thank you.*"

Alora stared back into those familiar silver eyes above the surface. "You're welcome."

A wave splashed over her boots, and when it was gone so was the mermaid. When the next came, Alora's boots had vanished. Another, and she was up to her knees.

The water was still rather frigid, a shockingly pure cold, and she looked out at the boundless sea, at the bare outline of a burgeoning moon, and closed her eyes.

She could feel morning easing nearer but thought Mrs. Flops could wait a bit longer. Mr. Zanfold had promised to check in on her, and Alora had not gone to the ocean in so long.

In her hand, dangled her membership card.

"Thoughts of joining the mermaid?"

Alora's body responded to that voice, though she did not turn. Or open her eyes. "Perhaps. Do you think I might imagine myself gills? Or maybe just bigger lungs, like a sea serpent."

The crunch of sand changed in her ears. He'd dismounted, coming toward her. Alora shook her head. She'd left him behind to see to the continued dismantling of Opulence. Either it hadn't lasted so long as she thought, or he worried she'd become entrapped again.

Or fall to the depths in melancholy.

"Lungs, probably. So you can go between land and water."

"That would be wiser, I suppose."

A touch on her back, and an arm was easing around her waist, dragging her backward, onto the beach. "Are you well?"

Alora stared up at Bash. He'd donned the vest again, the silver setting off his coloring. His eyes were warm, concerned.

She said, "Opulence is finished, everyone freed. Soon, it will be a bad memory. Why wouldn't I be well?" At his raised eyebrow, she huffed, scowling. "What? Did you think I would fall apart that we didn't break it? That I'm still entranced? At least I am entranced by a *good* person. A friend. She won't hurt me or convince me to commit diabolical things."

When he shifted at her words, her eyes dropped, and when they did, she noticed what was tucked beneath his arm.

Alora stumbled backward, her feet sinking into cold, wet sand. "What are you doing?"

Bash brought the skull to his middle. "Hear me out, Alora—"

"Bash, no!"

His jaw hardened. "I *need* you to hear me out. Will you?"

She dropped her head into her hands, as if she could wipe the beach clean of him by blocking her sight.

But she couldn't. She *wouldn't.* "Tell me."

"You can look at me. I'm not my—I'm not him."

Alora lowered her hands at once, her mouth parted. "I would never even *think* that! I only don't want you to repeat to me of your leaving."

Bash's eyes cleared, the darkness receding. "It isn't that. I only thought of it after everything was done, and I had time to consider it all."

"And what have you thought of?" Her eyebrows met, awaiting his explanation.

"Allow me to transfer your entrancement to me. To try this one thing. If it doesn't work, we can transfer it again. Back to Lennox." At her silence, he pressed, "Do you trust me?"

Alora gazed up at him—at his hard earnestness—and said, "Completely."

Bash's shoulders lowered.

He drew a deep breath to respond—only she interrupted. This was a quiet moment if she'd ever experienced one, and she couldn't hold it in any longer. Couldn't fathom how long he'd held it in himself.

"Merridon told me about you as a child," she began. "Only a little, but he told me about the two boys he traded for. To hear it from him… I'm so sorry, Bash."

The lantern's light struggled in the deep night, but it did fine in revealing an old hurt in Bash's eyes. His throat hitched before he scoffed. "Miserable years. Topped with a promotion. Quite the gift it was to be named a captain of my adoptive father's band of henchmen. Even better to discover the name to be a repurposing of an old insult. I'm surprised he told you."

Alora could not quell the welling of her tears. "He was despicably cruel."

Bash's gaze fell to the sand. "It's embarrassing to admit that a decade ago, I still had hope that I could fix it. Mend or mold our relationship into something resembling a real family. I signed that contract willingly. It was my greatest mistake, and I will spend the rest of my life in atonement for what I've done."

"Bash…" Alora blinked and wet coated her cheeks. "You couldn't have known."

"I read the contract, Alora."

"And did he also list out all the plans he had for you and the men you'd eventually lead?"

He swallowed. The pause stretched. "No. But it was all there, between the lines."

"His trickery is not your fault. An enchanted contract where you aren't to question his authority? That is not your *fault*. You did all right at hiding your good heart from me in the beginning, but it didn't take long for me to sense something was amiss in the details. I knew you didn't fit in the roles you'd been assigned—and I wasn't wrong. I'm sorry to have made you feel like your past doesn't deserve forgiveness. It does, and I trust you wholeheartedly. That you will do your best to right every wrong. That you won't hurt me. I really do feel that."

His eyes snapped to hers, intense and dark. "I sincerely don't think I deserve you."

"Why not? Because you're imperfect and I'm not?" Alora snorted at the ridiculousness. "Let me be imperfect with you. It's better than being it all alone."

He watched her steadily. If he thought it would intimidate her, he was very wrong. But he said, "Does this mean you'll try with the skull?"

Alora gulped, pulling strands of hair from where they whipped against her face. In her clenched palm, her membership bent, and in her chest, her heart hammered against her ribs. "If you really want to." Bash smiled at her response—though it didn't look quite real to her; his dimple hardly showed. When he made to turn the skull around, though, she threw a hand over eyes. "Wait! You're not going to tell me the details?"

"No."

Alora made a low sound, almost a growl, and widened her fingers. Did he not believe her when she said she trusted him? Apparently not.

She dropped her hand in a sudden rush. Like with the mermaid, she would prove herself true to her word. Alora stared into the ruby eyes of the cursed crystal skull and was immediately pulled down.

"Alora. Look at me."

Alora's gaze snapped upward.

"Good. It's worked."

"Maybe I only wanted to look at you."

"Did you?"

She couldn't refuse an answer. Or lie. "Yes. But it's also worked." Bash didn't seem all that pleased, however, considering she'd done as he'd asked. An anticipatory flutter rushed about her insides. "What next? Will you demand I kiss you?"

He frowned down at her. "Isn't that immoral?"

"Very." Though she'd be more than willing. If it mattered. Bash shifted again, rolling his shoulders. "You look nervous," she said.

"Do I? I suppose I am." He cleared his throat. "All right. Here goes. Alora Pennigrim…"

Alora's eyes widened at his use of her full name, and not all of it due to entrancement. Her heart rose until it lodged somewhere in the narrowing of her throat.

"You are my greatest desire. Your frightening amount of bravery. Your ability to realize the beautiful in all things. Your mesmerizing, imperfectly real smile. I desire *you*, wholly beholden only to yourself. Give me that."

Alora's breath caught.

Bash's wish—

His desire—

Good gracious.

Alora imagined the cursed skull vanished from the world.

Then she flung her arms up and kissed him.

Chapter Forty-Nine

ATTN: Restoration of Lost Memories

MS ALORA PENNIGRIM, Owner of **Pennigrim's Projects & Designs**, would like to invite those suffering from acute memory loss related to baton bludgeoning to attend a free consultation and treatment.

THOSE UNSURE OF INJURY ARE STILL ENTITLED TO ASSESSMENT.

Every **TUESDAY** for the month of **OCTOBER**, two o'clock to five o'clock in the afternoon.

006 Mugwort Alley, Enver

Alora closed the paper, pleased both with her newfound skill in opening the locked boxes of memories in people's heads, and with the ad. It had been the second time the good printer, Mr. Zanfold, had spoken to her.

The first being, *"Your wild rabbit ate my laces."*

She glanced over the cursed and broken tub, across the Room of Forgotten Memories, to where Bash labored, his shirtsleeves rolled tight across his upper arms. He swung the sledgehammer again, at last sending part of the wall crumbling.

Sweat beaded on his forehead, which he wiped with one forearm. It glistened on his collarbones. When he caught her watching, he shot her a glare. "You could have imagined it loose from the beginning."

"You were already started when I arrived!" said Alora, grinning as he swung again. Who was she to interrupt?

A third blow, and the wall came free. Behind the mirrors had been stone, thick and gray, and behind that—

Alora edged closer now that the dust had begun to settle. Her shoulder pressed against Bash's arm, both peering into the gloom. A gold vat waited for them, a pipe leading from its end, traveling beneath the floor.

"The vat is full of memory oil?"

"A fortune's worth. Hundreds could live out their lives on it."

"How did he get it in there?"

"I'm not sure. Though I doubt it's ever needed refilling. It only takes a few drops for the bath."

Alora straightened. "Was this what you brewed most often?" Bash nodded and cleared his throat roughly. She'd made him uncomfortable, talking about his past, but he'd asked her not to stop. That it helped. "Should I?"

"Unless you'd rather I pull it from the wall and heave it off the balcony."

Alora feigned needing time to decide. When Bash realized she teased him, he grabbed her around the waist and dragged her against him. She faced the dust-streaked container, her back to his chest, the scent of vetiver all around.

It was quite nice, considering.

Only water, she imagined.

"Done. Memory oil is officially purged from Opulence."

"And outside it," said Bash. "I burned the batons and shredded the recipe. Though, do you know what I found in that old book while doing it?"

"I certainly don't."

"A potion to regrow bones." Alora spun in his arms. A corner of Bash's mouth lifted. "It's a painfully long and particular list, but for not fitting the role of a potion-master, I should be able to manage."

Alora could not close her mouth no matter how she tried. Instead, what she managed after some moments was, "I'm incredibly in love with you, Bash Syntaine." He tensed beneath her hands, but she rushed, "And if you're an obsessive type—well—so am I."

In response, she received one of his rare, full smiles, dimple and all, and she relished the lightning strike.

"In your singular case, Alora, I am. I knew I'd be in trouble from the first step you made into my shop. I tried to fight it; you were too bright and too beautiful for someone like me. But..." His thumb pressed to her lower lip then, and he murmured, "I undeniably love you. Beyond even what I thought myself capable of."

Alora grinned beneath his touch. "Our fates are linked, yours and mine. I felt it from the start."

Bash stared down at her awhile, gaze heating, and Alora could only fidget, her heart near bursting, the rest of her on fire down to her very marrow, when he asked at last, "Do you think it's appropriate to kiss you in such a miserable place?"

"More than fine," she rushed.

His thumb left her lip at once to cradle her face, angling it higher. His opposite pressed hard into her low back. "You are divine. I'm only sorry I'm covered in dust," he said, his breath brushing her mouth.

Alora grinned with her sudden ideas. She imagined three things all at once:

A room free of dirt and debris.

A luscious bed in place of a bathtub.

And Bash, every button, zipper, and lace undone.

He laughed as his mouth met hers, not protesting at all when she fed her inspiration and tacked on a final fourth. And the feeling overwhelmed her. It was so much *more* now. More than satisfying any craving or grasping for a distraction. Bash shrugged out of his shirt in the same breath he dragged at her lacings, and Alora broke from him gasping to kiss each scar she could see.

The wound she'd inflicted upon him with the hairpin did not leave a lasting mark, but she hated that he was marred from the time he'd known her. She would add a new layer of memories over those harsh ones now. They wouldn't ever go away, but perhaps she could dull their sharp edges for him. She was nothing if not hopeful.

"What have you done, Alora?"

She allowed Bash to tilt her chin away and toward the wall. And she looked at the pair of them. Standing there, skin to skin, bared to the room. His kohl-lined eyes were dilated and dark to mimic her own, his fingers pressed firmly into the soft flesh of her hip and her jaw. She flushed in seeing them together this way; it almost felt unreal.

And she could only smile. "I cleaned the mirrors," she said—and promptly pushed him onto the bed.

Outside the grounds, Bash wrested the chains holding the gate back into place. The key on the padlock clicked, echoing against the pale stone. It didn't look so intimidating now, and not only because there was no gold-armored guard. It looked tired. Worn. Not the least bit enchanted. Alora shoved her mangled membership card into the links.

"That's that, then," he said, seeing it.

This time, it really did feel like the blessed end.

"Did I mention Reginald is Reginald again, and Ellie Turkens hired him for her bookstore? She said she's always wanted a handsome young man about, and he's happy to be out of the sun. Mister

Macaw did take your advice, too, and rented that land for his nursery. Also! Lennox bought her own flat! It might have more windows than mine."

"Good, they deserve it." But a muscle feathered in Bash's jaw. "And that bakery?"

"You know the name."

His tone dropped, almost a growl. "Have you gone?"

"No," sighed Alora. "But I did see Mister Whitters the other day and he seemed happy with the arrangement. He doesn't remember anything at all, Bash."

"I'd rather he not be anywhere near this town."

"He goes by Will now, I'm told. Mister Whitters says he's hard-working, wakes up to start the ovens every morning. Likes the heat, he thinks—"

"He should be clearing sewer drains."

Alora pursed her lips. She'd neither forgive nor forget what William had done either, and she might always have her bakery items delivered by bicycle. But Mr. Whitters knew the entire story and seemed willing to report any concerns. So far, there'd been none.

If there were, Alora knew Bash would see William removed in a heartbeat.

Bash whistled and Necros trotted toward them. When the horse neared, he gripped her waist, lifting her up behind the saddle. He followed soon after.

They'd made it onto the not-so-secret-anymore path through Renwick Forest when Alora, smiling devilishly, dipped wandering hands beneath Bash's coat, pressing her body against his.

She yelped when his hand gripped her wrist, hauling her around the front and into his lap.

His mouth bent to her ear, where he rasped, "This won't end the same as last time."

Thank heavens, she thought.

Epilogue

"He stole my case of cigarillos once," said Lennox to Alora. Her thickly stockinged feet tapped disjointedly on Alora's terrace stones, and she twirled a flower in her fingers.

"He did?"

"He did. I caught him with one, lit and all, and plucked it right out of his filthy mouth."

Alora sipped her tea, intrigued. "What did he say?"

"He didn't. He plucked it back. So I snatched one of his earrings." Lennox lifted Mrs. Flops onto her lap, nuzzling into the rabbit's soft, white fur. "*That*, he didn't like. He shouted at me."

Alora scowled at once. "He *shouted* at you? Whatever for?"

"Because he's an impulsive thief who can't handle the taste of his own medicine."

"But he seems so even-tempered… And he's a healer."

"Oh, he makes a great first impression with his pretty smiles and prettier words. Just wait until you have something he wants."

Alora blinked at the bitterness in her best friend's tone. "How long ago was this?"

"A year."

"Did he apologize or explain?"

"Yes. And no."

"So you've hated him all this time?"

"Wouldn't you? If he stole your rabbit?"

Alora huffed a laugh. "Mrs. Flops? She's the most precious thing I have."

Lennox nodded in vindication. She fed the creature her bloom. "Precisely."

Acknowledgements

This book! This book was written on some of my happiest days. Which nearly all involved trees, flowers, bees, and butterflies. I try my best to romanticize all my usual moments, to seek out whimsy, to realize the very real enchantment that goes into creating a story. Sometimes I forget—but like the main character in this book, I remember eventually. To create new worlds is my dream come true, after all, and I feel so lucky to do it.

Thank you to my family. Especially Gemma, whose art of Mrs. Flops inspired me to keep going even when the story felt wedged in mud. Your excitement was all I needed on the hard days.

Thank you to my early draft readers. Your feedback, your DMs, your reactions along the way—I hope you realize how much your thoughts and encouragement means to me. I could not do it without you.

Lastly, thank you to my readers. This is my second go-around, and while I'm not any less nervous, I am infinitely more excited knowing what's to come. Thank you for picking up my book. I hope you enjoyed it. Your support makes all of this possible, and I am endlessly grateful.

About the Author

Gloria Bottelman is a fantasy writer and registered nurse. While living in the Midwest (and dreaming of the PNW), she spends her time trying to make sense of her many book ideas and walking in the woods—usually at the same time.

Potions & Peculiarities is the first installment of a planned series of interconnected standalone novels.

Connect with her at
www.gloriabottelman.com or scan the QR code below!

www.ingramcontent.com/pod-product-compliance
Lightning Source LLC
Chambersburg PA
CBHW011316310726
48973CB00011B/2951